I lay sleepless, thinking about the future, as I saw it then a future without love. I was going to be one of those girls who lived a gentle existence with their parents, to end up as everybody's aunt, looking after nieces and nephews, and who no man would ever have wished to marry.

I'd be a rebel. They would cut my photographs off family groups; I'd do something outrageous relatives and people who knew us would simply say, 'She's just like her Aunt Alicia.'

But what had Aunt Alicia done to deserve such recriminations? That night while the sound of music floated upwards from the festivities below I vowed that I would ask Aunt May about my father's forgotten sister.

My mother wouldn't tell me anything; there was only Aunt May who I knew would at first decline to speak but would later change her mind. When had she ever been known to keep a secret? Aunt May had always thrived on gossip and this time she'd tell me all I needed to know.

THE LAST WALTZ

Sara Hylton

First published in Great Britain 2002 by Judy Piatkus (Publishers) Ltd.
Paperback edition 2006
by Harlequin Mills & Boon Limited, Eton House,
18-24 Paradise Road, Richmond, Surrey TW9 1SR

THE LAST WALTZ © Sara Hylton 2002

ISBN-13: 978 0 263 85104 5
ISBN-10: 0 263 85104 4

169-1106

Printed and bound in Spain
by Litografia Rosés S.A., Barcelona

To Peter, whose fascination with European history, and particularly with Vienna, was an enormous help to me in the writing of this novel.

CHAPTER ONE

STEVENSON SQUARE WAS considered the most prestigious square in the town since it consisted of tall Georgian houses with large lofty rooms, a conservatory at the back and a side entrance leading down to the basement where the servants lived.

Tall maples lined the square and although the gardens were small they were well kept, with short front drives, gleaming brass knockers on every door and well-scrubbed entrance halls.

My grandparents moved into number four after their wedding and it was there they raised their family of three sons and one daughter. My father Robert was the eldest, then came Uncle William and Uncle Alec; their daughter Alicia was the youngest, but more of Aunt Alicia later.

The three boys married. My father married Miss Elizabeth Starkey, who was visiting relatives at number seven and had been invited to attend my Uncle William's twenty-first birthday party. Mother always said it was love at first sight.

Uncle William went on to marry May Jarvison, whose father was the head clerk in the firm's general office, and Uncle Alec did rather better for himself, marrying Jane

Thornham, who was the only daughter of Sir John Thornham. The Thornhams considered themselves to be landed gentry and were not even remotely interested in anything that could be considered trade.

Uncle William had two sons, Sydney and Simeon; Uncle Alec had a son, Gordon, and a daughter, Edith. My parents had three girls: Della, Ruth and me. I was christened Alexandra but everybody has always called me Alex.

We lived across the park in Cromerton Road. It was my duty every Sunday after church to walk across the park to visit my grandparents. I was only just tall enough to reach the bell which had replaced the door knocker since it could be heard in the basement. In just a few minutes the door would be opened by Mrs Pearson. She was primed for my arrival and didn't trust the maid Polly to instruct me to take off my shoes and put on my slippers before entering the drawing room.

She would fix me with an eagle eye, saying, 'There now, Miss Alex, take off those muddy shoes. Your slippers are here behind the door.'

I would have given anything to be let off those duty visits which my sisters were excused from attending so that Della could do her homework and Ruth could practise the piano. They were always the same.

Grandfather would be fast asleep in the big chair in front of the fire, snoring gently, an empty glass which had contained a hot toddy on the table near his chair, and Grandmother sitting opposite working on her embroidery. She would look up with a smile; I would dutifully kiss her cheek and go to sit on the soft leather pouffe close by.

Conversation, if there was any, would be conducted in

whispers so as not to wake Grandfather, and promptly at three o'clock Polly would come in carrying a tea tray on which rested a silver tea service, three cups and saucers, three plates and a large plate containing home-made scones.

Grandmother poured the tea. I handed round the scones and Grandfather invariably said, 'Good afternoon, Alex, how are you?'

'Very well, Grandfather,' I would reply.

'Mmm. These scones are very good, are we agreed?'

We were agreed, after which Grandfather resumed his sleep and Polly came in to collect the tray. She favoured me with a swift smile and I looked at the clock: another half-hour to go.

I wonder if Grandmother ever noticed that I jumped to my feet with great alacrity when the clock struck four. It was her signal to rise to her feet, look in her handbag and extract from it three new threepenny pieces, one for me and the other two for my sisters.

At the door Mrs Pearson would admonish me to go straight home, not talk to anybody and keep my feet out of the puddles.

I was always under the impression that I was not a favourite with Mrs Pearson. I couldn't sit still; I fidgeted while my two sisters invariably sat with their hands folded decorously on their knees, their expressions polite and vacant, while I responded to Polly's swift smiles and listened too closely to grown-up conversation.

The times when we were all together as a family usually fell at Christmas and on Grandmother's birthday. Then we would all arrive clutching our gifts and the grown-ups would sit in the drawing room exchanging conversation and we would be relegated to the huge nursery upstairs to play games.

My boy cousins were boisterous and I learned to give as good as I got; consequently we were friends of a sort, since my two sisters kept a discreet distance from their teasing. My cousin Edith wasn't much fun. She always dressed beautifully and had received instructions from her mother not to get her dress soiled, to chat to her girl cousins Della and Ruth, who were really quite nice, but not to have too much to do with the boys or Alex.

After the evening meal Ruth played the piano and Edith played the violin. I was really rather young to appreciate their talent but I was informed that they were both very gifted and could go far. I hadn't the faintest idea what was meant by that in Ruth's case, since she hated travelling, was invariably sick on the shortest journeys and as a result spoiled the day for the rest of us.

There were certain aspects of those visits to Stevenson Square that intrigued me, mostly concerned with whispered conversation between the grown-ups which without fail ceased whenever the younger element went near them.

'Why are they always whispering about something?' I asked Ruth, 'and why do they always shut up whenever they find us looking at them?'

She confessed not to know, and maybe she didn't, but I was determined that one day I would find out even if it meant listening at doors.

I didn't much care for Aunt Jane. I considered her frosty and autocratic, and when I said as much to Della she said, 'Oh well, she's gentry, isn't she?'

'What's that supposed to mean?' I asked.

'Her father's a baronet and her mother's Lady Thornham.'

We were never allowed to forget it, but I did like Aunt May. She was fun even if she did speak with a broader accent than the rest of the family. She dressed more flamboyantly, her hair was a bright shade of auburn and she was not in the least intimidated by Aunt Jane's superior air.

I remember most vividly the quarrel that began on Christmas morning and continued on and off for the rest of the day. Two days before Christmas had been the occasion of the works Christmas party for the workpeople and the office staff, followed in the evening by dinner for the managerial staff at the town's most expensive hotel. Apparently Aunt May's behaviour had given rise to much gossip and Aunt Jane was quick to raise the matter over lunch on Christmas Day in spite of Mother's obvious attempts to silence her in front of the younger element.

'What has Alec had to say about your disgraceful behaviour the other evening? Mr Jefferson was a guest; did you have to flirt with him all evening? It made me feel quite embarrassed.'

Aunt May tossed her head saying, 'I've known Jimmy Jefferson longer than I've known William. If you're narrow-minded enough to read more into it than that, you're very welcome.'

'Setting all those tongues wagging, everybody was talking about it.'

'Then they're a lot of interfering old busybodies. You didn't notice anything out of the ordinary, did you, Liz?' she said, addressing my mother.

'I wasn't sitting anywhere near you,' Mother said softly.

'Well I was, and she made it so obvious,' said Aunt Jane.

'I'm a chatterbox,' Aunt May said defensively. 'I like to chat, it keeps the party moving along, and heaven knows it's not easy with the Clarksons and with you, Jane. You never make much of an effort to chat to anybody.'

'I don't smother people with my attention,' Aunt Jane retorted. 'The poor man looked most embarrassed at times.'

'Well if he did it's the first time ever, because I've flirted with him on and off for years. Most people thought I'd have married him until William came along.'

'Hardly a subject to trot out in front of your husband's family as something to be proud of.'

'That's enough, Jane,' Uncle Alec said testily.

'Surely we've had enough scandal in this family with Alicia without you subjecting us to more,' Aunt Jane snapped, whereupon Grandfather banged his fist on the table and in a voice like thunder stormed, 'I've said before I'll not have her name mentioned in this house by any one of you. When she walked out of this house she walked out of our lives.'

'I'm sorry,' Aunt Jane murmured. 'I merely wanted to warn May that we've suffered enough from gossip; we don't want any more.'

Somehow a blight seemed to have descended upon the entire day. Uncle William and Aunt May left with their boys as soon as the meal was over and Aunt Jane sat sulking in silence until they departed a little later, much to my relief.

Grandfather retired to his study and Grandmother said feelingly, 'He'll be like that for the rest of the day. Whatever possessed Jane to go on and on all over our meal? Surely she must have known there would be trouble.'

We left in the early evening with Grandmother's anxieties still troubling my parents. On our way home Ruth and I trailed behind and I whispered, 'Who's this Alicia they were talking about? Why does Grandfather not want to talk about her?'

'I don't know. I saw a photograph once of Grandfather and the family and somebody had been cut off the corner.'

'Somebody young.'

'Alex, I don't know, but I shouldn't think so. How can Grandfather be angry with somebody young like us?'

'Why don't we ask Mother?'

'You ask her, I shan't. She won't want to talk about it anyway.'

'I don't like Aunt Jane nearly as much as Aunt May. She's always so stuck up and unfriendly, and I think she's jealous of Aunt May because she's pretty and lively.'

'Well, I'm not taking sides with either of them, and you won't if you've any sense.'

Actually, at ten years of age I don't think I had a lot of common sense. I had feet that danced when they should have walked. I had a happy-go-lucky nature that was rarely otherwise and saw the funny side of most things even when they should have been taken more seriously.

The fact that Aunt Jane and Mrs Pearson despaired of me didn't matter. I was young and loved life, and I was happy in that house across the park with friends at the school I attended close by.

My school reports said that I was a bit of a dreamer, not destined to be academic. I loved the dancing lessons and strangely enough I enjoyed history connected with the royal houses of Europe and the intrigues of court romances which

Mavis Longworth passed on to me and which I read under cover of the bedclothes.

In my heart I expected this happy-go-lucky life to go on uninterrupted but that was not to be. It came to an abrupt end on the death of my grandfather from a heart attack, sitting at his desk at the works. He was sixty-nine and I think the day of his funeral will live in my memory forever.

The huge black hearse was pulled by four coal-black horses, their coats gleaming like satin, their heads adorned by waving black feathers, vying with an array of brass fittings.

Grandfather would have been delighted with the spectacle as well as with the dozen or more carriages that followed him to the graveyard, all bearing respected citizens of the town.

The streets were lined with men clutching their caps in respectful silence, women in tears and wide-eyed children. Most of the men had been employed in Grandfather's engineering business and many of them could not remember a time when he had not been the man in charge.

I sat with my family in the first coach in something of a daze. Grandfather had always seemed a remote figure in spite of my Sunday visits, and my thoughts on that morning were concerned with those visits and how long they would continue now that Grandmother was on her own.

While we clustered round the large ornate tomb in the parish church graveyard I looked around me with interest. Grandmother leaned heavily on my father's arm while we stood behind them. My mother and the aunts wore deepest mourning. The boys were in their Sunday best dark suits and the girls wore grey, all new and bought for the occasion.

Mrs Pearson and Polly wept copiously and catching my interested stare Mrs Pearson frowned; I should have been weeping and suffering some form of distress in accordance with my loss.

The banquet after the funeral was much to my liking. It was held in the town's most salubrious hotel and was attended by local dignitaries and a great many business associates. Aunt Jane's family were there in force and Ruth whispered to me that the boy chatting to Della was destined to be the next Sir John Thornham after his father.

At that moment the boy caught my eye and he smiled, a smile that was to haunt my dreams for many years.

Ruth whispered to me, 'He's very handsome, isn't he? Look at Della, she's thrilled to bits to be talking to him.'

'Why isn't it Edith he's talking to?' I asked.

'Well, they're cousins, aren't they, that wouldn't do at all.'

At that moment I wished I was older. I had never felt inadequate before, hadn't cared; now it seemed I suddenly cared too much. But I was not left long to contemplate matters; the mourners were moving away and Mother said, 'I think we're leaving now, dear, so keep close to me; we're taking Grandmother home. There are many things to be sorted out.'

'What sort of things?' I asked.

'Well, what she's going to do now that she's on her own. Do hurry up, Alex, your father's waiting at the carriage.'

When we eventually pulled up outside number four Stevenson Square it seemed that the rest of the family were to join us and once inside the house Mrs Pearson and Polly were already banking up fires and pulling back the long velvet curtains that had been drawn across the windows.

Aunt Jane said, 'Perhaps the children should go up to the nursery so that we can talk.'

'A fire hasn't been lit in the nursery,' Grandmother said. 'It will be very cold up there. They can stay here if they promise to be good. There are books to read and they can all sit in the window space.'

Books were produced, and magazines, but I was more interested in the conversation going on behind me.

'Have you thought seriously of what you are going to do now, Mother?' Father was the first to ask.

'I've thought of little else since your father died. This house is very large but I don't want to move,' she replied.

'It's far too large to live here on your own, Mother, even with Mrs Pearson and Polly. Don't you think you should look for something smaller?'

'If I look for something smaller it won't be here in this town. Your father liked this house, and the Favershams have a standing that demanded we lived here. Now I shall have no connection with the works apart from the income I derive from them. However I am not going to have people saying circumstances have driven me to look for something more modest.'

'Would they say that, Mother? Surely people would have the sense to see that the house is unsuitable for an elderly lady living on her own, besides which it's nobody's business but yours.'

'I do agree with Robert,' Aunt Jane said adamantly. 'The house is too large for you, Mother-in-Law, unless one of us moves in with you, or we exchange properties.'

For a long moment there was silence then Father said, 'What are you suggesting, Jane?'

'Just that. That one of us moves in here, your family, our family or William's family, although I hardly think May would enjoy living in Stevenson Square.'

'Why not?' Aunt May snapped.

'Haven't you always said the houses in the square were pretentious and far too old-fashioned? I assumed you preferred something more modern.'

'Well I do, but my saying that shouldn't exclude us. After all William is a son just as your husband is.'

'Well, Alec and I would not object to moving here. My brother and his wife have recently bought number nine and they'll be moving in in the spring. It would be nice to be close.'

I was watching my mother's face, filled with doubts, looking round the room in search of inspiration, but it was Grandmother who said, 'Your father always said that he would like Robert and Elizabeth to move in here either when one of us died or if we moved out of the area. Now one of us has died, but I don't want to move away, and the house is big enough for all of us. What do you say, Robert?'

My father looked at Mother for some sign of agreement or otherwise, and quick to follow up her suggestion Grandmother said, 'It would be ideal, Robert. There is a grand piano for Ruth, and there are five bedrooms. Mrs Pearson will stay on, as will Polly, and you would be able to take on other domestic help to cope with all of us. I wouldn't be a problem, you'd hardly know I was here.'

Father looked across the room at us. Ruth was all smiles as she thought about the Bechstein grand and Della too seemed happy, obviously thinking about John Thornham who would be living across the square. I, it seemed, was the only dissenting voice. I loved our smaller house across the park, I loved my friends and the school, now Uncle William was saying, 'It all sounds cut and dried to me. The rest of us are not going to have any say.'

'This isn't something I've arranged,' Father said testily. 'Mother's suggestions have come as a surprise to me, but all the same, Mother, Elizabeth and I have to talk about this, and we do need to consult the children.'

'Of course, Robert, but do try to remember that this house has been our pride and joy. It has reflected our standard of living and you were all happy enough to be brought up in it. I'm sure when you've had a chance to talk it over you'll see the solution is an ideal one.'

We talked over every aspect of it that evening and I soon became aware that I would have no influence on the outcome. To live in Stevenson Square was tantamount to living in the best the town could offer. It would open all sorts of doors into the future, and at the end of it the right sort of marriages, which were not readily available for three daughters.

Only two people resented the move. I was one and Aunt Jane was the other. She would dearly have liked Stevenson Square for her own family, and Aunt May was delighted with her jealousy.

Our house was quickly sold to a local councillor and his family and in no time at all we were installed at number four. I had my own bedroom, which was chilly and far too large, I was enrolled at the same school my two sisters attended and we got two more servants, Mrs Cloony the cook and Jenny, who promptly got under Polly's feet so that the rows they had were endless.

Grandmother had her own sitting room and kept herself very much to herself, and at the end of the first month I had to admit that perhaps life in Stevenson Square would not be as bad as I had pictured it.

Although I had been a constant visitor to the house for years I had never really known any of Grandfather's neighbours. Now they were calling to be entertained to afternoon tea when we were at home or they would leave visiting cards and Mother would invite them back. There was only one boy of my age, Harry Stevenson, the great-grandson of the man who had built the houses round the square. He had little conversation beyond his model railway, was small, rather pompous, and unfortunately spotty.

Aunt Jane's brother and his wife called but to my disappointment their son was not with them. They explained that he was in his last year at Oxford and I do not know who was the most disappointed, Della or me.

It was a funny sort of year. We had Cousin Edith for three weeks so that her parents could go to Madeira after Aunt Jane's appendix operation, and it was from Edith that I learned a little more about Aunt Alicia.

I was vastly intrigued but kept the information to myself. This wasn't difficult since Aunt May was providing the family with more of her indiscretions, even though they were largely light-hearted.

Life in Victorian England was very staid and proper. We had a queen on the throne who was a total recluse after the death of Prince Albert, whom she had adored. We were proud to be British; there was a great sense of dignity and stability about an Empire upon which the sun never set, and our heroes were men of achievement, men who had done great things to make our country even stronger. I could not believe that it would ever change.

Our new neighbours were local dignitaries, aldermen and councillors in the town, as well as high-up civil servants and factory owners. They held dinner parties and banquets to which my parents were invited and for the younger element there were parties and charabanc trips to the seaside. I grew so tall Ruth's hand-me-downs were now too short for me and I had to be given a whole new wardrobe.

Contrary to all my misgivings, growing up in Stevenson Square was something far better than I had expected and I was learning more about my family from new friends than I ever learned from the family itself.

CHAPTER TWO

THERE WERE TIMES after school when a few of us would wander into the centre of the town to go to the museum or into the library where Mr Jefferson was the librarian, and it was there on a miserably wet afternoon in spring that we observed my Aunt May tripping lightly across the cobbled square to enter the library doors. Inside there was no sign of her, but we heard the sound of laughter coming from Mr Jefferson's private office and I did not miss the exchange of glances between his assistants.

Stephanie Anderson giggled and in answer to my look of annoyance she said, 'Everybody's talking about your aunt, Alex, she's such a flirt.'

'She's very nice,' I defended her.

'I'm not saying she's not. She's awfully pretty, but Mother says she's got quite a name in the town.'

I was resentful. I thought about Aunt Jane's condemnation of her antics, I thought about my mother's embarrassment whenever the family was threatened, and I leapt to her defence.

'She's known Mr Jefferson for years, they're old friends. Why shouldn't she call to see him when she's in town?'

The girls looked at me in pitying silence, and it was only on our way home that Stephanie said, 'I'm sorry I've upset you, Alex. I really didn't mean to but I thought you'd know.'

'Know, know what?' I demanded.

'That she's talked about.'

'That's because she's pretty and very nice. Men admire her. I admire her—I'd like to be like her.'

Beatrice Roper said vindictively, 'Well, you're in with a good chance, you've two aunts who caused an awful stir in the town.'

'Which aunts? Aunt Jane would never cause any scandal. She's far too circumspect.'

'Not your Aunt Jane, silly. Your Aunt Alicia.'

'What do you know about my Aunt Alicia?'

'Only what I've heard Mother talking about. Don't you know?'

'I don't know what you mean.'

'Oh well, then, it's not for me to tell you.'

I didn't like Beatrice Roper but I was intrigued and when I passed her words on to Ruth my sister simply said, 'Mother and Father never talk about her, Alex, and you shouldn't either. Has Mother told you we're invited to a party at the Thornhams' on Friday evening? John is home, it's his birthday.'

'Are we all invited?'

'Of course. Mother and Della have gone shopping, she's to have a new dress.'

'Why Della, why not us?'

'Because I shall wear the new one I had at Christmas, and you'll probably be wearing that blue one you had for your birthday.'

Up in my bedroom I stepped into the blue dress and hated

it. It had a round neck adorned with a ruched frill and the skirt flounced above my ankles. I was thirteen but I had no shape and I looked about ten. The colour suited my blonde hair and blue eyes but there was nothing graceful in the stiff taffeta and I thought about the dress Della would be choosing, something elegant and grown-up. I didn't want to go to the party looking like some Victorian doll but I desperately wanted to see John Thornham again.

It was even worse on the night of the party. Della looked very beautiful in peach satin and Ruth too seemed suddenly grown-up and pretty. I decided that nobody was going to look at me, certainly not John Thornham, who would be surrounded by older more beautifully dressed girls.

I spent most of the evening sitting on the stairs with the Stevenson boy who went on and on about his model railway and invited me round to see it in action. He seemed taller and a little less spotty, but I was dismally aware of the laughter below us and the music from the next room.

John Thornham spoke to me once and that was to ask if I was enjoying myself and did I like living in Stevenson Square. I answered yes to both, then with a brief smile he walked away to ask his cousin Edith to dance.

Aunt May was enjoying herself as usual, surrounded by a group of men she was entertaining with her conversation, and Ruth whispered, 'Look at Aunt May, she's not danced with Uncle William once, and look at Aunt Jane's face filled with disapproval.'

I desperately wanted to be like Aunt May: vivacious, pretty and popular with the men. Her dress was bright scarlet with a low neckline and she wore red poppies in her hair; I looked down at my blue taffeta and wished I was dead.

Over breakfast next morning the party was talked about. Della talked about John Thornham to the exclusion of everything else, but Mother advised her to be very circumspect and not read too much into his attentions too soon, and pouting prettily Della said, 'He likes me, Mother, I can tell. He danced with me more than any of the other girls.'

'I know, dear, but don't be too readily available.'

'Not like Aunt May,' I snapped. 'They were all talking about Aunt May.'

'Alex, don't say such things! You're far too young to be talking like that and don't let your father hear you.'

'Isn't John Thornham going back to Oxford?' Ruth asked.

'Yes of course, but when he gets his degree he's coming back to work in the family firm, and he told me he expects to see much more of me then,' Della said brightly.

'So John is going to be a solicitor,' Mother said.

'I suppose so.'

'Well, we'll have to see that you do well at school, have the right sort of clothes and the right sort of conversation, Della. John Thornham's family will expect nothing less from the girl John marries.'

I wanted the conversation to end; I had no appetite for my breakfast and I wasn't too fond of my sister Della.

There were many changes during the next six years. Queen Victoria died on the 22nd of January in 1901 and we had a king on the throne, her son Edward. Suddenly life seemed more colourful, music more tuneful.

A change more close to our family life came when Grandmother elected to leave the square to make her home near to an old friend who was now living in Torquay. Nothing my father said could dissuade her since her friend was writing long enthusiastic letters proclaiming how much more Torquay had to offer than the staid, time-worn interests of Stevenson Square.

My parents helped her to find a suitable property and we visited whenever it was possible. She seemed entirely happy there with a new circle of friends and appeared more youthful than she had for years.

Ruth was the one who caused my parents the most disappointment. They had expected her to do great things with her music and her reports from the College of Music she attended were excellent, but then Ruth fell in love with a boy she met while travelling to the college, a very handsome boy who worked in one of the city stores, the shoe department to be exact, and all thoughts of becoming a musician were swept from her mind.

There was nothing wrong with the boy, who was good-looking, very polite and adored Ruth, but it was the loss of her music that my parents deplored.

Father found him a job in the works office; he was bright and intelligent so that promotion could be expected at some future date.

They opted for a quiet wedding, preferring the money instead, and we were all delighted when Grandmother came up for a week's holiday to enable her to be there. Aunt May looked predictably glamorous on the arm of Uncle William and Aunt Jane gave us all the benefit of her disapproval from the moment she stalked into church to the moment she left the house after the reception.

Nothing of that could dampen the enthusiasm of the couple exchanging their wedding vows. Ruth was very happy to be Mrs Atherton.

My parents bought them a small house at the other side of the town and Ruth settled down to domesticity. The year after they married Sally was born and although she had caused my parents so much disappointment they realised she was happy with her life and they adored the baby.

Della's wedding to John Thornham was an entirely more elaborate affair and one that caused me despair, particularly when I was expected to act as a bridesmaid.

For too long I had cherished a hope that he would care for me as I grew older, and there had been that one occasion on my fifteenth birthday when he had kissed me and I had clung too tightly to him so that I did not miss the sudden awareness in his eyes when he released me.

After that I never missed an opportunity to chat to him, laugh with him, dance with him until Della said peevishly, 'You embarrass John, Alex, always fussing round him. Why don't you leave him alone?'

Mother too remonstrated with me and John was avoiding me. I was too young. Compared to Della I was a girl with no shape, little dress sense and my conversation was childish. On the day of their wedding I acted my part but at the reception I was sulky and in so much pain I pleaded a terrible headache and was excused from the festivities.

John's parents had moved out of their house across the square and Della and John moved into it. That meant they were our neighbours and I did my best to avoid seeing either of them. John went into his father's law firm and Della entertained her friends to afternoon tea and garden parties; Mother commented that they seemed to be entertaining the entire town but they could obviously afford it.

Another incident happened during my growing up period, but this was of a rather more sad nature. Uncle William died from a heart attack at the age of forty-six and when Sydney left university he went into the family firm to take his father's place. Aunt May was devastated. We saw her every day with tears rolling down her cheeks, sobbing her heart out, while Aunt Jane eyed her with the utmost disdain, saying privately that it was guilt that had brought on this overdone show of grief.

Indeed as the months wore on Aunt May came to our house less and less until in the end it was Father who said, 'May seems to have recovered remarkably well. Sydney tells me his mother is enjoying a holiday in Bournemouth with Jimmy Jefferson.'

'Doesn't Sydney mind?' Mother asked.

'What if he does? We all know May has only ever done what May wanted. She's a widow; I suppose she's every right to please herself.'

'I know, dear, but it's only months since William died.'

Father merely smiled, and I thought about the laughter we heard issuing from Mr Jefferson's private office at the library.

Aunt Jane thought it was scandalous, and at our usual Christmas gathering was not afraid to say so, to which Aunt May retorted that since Uncle William had elected to leave her an income rather than a lump sum and that most of his money would go to her boys, then she obviously had to think about herself.

After Aunt May had departed to attend a musical evening at the City Hall Aunt Jane commented, 'William evidently knew what he was doing; she'd have gone through her money like wildfire. At least this way the boys get their proper share—no doubt her behaviour over the years prompted him to take that step.'

I still liked Aunt May. I saw her many times in the town, beautifully dressed in spite of her so-called reduced income, always affable, greeting friends with her pretty smiles and laughter, treating me to afternoon tea in one of the local cafés she favoured.

'You know, Alex,' she said one day. 'I really did love your Uncle William but he was happy spending all his time in the garden or down at the cricket club, it never entered his head to do what I liked, you know, the theatre and the music halls. Your parents are happy because they like the same sort of things, and your Uncle Alec does as he's told.'

She made me laugh. She was audacious and pretty and I made up my mind that one day I would ask Aunt May to tell me about Alicia. I often looked in the photograph albums and found several where somebody had been cut out of the picture.

I desperately wanted to ask Mother who that person might be but somehow I believed it would be Aunt Alicia who nobody wanted to talk about.

It was the occasion of my eighteenth birthday and as I stepped into my new party dress I asked myself silently where the years had gone. I was the daughter who stayed at home and went shopping with Mother, entertained her guests and learned how to be a good wife to some man who would with luck one day ask me to marry him.

If I'd been born in less salubrious surroundings I would

have found myself a job in a shop or factory, but I'd been educated for better things and instead I learned embroidery, how to paint pretty watercolours, serve the right sort of food on the appropriate crockery, and know which wines went with what. I learned how to dress and how to dance, while attending the local academy, and I now had a shape.

I was tall and slender, my hair was a vibrant strawberry blonde and I had no difficulty in finding dancing partners of the right social background whenever I attended functions my parents thought it right and proper for me to attend. All in all most people thought I was a very fortunate girl; none of them was to know that I was totally bored with the sameness of my existence.

There was constant activity going on in the house and guests were beginning to arrive for the party. I could hear the sound of their vehicles as they drew up and all around the square lights shone out of the windows and people were coming out of their doors to walk across to us.

All our neighbours had been invited, even grumpy old Mr Stokes and his wife who lived at number ten. Mother said nobody must be left out and before I turned away from the window I saw Della leaving their front gate. I knew that she would look beautiful, she always did, and I would see her dancing with John, gazing adoringly up into his eyes, and my heart would be sick with jealousy.

I took a last look in the mirror and was not displeased with what I saw. The dress was lovely, my favourite colour of blue; it swirled round my feet in rich silken folds, showing off my creamy shoulders and emphasising my slender waist.

Mrs Pearson came into my bedroom to view the finished

result and from her expression was not entirely pleased. As fast as she pulled up the bodice I pulled it down again, until in despair she snapped, 'Really, Miss Alex, you are supposed to be a well-brought-up young lady with a sense of decorum. A married lady could show off her décolletage, but a young unmarried girl must be seen to be modest.'

'The dress looks prettier like this, Mrs Pearson,' I protested.

'Well, have your own way, you always have, but you'll not find your cousin Edith wearing a bodice like that.'

Silently I agreed with her. Edith was a faithful copy of her mother, inclined to be plump, stiff and unbending, and men never flirted with Edith, nor she with them.

Mrs Pearson gave me a hard look and left the room in something of a huff; in the next moment there was a little tap on my door and Ruth came in. She was wearing a pink taffeta dress that I recognised as having once been Della's and seeing my half smile she said, 'You recognise it, don't you, Alex.'

'Yes, but you look lovely in it, Ruth.'

'I was so pleased when she offered to give it to me. I like to spend any spare money I have on the baby; she's so beautiful and she needs things more than I do.'

'I suppose Della's wearing something quite expensive and flattering.'

'Of course, and looking very beautiful. Aren't you coming down? I think everybody has arrived.'

So we left the room together and I quickly became surrounded by well-wishers and the air was filled with laughter and music.

Mother said, 'You have a great many presents, Alex, all in the morning room. When you've opened them I suggest you spread them out on the table so that people can see them.'

Indeed I was both touched and overwhelmed by the gifts I received, from expensive family presents to small tokens of affection from the servants. Helping me to set them out Ruth said, 'I'm feeling very envious, Alex. I had the money instead, because it seemed more important when Paul and I had a house to furnish.'

'But you did get presents, Ruth. I bought you a bracelet and I know Mother and Father bought you a gold watch.'

'That's true, but it was nothing like this. I remember when Della was twenty-one the gifts were all over that huge table in the Town Hall, and yours will be too when you come of age.'

At that moment Della and John came into the room. Della placed a gaily wrapped package in my hand and with a bright smile said, 'I had nothing to do with choosing your present, Alex. John selected it—I thought that would please you more.'

When I stared at her in some confusion she said, 'Open it, Alex, and tell me what you think. Here is John: you can tell him yourself how much you like it.'

The velvet box contained a gold necklace with one single sapphire hanging from it, a stone that sparkled under the lights. With a little laugh Della said, 'I thought you'd be wearing blue. Here, let me fasten it for you.'

I thanked them both and as my eyes met John's I felt that between us was something personal, a new awareness that spoke volumes.

'Do hurry up and join us, you two, everybody's wanting to get on with the dancing and that three-piece orchestra

Mother's managed to get hold of from the George Hotel restaurant is straining at the leash,' Ruth called.

I thought about Aunt May, who had found Mother's choice
of an orchestra rather hilarious: three plump middle-aged
ladies, piano, violin and cello as she called them.

It was later in the evening when Mother asked me to tell
everybody that a buffet was laid out in the dining room. I was
on my way into the conservatory when I met John and his
swift sweet smile lit up my day. Taking hold of my hand he
said, 'I remember that you gave me a warm embrace on your
fifteenth birthday, Alex, yet I think this evening you've been
avoiding me.'

I would have pulled away but he drew me closer into his
embrace then he was kissing me as ardently as on that other
time and only stopped when a man's voice behind us said,
'Well, well, that's what I call a happy birthday kiss.'

John released me and, while I stood there blushing furiously,
he merely smiled, saying, 'Alex is young, beautiful and eighteen.
I thought she deserved to be kissed like that. Are you going to
sample the buffet, Edgar? I think we'll find our wives in there.'

Strangely bemused, I had no appetite for what was laid out
in the dining room. Instead I went up to my bedroom and
stood staring out of the window. A thin mist hung around the
square, lingering on the trees and the lines of parked cars, and
my foolish young heart agonised about a future where John
loved me and because he was my sister's husband there was
nothing we could do about it.

I sat on the edge of my bed hugging my knees and it was
Mother coming in search of me that brought me back to earth.

'Alex! What are you doing here? This is your party, every-body is asking for you and toasts are waiting to be drunk. Have you eaten anything?'

I shook my head.

'Why? Aren't you feeling well? You were perfectly all right a little while ago.'

'I'm too excited to eat, Mother. It's a lovely party, I'll come down with you now.'

'Well, just let me look at you; you're rather pale.'

'Honestly, I'm all right, Mother.'

I moved towards the door and doubtfully she followed me.

The people assembled in the dining room, greeted me with cries of welcome and standing with his arm around my shoulder Father proposed my health and a future filled with nothing but joy.

The three-piece orchestra was well received; the three ladies had eaten well and were anxious to show off their ac-complishments on their different instruments and everybody was anxious to dance or listen to them.

I danced with Father and a good many other of our male guests but I wasn't asked to dance by John, who danced all the time with Della. It was just after midnight when Mother said, 'Mr Jefferson is putting on his overcoat, Alex, and I don't know where your Aunt May is, so do be a dear and see if she's in the conservatory. Be very discreet—you know what Aunt May is like.'

CHAPTER THREE

ONLY LOW LAMPS burned in the conservatory and not until I stood on the threshold did I hear a man's voice saying, 'Nice party, John; your little sister-in-law is promising to be quite a beauty. Good job Della didn't see that warm embrace you gave her.'

There was laughter before John said, 'I had Della's permission to give Alex that birthday kiss—it was the last thing she said when we left the house. "Don't forget to kiss Alex, John, it'll really make her day. She's had a crush on you for ages."'

'Oh well, nice to have the wife's permission. My wife wouldn't have been so accommodating, but then I've never had any desire to kiss my sister-in-law. She's hardly a nubile enchanting eighteen-year-old!'

There was more laughter and I stepped hastily into the cloakroom while the two men walked out of the conservatory.

I sat down trembling on the only seat in the room, my thoughts in chaos. Della had asked him to kiss me, and it was a kiss that had meant nothing. I'd been stupid, I'd built my dreams around a shadow: John didn't love me, had never loved me, but he believed I loved him and at that moment I hated him more than I had ever thought to hate anybody.

I knew that hatred wouldn't last and love would die slowly and bitterly in the time ahead. It was my first brush with reality, with a man's duplicity and a sister's thoughtlessness. Pulling myself together I went in search of Aunt May and on entering the conservatory I heard her laughter from the far end.

I found her sitting with Mr Dryesdale, one of my father's business associates whose wife was a friend of my mother's. They were drinking champagne and evidently enjoying each other's company. When they saw me Aunt May called out, 'Has Jimmy sent you, Alex?'

'No, but he's waiting for you rather impatiently, I think.'

She rose to her feet and with a rueful smile said, 'I'd better go, then. Lovely party, Alex. I don't know why we have to leave so early—it's not as though he's driving himself.'

She embraced me warmly before she and Mr Dryesdale left the room. I didn't wish to return to the festivities; I felt sick with humiliation and instead of returning to the music and the laughter I went up the back stairs to my bedroom.

It was there some time later that Mother found me and she stood staring down at me with deep consternation in her eyes.

'So this is where you are, Alex. Have you been crying, is something wrong?'

'I felt sick, Mother. I've eaten too much. I thought if I came to bed without seeing anybody I wouldn't be missed.'

She sat on the edge of my bed and I wished fervently that she'd leave me alone.

'You were so looking forward to the party, Alex, it's a

shame you're not feeling well. Shall I ask Polly to bring you up some warm milk? I'll make your excuses to the guests.'

'No really, Mother, I don't want anything; it'll be better in the morning. They'll be leaving soon, surely.'

'Well yes, some of the older ones. Your sister Della and her husband are still enjoying themselves, Ruth and Paul have left and so have Aunt Jane and Uncle Alec. Who was Aunt May with?'

'Mr Dryesdale, they were just leaving the conservatory when I met them.'

She didn't answer and I wondered stupidly why I felt it necessary to lie to protect Aunt May. After all they'd only been chatting, and yet somehow wherever Aunt May was indiscretion had to be part of it.

'Well if you're sure you don't want anything, Alex, try to get some sleep. I'm so sorry you've had to leave your party; it really has been a great success.'

I lay sleepless, thinking about the future, as I saw it then a future without love. I was going to be one of those girls who lived a gentle existence with their parents, to end up as everybody's aunt, looking after nieces and nephews, and who no man would ever have wished to marry.

Eaten up with self-pity I promised myself that I would never set foot in my sister's house to have Della smiling at me with a sympathetic glint in her eyes, embracing John in front of me with a proprietary air as if to say: This man is mine, he only kisses other women when I allow him to do so.

I'd be a rebel. They would cut my photographs off family groups; I'd do something so outrageous relatives and people who knew us would simply say, 'She's just like her Aunt Alicia.'

But what had Aunt Alicia done to deserve such recriminations? That night while the sound of music floated upwards from the festivities below I vowed that I would ask Aunt May about my father's forgotten sister.

My mother wouldn't tell me anything; there was only Aunt May who I knew would at first decline to speak but would later change her mind. When had she ever been known to keep a secret? Aunt May had always thrived on gossip and in time she'd tell me all I needed to know.

The party faded into limbo and my life resumed its familiar pattern. John came round several weeks later with an invitation to one of Della's garden parties and found me alone writing letters. He came naturally to take me in his arms but I slipped quickly away, saying, 'It's not my birthday today, John. I'm not expecting you to kiss me.'

Doubtfully he said, 'But it doesn't have to be your birthday, Alex. Don't you want me to kiss you?'

'No, why should I? Paul doesn't kiss me every time we meet.'

'But I'm not Paul. I rather thought you and I had a special relationship.'

'Oh, we do. You're my eldest sister's husband and I'm growing up.'

He frowned, left the invitation on the table in front of me and departed in something of a huff. I wondered if he would repeat our conversation to Della.

I was determined I would not go to the garden party. One half of me was desperate to go; I still had forbidden feelings for him but I was also smarting from those words I had heard on the night of my birthday.

I ate nothing that morning and Mother asked anxiously, 'What is it, Alex? You usually eat a hearty breakfast.'

'I'm not hungry, Mother. I have a terrible headache and I didn't sleep well.'

'Perhaps I should call the doctor, there's flu about.'

'Oh no, Mother, I'll stay in today, and I'll be better tomorrow.'

'But the garden party, dear. Della and John will be so disappointed if you don't go.'

'There'll be plenty of guests, Mother; I'm sure I won't be missed.'

All morning she pampered me with hot drinks and potions but when she came no nearer to making me change my mind I watched her depart in the early afternoon with Father, who I thought seemed a rather reluctant guest.

From my bedroom window I could see the square rapidly filling up with people and I noticed Aunt May arriving with a gentleman escort I hadn't seen her with before. I could see Aunt Jane and Uncle Alec arriving with Edith in the company of a young man. No doubt I would hear plenty about this occurrence in due course.

It was later in the afternoon when I saw Aunt May tripping across the square in the direction of our house and I ran quickly down the stairs to open the door.

'Why Alex,' she greeted me. 'Your mother said you didn't feel well. Are you feeling better?'

'Much better, Aunt May.'

'Why don't you get changed and come back with me? It's really quite nice over there.'

'I still have a headache and the party will soon be over. I saw you arriving.'

'Well if you're sure, dear, perhaps I ought to be getting back. I'm with Graham Stedman, I met him last week at the Durrants'. He's come to live in the town, bought that new house at the end of The Crescent.'

'What happened to Mr Jefferson?' I couldn't resist asking, and with a dimpled smile she said, 'We're still good friends, Alex, but we've known each other too long, since we were children, in fact. Don't be reading any more into this than there is, dear, it's all very recent. Perhaps I'd better be getting back to the party.'

'Aunt May, there's something I very much want to ask you. Can you spare just a few minutes?'

'Well dear, they'll all be wondering where I am. Can I meet you tomorrow in the town?'

'I want to meet you without Mother.'

'It all sounds very mysterious.'

'Please Aunt May, a few minutes, that's all it will take.'

'Oh, all right then. I usually go missing at parties and there's always speculation as to where I am and who I'm with. I don't suppose today will be any exception.'

She followed me into the drawing room and I went immediately to the bureau and took out the photographs which I had found hidden there. Handing them to her I said, 'Why is there somebody cut off from all these pictures, Aunt May? Is it Aunt Alicia?'

For several minutes she stared down at the pictures before she looked at me doubtfully.

'Please, Aunt May,' I pleaded. 'Ever since I can remember there's been some sort of mystery surrounding Aunt Alicia. My parents never talk about her and there was that awful row on Christmas Day when Aunt Jane mentioned her. Can't you tell me?'

'It shouldn't really come from me, dear. Heaven knows, I'm not favourite number one with any of them.'

'You are with me. It's only Aunt Jane who has a lot to say.'

She sat down in front of the fire still holding the photographs and I prompted, 'It is Aunt Alicia, isn't it?'

'Yes dear.'

'But why?'

'Nobody was permitted to talk about her after she went away. Your grandfather laid down strict rules about that, and your great-grandfather was even more adamant.'

'But what had she done that was so terrible?'

She sat for a few moments staring into the fire and I asked uncertainly, 'What was she like, was she very beautiful?'

She looked up with a smile.

'Oh yes, Alex, she really was, and strangely enough you're the most like her of all the family. I used to see her about the town or in the country lanes riding her horse. She was lovely with hair the colour of yours and she had a beautiful alive sort of face that always seemed to smile. I never thought I'd ever be a member of the Faversham family; my father was only a clerk in the general office, but even then Alicia Faversham was my ideal. I so very much wanted to grow up like her.'

'But you have, Aunt May, you're so pretty and you're so much fun.'

She smiled. 'But your Aunt Alicia, Alex, she was beautiful. I think every man in the town must have been in love with her and I can't believe what she did to destroy it all.'

'But what did she do?'

'She went to some private school with a group of other girls from well-heeled families and she had a special friend called Janice Goulden, whose family were gentlemen farmers in the fells above the town. Most weekends Alicia spent with them, riding and going to parties at nearby houses. She went there one weekend and never came back.'

'Never came back? But where did she go?'

'Your grandparents were frantic with worry. Your father and William were sent immediately to the Gouldens' house but the story they came back with was unbelievable. She'd been there on the Saturday evening at a party as usual. One of the guests had been a cousin of the Gouldens', a young man who was a junior officer on a merchant ship, and Alicia had met him several times at similar functions before. They went off together and all that was left was a brief note saying she was in love and intended to marry him. She asked the family to forget her, not to look for her, and there was nothing any of them could have done to make her change her mind.

'Your grandmother was in despair, your grandfather was bitter, and I think you know the rest, Alex. Every trace of Alicia was obliterated from photographs like these; no mention of her was to be made; if she ever wrote her letters were never opened and none of us have ever seen her since.'

'But this man she married, did none of you ever know him?'

'No. The Gouldens knew him. They said he was a distant relative who spent time with them when he was on leave from his ship, was handsome and well spoken, but had little money. Since he was a merchant seaman she would be allowed to sail on his ship with him.'

'But it's all so cruel, Aunt May.'

'She cut herself off, Alex. Nothing could be done.'

'But why couldn't she have talked to the family, brought him to meet them?'

'You never knew your great-grandfather, Alex. He was stiff-necked and proud. If he'd been alive when I met William he'd never have been allowed to marry me; we had trouble with your grandfather, and it was your father who got him to change his mind about us.'

'I didn't know.'

'Let it be a lesson to you, Alex. Find some young man with money and position, otherwise you too could have trouble.'

Grimly I thought what sort of trouble would I have been in if the family had had any inkling that I was in love with my sister's husband; but that was something I had to forget about one way or another.

In the days that followed I combed the house for any lingering trace of Aunt Alicia. I even searched the kitchens when the servants were busy elsewhere and Mrs Pearson was out.

Nothing remained of her. No more photographs with her excluded, no small mementoes revealing that my father and his brothers had ever had a sister; it became an obsession with me.

Cousin Edith's engagement to a certain Mr Algernon Buckley was discussed at great length whenever Aunt Jane called to see us and she called often in the next few weeks. Mr Buckley was the son of a yeoman farmer with a great deal of land and a lucrative farm on the fells above the Thornham mansion. As an only son with two sisters, it would appear he had a great deal to offer Cousin Edith.

Della was amused by it. 'You're lagging behind, Alex,' she taunted me. 'Here's Edith, as plain as a pikestaff, while you've always been considered the beauty of the family. Could it be that you're secretly pining for somebody else?'

'You're behaving very spitefully, Della,' Mother said in some annoyance. 'What's got into you? I thought you were friends.'

'Well we are, Mother, it's just that Alex is being perverse. She didn't come to our garden party and she never visits us. She's the difficult one, even John's remarked about it.'

'Alex wasn't well on the day of your party.'

'There's been plenty of time for her to make up for it, though. Did you know Aunt May's gone to Broadstairs with that man she brought to our party, who's very rich? Trust Aunt May to find somebody like that.'

I was beginning to hate my life with the constant tittle-tattle and vague innuendoes. It was one evening several days later when I realised something had to change.

I was in the garden at the back of the house. Mother had gone to one of her various committees, Father was at work and the garden could not be seen from the kitchen window. Our gardener was ill so I had promised my father to do some weeding and I was so engrossed that I did not hear the catch on the wicker door, then suddenly two arms were encircling me and I was pulled back into John Thornham's embrace. He was laughing down into my eyes, saying, 'Why didn't you come to our party, Alex? Surely you knew I would miss you?'

The more I struggled the closer his arms held me, and then suddenly I heard my sister's voice. 'I followed you, I knew you were coming here.'

He released me so suddenly I had to hold on to the archway

to stop myself from falling, while John faced his wife, who was standing near the gate, with a furious expression on her face.

'Darling, it was nothing,' he said. 'I was simply teasing Alex that she hadn't been at our party.'

'You fool, John,' she stormed. 'She's crazy about you. She's been after you since the day she saw you.' Then turning to me she said viciously, 'He's mine, Alex, never forget it. I'll have something to say about this to Mother when she gets home.'

That was the start of it. Long strictures on an infatuation that was doomed and should never have been from both my parents, and the worst of it was that Aunt Jane knew about it.

'Really, Alex,' she chided, 'whatever possessed you to think John cared anything about you? He's your sister's husband and they're very much in love. You should put him out of your mind right now.'

The irony was that I had now done so. Whatever romantic ideas I had ever entertained for John Thornham were history and I was furious with myself that I should ever have harboured them.

Aunt May was the most sympathetic person I could talk to. 'You don't really like him, do you, Alex?' she asked gently.

'I thought I did once, but I don't any more.'

'Don't worry, Alex, they'll get over it and you'll meet some nice young man who doesn't belong to somebody else.'

In the days that followed I thought that everybody in Stevenson Square knew about the episode. I felt that everybody was talking about me, and at home even my parents watched my comings and goings with doubtful expressions.

I felt that the servants knew about it. Never a favourite with

Mrs Pearson, I became accustomed to her frowns of reproach and the younger servants' sympathetic smiles. Della ignored me whenever she came to the house but it seemed John Thornham had escaped without censure of any kind.

I became lethargic and anxious about my future. What was there for me in this house reminiscent of my grandfather's days? I felt destined to becoming an old maiden aunt who would live out her days in genteel obscurity and the thought of it appalled me.

I, who had always been the happy-go-lucky one, the one who had laughed and danced her way through her schooldays, now felt stifled by a future that was both uneventful and predictable.

Mother was worried about me to such an extent that she suggested she and I should take a few days' holiday with Grandmother in Devon. It was something I couldn't face when I remembered Grandmother's long diatribes on how young ladies should behave and behind all the strictures would be thoughts of Aunt Alicia and how she had betrayed all of them.

I lost interest in clothes; I didn't want to go to the shops or the concerts in the town, and Aunt May said one Sunday, 'I think it's disgusting that everybody's blaming Alex when it takes two to cause an uproar like this one. Nobody seems to think John Thornham had anything to do with it, but he was here with Alex in the garden and she hadn't invited him here.'

Quick to defend her nephew, Aunt Jane said, 'He merely came to ask why she stayed away from their garden party. It was Alex who threw herself at him.'

'Why is everybody so anxious to believe him rather than Alex?'

'I've always found my nephew to be very circumspect and

honourable,' Aunt Jane snapped. 'Alex has always been the flighty one.'

Her looks said it all. Another Alicia, another Aunt May, and I felt trapped in an environment from which there was no escape.

The only relief came from the fact that Aunt May decided she would go on a cruise liner in the company of a gentleman she had met at the music circle. None of us knew him or anything about him. He was new in the town and Aunt May did not enlighten us.

She smiled at me mischievously across the dining table, saying, 'Well at least my misdemeanours will take some of the heat off poor Alex. I'm looking forward to spending some time in the sun. We're sailing to the Canaries and on the way back we're docking in Barcelona. It's time you launched out, Jane, you and Alec only ever seem to go as far as Bognor.'

'Foreign places don't interest us—there's enough to see in this country,' Aunt Jane snapped. 'We once spent three weeks in Madeira and it was too hot for me.'

'Well, of course if you never feel adventurous…One of these days, Alex, you and I will take a trip abroad: it will broaden your horizons.' Aunt May's sentiment was ignored by everybody else round the table.

CHAPTER FOUR

AT THE BEGINNING of May Della and her husband departed for a holiday in America and Aunt May and her gentleman friend left on their cruise liner. Cousin Edith announced that she would marry at the beginning of July; I was not elected to be one of her bridesmaids.

This did not trouble me in the slightest but I wondered how long I would be frowned upon by all and sundry for a childish infatuation and a snatched embrace that had not been my fault.

Only Ruth seemed to be happy with her lot. The baby was enchanting and her husband had worked so diligently in his job my father promoted him to something decidedly more lucrative, so much so that they moved from their small terraced house into new property being built in the town.

When my parents decided they would travel down to Devon to stay with Grandmother at the end of June I was invited to go with them, an invitation I was quick to decline.

I was convinced that by this time my grandmother would have been made fully aware of my indiscretions and I wanted no more strictures. I refused to go with them, much to Mother's annoyance.

'But what will you do all on your own?' she asked plaintively. 'Your Grandmother would like to see you, and there'll only be the two young girls to look after you and the house. Mrs Pearson's going to Wiltshire to spend time with her sister.'

'Mother, I don't need looking after. I can do that for myself.'

'All the same, Alex, I would have thought you would want to see Grandmother. Why, you were the one who always took the trouble to visit them every Sunday.'

I watched them leave in a flurry of light summer rain and when I closed the front door I became aware of a feeling of utter loneliness. When I walked out into the square I felt that I had been cast in the role of femme fatale, a girl who had designs on her sister's husband, and that all the people I met were aware of it.

Mrs Pearson departed for Wiltshire but even in that short space of time I became miserably aware of her frowns of disapproval. It was during one of my morning visits to the library that I met Beatrice Roper, my one schoolfriend who could be relied upon to demonstrate the utmost spite.

'Alex Faversham,' she greeted me in a loud voice. 'Where have you been putting yourself these last few weeks? Afraid to venture out?'

'No, Beatrice, why should I be?'

'Well, you know. Your sister's spread it around that you had designs on her husband. I can't think why, he's an awful stuffed shirt.'

'No, I can't think why either, and you're right, he is a stuffed shirt.'

'Then why, Alex?'

'Growing-up pains, I expect.'

'Della's obviously spirited him off to America to get over things.'

'There's nothing to get over. They've gone on a holiday, not to escape triviality.'

'Your Aunt May's off with another admirer too. I must say she gets around.'

'Yes. I'm so glad, she's a widow, she has a right to please herself without a lot of silly women gossiping about her. It's a great pity they've nothing better to do.'

'Oh I do agree, Alex. We really must see more of each other; we were such friends at school.'

I ignored the suggestion. Beatrice and I had never been great friends, and I had always found her malicious and spiteful, the sort of girl who delighted in other people's misfortunes, but my meeting with her had unsettled me yet again.

We walked together from the library and when we neared Stevenson Square Beatrice said, 'All this was very smart. Now there are so many new properties going up all over the place. Your sister Ruth is moving, I believe.'

'Yes. Their new house is very nice.'

'She didn't do much with her music, did she?'

'She still plays the piano but has no intentions of making a career in music. She's very happy with her husband and baby.'

'That's nice. But who is he? I never heard of him.'

'Why should you? He's extremely nice and doing well in the firm.'

'How nice! And what about Edith, she's getting married soon. I must say I was surprised that she's beaten you to the altar, Alex, after all, she was no great shakes as a beauty.'

I was tired of her comments and her company, and was glad when she reached the square so that we could part. She kissed me effusively, then looking up the square said, 'There's a large motor car parked there. Is it outside your house, Alex?'

I followed her gaze and indeed there was a large grey car parked there, but I didn't recognise it. Beatrice was staring at it curiously. 'It *is* at your house, Alex, there's a chauffeur sitting inside it and there's somebody standing at your front door. It all looks very exciting.'

'Goodbye, Beatrice, I'd better see who it is,' I answered her quickly, and hurried away. I turned at the gate to see her standing where I had left her but as I walked up the path a woman who had been waiting on the doorstep turned round to smile.

She was elegantly dressed in silver grey and round her shoulders was the sheen of furs. She was tall and slender with a small velvet hat positioned attractively on her blonde hair. We stared at each other for several minutes before she said, 'Which one are you, I wonder? I suspect it is Alexandra.'

I had never seen her before, but in those first few moments I had the oddest sensation that somehow my entire life was going to change. She was incredibly beautiful and she was looking at me with a degree of intensity that seemed peculiar from a total stranger.

'It is Alex, isn't it?' she asked gently.

'Yes, but I don't know you.'

'My dear, how could you? I'm your Aunt Alicia.'

I stared at her in amazement, and of course she couldn't be anybody else. This is how I had imagined she would look. Tall and graceful, elegantly beautiful, and she was smiling at me; her face was so reminiscent of my own that had looked back at me from mirrors as I grew older.

Her hair was the same colour as my own, her eyes as steadily blue, her smile was my smile, and when people had said over the years that I reminded them of Alicia, whenever they dared mention her name, I now realised they were right.

'You must be very surprised to see me, Alex. I don't suppose you know anything about me,' she said softly.

'But I do. I asked Aunt May, because I wanted to find out. I'm just so surprised to see you here at last.'

'I'm in England for a very short time. Against all my better judgement I had to come here, had to see the old square, I'm not expecting a welcome.'

'There's only me at home. My parents are in Devon with Grandmother.'

She looked upward at the facade of the house and anxiously I said, 'Please, please come in and talk to me. We can have tea, oh please, you have no idea how often I've wanted to meet you.'

My fingers fiddled nervously with my door key then at last the door was open and I was ushering her into the hall where she stood looking around her. I went to open the drawing-room door and she went before me into the room with a strange haunted expression on her face. At last she said, 'But it's just the same! This is exactly as it was, your parents haven't changed a thing.'

'No. Grandmother said this furniture was too large for her new house so she took some of ours and Mother and Father decided to keep this. It is right for the house, Father said.'

'Well, yes. That was always your grandfather's chair, and your grandmother would sit across from him doing her embroidery.' She smiled. 'My mother preferred to sit in the window, since it was light there. Oh Alex, whenever I closed my eyes I could picture this room just as it is now, and the square. I never really left it.'

I knew in those first few moments as she walked around the room that she had forgotten my existence. She was reliving her girlhood in this house, in this room. Her face was reflective as she occasionally picked up an ornament or a photograph and when at last her eyes met mine I was aware that hers were swimming with tears.

'Please sit down, Aunt Alicia. I'll ask one of the girls to bring in tea.'

'No, Alex, I have a better idea. I'm staying tonight at that new hotel in the High Street. Why don't you dine with me? Unless of course you have something better to do.'

'Oh no, no I haven't. How awful that you feel you have to stay there when you could stay here.'

'I would prefer to stay there, it's really very nice. I preferred it to the George—there are no memories associated with the Adelphi.'

'No. It was only built last year. I'll have to change, I don't feel properly dressed for a meal out.'

'Then I'll sit here in front of the fire until you're ready. Are there some photographs I could be looking at?'

'I never know where they are, but you can look at Della's and Ruth's wedding photographs.'

'Yes, that will be nice. I don't suppose there are any of me lying around. I forfeited all right to be remembered in this household a long time ago.'

I left her poring over the wedding photographs before I

hurried upstairs to change. Tonight I was determined to learn more about Aunt Alicia's adventures after she turned her back on Stevenson Square forever.

I was well aware that people were staring at us as we climbed into the large Daimler and throughout our progress round the square curtains were lifted and I was certain the tale would be well and truly hashed over in the weeks to come.

The Adelphi was grand. We were waited upon by a foreign waiter who made me feel incredibly important as he summoned the wine waiter and carried out his duties with great style and aplomb.

After we had eaten and we were walking out of the dining room she said, 'We'll go up to my room, Alex. It's a beautiful room overlooking the gardens but we can talk there without anybody coming into the hotel who might recognise you. It's unlikely anyone will recognise me.'

Coffee was served to us in her room which was certainly luxurious and as she took her place beside me I was aware of the subtlety of her perfume and the sheen of jewels round her throat and on her hands.

'Now,' she prompted me, 'tell me about yourself.'

'There's not much to tell; I'd far rather hear about you.'

'Tell me what you know.'

'It's only what Aunt May said. I couldn't ask Mother and I was curious.'

'You didn't know your father had a sister?'

'Yes. Now and again somebody somewhere let something slip. It was always hushed up, then there were the photographs.' At her raised eyebrows I said nervously, 'There was always one person who had been cut away. With such a mystery about it, I had to find out.'

'I never really knew May. She was just a young girl I used to see about the town; I think her father worked for my grandfather. So she captured William?'

'Yes, and he died. She has two boys, and she's nice and jolly. I've always liked her.'

She smiled. 'And Jane, Alec's wife?'

'She's all right, I suppose, but I prefer the other one. They have a daughter, Edith, who's just got engaged to be married, and a son, Cousin Gordon.'

'And my father died?'

'Yes, so Grandmother left here and we moved in. Sometimes I think I'm destined to spend the rest of my life in Stevenson Square.'

'That's exactly how I felt, my dear. It was either some boy the family found for me, eminently suitable, or a lifetime as the daughter of the house, the maiden aunt, caring for my parents and my nieces and nephews.'

'It's the same for me.'

She smiled. 'I've heard many times that history can repeat itself. You don't feel happy with that sort of future, Alex, and it's beginning to worry you.'

'You have no idea how much.'

'But you're so young! What are you, seventeen, eighteen? Younger than I was when I ran away.'

'I'm eighteen. I've been such a fool, and now nobody has a good word for me and I can't see things ever getting any better.'

'Tell me about it.'

So I told her about John Thornham and a silly young girl's love that had turned sour, leaving me the predator and John strangely unsullied.

She listened without interrupting me and when the sorry tale was told she said, 'It'll pass, Alex, but it will be hard with your sister and her husband living so close. I suspect she's making the most of it.'

'Oh yes, yes she is. I don't want to talk about it any more. I'd much rather hear about you. Please, Aunt Alicia, right from the beginning, from the night you left home. Aunt May said it was too romantic for words.'

'Romantic! Perhaps it was for me, for Johnny too, but there were so many people I hurt that even when I've been most happy the pain never went away. They apparently forgave me and I never forgave myself.

'I knew Johnny Cameron well. Over the years whenever he came home on leave he came to my friend's parents' house and we had such fun there. They were a jolly family; they had parties and picnics and there was always so much going on so I spent weekends there. My parents didn't mind. One of my brothers escorted me there and came for me to take me home. On the weekend I left home for good I told them my friend's father would bring me home. I didn't want them finding out too soon that I was never going back.'

'You went with Johnny?'

'Yes. He was a junior officer in the merchant navy. He was handsome and such fun to be with. I believed I loved him rapturously; we loved each other. We were married by his captain on the ship, and I sailed with him to Australia.

'For those first few years it was wonderful. We went everywhere, all the exotic places I'd only dreamed about. We bought a small cottage for those times we spent in England. It was poky and the windows fitted badly so that the rooms never seemed to get warm, and the chimney smoked terribly. I hated it. I thought about the luxury of Stevenson Square and became miserably aware that I could never go back.

'When my daughter Sophie was born Johnny went to sea and I had to stay on with her in that tiny cottage. Johnny knew I was unhappy and then he decided to change to passenger ships.

'He was Junior Fourth Officer, but once again I could sail with him and things were better between us. Then as he got promotion and moved on to larger ships, more salubrious ships, Sophie was left at home in England at a good school and I thought I was having the most wonderful time. I was pretty and the ship abounded with rich men only too willing to flirt with me and flatter me. I absorbed it all as my right and things between Johnny and me were becoming impossible.

'I had married a nice boy with ambition in his chosen profession; he had married a spoilt foolish girl, ridiculously at variance with her family and her life and eager for what she thought of as adventure.

'Johnny divorced me.'

She was sitting staring down at her hands resting on her lap, idly twisting the rings on her fingers, and I waited anxiously to hear the rest of it. Her thoughts were in the past and I was momentarily forgotten. At last she raised her head to look at me and there was so much pain in her eyes I felt the burning sensation of tears in mine.

'It isn't a pretty story, Alex,' she went on. 'When we returned to Southampton I went back to the cottage. The man I had believed loved me vanished like a summer storm and there was Sophie to think about. I loved her, but I couldn't provide for her. Johnny had received promotion but he was at sea more than he was at home, and although he was generous with money I couldn't visualise my life on my own with a young daughter to think about.

'On the last voyage I'd become very friendly with an older woman who was an avid traveller. She'd seen how things were doing and her last words to me before she left the ship at New York was that we should keep in touch. "I'll be dying to know how you resolve all this, honey," she said, "promise you'll let me know." Her name was Violet Polenski. She was the widow of a Polish Jew.

'I wrote to her and waited eagerly for her reply. When it came I could hardly believe the solution she was offering me. She was rich, she wanted a travelling companion and I fitted the bill in every respect.

'My acceptance of her offer gave Johnny all the leeway he wanted. We would both be travellers on the world scene but he had a mother and a sister who could give Sophie a home and a stable background. I was granted the right to see her whenever it was convenient, but in essence she would belong to Johnny.

'I'm not asking for sympathy, Alex. My life was a mess and it had all been my fault. I had lost my family, my husband, my daughter and my home, and I had also lost the man who had been my lover. All I now had was an uncertain future with a woman I hardly knew in a life I could only speculate on.'

'Did you see Sophie frequently?' I asked.

'Whenever I was in England, which wasn't very often. She was a beautiful girl but I never really got to know her. She was always polite, never demonstrative, and her aunt and grandmother kept her on a very tight rein. They resented my visits; they had very little time for me, rightly so I suppose, but after each visit I felt I knew her less and less until after the last one I realised we had had very little to say to each other.

'I talked about our travels: Paris and Rome, Vienna and Athens, but I learned very little about Sophie beyond the quite expensive boarding school Johnny was sending her to, and a voyage she would be taking with him during her summer holidays. There would be no regrets on Sophie's part if I disappeared into oblivion.'

'Were you happy travelling the world with your new friend?'

'At first, perhaps; later it was more difficult. Violet was the one with the money and she paid me a salary to act as her companion. She could afford the clothes and the jewels and she was annoyed when the men we met paid more attention to me than they did to her.

'She was fifteen years older than I, she was plump, not particularly attractive. If they flattered Violet they were aware of her money, whereas when they flirted with me they had more amorous intentions. We squabbled and made it up, we said our liaison had been a mistake and decided to separate, but she needed me perhaps more than I needed her.'

'Are you still with her? Is she here in England with you?'

She smiled. 'No, Violet and I parted a long time ago. She wanted to go to Vienna; she drooled on and on about the

Empire of the Habsburgs, the endless waltzes, the sheer glamour of Vienna with its operettas and its palaces.

'On our first night she wanted to go to the opera. They were performing *The Merry Widow* and all Europe was waltzing to its melodies. Everybody dressed up for the opera house: the men wore their orders, the women tiaras and their jewels and there were countless glamorous uniforms among them.

'I borrowed a dress from Violet and spent all day taking it in to fit me. It was pale blue, unadorned and hardly a dress to invite attention, whereas Violet wore a new cream satin confection and every item of jewellery she possessed. The only thing she didn't have was a tiara so she ordered orchids for her hair which seemed to make her singularly overdressed.

'She was ecstatic with the appearance of the Emperor and his Empress, he a slender grey-haired man, the Empress quite beautiful. By hook or by crook Violet had succeeded in obtaining a box from which we could see everybody in the royal box and since I was sitting hidden away behind her voluminous skirts all I had was a commentary on events taking place.

'It was much later on the staircase that Violet dropped her purse and we were surrounded by people anxious to help her find it and alleviate her very evident distress.'

I could tell from her expression that her entire thoughts were focused on another time and place. Her eyes were strangely sad, her mouth set in a wistful smile and when at last her eyes met mine I was dismally aware of the feelings of regret that she was unable to escape from.

She sensed the anticipation in my eyes. There had to be more, much more, and she said softly, 'That was the moment I looked up into his eyes without realising that once again fate was being unkind. It would have been better if we had never met.'

CHAPTER FIVE

I SAT WAITING PATIENTLY for her to continue with her story but as before her thoughts were concentrated on a past tinged with regret and burdened with bitterness. At last I was prompted to ask, 'Why are your memories making you so sad? Are they to do with that man?'

She nodded. 'So many of them are sad, Alex, but so many more are wonderfully happy. We stayed on in Vienna and Violet was happy to spend her money to ingratiate herself with a crowd of hangers-on, people who lingered on the edge of the Viennese aristocracy; many of them had escaped from their own war-torn countries, holding on to titles that meant nothing, but they saw nothing wrong in cultivating a rich American lady who was happy to be with them and finance many of their dubious enterprises.

'We went to the opera and the garden parties, to the musical evenings where they gained entry as a result of their titles and Violet was welcomed because of her money. I was the paid companion. I stayed in the background sometimes wishing I was miles away, while Violet exulted in the lime-light and her ability to pay for it.'

'Was this man one of the people you're talking about?' I asked her.

'No, Alex. He was Hungarian, an aristocratic officer in the Emperor's Guard, and he was quite uninterested in Violet's new friends. He was interested in me and while Violet amused herself with her crowd Zoltan and I went to the opera and the ballet. We spent evenings in Grinzing listening to music in the beer gardens and taverns and I felt that I had never been so alive before, or so much in love.'

'But you said it would have been better if you had never met.'

'Yes, that is true. Violet woke up to the fact that she was seeing little of me and it was then that resentment began to take the place of friendship. She accused me of using her, even of deserting her, and stated her intention of moving on. She was tired of Vienna, tired of the superficial crowd who surrounded her, and I realised that she was expecting me to go with her. She resented Zoltan; there was so much jealousy I was subjected to long silences or accusations that I had neglected her. In desperation I told Zoltan that I could not see him any more, that I was leaving Vienna. Violet said he would let me leave without a protest, that he had no deep feelings for me, and I should be glad to get away from the city and a love affair that was going nowhere.

'Zoltan persuaded me to stay. I had little money, but he found a modest pension for me in Grinzing and Violet departed after telling me I was a fool to expect anything more from Zoltan beyond a brief affair.

'It was an enchanting summer. The owner of the pension found me work sorting out his disastrous accountancy methods and I could speak German fairly fluently. The evenings were spent waltzing to music that was so romantic and melodious I had few thoughts beyond the time we were together and none at all as to where we were heading.

'Zoltan told me he was returning to Budapest to see his family and would be away two weeks, then when he came back we would speak of marriage after he had told his family about me. The days seemed endless as I waited for the evening he promised to meet me in our favourite tavern.

'I remember dressing up for the occasion, and how my feet danced along the street that night. There were lanterns in the trees and music poured out of every door. Young lovers walked under the linden trees and I was sure that my future would be in Vienna with the man I loved, and nothing that had gone before and nothing that would come after would have the power to take away what we would have that night.

'I sat at the table near the window so that I could watch the people walking from the gates across the garden. I was intensely aware of the music and the laughter around me until the laughter died away, the stars paled and the musicians looked at me with weary eyes; everybody else had gone home. At last they began to put away their instruments and the owner of the café came to the table and looked down at me with sympathetic eyes, saying, "He will not come now, Fräulein, it is very late."

'Even then I couldn't believe that it was over. He had been detained, Budapest was a long way away, he had duties with his regiment. Everything under the sun had delayed him; tomorrow he would come.

'I went every night for a week to that café and every night those people around me looked at me with curious sympathy and the café owner shook his head sadly, his eyes filled with pity.

'I don't remember anything of the street when I walked

back from the inn on the final night. I had almost reached the pension when a horse-drawn carriage pulled up at the entrance and a man descended into the road. He held the door open for me to pass in before him, then to my amazement he said, "Am I addressing Fräulein Faversham?"

'I had reverted to my maiden name but I did not know the person speaking to me and I looked up at him in surprise. He was tall, silver-haired and he bore an aristocratic air; his voice too was cultured. He repeated his question, and I nodded dully.

'"Is there somewhere we can talk, Fräulein?" he asked, and indicating the office behind the bar he followed me there. I did not know this man, I couldn't imagine what he wanted with me, but I was not left too long in doubt.

'"I have seen you in the café waiting for Zoltan Bartok. I did not wish to speak with you there, but I need to speak to you tonight."

'I looked up at him expectantly. This was it, Zoltan had sent him with an explanation, but his expression sent my hopes crumbling. It was not unkind, but nor was it reassuring.

'"Zoltan is my nephew, Fräulein. He is with his regiment in Slovenia and you will not see him again," he said.

'I was aware of the tears filling my eyes, my hands were trembling, and then not unkindly he pulled forward a chair and told me to sit down. "I am sorry to bring you this news, Fräulein, but whatever hopes you possessed regarding my nephew were entirely misplaced. He has no money of his own. He is dependent on his family for finances and on his pay from the regiment. If he marries it must be to a woman chosen by his family, so I see little point in trying to cover it with a gloss that means nothing."

'He was looking down at me with an expression I couldn't read, but all I wanted was to be left alone. I couldn't trust myself to stand up, if I did I felt sure I would make a fool of myself by fainting, then he said, "You are staying here and have work here, Fräulein?"

'I didn't answer him. Why did he know so much about me? Zoltan had told him, but it had nothing to do with him, and why should he care?

'He pulled up a chair and sat opposite me.

'"I do not know how long you intend to stay here now, Fräulein, but you need money." He opened his wallet and took out a wad of banknotes which he placed on the table near us. It was then some remnants of pride came to me and I snapped, "I do not require your money, sir. As you say, I have work here."

'"But you are English, are you not? Why should you wish to remain here?" he asked.

'I didn't answer him; I didn't think it was any of his business. He put his money away and left. I gave him no further thought, since I did not expect to meet him again, but the machinations of fate are unpredictable.'

'You met him again?' I asked curiously.

'Yes, and I met other men, army officers, businessmen who came to the inn. They were intrigued by an Englishwoman who paid them little attention and didn't respond to their flattery.

'The innkeeper began to rely on me for inspiration as to how he could improve the entertainment in the inn and in the tea garden, and I had all sorts of ideas so that eventually the inn became the most successful in Grinzing. Every weekend people drove in from Vienna to hear singers from the opera house singing operetta and one day he came with a group of aristocratic people.'

'Do you mean Zoltan?'

'No. Count Bruckner, Zoltan's uncle. He made it his business to talk to me. It was civilised and no reference was made to the past by either of us.

'He was Austrian and I learned much later that his sister was Zoltan's mother. He was an aristocrat and very rich, he mingled in court circles and had a vast estate in the country outside Vienna. He was charming and courteous and he revived my shattered pride like no other.

'Over the months that followed he introduced me to the upper echelons of society. I was flattered to be in the midst of a circle in which Zoltan was a mere serving officer and whenever we met I sensed the jealousy and bitterness in his eyes. I had no thoughts of where our friendship was going— to me, Franz was an escort. I refused to accept the jewels he offered me but as time passed his friendship became very important to me. We were not lovers.

'I couldn't believe it when he asked me to marry him. I was twenty-nine years old, he was forty-five. We came from different worlds, and for the first time I thought about returning to England, but to what?

'Franz was persuasive, and he was offering me a safe and luxurious future. There were more things for it than against it, and in the end I agreed to marry him.'

'Have you been happy?' I asked her.

'I have been content. Franz has been a thoughtful and considerate husband. I respect him, although I have never loved him and it has been a marriage to suit us both. I have been hostess to his friends and mistress of his house. We have both played our part, and that is all I can say about the situation.'

I stared at her doubtfully before saying, 'Where is he now, in Vienna?'

'No, he is in London at the embassy. I came up here alone. I have been to see the girl I was at school with; strangely enough from time to time we corresponded with each other, and it was from Janice that I learned my father had died and what was happening to the rest of the family. I learned about Johnny and Sophie too. Johnny has married again, very happily, I'm glad to say, and he has two boys. Sophie is married also and living in Canada, so we all have new lives. Johnny doesn't figure in mine nor I in his.'

'But you had decided to see us.'

'I stood on the doorstep but I did not knock on the door. I was about to turn away when you came and that is why we are here.'

'But you'll come again, Aunt Alicia? I'll talk to my parents, I'll tell them all that has happened to you, then surely everything will be forgiven and forgotten.'

She shook her head. 'You forget that Vienna is a long way away, Alex, and that is where my home is. You are so like me, but don't be. Whatever worries you have now, this is where your heart is, not on some wild goose chase after excitement and fantasies. I was a very foolish and selfish young girl with little thought for anything and anybody outside myself.'

'But it must be wonderful to live in Vienna, and in such style. I've read all about the Habsburg Empire, all about the operettas and the waltzes. How can this stodgy existence we live compare with all that?'

'It can't my dear. But the heady imperial Vienna that you

have read about is dying on its feet, the waltzes are sweeping to an end, oh perhaps not tomorrow or next year, but soon Alex, believe me.'

I looked at her in agonising silence, then with a little smile she said, 'Come, we must get you home, it's very late. Is there nobody at home to worry about you?'

'No. Only the two housemaids and they'll be in bed by this time.'

As we drove through the empty streets to Stevenson Square I murmured, 'I'll bet the streets in Vienna are not like this. The cafés will be crowded and there'll be waltz music pouring out of all of them.'

She laughed.

'You could be right, Alex, but underneath the music and the waltzes, there is often a sense of the old Vienna that is already doomed.'

'When will you go to London?'

'In the morning, Alex. I promised Franz I would return then.'

'Will you ever come back, do you think?'

'To England probably, but not to Stevenson Square.'

'Then I shall never see you again.'

She smiled gently. 'No, Alex, but although we have only met briefly I am glad that we have done so. Think of me kindly, my dear, but never never attempt to emulate me.'

'I want to! Everybody has always said I resemble you, which is a good start.'

'This is a changing world, Alex; new songs will be sung, new stars will appear. Think of our meeting today as our little secret, then make the very best of your life, even when it appears most difficult.'

She reached out and embraced me. I could smell her perfume, feel the velvet softness of her cheek against mine; then with a little smile she turned and walked back to her car.

They waited until I had unlocked the front door and entered the house then I ran to the morning-room window so that I could watch them driving away. There were no lights in the square and looking at the clock I was surprised to see that it was well after midnight.

I felt both restless and exhilarated by our meeting. Aunt Alicia had always been a phantom figure every time I came to the house as a child. I had pictured her running down the stairs, sitting at the piano, walking in the garden, and I had pictured her looking like me. Now we had met and the real Aunt Alicia was more enchanting than any of my imaginings.

She had not sought to glamorise her life to me, but now I was doing that for her. The cruise ships with a handsome young husband in spite of the fact that they had parted. The allure of Vienna and its eternal waltzes, the handsome Hungarian officer she had been in love with and the husband she was married to. Rich, aristocratic, and yet a vague shadowy figure I could not as yet put a face to. It was the stuff of every romantic novel I had ever read and I wanted to shout her story from the housetops, tell all my friends about her, tell the family.

Life in Stevenson Square got back to normal. My parents came back from Devon, Aunt May returned from her cruise, filled with enthusiasm for more of the same, and obviously well suited with her latest gentleman friend. Della and her husband returned from America, equally delighted with all they had seen; how I longed to silence them all with the story I could tell about Aunt Alicia.

Grandmother had been disappointed that I had not seen fit to visit her and life assumed its familiar pattern: shopping in the High Street and visiting the library. Ruth and her family came every Sunday for tea, Della continued to give her parties to which I was now invited, even when I was dismally aware of her watchful eyes on me and her husband's very obvious distance.

I longed to tell Aunt May about Alicia's visit but I knew that she had never been able to keep a secret and would delight in telling everybody, particularly about Alicia's life-style and her aristocratic husband.

Cousin Edith was to be married in early July and had chosen her bridesmaids from her mother's side of the family, a fact that didn't worry me in the slightest even when Mother was hurt about it.

'Really, Alex,' she said mournfully, 'whatever have you done to turn them against you? You're the only cousin she has on her father's side of the family who is unmarried. Wouldn't you just have thought she'd want you as her bridesmaid?'

I was invited often to parties in the homes of old school-friends and there were a host of young men anxious to dance with me and invite me out, but they were all of a pattern: young men my parents would have approved of with decent professions and great expectations. I thought about Aunt Alicia and Johnny. Would there ever be a young man I could contemplate leaving home for?

One young man was more persistent than the others. His name was Noël Belsize and his father was a solicitor in the town. Noël was also in the family business and destined for better things.

My parents and the family generally seemed pleased with our friendship. Noël was very presentable, good-looking and well educated, and even Aunt Jane decided to invite him to Edith's wedding. We were beginning to be looked upon as a pair until he invited another girl to the Law Society's ball.

Millicent Downing was my age, a nice quiet girl of no great beauty, but her father was a great friend of Noël's parents. My parents were annoyed by his act. They called it insensitive; Aunt May was furious, Della strangely noncommittal. He turned up later like a bad penny to invite me to the Mayor's ball and when I mounted my high horse and refused his invitation we had words, from which I learned that my sister had been spreading it around that her husband and I had been rather more than friends.

That was the occasion when I decided I'd had enough of Stevenson Square and the people in it.

I loved my parents, Ruth and her family were sufficient unto themselves, and I knew that whatever I did I would have Aunt May's blessing, but how to get away was a different matter.

Fate must have been on my side that morning when I visited the library to find Beatrice Roper poring over a magazine in the reading room and evidently enjoying what she was reading. She called me over with a bright smile saying, 'My granny used to take this magazine. She enjoyed reading the advertisements, they're so grand.'

I took the chair next to hers and together we scanned its pages. It was filled with columns of well-off ladies seeking

companions, housekeepers, friends for travelling and governesses for their children.

'Look at this one,' Beatrice cried. '"Urgently wanted,
educated young lady to act as companion to middle-aged
widow, interested in travel, music, visiting the theatre. Salary
commensurate with suitability."'

'I wonder what sort of a woman she's going to get?'
Beatrice said. 'I'd love to reply to some of these but I'd never
be able to do anything about it.'

'Why not?'

'Oh come on, Alex. My mother'd be horrified. I'm
destined to help with the shopping and the housework until
some man takes me off her hands. Isn't that what you'll be
doing?'

'Probably.'

'There's no probably about it. Look at your two sisters.
Della was academic but she married the first man who asked
her, and Ruth never did do much with her music, did she? You
were always going to be the stay-at-home one.'

'What makes you so sure?'

'Well, what sort of work could you do? Your sister's having
an awful lot to say about your fancying her husband.'

I stared at her in angry resentment. 'I'm sure she hasn't
said anything to you,' I retorted.

'No, but she's said it to my sister, and to some of the girls
she was at school with over the teacups.'

I turned away to go to the shelves and she called after me,
'Do look at these sometime, Alex, you'd find them very
amusing.'

I waited until she'd left the reading room and the library

before I picked up the magazine she'd left on the table. It was one my grandmother had liked called *The Lady* and on my way home I called at the newsagent's in the High Street to see if they had a copy.

'Bless ye no, love,' the newsagent said with a broad smile. 'One gets delivered to the library every Friday but it's a bit too grand for most of me customers. If ye wants to order a copy I can get ye one.'

'Yes please. When will it be in?'

'Next Thursday. Will ye be calling for it?'

'Yes, of course.'

On the way home I thought I had done a stupid thing. What possible interest could I have in reading about people needing travelling companions? Yet Aunt Alicia's story was still fresh in my mind. Wasn't that what she had been to Violet? Why shouldn't I find a Violet to travel the world with?

Of course it was ridiculous. Aunt Alicia had left home because there had been Johnny. There was no Johnny waiting for me, and, like Beatrice had said, my parents would be horrified at any other escapade I was likely to come up with.

CHAPTER SIX

I READ THAT MAGAZINE in the privacy of my bedroom every evening, trying to imagine if I was a suitable applicant for any of the positions advertised. I wasn't interested in being a housekeeper, a nanny to young children or a companion to an invalid, and in the main these were what was available. For weeks I went into the public library and read each new copy of the magazine; on one occasion Beatrice found me there.

She laughed when she saw what I was reading.

'Is there anything you fancy?' she asked pertly.

'No, of course not. I wonder if they ever find anybody.'

'No doubt some silly woman who is down and out and looking for a home. I don't suppose they'll pay much.'

She was probably right. I was being foolish in even thinking about such things, and then one morning an advertisement leapt out of the page at me and I reached inside my bag for my diary and wrote the entire sentence down in one of the blank pages.

SINGLE LADY REQUIRING A COMPANION FOR FOREIGN TRAVEL. SOMEBODY WHO MUST BE INTERESTED IN

HISTORY, MUSEUMS, MUSIC AND OPERA. ALL TRAVEL AND
HOTEL BILLS PAID, SALARY FOR SUITABLE APPLICANT TO
BE ARRANGED.

The lady lived in Devon and a post office box number was
given to reply to.

It was hopeless but the more I read the advertisement the
more excited I became. In any case I probably wouldn't be
suitable. I'd be too young, too unworldly, she would have a
thousand and one applicants more suitable than myself, but
still the notion lingered until I couldn't think about it any
longer. I had to write.

Every morning I was the first downstairs as I waited for
the postman, and I began to think nothing would come of it.
She'd already found someone suitable, a person who lived in
Devon so that they could meet immediately, not a nineteen-
year-old who lived in the Midlands. Then I thought of
Grandmother. If the lady answered my letter, I would go to
see my grandmother so that we could meet.

The letter arrived a week later and I took it into the conservatory to open it with trembling fingers.

She was a Miss Emily Parsons and she lived at the Old
Vicarage, Chancery Close, Witherington, South Devon. She
had to interview several applicants and would like to see me;
she did however realise that I lived some distance away but
she was prepared to reimburse me for any travel expenses.
Would I please let her know as soon as possible when it
would be convenient for me to visit her.

I willed myself not to read too much into the letter. She
had said there were other applicants; all the same I suggested

to my parents that perhaps I should make the effort to visit Grandmother. It was something that pleased both of them enormously. They were none to happy about my travelling alone, however. Father took me to the station and saw me safely on the train, and it was only then that I truly realised the enormity of what I was doing.

I should have been able to tell them, but the shade of Aunt Alicia haunted us still. Girls in my circumstances didn't do this sort of thing. They went to church on Sundays and listened to the band in the park every Saturday. They shopped with Mother and took tea in friends' houses. They went to balls and parties with the right sort of young men, and they did not converse with strangers or write to people they hadn't been introduced to.

My guilt increased when Grandmother embraced me warmly on arrival; that fact that I was using her made me feel very ashamed.

I had no idea where to find Witherington. I couldn't ask Grandmother, she'd only be curious as to why I wanted to know, so I waylaid the postman who told me Witherington was a small village four or five miles further along the coast. It could be reached by train and he went on to say, 'There's nothin' much there, miss. Just an old church and some nice little cottages.'

'Do you know the vicarage?' I asked him.

He rubbed his head thoughtfully. 'Well, there's the one near the church where the vicar and his family live. Be that the one?'

'I really don't know. Is that the Old Vicarage?'

'Well now, let me see. The church is St David's and the

vicarage is fairly new. The vicar's young and they have three or four children. I can't rightly say I know some old vicarage.'

'Oh well, perhaps I've got the wrong address.' I didn't want to involve the postman so that he knew exactly where I was going. My hopes of being suitable for the position were not very high, but thinking back on Aunt Alicia a great many people had been questioned about her activities prior to leaving home.

The day I had chosen to visit Miss Parsons was not very convenient for my grandmother.

'This is my day for visiting Dolly and Arabel Foster,' she said shortly. 'I told them I'd take you with me. Why is it so important for you to visit your schoolfriend today, Alex?'

'But she's only here for a few days, Grandmother, she's staying in a very nice hotel with her mother, and they've invited me to have tea with them. I'm so sorry. Can't we visit the Fosters another day?'

'I don't know. How long are you intent on staying here?'

'I'm not sure, Grandmother, but we'll think of something.'

I watched her depart for the Fosters' halfway through the morning then I rushed down to the station to catch the train which ran through sleepy villages along the coast; after several stops it arrived at a well-cared-for station and I got my first sight of Witherington.

The postman had been right. The village was pretty, but there was very little of it. A rather large stone church stood at the top of a hilly main street with its shops and cottages. There was an inn called the Gantry Arms halfway along it and next to the church a fairly large stone house which I deemed to be the vicarage.

I stared at it curiously. There were three young children playing in the garden and I paused at the gates to look at them. A woman tying up some dahlias looked up and seeing me standing there smiled and walked towards me.

She was young and pretty, and one of the children ran towards her and took hold of her hand, smiling up at me in a friendly way.

'Are you looking for someone?' the woman asked.

'Is this the vicarage?'

'Yes. I'm Mrs Howells, the vicar's wife.'

'The Old Vicarage?'

She laughed. 'Oh no, this is the new vicarage. The old one is at the top of that lane there. You mean Miss Parsons' house?'

'Yes.'

'People do get confused. That used to be the vicarage for the church when her father was the vicar but they built this new one when he decided to retire. She doesn't often go out, and you'll probably find her in the garden as it's such a nice day.'

I thanked her and as I turned away the children came to wave goodbye.

The Old Vicarage was a low rambling building where clematis clung colourfully round the door and there were extensive lawns and large leafy trees. A cobbled path led up to the front door and there I found an old-fashioned bell pull which I could hear loud and shrill behind the door.

After only a few minutes the door opened and a large woman stood there with a smile on her face. She wore a brightly coloured apron over her skirt and she had a rosy country face and a shock of dark grey hair.

'I have an appointment to see Miss Parsons,' I said somewhat nervously.

'You be Miss Faversham, then?'

'Yes.'

'Come in then. Miss Emily's in the garden, I'll tell 'er yer 'ere.'

She ushered me into a low-ceilinged room with dark rafters and small-paned windows. It was a gentle room of water-colour pictures and chintz covers, soft oriental carpets and vases of garden flowers everywhere. Against one wall stood a piano; there were several small tables and a walnut bureau.

Over the mantelpiece was a large painting of a young girl and I went to stare up at it. The girl was pretty, with soft light brown hair and a sweet delicate face. I did not hear anybody coming into the room but a pleasant voice said, 'That was me when I was fifteen years old.'

I looked down at a small, very slender, middle-aged woman whose expression had hardly changed from that on the girl's face in the painting.

She held out her hand saying, 'I'm Emily Parsons and you must be Alexandra Faversham. Come and sit over here and we'll have tea.'

The woman I had seen earlier came in carrying a tray which she put down on the table in front of her, and Miss Parsons said, 'This is Flora. She's been with me many years, and she worked for Papa for years before he died.'

Flora smiled saying, 'There's fresh scones and cream to go with 'em. I expect the young lady'll be ready for a cup o' tea.'

'Flora has always been a treasure,' Miss Parsons said with a smile. 'She's not at all happy with my ideas for travelling abroad.'

'Have you been abroad before?' I asked her.

'No, never, but not through choice. Papa never wanted to travel. He loved it here in the village; he never even ventured into the larger towns. He would be horrified if he could know how very much I yearned to go further afield. Now what about you, my dear? You're very young.'

'I'm nineteen and I've never been anywhere either.'

'I'm forty-nine; time is flying underneath my feet. You have more time in front of you, Alexandra.'

'Will you please call me Alex? Everybody does.'

'And who is everybody? Your parents, your family in general?'

How easily the lies sprang to my lips. 'My father's a seaman, my mother travels with him. There is nobody else.'

'You mean you are left on your own in England? Don't you wish to travel with them?'

'It isn't possible. I had to receive an education.'

'Ah yes. Our people sustain an empire, but their children live in a different world.'

Her expression was pensive, then with a little smile she said, 'How did you come to see my advertisement?'

'I read it in a magazine.'

'And saw it as a means of fulfilling your dreams?'

'Something like that.'

'Who do you live with if your parents are overseas?'

'With different aunts and cousins. I'm a bird of passage; they'll not be sorry to see me find something I like. Have you thought where you intend to go, Miss Parsons?'

'Yes. I want to go to Rome and Florence, to Venice and Athens. I want to see their cathedrals and their museums, absorb their culture. Are they places you would like to visit?'

'Oh yes, very much so. And Vienna and Budapest, don't they appeal to you also?'

'My dear, everywhere in the world appeals to me. Papa was always in control. I loved him dearly but the pattern of our lives would never change. I always knew that. He died from a heart attack at the age of seventy-five, and for the first time in my life I felt like a horse suddenly deprived of the harness that restrained me.

'I never thought of Papa in relation to money. We had enough, our tastes were never extravagant, so it took me a long time to realise that he had left me very well provided for. All those years when he was sitting on a fortune and we never went beyond the village street! Church three times on Sunday, weddings, christenings and funerals; beyond that my joy and my work was in the garden.'

'Flora wouldn't travel with you?' I asked curiously.

She laughed. 'Indeed no. Flora is happy with her lot. She'll wish me well, care for the house and my cat, and she'll welcome me home with much fussing.'

I had to ask the next question. 'How long do you intend to be away?'

'As long as it takes, my dear. To satisfy the longings of so many years, enjoy the sense of freedom I've never really known.'

She was looking at me with a strangely questioning smile.

'And you, young lady. You're a very pretty girl, isn't there some nice young man waiting to sweep you off your feet?'

'No. Nobody special.'

'I have interviewed several people during the last week, and you are the youngest. Can you really think you would be happy travelling around Europe with somebody of my age?'

'Oh yes, yes I do. I think you are very young at heart.'

She laughed. 'I have to tell you, Alex, that I still have two other would-be travellers to see. One of them lives in the village and I have known her a great many years. Her father was a schoolmaster at the village school and in the summer they used to go off walking and painting. She never married and I have the strongest feeling that, like me, she's missed an awful lot.'

'She sounds like the ideal travelling companion, Miss Parsons.'

'Two middle-aged English ladies searching for youth and adventure! I'm not so sure, but I have to see her. The other lady comes from London, she's a widow; I would have thought London was adventure enough for anybody.

'As soon as I have made my decision, Alex, I will write to you, probably in a week's time. Do you have a passport?'

'No, but I can get one.'

She smiled. 'Then can we leave it at that. It has been nice to meet you; perhaps we shall meet again. Are you travelling home today?'

I nodded. She didn't know anything about distances. She wasn't curious about where I lived and I had no intention of mentioning my grandmother.

She came to the garden gate with me and stood there until I turned the corner into the village high street. I had no hopes that I would be the successful candidate when I thought about the two women she had yet to see. I was too young, and yet I believed I possessed a sophistication she had still to acquire.

My grandmother wanted to know how I had spent my day but quite deliberately I made no mention of Witherington and the country train that took me there; instead I talked about the lanes above the town and the shops on the main street.

'I hope you'll come to see me often, Alex. I'd like all of you to come, because I'm not thinking I shall be doing much travelling; after all I'm getting old,' she said with a wry smile.

Thinking over the day's events I could hardly believe that I was destined to be Miss Parsons' travelling companion. I was too young, and of course it would be impossible; too many lies would have to be told and I was wishing Aunt Alicia had never appeared in my life.

She'd furnished me with stories I had used to fill the gaps. I'd turned my parents into merchant sailors simply because she'd told me about Johnny and herself, and I'd had to ask about Vienna and Budapest because she'd fired my imagination with talk of waltz music and the decadence of the Habsburg Empire.

All the way home I thought about Emily Parsons. She was surely the sort of nice gentle woman my parents would approve of, and yet it wasn't possible to be sure she was somebody I could travel Europe with. She was a stranger and I had only been home three days when it was brought home to me how unlikely it was.

My sister Della was in the habit of calling round most mornings for coffee. There was a very uneasy peace between us, but Mother insisted that we sit and chat together and this particular morning Della had a lot of news to impart.

'What do you think about Janice Roper?' she said as soon as she'd made herself comfortable in the morning room.

'What about Janice Roper?' I asked.

'Well, you're friendly with Beatrice, hasn't she said?'

'I've been away. I haven't seen Beatrice since I got back.'

'She's gone off to Bath to act as nanny to two children. Saw the advertisement in some magazine or other.'

'But that's awful,' Mother said. 'Wasn't she more or less engaged to the Gibson boy? She doesn't need to work, the Ropers have plenty of money. I wonder what her parents have to say about it.'

'They're horrified. Her father went down there and read the riot act, ordered her to come back apparently, but she refused and he told her if she decided to return home she wouldn't be welcome.'

'How terribly ungrateful of Janice to treat her parents in that way,' Mother said. 'She had a good home and a very nice young man. What will she get out of it in the end?'

'I should think your friend Beatrice is rubbing her hands with glee,' Della went on. 'She's already being escorted by Stanley Gibson. Like you, Alex, she must have had an eye on her sister's fiancé?'

'That was uncalled-for, Della,' Mother snapped. 'It's time you stopped making snide remarks about something that was perfectly innocent.'

'Innocent, Mother!'

'Of course it was. Now, can we change the subject?'

For a while we talked about something else until Mother said, 'Did you say Janice Roper found that position from a magazine?'

'Yes. The one Grandmother used to get. It's filled with advertisements for governesses, housekeepers and the like.'

How glad I was at that moment that I hadn't left the copy I had bought lying about the house for everybody to see.

Della was smiling. 'At least it's found people something else to talk about besides Aunt May and her conquests. It seems to me we've had more than our share.'

'What do you mean by that?' I asked her.

'Wasn't there Aunt Alicia?' Della retorted.

'And Aunt Alicia is somebody we don't talk about,' Mother said. 'You know it displeases your father just as it displeased your grandfather.'

'Do none of you ever care about what became of her?' I asked. 'Whether she's alive or dead?'

'Alex, she's never thought about us. To go off like that without a backward glance, never to write, never to ask forgiveness. I don't want to talk about it. Neither of you knows the full story so it's better we say nothing at all.'

'But it was so awful, Mother. To destroy her photographs, everything she ever owned, just as if she were dead. Didn't you like her?'

Mother got up from her chair and started to put the coffee cups on the tray before she said. 'As I said, girls, I don't want to talk about it. It's all over and done with a long time ago. She's never likely to come back into our lives, is she, so neither of you will meet her.'

Della grinned at me ruefully and when Mother had left the room she said, 'If you see Beatrice Roper get to know what is happening about Janice, none of my friends seem to know the full story.'

I had no thoughts of questioning Beatrice to satisfy Della's curiosity but I was beginning to hope that Miss Emily Parsons would find a suitable companion from the ladies she had already interviewed or was yet to interview. My foolish fantasies were impossible. Why ever had I thought they would come to anything?

All the same I got up very early in the morning to waylay the postman. Just in case, I told myself, without thinking for a moment that a letter would arrive offering me the position.

It came at the beginning of the following week and I ran with it up to my bedroom and sat on the corner of my bed for a long time before I found the courage to open it. The letter was two pages in length, written in Miss Parsons' neat precise handwriting, and addressing me as Dear Alex. She had completed her interviews, made her decision and had picked me. She was hoping to travel at the beginning of September with all of autumn before us, and it would give me sufficient time to obtain my passport and take my farewells of friends and those I was staying with. She would like me to join her in Witherington in mid-August. This would allow us to plan our journey, purchase the necessities, get to know one another. Would I please confirm?

More than anything in the world I wanted this position, but I didn't think about confirming it without hours of heart-searching. I loved my parents, although I didn't love the sort of life they wanted for me, and I wouldn't go without a word like Aunt Alicia had done. They deserved better than that.

CHAPTER SEVEN

I SPENT LONG HOURS in my room composing the letter I intended to leave for my parents. I told them I loved them and asked them to forgive me. I promised to write to them often to tell them where I was and what I was doing, but I made no mention of Miss Parsons or how I had come by her.

I told them something of my frustration with my present life and what I saw as my future and I asked them to think of me kindly and pray for me. I ended my letter by saying that I would always love them and miss them.

I read the letter many times and each time it seemed inadequate and cruel but there was nothing else I could say.

The next hurdle was acquiring a passport and a visit to the bank where I had a savings account for money accrued over the years from birthday and Christmas presents. I was somewhat surprised to find that there was over a hundred pounds in it and I withdrew most of it: I did not miss the bank clerk's look of surprise when he handed me the money. I smiled at him disarmingly, saying, 'It's for a very special occasion.'

The bank manager was a friend of my father's; I didn't

want him speaking to my father about it, although I wasn't really sure if bank managers did that sort of thing.

I knew too that old Mr Hathershaw was a magistrate and also a friend of my father's, and I had to ask him to sign my application for a passport. Fortunately on the day I called to see him he was rushing off to attend court and seemed anxious to be gone. He was also somewhat forgetful and I prayed no word would get round from that source.

I wrote to Miss Parsons to inform her when I hoped to arrive, after which the next thing was to plan my departure. It had to be on a day when my father was at the works and my mother was out for rather longer than a shopping expedition. It was easier than I had thought.

Aunt May invited her to take tea so that she could meet a certain Mr Billingsworth. We had heard all about him from Aunt Jane who as usual was disapproving and spiteful. He was a widower and without children. He had come to live in the same road as Aunt May and neighbours had been commenting that he seemed to be spending a lot of time at her house.

'Why don't they all mind their own business?' I asked Mother.

'They never do, dear,' she answered. 'Her other gentleman friends have all had children. Perhaps that is why this particular one is so much more suitable.'

'It would be nice for Aunt May to get married again. The two boys won't be with her forever and she's very pretty,' I said.

'Why don't you come with me, Alex? You've always been quite a favourite of hers, she'll be so glad to see you.'

I was quick to make an excuse. This was the day I had

longed for, when I would have the house to myself and I could pack my suitcase and with luck leave when the servants were in the kitchen and Mrs Pearson would be at the shops.

I had to be very careful when I removed a suitcase from the loft in case I was seen, but somehow or other fate was on my side. Then came the problem of what to take with me. Would there be an occasion to wear party frocks, surely there would, hadn't Miss Parsons talked about concerts and the opera?

By the time I had finished packing the suitcase was very full and extremely heavy. I had ordered a taxi to pick me up at two o'clock and I waited anxiously, looking through the front window until I saw it drawing up.

By the time he arrived at the front door I was already standing there with my suitcase and as we drove away I could hardly believe that in the end nobody had seen me, and the square was relatively deserted.

It was not until I was on the train, however, that I felt really safe, and then I began to agonise over what I had done.

I was not proud of myself. I had left a loving home with loving parents for an unknown future. I knew what everybody would say: that I was Aunt Alicia all over again, and they would all think I had become involved with somebody like Johnny. Speculation about where I had met such a person would be rife, and one by one the boys in the town would be eliminated. Perhaps when I visited Grandmother, but then I had only been with her two weeks. Surely I wouldn't leave my home for a boy I had met briefly on a two-week visit to Devon?

I could picture my mother, bitterly distraught, my father

angry, inwardly comparing me with the sister who had deserted them, and Della, too quick to declare that she'd been right about me all the time.

Even Mrs Pearson would fail to be surprised, for hadn't she always thought that I was the wild one?

It was early evening when the train arrived in Exeter and I made enquiries at the station as to where I could find a small hotel to stay in for the night. I was directed to one just outside the station, unpretentious, clean and inexpensive, and I had a plain but satisfying meal in a small dining room occupied by several others, mostly businessmen.

The landlady was disposed to be chatty.

'Are ye travellin' alone then?' she asked me.

'I'm visiting a friend in the morning, in a small village near the coast,' I replied.

'So you'll be catchin' the early mornin' train?'

'Yes, that's right.'

'Well, you'll probably be wantin' breakfast around eight o'clock, that be no problem. I likes the autumn on the coast although we're not fro' round 'ere originally.'

At that moment a gentleman sitting in the window seat called her over and with a brief smile she left me to my thoughts.

I didn't sleep well that night in my unfamiliar room. I was plagued with thoughts of family and home. In my imagination I could see the meeting they would have, my mother's tears, my father's anger, my sisters' disbelief. Then there would be John; I didn't know what he would be thinking.

The fact that I had slept badly reflected in my eyes

when I looked in the mirror the following morning. What would Miss Parsons think about my lacklustre appearance? I unlocked my suitcase and took out another blouse and skirt which went some little way towards enlivening my appearance.

It was two trains later and another taxi before I arrived at Miss Parsons' house in the early afternoon and Flora came out of the house smiling and picking up my suitcase as if it were thistledown.

'Miss Parsons has gone down to the church to put flowers on 'er father's grave, miss,' she informed me. 'Every Tuesday without fail she goes, and when she's away I'll 'ave to do it for 'er.'

'She knows I'm coming today, though?' I asked anxiously.

'Oh, that she does, but nothin' must interfere with the trip to the churchyard. Come in, love, and I'll make ye a cup o' tea.'

I sat down in the window seat beside a large tabby cat that sat there washing his face, and Flora said with a smile, 'Allus sits there lookin' down the road 'e does, 'e's goin' to miss 'er.'

'What's his name?'

'Thomas. 'E wasn't allowed in 'ere when the old man was alive, but now 'e can go where 'e pleases. Do you like cats, love?'

'Oh yes, and dogs.'

I was thinking about Sally, our cocker spaniel. It wasn't just the family I was going to miss, it was Sally and the canary too.

She was full of apologies when she returned to the house, but I sensed in her an excitement too. With my arrival her dream was coming to fruition and I couldn't help asking, 'Didn't you care for the two ladies you had to interview after I left, Miss Parsons?'

'Please call me Emily, Alex, it is so much more friendly, and I'm not your schoolteacher. That is exactly how I viewed the lady from London. She gave me a long lecture on the dangers of two ladies travelling Europe alone and unescorted—foreigners and money problems, languages we wouldn't understand and sickness from eating foreign food, not to mention insect bites and the like.'

'If she was so aware of all those dangers why did she ever think of travelling with you?' I asked.

'She had recently lost her husband and I rather gathered he hadn't left her very well provided for. That really wouldn't have mattered, but I think I told you that my father was domineering. It was something I lived with because I dearly loved him, but I didn't want another such figure in my life.'

'And the local lady?'

'Oh, she was never the sort of person I wanted. I'd known her a long time, she knows everybody's business throughout the village and very soon they would all have known everything about my plans and other matters as well.'

'I couldn't believe it when you chose me. You said I was the youngest applicant.'

'Perhaps that's why, Alex. Somebody young and smiling. Somebody to bring enthusiasm into my life. It's been so exciting planning where we're going to go. Did you get your passport?'

'Yes, and most of the money out of the bank.'

'Well, I shall pay for everything, the hotels, the concerts, so your money can be spent on souvenirs and anything else you fancy. I shall pay you a salary for being my companion, and I hope we shall become very good friends. Did you say your farewells to your friends at home?'

'Yes, of course.'

'I think the people here in the village think I'm going senile. None of them have travelled, not even the new vicar. I'm still calling him new although it's years since Father died. He's a very nice man, and he at least has shown a little interest in our plans. I thought we'd start our adventure in Brussels, Alex; the vicar's been so kind in helping me to work out our route, and I'm sure you'll approve of everything.'

The days leading up to our journey were spent visiting the shops in Exeter, largely to replenish Emily's wardrobe which consisted of staid skirts and blouses and the occasional afternoon dress, navy blue or brown.

'What do you think of them?' she asked me dismally.

'I've never been to Europe but I've seen pictures. None of them look very appropriate for visiting capital cities and the opera.'

'No, that's what I thought. Father was always insistent that I dress correctly for church on Sundays and the various meetings I attended. This isn't so bad; I wore it for a wedding in Totnes.'

She brought out a floral silk dress that my mother might have worn several seasons ago and seeing my doubtful expression she said, 'If you're not sure, Alex, then you'll simply have to come to the shops with me and help me choose.'

When I showed her what I had packed for our travels she said, 'They're all so very pretty, Alex. Your parents must have kept you well supplied with money to buy all these, and you must have found many occasions when you could wear them.'

I invented rich friends, and realised that I would have to tread very carefully.

'Aren't your friends concerned about you travelling abroad with somebody they haven't met?' she asked curiously.

'Not at all. They think I'm sensible and old enough to be a good companion and handle the future.'

I was clearly the sophisticated one. Emily had dreams of all she wanted to do. She had followed advice from the vicar on where she should go and how to get there, but I quickly grasped that I would be the one with my feet on the ground. I wished I'd paid more attention to my French mistress, because schoolgirl French was all I could lay claim to, and Emily had none at all.

'Father maintained I would never need it,' she explained. 'I went to a private school but on reflection my education was pretty basic.'

Looking back to our journey across the Channel to Le Havre I find it hard to believe that we achieved it without problems. We must have appeared like two complete innocents, but we found that people were kind and willing to help us.

Gentlemen who were prepared to carry our hand luggage, assist us in finding the cabin we had booked for the night journey and the dining room. Young officers who held doors open for us and escorted us along decks that had suddenly developed strange weaving patterns when we were out on the open sea.

I discovered that we were both good sailors and there was a new sparkling awareness in Emily's eyes as she looked around the dining room acknowledging smiles from nearby tables.

I liked her: she was sweet and innocent, and whenever I

found myself dwelling on home and the people there I tried to think of other things quickly in case my unease showed itself too plainly.

I had seen Emily's itinerary for which she had been quick to ask my approval. How could I not approve it? If she'd suggested we go on to the South Pole I would have said yes; as it was we were to start with Brussels, move on to Paris, then to Italy. Rome and Florence, Venice and Naples, and if so far there had been no mention of Vienna I felt sure she would agree that we should go there.

When a young officer smiled as he passed our table she said, somewhat wistfully, 'You're very pretty, Alex. You'll want more from this journey than visits to the museums and the art galleries.'

'There's plenty of time to think about other things, Emily. For now I'm simply thrilled to be doing what we planned. Did you never fall in love?'

She blushed, looking momentarily disconcerted, then she said, 'I did like somebody once, somebody very nice, but my mother was an invalid for many years and I think we both realised nothing could come of our friendship. Father relied on me for support to care for Mother, and when she died to be there for him. He was a good vicar; when he died all the village mourned him and my satisfaction is that I was a good daughter and gave him all the love and help that I could.'

She made me feel ashamed. That I'd been an ungrateful wretch to parents who had been good to me, and yet listening to Emily talking about her father I felt that he had been unfair, he had crushed her spirit, deprived her of love. It seemed to me that the only thing he had given her was the money he had left behind and I was determined that she should enjoy every last penny of it.

That night I lay in my bunk listening to the sound of the waves breaking against the ship, the rush of the wind and the ship's engines, and I realised that I would get little sleep. Up to the time when we retired for the night Emily had paid for everything and I began to feel guilty. I had some money; I wanted to pay my share. After all I had over a hundred pounds in my purse and although the job she had offered me had set out plainly that she would pay and give me a salary also I had not been brought up to be a passenger.

She was too nice a person to be treated like a fairy godmother. All I had wanted was a companion, somebody I liked, to travel with and give me an excuse to change my life. When I talked about it over breakfast next morning, however, she wouldn't hear of my spending my money at all.

When I prevaricated she said, 'Alex, I advertised for a travelling companion. I was going to pay everything and now I cannot allow you to share the expenses. If Father taught me nothing else he taught me to keep my word and that is what I intend to do.'

'But it's so unfair,' I protested.

'My dear child, you have all your life in front of you when you are going to need your money for other things. If I end up destitute then we'll have words again, but for the time being can't we leave things as they are? I'm quite happy with the arrangement and you should be too.'

I had behaved very badly towards my family and I was ashamed of my deceit, yet at the same time I was entranced with all the wonderful things we were seeing.

I wanted to write to them but I was afraid that Father would begin to delve too deeply into the way I had run away. They would remember Janice Roper and the magazine. Beatrice would not be averse to discussing my interest in the same magazine and suppose Father followed it up from there. I did not want to involve Emily in any of it: she was too nice, too kind.

I would not be like Aunt Alicia, who never went home. One day when our travels were over I would go back, explain and pray for their forgiveness. But for now there were so many wonderful things to see, so much to be enjoyed as we moved on through France and into Italy.

It was Italy I fell in love with. The beauty of her cities, the enchanting scenery of her coastline and her country-side. We went to the opera in Milan and Naples and we wandered enchanted through St Peter's in Rome. We climbed the long hill to the monastery of St Francis in Assisi and we explored the winding canals in Venice and sat entranced listening to the orchestra in St Mark's Square.

Everywhere I went I collected vast amounts of picture postcards which I hoped one day to take home with me but I never quite knew if this promise was meant or if it merely represented a sop to my conscience, that one day all would be well.

Much as I enjoyed the museums and the operas there was another part of me that watched the dancers in the ballrooms of the hotels we stayed in. Young people dancing the night away, young lovers strolling with their arms around each other in the city squares. I knew that what we had was not enough for me.

Not for a girl of nineteen whose feet tapped out tunes

underneath the tables, a girl whose eyes followed in the wake of handsome young men and longed to dance with them.

There were many times when I was invited to dance, to take walks in the gardens or the city streets, but always I returned to the table where Emily sat waiting for me, and the young men bowed their heads and walked away.

As time passed I started to think about what would happen when the travelling days were done. She received letters from Flora, and constantly wrote back because she was concerned about her cat, the people in the village and what might be happening there. One day she asked, 'Do you never write letters to anybody, Alex, not even to your parents?'

'I never really know where they are,' I prevaricated.

'You poor child. It must be very sad for you sometimes, but you never hear from your friends or other relatives.'

'No. They all lead very busy lives, they don't go anywhere or do very much, so I don't want to make any of them envious.'

'Who will you go to when we go home, then?'

'I haven't really thought about it.'

'Well, you can stay with me as long as you like. It will be nice to have young company in the house and the vicar will no doubt be able to involve you with his hundred and one things connected with the church.'

Listening to Emily describing her life in the village I couldn't think why I had ever called my life dull. There had always been parties and family. Aunt May's doings would have scandalised Emily, and Aunt Alicia would have seemed like a scarlet woman from the pages of the romances she was fond of reading.

* * *

It was our last night in Venice; in the morning we were moving on to spend time at Stresa on Lake Maggiore and Emily said, 'We're travelling northward, Alex, can you not feel that our holiday is nearing its end?'

I nodded. We had been in Europe almost eight weeks and on the way south I had never thought about the journey back. It had seemed to me that we would simply go on indefinitely looking for something new and wonderful, but now I was being made to realise that time was not on our side.

'Italy was always my dream,' she was saying. 'I really do think we've made the most of our time abroad, don't you, Alex?'

'We haven't see Vienna, Emily.'

I had to say it. There still remained Vienna and Budapest, still the Balkans, but of course Emily had to be the one to decide what happened next and I had no means of knowing if she had sufficient money and the desire to see these places.

CHAPTER EIGHT

I HAD NEVER SEEN anything more tranquil than the sun shining on the beautiful blue lake and its procession of small boats sailing towards the Isola Bella in the centre of the lake. We were sitting on the hotel veranda, having arrived in Stresa a few hours earlier.

Neither of us was in the mood for conversation. My thoughts were on what I was going to do when we returned to England. Emily had said she hoped I would stay on with her, I would love Devon, the village, and the people in it, but in my selfish little heart I only believed I would be exchanging one humdrum existence for another. I was very fond of Emily, she'd been a wonderful friend, a charming companion, but there would be more excitement in Stevenson Square than in the sort of life she was offering me.

'You're very pensive, Alex,' she said with a wry smile. 'Is it because we're on our way home?'

'Perhaps. It's all been so marvellous. Anything that follows these last few weeks can only be an anti-climax.'

'I suppose so.'

'We should make the most of what we have left. Would you like to sail across to the island this afternoon, Emily?'

'I thought in the morning, dear, when it might not be quite so busy. Why don't you go?'

'Would you mind?'

'No, of course not. I'll see you for dinner.'

I had risen from my chair and was moving away when a man stopped at our table saying, 'Emily, is it really you?'

I looked up at him. He was of medium height, nice-looking and with an agreeable smile, and he was looking at Emily with the utmost astonishment. Her face was suffused with a warm blush.

He was holding her hand, and in a breathless voice she was saying, 'Edward, what are you doing here?'

I stood at the table looking uncertainly from one to the other. Collecting her thoughts, Emily said, 'Alex, this is Edward Danson. We grew up in the same village. Edward, this is Alexandra Faversham. We've been travelling Europe together and enjoying every minute.'

He took my hand in a firm grip and Emily went on, 'Alex was just on her way to the island. We were meeting later for dinner.'

'That is where I was heading too. Suppose we all three go?'

'Are you alone, Edward?' she asked in some surprise.

'Yes, quite alone. I've been spending some time in Switzerland and now Italy.'

'Isn't Margaret with you?'

'No, Emily. Margaret died eighteen months ago—she'd been an invalid for several years.'

'Oh Edward, I am so sorry. We lost touch when you

moved away from the village, and none of our old friends heard from you.'

'No. Margaret didn't want anybody to know that she was ill so we simply moved on.'

'Did you have children?'

'No.'

I sensed in him at that moment a vague feeling of regret because almost immediately he said, 'What do you say to our taking that boat ride, ladies? I'll be very glad of your company.'

So we sailed across the lake in a small sailing boat and we walked enchanted round the small island with its beautiful villa and gardens. It was later when we stepped off the boat on to the jetty that Edward said, 'Why don't you both join me for dinner? We've so much to talk about, Emily, that's if Alex doesn't mind two old friends reminiscing about the past.'

'Why don't you two have dinner together? I can quite easily wander down to one of the little cafés in the square and listen to the orchestra,' I suggested.

Neither of them would hear of it, but all through dinner I felt superfluous, although neither of them was responsible for this feeling. They included me in their conversation, but there was so much in the past that I wasn't aware of, and it was only later in our bedroom that Emily said, 'I do hope our talk of the past didn't bore you, Alex. It's so long since I saw Edward and there seemed so much catching up to do.'

'You didn't bore me, Emily. Is Edward the man you were in love with?'

She blushed, her smile nervous as she said, 'Well, yes he is, but it was a long time ago.'

'He's nice. Why did you let him go out of your life?'

'As I told you, Mother had died after a fairly long illness and Father was helpless without her. He had so many commitments at the church I had to help him and Edward was going to live in Exeter. He was a solicitor, so all his future was in the city, never in our little sleepy village.'

'Did you know his wife?' I couldn't resist asking.

'Margaret. Oh yes, she and I were school friends and I knew that she too liked Edward. Her father was the local headmaster and she had other sisters older than herself. Margaret could go anywhere, do anything; when she married Edward I was so sure they would be right for each other.'

'But you minded, Emily; it was all terribly unfair.'

She looked at me uncertainly before saying, 'Oh no, Alex, it wasn't unfair. I couldn't leave my father and I couldn't expect Edward to wait for me. I'm sure he and Margaret had a very happy life together, although it seems such a shame that they didn't have children.'

'He's back in your life, Emily, and he's very pleased about that. You're both going home—don't let him go out of your life again.'

'Oh my dear,' she cried. 'I'm sure Edward isn't thinking about me in any way except as a very good friend. The young are so romantically minded! What Edward and I had was a long time ago.'

'Well, tomorrow I'm setting out on my own and I'm leaving you two together to recapture the past. I mean it, Emily, please don't try to dissuade me.'

'But I can't have you going off on your own, Alex. This is Italy, you don't know your way around. Besides, I've seen those handsome Italian boys looking at you and they're very flirtatious.'

I smiled. I too had seen the glances aimed at me from dark Italian eyes and it hadn't bothered me in the slightest.

We had the same argument over breakfast but nothing she said could persuade me to join them on their tour around the lake. One thing did disconcert me however and that was when Emily said, 'Alex is coming home with me at the end of our journeying, Edward. Her parents are both overseas and we've become such good friends I've told her she can stay with me as long as she likes.'

Edward merely smiled. I on the other hand was as determined to move on as I had been to leave Stevenson Square.

As I walked along the promenade that morning after seeing Emily and Edward leave on their tour my mind was obsessed with how I was going to accomplish it.

There would have to be more lies, more imaginings, and probably more tears. I wished I could develop a skin so thick that I didn't care about people too much, so that I could simply walk away without a backward glance and too many memories, but as yet I hadn't acquired the ruthlessness that had been Aunt Alicia's.

When we first set out on our travels I had dwelt on home and family constantly, but now more and more they were becoming like a dream. I loved them, but I seldom thought about them. I prayed to God to forgive me and constantly reassured myself that my prayers had been answered; otherwise why had it all been so easy? It was God's will that I had met Emily, His will that our travels had been so wonderful and now it was His will that Edward had arrived just at the right moment to make up to Emily all she would lose in me.

As I crossed the road two young Italians smiled at me in the most flattering way and I smiled back. There would be other men, but not here. I had already set my sights on the long tortuous paths Alicia had followed, but without making her mistakes. I would be wary, I would not fall in love unless it was returned in full measure, and I would prosper without falling into any of the holes Alicia had dug for herself.

Emily constantly voiced her anxiety in leaving me to journey on alone, and in spite of my reassurances she delivered a lecture every day on the dangers which would surround a girl of my age travelling on to central Europe.

Her expression was filled with trouble as she said, 'Alex, please return to England with us. One day when you're older you can go to Vienna, I'm sure, one day when some nice young man can accompany you. I am totally against you going there alone, and Edward too is very concerned.'

I had never intended to tell her anything about Alicia, but now in desperation I said, 'Emily, there is really no need to worry about me. I have an aunt in Vienna, my father's sister. The family lost touch with her for years, but she knows me, and she'll be delighted to see me.'

'But you've never mentioned her before, Alex. Are you sure she'll be glad to see you?'

'Yes, of course.'

'Would you have been happy for me to meet her?'

'Of course. I'd have been thrilled, but you never mentioned going on to Vienna and it wasn't for me to suggest it. I did mention it once but you never took me up on it.'

'I would have done if you'd told me about your aunt, Alex.'

'No matter; it isn't important now, Emily. You have Edward and a wonderful future to look forward to.'

'Tell me a little more about this aunt of yours, then.'

'She's my father's youngest sister. She's beautiful and she is married to a member of the Austrian aristocracy. They have a house in Vienna and a large estate in the country.'

She was looking at me with a half-smile on her face and I knew she wasn't believing a word of what I was telling her. To Emily it as a fairy tale, nothing more than a young girl's fantasies, and in a way it was true. I had absolutely no intention of seeking out Aunt Alicia in Vienna. I was going to make it on my own, just as she had done, but with considerably less trauma.

Up to that moment everything had fallen into place as if a guardian angel had planned it for me. Emily and our journey, even Edward who had appeared just at the right moment. I had no reason to think that one day my dreams and wishes would fall around my ears. That my guardian angel would desert me.

On the morning Emily and Edward left for England I went to the railway station to see them off and the farewell was emotional for Emily in particular. She hugged me close to her and there were tears in our eyes as we uttered our farewells, then to my surprise she handed me an envelope, saying, 'I want you to have this, Alex. You've been a wonderful companion, the sort of daughter I shall never have. I shall feel happier leaving you behind if you have enough to sustain you in the future you have planned for yourself.'

I stared down at it in some confusion and she said, 'There is no need to open it now, dear, and promise you'll write to me and let me know where you are and how you are faring.'

'I promise, Emily, I will.'

'You're sure you can rely on this aunt of yours, Alex?'

'But of course, she'll be delighted to see me.'

My innocent expression went some way to reassuring her, and after another embrace she climbed up into the train. Edward shook my hand and I said, 'You'll take care of Emily, won't you, Edward. She's a lovely lady and I'm going to miss her.'

His smile was warm as he said, 'You know I will, Alex, and you take care of yourself. This is a precarious adventure you are embarked upon, my dear.'

'Why do you say that? Vienna is a beautiful city. Their empire is surely as solid as our own?'

He shook his head, saying, 'You listen to their waltzes, Alex, and admire their style. It is true their empire has lasted a great many years but it is nothing like ours. It is composed of angry volatile nations who are plotting and scheming to end it and underneath its glamour and charisma the Vienna the world waltzes to, the old imperial Vienna, is already doomed.'

I stared at him uncertainly and taking hold of my hand he said, 'Don't be tempted to stay too long, Alex. This is only a visit you are embarked upon. Enjoy it while you may then bid Vienna a fond farewell. We shall be waiting to hear from you.'

I waited on the platform until their train was out of sight then I walked slowly back to the hotel. His words had troubled me, yet surely he must be wrong. I thought about Alicia's words that the old imperial Vienna was not the one the world outside it remembered and yet I had to see it for myself; it was something as compelling as leaving England had been, as though some force outside myself was propelling me onwards into a strange fairy-tale world.

Emily and I had spent weeks poring over maps and routes throughout France and Italy; now I would have to do it alone. The prospect was daunting and exciting, and as soon as I reached the hotel I went immediately to the wardrobe to find our maps. It was then I remembered the envelope Emily had given me and which I had placed in my handbag. I felt sure it contained money but I stared down in amazement at the wad of notes in my hand: there was well over a hundred pounds.

Her generosity made me feel suddenly ashamed. I had loved her, but I had used her, telling her innumerable lies. I had been glad that she had found Edward, but my joy had been tempered with relief that I could journey onwards on my own. I had not wanted to go back to England with Emily, and if Edward had not appeared at the right moment I would have found some excuse to leave her.

I was not very proud of myself, but I vowed that I would try to be a better person, to think of others instead of myself.

I was impatient to leave Stresa. I planned my journey to Vienna and in two days' time I had packed my belongings and was on my way to Milan to board my train for Austria. It was the end of November and although the sun was still warm as I waited on the station platform I noticed that all around me people were carrying travelling rugs and were clad more warmly than myself.

A handsome smiling young man held the carriage door

open for me; behind him was another man wearing a deer-stalker hat and horn-rimmed spectacles. The first man helped me put my luggage on the rack and it seemed we three were the only people sharing the compartment.

I felt strangely sad to be leaving Italy with her history and her sunshine, and as we moved out of the station I felt the sudden prick of tears in my eyes. Wiping them away swiftly I saw that both men were looking at me and the man who had helped me said something in German. When I shook my head he said, 'You are English, Fräulein?'

'Yes. I don't know any German, I shall have to learn.'

'You are staying in Austria some time, then?' he asked with a smile.

'I hope to.'

The other man listened to our conversation but offered none of his own, quickly reverting to his newspaper. The first man was inclined to chat.

'My name is Karl von Winckler, Fräulein, and my home is in Vienna. I serve in the Emperor's guard.'

'My name is Alexandra Faversham.'

'So. Why are you hoping to stay in Vienna?'

'I've read about it; I love her music; it's a city I've always wanted to see.'

For the first time the other man spoke, eyeing us over his spectacles rather sternly. 'There is more to Vienna than waltz music,' he said, speaking in perfect English. 'Vienna is also a questionable city for an unescorted English girl to be visiting.'

The Austrian laughed, saying, 'Our English friend is disapproving, Fräulein. Enjoy Vienna while you may. I very much doubt if you will be long without an escort.

His smile was audacious. He was the sort of man I had
associated with Vienna: tall and handsome and smiling. I
could imagine him in uniform dancing in exquisite ballrooms under crystal chandeliers and I warmed to him.
While the Englishman perused his newspaper we talked
and I had the utmost conviction that my guardian angel
was still on my side.

As we journeyed onward I became increasingly aware that
the weather was changing. Instead of Italy's brilliant sunshine
there was now snow on the mountains and fine particles on
the windows of the train. It was warm in the carriage but I
thought dismally about the summer dresses packed away in
my trunk and even the travelling clothes I was wearing were
hardly adequate for snow-covered streets and cold winds.

As if he understood my thoughts Karl said, 'You will find
it much colder in Vienna, Fräulein Faversham, so I trust you
have brought warm clothing.'

'Not really. I shall have to shop for some.'

At that moment I blessed Emily for the money she had
given me. It would be sorely needed.

I had the strongest feeling that the Englishman had given
up on me. I was going to a city because I enjoyed waltz music
and the operatic glamour of a frivolous empire. I did not have
appropriate clothing and I was happy to chat to a young man
I had only just met as though I had known him for years. I
felt quite sure that the young woman of his acquaintance
would not behave in such a foolish fashion.

He did not join us in the restaurant car but elected to dine
in the company of an elderly cleric. Seeing my rueful smile
Karl said, 'I'm afraid our English friend does not approve of

us. He would be happier to make his journey in silence without having to listen to talk of music and amusement.'

'I suspect he disapproves of me.'

'Perhaps so. Have you anywhere to stay when you arrive in Vienna?'

'No. I hope to find a small inexpensive inn for the first few days until I know what I am doing and exactly where.'

'I know of several small inns near the railway station with good reputations. The hotels around the Ringstrasse would be very expensive and you did say you had shopping to do for appropriate clothing.'

'Yes.' I thought he was being very kind and I was happy to lean on his advice for somewhere to stay. After all he was Austrian, and the dour Englishman had hardly been a tower of strength to a fellow countrywoman.

When we returned to our compartment he was sitting staring out of the window and Karl said, 'The weather is becoming worse. I fear Vienna will be very cold and possibly there will be snow.'

Shrugging his shoulders the Englishman said, 'I am leaving the train at Salzburg; I was expecting this sort of weather.'

When we arrived at Salzburg he gathered his belongings together and fixing me with a rather stern glance he said, 'Enjoy Vienna, Miss Faversham. I'm not a lover of Strauss; I find his music too light. I prefer Mozart.'

I smiled. 'I take it you're not a dancer, then?'

'Only if I have to.'

'I love dancing, and I love waltzes, particularly those of Strauss.'

'That is fortunate then. You are going to the city of Strauss waltzes and the operettas.'

'Oh yes,' I breathed. 'I'm so looking forward to those.'

In the next moment he had gone and the last I saw of him he was trundling his luggage along the station platform toward its exit.

Karl smiled. 'Our friend will enjoy Salzburg,' he said. 'He will find it less dissipated and more in keeping with his English reserve. But what about your English reserve, Fräulein?'

'I have yet to discover Vienna so how can I be sure how my English reserve, as you put it, is affected? Will you be staying in Vienna?'

'For two days only and then I join my regiment.'

'I would like to go to Grinzing.'

'Ah yes, you should go to Grinzing. It is pretty, romantic and awash with music. I make it a duty and a delight to go to Grinzing whenever it is possible. Who knows, perhaps we will meet there.'

I smiled but offered no comment. If Karl was an example of the young men I was likely to meet in Vienna the future promised to be all I expected of it.

CHAPTER NINE

I HAD BEEN FOUR days in Vienna and already I had fallen in love with it. I had explored the museums and the beautiful churches, wandered along the city streets and through the vast parks and I had spent considerably more money than I should have.

The inn was not over-expensive but it was some way from the city centre so I was constantly using whatever transport was available to take me to the shops, which were exclusive. I began to realise that very soon I would have to move out of Vienna to some smaller place where my money would go further.

I learned, however, that Grinzing, which was very popular with the Viennese, would be equally expensive but I had ideas about Grinzing. I would look for the sort of inn Aunt Alicia had found, I would have German lessons and if she had been able to find work so could I.

The taxi driver who took me there was very helpful and as we drove along the main street of the village he pointed out different inns. How I loved Grinzing, with its flowers and its lights, the music that poured out of every doorway and the sweet gay charm of its smiling face.

The inn I found was small compared to the others, but the innkeeper received me with a charming smile and the bedroom he showed me into overlooked a courtyard of cobbled stones edged by small tables covered with bright red and white checked tablecloths and where he assured me a small band played every evening for his customers.

I quickly discovered that his customers were ordinary, sometimes elderly, and hardly what I had hoped for. At the same time I enjoyed listening to zither music and had no complaints about the music the small band played.

I was impatient for life and it was going too slowly for me. I felt that time was slipping underneath my feet when I should be waltzing in more salubrious surroundings and on the third evening I ventured out along the street where I saw elegantly clad women on the arms of uniformed young men entering larger inn gardens where the music was lilting and the ambience more pronounced. I had no escort and was unsure if I would be welcome without one, but the young man standing at the gate smiled at me, holding the door open and pointing to one of the tables set near the wall.

This was the sort of evening I had been waiting for. Young men clicking their heels before me as they bowed and invited me to dance. Music from the operettas that were sweeping Vienna, and waltz music that went on and on until the stars paled.

I had been aware that from across the room a man had been staring at me constantly. He had arrived halfway through the evening, sauntering between the tables, standing surveying the scene from the garden steps, and then speaking to the proprietor so that they both stood gazing at me to my utmost embarrassment.

Dancing with a young army officer I asked, 'Do you know the man standing near the steps?'

'You mean Herr Gruber, the proprietor?'

'No, the other man.'

'Yes, that is Herr Windisch. He owned this inn before the Grubers took it. Why do you ask?'

'He was staring at me as though he knew me but I have never seen him before.'

'Can a man not stare at a beautiful girl?' he said, smiling. 'He lives here in Grinzing, I believe.'

By this time we had grown close to him and meeting his eyes I could see that his were filled with speculation. When we reached our table my dancing partner said, 'May I be allowed to escort you back to your home? I have to get back to Vienna tonight.'

'Thank you, but I only live at the inn at the top of the street, so there will be many people going my way, I'm sure.'

He bowed gallantly, saying how much he had enjoyed our dance and hoping to see me very soon.

The band had left the dais momentarily to take some refreshment and I was beginning to wish I had left with the young officer, particularly when the man who had been staring at me started to walk across the room, pausing at my table to bow his head, saying, 'This is not a cliché, Fräulein, but have we not met before?'

'No, I'm sure we haven't. This is my first visit to Austria.'

'You are English?'

'Yes.'

'My name is Herr Windisch and this was once my inn.'

I stared at him uncertainly, and he said, 'May I join you

for a few moments, Fräulein? I can assure you I am not
sinister, and I am well known here. The proprietor himself
would be happy to vouch for my credentials.'

He had spoken to me in English and that in itself went
some way to reassuring me that there was nothing ominous
in his interest.

'If we have never met, Fräulein, you remind me of a lady
I met here in Grinzing. An English lady like yourself; indeed
she came to work for me at the inn. I was devastated when
she left, because she had become indispensable to me.'

'I remind you of her?'

'Very much so. Your colouring, the way your head turns
so, and your smile. Oh yes, it is not just that you too are
English. It is much more than that.'

I had vowed to myself that I would not follow in Alicia's
footsteps, but how could I ignore something that was inevitable?

'What was her name, this lady who you say looked so
much like me?'

'Her name was Alicia. She is now Countess Bruckner. She
left me to marry an Austrian aristocrat so she is now happy
to be Austrian.'

'She lives here in Grinzing?'

'No. She has a house in Vienna and a large estate in the
country. Very occasionally she comes here, but her husband
is not one for frivolity. That part of Vienna which his Countess
found so enchanting he finds degenerate. It is a pity, I think,
for this is the part of Vienna that will live on when old imperial
Vienna is part of the past.'

With a little smile he had risen to his feet and was preparing to leave the table. Honesty warned me that I should let

him go, but perception told me that I needed him. I needed a friend, I needed work; it wasn't as though I was using Alicia to get what I wanted, indeed I need never meet her, but surely I was entitled to use her name to help me now.

He bowed over my hand and I smiled. Then, taking my courage in both hands, I said, 'I know the lady you speak of, Herr Windisch. She is my aunt, my father's youngest sister.'

He stared at me, then sat down heavily in his chair.

'If she is your aunt why are you here alone?' he asked.

There was nothing else but to tell him about her early history, the way she had left home, and how she had arrived in Vienna.

'How do you know all this if she was estranged from her family?' he asked astutely.

So then I had to tell him of her visit and that I had been the only one to see her.

'But how do you come to be here?' he asked.

I told him my story after which he said, 'Two adventurous English ladies cut from the same mould. And what do you intend to do now, young lady? Go home to England, or visit your aunt in Vienna?'

'I have no intentions of visiting her. I do not want her to feel responsible for my behaviour.'

'And what is left, Fräulein?'

'I want to do what she did. I want to work here, at least for a time. If she could do it so can I.'

'So you are looking for a benefactor. Your aunt found me, but I no longer own an inn in Grinzing. I am retired from that life.'

'But you might know somebody who is looking for help in his inn. I will learn the language and I will work hard. You helped her; can you not help me?'

He laughed. 'I can see, young lady, that you are every bit as enterprising as I found Alicia to be. My customers admired her, she was efficient and respectful, and I was very sorry to lose her.'

'She left you to marry?'

For a long moment he stared down without answering, then with a brief smile he said, 'She left me for the high life in Vienna. I heard later that she had married. She has been here only once to my knowledge since she moved away. She was with a party of aristocratic people who no doubt came on a whim, to waltz the night away in less salubrious surroundings than the ballrooms of Vienna.'

'Was her husband with her?'

'I believe so but I cannot be sure. I was an innkeeper, Fräulein; Count Bruckner was not an acquaintance even if his nephew was.'

'Zoltan Bartok?'

'So you know of him. Occasionally he comes here to Grinzing, always alone, although I heard he married, briefly. He is not a man I admire.'

'You have not said if you can help me, Herr Windisch?'

He smiled. 'Alicia had a little German. Do you have any yourself?'

'I'm afraid not, but I am willing to learn. Everybody seems to know some English.'

He laughed. 'That is so. We pander to our English cousins who think they need not know anything outside their tight little island. Nevertheless, Fräulein, it would help if you spoke some German. It would be polite, you understand?'

'Of course.'

'And I will speak to the innkeeper, who remembers well the lovely Alicia. Come here tomorrow evening, I may have some news for you.'

With a polite bow he left me to walk out into the night.

I was glad of the warm woollen stole wrapped around my shoulders, since the wind whistled down the street so that the lights strung in the trees shimmered eerily through the bare branches and people were hurrying to their homes ahead of the impending storm.

I hoped Herr Windisch would have good news for me. My money was dwindling and soon it would be Christmas; I had been told that Christmas in Grinzing could be wonderful but expensive. The inns would put up their prices and so far as I was concerned everything was going out and nothing was coming in.

When I reached the inn I ran quickly to my bedroom and sat on my bed to count the money I had left. In some dismay I realised that I had less than sixty pounds remaining out of the money I had brought with me and the sum Emily had given to me. I simply had to find work of some sort. If it was not forthcoming I would need whatever I had to take me home to England.

With all the optimism of youth I refused to believe that I had come so far to be beaten now.

I stood in the inn doorway in the early evening the next day watching the rain dripping from the trees sweeping across the garden paths in unremitting fury, and seeing me standing there the innkeeper said, 'You are not venturing out into the storm, Fräulein? Few people will be about on such a night.'

'I have an appointment to meet someone at the Golden Pheasant—I promised to be there.'

'Will they not call for you here?'

'He does not know where I am staying.'

He shrugged his shoulders. 'Then be very careful, Fräulein, the storm is bad. I cannot think there will be dancing at the Golden Pheasant tonight.'

As I hurried down the road with my feet slipping and sliding into numerous puddles and the rain lashing against my face I found myself agreeing with him. There were no lanterns lighting up the trees, and beyond the garden the lights of the inn were dim so that it seemed singularly deserted.

There was no sign of the orchestra, and only one man, playing a zither, seemed more to be entertaining himself than expecting to be listened to. The tables were deserted. The inn-keeper stared at me curiously and as I sat at the same table I had occupied the evening before I reflected that only a fool would turn out on such a night.

I knew exactly how Alicia had felt sitting alone waiting for her lover; only Herr Windisch was not my lover, simply a man I had pinned my hopes on and who did not think me worthy to face the storm for.

A waiter came to the table, eyeing me curiously with a dejected air, and I ordered a glass of wine. As he turned to go I asked, 'Do you know if Herr Windisch has been here?'

He stared at me and I realised that he understood only a modicum of English; shrugging his shoulders he walked away. I decided then that I would drink the wine and walk to my lodgings. By this time even the man on the zither had had enough.

If anything the storm was getting worse. Heavy branches were being torn from the trees, bringing the lights crashing down with them. The innkeeper surveyed the scene with an anxious frown, and catching my eye he too shrugged his shoulders despondently and turned away.

I finished my wine and left. He would not come tonight and I was dreading the walk along the deserted street. I had almost reached the gate when a man entered trying desperately to gather his coat round him, and I watched his feet sliding along the path until he reached the shelter of the inn. Then with incredulous joy I looked up into his face and saw that he was indeed Herr Windisch. He smiled and, taking my arm, drew me into the corridor and from there into a small room which he was evidently aware of.

I watched while he divested himself of his coat, then he spoke. 'I was not sure you would come out on such a night, Fräulein, indeed I told myself mine would be a wasted journey. However, here you are, which goes to show how eager you are to stay with us in Grinzing. Now, Fräulein, we will call upon Herr Gruber and find out how accommodating he is going to be.'

He left me for a few minutes, returning with Herr Gruber who acknowledged my presence with a swift smile and correct bow.

'This is Fräulein Faversham, Herr Gruber. Perhaps you will remember her aunt, who worked for me many years before she left for the high life of Vienna and marriage to Count Bruckner. This young lady has also fallen under the spell of Austria and wishes to remain here to work.'

Herr Windisch had delivered his words with a smile but it was evident the innkeeper had questions he needed to ask.

Addressing me he asked in English, 'You say you wish to

find work, Fräulein. Would it not be more sensible to be with your aunt in Vienna?'

'No, Herr Gruber. I wish to find my own way here. My aunt doesn't know I'm in Austria; we need not even meet.'

'Is there some conflict, then? Occasionally the Countess comes with friends, and I would not like there to be problems if you are estranged.'

'We are not estranged. We simply are hardly known to each other. I have only met her once, so it is even doubtful if she would remember me.'

'You are very like her. When you came to my inn I felt I had met you before, and now I know why.'

Turning to Herr Windisch he said, 'Colonel Bartok comes here. I would not like there to be trouble.'

'Why should there be trouble? We are talking about a different generation, about something that has no bearing on this one. Fräulein Faversham does not speak German but is anxious to learn. I was thinking that Frau Messel might help her; we know that she taught English to German students, so why not German to an Englishwoman?'

Herr Gruber stroked his face thoughtfully and Herr Windisch said quickly, 'You admired my English assistant, Herr Gruber. I have often heard you saying that you wished you could find someone like her to handle the disaster you make of your accounting system.'

For the first time Herr Gruber smiled without expressing a doubt. 'It is true,' he said. 'I will speak to Frau Messel, but there will be no problem in the meantime. Many of my staff speak English and Frau Messel is a good teacher. Where are you living now, Fräulein?'

'I am staying at Inn Danilo but I would prefer to live here if you have accommodation, because it would be less expensive.'

'Ah yes, we have the room your aunt occupied when she was here. It is a storeroom at present but it could be got ready for you in two days. My wife will see to that. One of my men will help you with your luggage from the Danilo. We will come to some arrangement about your salary and it will not all be work, Fräulein, you will be welcome in the gardens to join my guests in the evening.'

'Thank you, Herr Gruber, you are very kind. My name is Alexandra but I have always been called Alex.'

He smiled.

'I remember that your aunt was always charming, and popular with the guests. After that one disastrous love affair she remained most circumspect. The inn will abound with young officers, particularly in the springtime and at Christmas. Many of them are from aristocratic families; most of them are charming. You are young and very beautiful, but you are also English and may not know how they should be judged. Herr Windisch will advise you, I feel sure.'

Herr Windisch smiled. 'With an aunt in high places I do not think we need to fear that Alex will suffer the wrong sort of liaison.'

I stared at him doubtfully before saying, 'I would not like anything I say or do to be brought to my aunt's attention, Herr Windisch.'

'Nor will it, Fräulein, a figure of speech, no more than that.'

There were handshakes all round then I was plodding with Herr Windisch up the road towards the Danilo. I didn't care that the storm was lashing down and the wind tearing at the trees; this was the beginning, a new life, a new adventure.

I sat in my room listening to the sound of rain against the window panes and I thought about writing home to tell them where I was and how my future would be resolved, but then I thought better of it. My father would not hesitate to take things further. He would contact the Foreign Office and insist they look for me; he could even insist that I be ordered home. No. Sometime in the distant future I would enlighten them, one day when I was older and not even my father could tell me what to do with my life.

True to Herr Gruber's word the room at the Golden Pheasant was prepared for me. It was on the very top floor, but it overlooked the rolling countryside and the enchanting Vienna Woods. It was furnished with a large bed and wardrobe, a small chest of drawers and an easy chair, and it seemed like paradise.

I wrote to Emily, a great many pages filled with talk of Vienna and my new life, the heady glamour of her lilting waltzes and the wonderful imperial palaces. Then I went on to tell her that I had found work, was learning German and was wonderfully, unbelievably happy. I asked her to write to me soon to tell me about her journey home and to remember me to her gentleman friend.

Herr Gruber had been correct about the state of his accounts and I was amazed how easily I began to understand and speak the German language. French lessons had proved disastrous to me, but somehow or other there was much in the German language reminiscent of my own and the more I learned the more easily I coped with Herr Gruber's misman-agement.

In those early days I was too tired to spend much time in the garden but soon it would be Christmas and already I was helping to decorate the inn. A large Christmas tree had been brought in from the forest and everybody on the staff took a share in decorating it.

'You have Christmas trees in England?' Frau Gruber asked me.

I told her that it was Prince Albert, Queen Victoria's consort, who had introduced Christmas trees to Britain and how much we loved them.

More and more people were descending upon Grinzing for the festivities and new fairy lights were being strung among the branches of the trees; my memories of Christmas in Stevenson Square seemed pale by comparison.

As I pulled my prettiest party dress over my shoulders I thought about the family sitting down to dinner that evening, with Aunt Jane no doubt expressing harsh thoughts about two people who had walked out on them, as well as Aunt May's misdemeanours, which I felt sure had been continu-ing.

Della would be there with John, looking up at him with adoring eyes, and Edith with her new husband. It would not be all joy and laughter, I realised: in my parents' hearts there would be sadness for a daughter they had loved and who had hurt them cruelly.

CHAPTER TEN

FOR A LONG TIME I sat at my bedroom window watching people arriving for the evening's festivities. Girls in pretty frilly dresses hung on to the arms of young men in uniform or evening dress, and the music drifted upwards, as well as the laughter from people intent on enjoying every minute.

I knew that I would not lack for dancing partners because I was very popular with the people who came to the inn, largely I think because I was English and so obviously loved my new home. I was no threat to any of the young men who escorted their sweethearts for the simple reason that I was not interested in any of them, not even the young men who blatantly flirted with me. To me it felt wonderful to be heart-whole and contented with my lot and I was foolish enough to believe it would go on like that, carefree and innocent. As I made my way downstairs I was blissfully unaware that the pattern of my life would change dramatically in just a few months.

Everybody was in a party mood. The small orchestra played polkas and waltzes; I was greeted with smiles of welcome and invitations to dance came immediately. Herr

Gruber smiled as we swirled by him and ever more widely when Herr Windisch invited me to dance. Looking down at me he said, 'There are stars in your eyes tonight, Fräulein, which tell me you are happy.'

'Oh yes, I am. Everything is just as I thought it would be! I have so much to thank you for.'

'I made it happen, but you yourself did the rest. I know you do not wish to be associated with Alicia, but she too made things happen for her. Although she was sad and miserable when she came here, she survived wonderfully well and now she is in a position where she mingles with royalty and the aristocracy. I am very happy for her.'

'Is she happy, do you think?'

'Ah. Happiness is harder to define. For some it is riches, glamour, Alicia has all that. How much happiness is necessary to her perhaps I shall never know.'

I glanced up at him but he was no longer focusing on me. Instead he was looking towards the door where a man stood watching the scene. He was tall and swarthy, and there was an arrogance about him as he surveyed the dancers. Then his eyes met mine and I couldn't help the sudden feeling of menace from his piercing dark eyes.

'Who is that man?' I whispered.

'His name is Zoltan Bartok.'

'Why is he staring at me?'

'You remind him of your aunt. You are very like her, and once your aunt and Zoltan Bartok were lovers.'

'She told me of him. Herr Gruber warned me about him; he was afraid there might be trouble.'

'Come, we will leave the dance floor and join the people

I am with. The man is unpredictable but this is Christmas Eve. Herr Gruber will not want any problems tonight.'

I was made welcome by Herr Windisch's friends and my escort made sure that I was seated where the man standing at the door could not make eye contact. All the same I was aware of his presence and even when I could no longer see him I sensed his haughty brooding eyes boring into my back.

After a few minutes a man sitting at our table invited me to dance and encouraging me with his smile Herr Windisch murmured, 'Bartok has gone, you need not be afraid.'

As I walked with my partner to the dance floor there was the sound of laughter and a new group of girls and young men in uniform came through the door. My partner said, 'They have come from Vienna. They are here to enjoy themselves and bring the evening to life.'

Most of them joined the dancers, leaving two young men standing in the doorway chatting to Herr Gruber; as we danced by I stared at one of them in amazement recognising him as my friend of the train, Karl von Winckler. As I turned my head to look at him again our eyes met and his smile of recognition reassured me that I had not been mistaken.

We had not been long at our table when he came to me, bowing correctly over my hand, his smile warm, saying in English, 'So we do meet again, Fräulein, didn't I tell you that it might happen in Grinzing?'

I was suddenly aware that the people sitting at the table were impressed by this handsome young man in his splendid uniform and then he was inviting me to dance and my fairy tale was coming true.

We did not go back to the table. Instead we went to sit near the window from where we could look out at a garden shimmering with silver frost, where lights twinkled in the branches of the trees and where lovers stood wrapped in each others arms oblivious to the cold winter night.

As he poured the wine he said, 'It is obvious you have survived very well in Grinzing, Alexandra. I am eager to know how you have managed to do so.'

'I work here. I do Herr Gruber's accounts and I am learning to speak German. Sometimes I wonder why I bother, since they all know I'm English and they speak to me in English.'

He laughed. 'But of course. They hope to practise their English while you hope to practise your German.'

'You came with a crowd of people. Won't they be missing you?'

'If you mean do I have a girl to return to, the answer is no. I have been with my regiment in Hungary and only returned to Vienna yesterday. My friends invited me to join them this evening, because I was expecting to feel a little solitary.'

'You are returning to Vienna tonight?'

'In the morning; it is already almost midnight. Christmas Day, Alex. In just a few moments you will see how we Viennese welcome it in.'

He was right. It seemed that all around us was the sound of bells, and then we were dragged on to the floor in a swirling mass of people embracing each other; almost immediately afterwards we were walking along the village street in the direction of the church, heedless of the biting wind and with only Karl's arms around me to shield me from the cold.

* * *

It was almost dawn when I saw them driving their cars away to Vienna, a crowd of laughing happy people. Karl had kissed me, holding me close to him for several minutes while his friends laughingly urged him to hurry up. He had smiled down at me, promising that he would see me again very soon. 'Now that I know you are in Grinzing, Alex, there is an added incentive to come back here.'

My feet danced up the stairs to my little room already lit by the first tints of dawn. I was in love with a fairy-tale prince in a fairy-tale land in an evening filled with laughter and waltz music and all the romantic illusions of a girl brought up in a different world, a world of Victorian values and stern reality.

I joined in the revelry on New Year's Eve, my eyes searching the road, desperately hoping Karl and his friends would arrive for the festivities. But the hope was a forlorn one, and why, I told myself, should he come to Grinzing when the celebrations in Vienna would be far more wonderful?

I was standing at the window looking out into the gardens when a man appeared before me inviting me to dance, and I looked up into the dark piercing eyes of Zoltan Bartok. We danced without speaking, but all the time I was aware of his arm pressing me ever closer to him, and when I tried to edge away, his amused smile and the hard grip of his hand holding mine became excruciatingly painful.

When the music ended he did not immediately release me. Instead he asked, 'Who are you, what is your name?'

'Alexandra,' I answered curtly.

'Do all English girls look alike?' he said softly.

'Please let me go, you are hurting my hand.'

'What are you doing here?'

'I work here. Now please let me go, I have things to do.'

He released me so suddenly I almost stumbled and fell, but then he was stalking away and Herr Gruber was beside me whispering, 'Be very careful, Fräulein, I want no trouble here and that man is trouble. Didn't I warn you of him?'

'He invited me to dance, Herr Gruber, but perhaps I should have refused him.'

'That too would have meant trouble. I do not want you around when he comes to the inn.'

'I do not encourage him, Herr Gruber, I do not even like him. Why is he coming here?'

'He came here often when Fräulein Alicia was here; then it all ended. She moved away, and now for some reason of his own he is back here.'

He moved away still muttering to himself, leaving me with a sense of deep anger that a man who had once been my aunt's lover was capable of spoiling things for me.

For many days he came to the inn and I stayed out of his way. Then Herr Gruber said he had had the effrontery to ask if I still worked at the inn, and had been told that I was busy with my work.

His face was troubled and I asked, 'Did that satisfy him?'

'No. He said he came to the inn to dance, to dance with the English girl, and I should look to my business. Do not worry, he returns to Budapest soon so we shall not be troubled by him.'

'But he could come back?'

Herr Gruber shrugged his shoulders saying, 'Perhaps, but by that time, Fräulein, there could be some other young man, perhaps the young officer who came at Christmas.'

I had no such hopes. The months passed and I began to believe that I would never see Karl again. Then one morning in early June Frau Gruber came into the little office where I was working at the accounts with a bright smile on her face to tell me that a young officer was asking for me. When I stared at her anxiously she shook her head. 'No Alex, this is the young man who came at Christmas. He is wishing to stay with us for two whole weeks; he must be on leave from his regiment.'

The Grubers were generous in giving me time to be with Karl, two whole weeks to waltz with him, dine with him, and take long romantic rides through the Vienna Woods in his company. In those two weeks I learned more about Vienna than I ever had poring over history books, and he was ex-tremely knowledgeable about his country and the Habsburgs who had ruled over it for centuries.

He told me stories of the beautiful Empress Elizabeth who had been assassinated on her way to board a boat for a sail on Lake Geneva by a young hot-headed Italian who had murdered her for no apparent reason. He told me that the Emperor had a mistress, an actress named Katherina Schratt, and innocently I asked, 'Will he marry her, do you think?'

His smile was entirely cynical. 'No, *liebchen*. Men in high places seldom marry their mistresses. He has high regard for her, but there I think it will end.'

'You make Edwardian England seem very dull,' I said woefully, and he laughed, saying, 'But not any more, Alex. Your

King surrounds himself with an array of mistresses in a way that makes our ageing Emperor seem the epitome of discretion.'

'How do you know all this?' I asked him.

'I have served His Majesty in the Royal Hussars all my adult life. I come from a military family; my father before me and his father before him all served the emperors of Austria. We have always been in a position to see and know what goes on in exalted circles.'

That was the moment when I could have asked him about his family, but I had told him nothing about mine. It could well be that his family would know my aunt and her husband; he had not said if they were aristocratic or wealthy, only that they had been military. Instead I asked, 'Do you know Zoltan Bartok? I think he is Hungarian.'

'Yes, I know him. Not many people hold him in high regard. He is an officer in a Hungarian Regiment and unfortunately although Hungary is a part of our empire the Hungarians have been plotting for years to leave it. The Austrian Empire encompasses many domains; when you look at our flag you will see that the Austrian eagle is two-headed and surveys the empire from two sides. It is the Hungarians and the Balkans that give us most trouble.'

Ignoring the history lesson I persisted in asking, 'Why do you say Zoltan Bartok is not held in high regard, Karl?'

'Why are you so interested in him, *liebchen*? Has he been here, has he made trouble for you?'

'No, but I wondered about him. He looks arrogant and brooding, and he is always on his own.'

'His mother is Austrian, his father is Hungarian. His

mother's family are well connected, but I know nothing about his father's people.'

'Perhaps that is why he spends time here visiting his mother's family?'

'That I very much doubt. His uncle Count Bruckner does not acknowledge him, and I am not aware of any other relatives in Vienna.'

I decided it was not the time to dwell further on Zoltan Bartok's family history. The days were long and filled with music and sunshine, so why waste them in speaking of a man I disliked and for whom Karl had little regard?

It was one glorious afternoon at the end of Karl's leave when we drove through the Vienna Woods and came across a beautiful hunting lodge. I gasped with delight at the setting: the tall trees in their summer leafage, the exquisite architecture, and Karl said, 'You are looking at Mayerling, *liebchen*, that is the hunting lodge where Crown Prince Rudolf and the poor girl who was his mistress met their deaths.'

'But that is terrible, in such a beautiful place. How did they die?'

'If I tell you about it, *liebchen*, will you still be in love with Vienna, do you think?'

I stared at him uncertainly and he smiled, the sweet gentle smile that had made a slave of my heart, and taking hold of my hand he said, 'Come, let us walk towards the lodge. It is now a Carmelite convent occupied by nuns, perhaps the best thing that could happen to it.'

So we sauntered together in the grounds and I listened to Karl telling me about the tragedy that still haunted the courts of Imperial Vienna. The handsome Crown Prince had been married to Princess Stephanie of Belgium, but the marriage had been thrust upon them both. She was fifteen years old, thrilled with the idea of becoming the next Empress of Austria, while he was a man who had had many mistresses, and had lived a life of debauchery with drink, drugs and women. His father despised him, and although Rudolf idolised his mother she was seldom in Vienna, preferring to spend her time anywhere but at home.

The marriage was not a success; it was an arranged match that should never have taken place and very soon Rudolf was back with his old mistresses, Countess Marie Larisch and Mitzi Kaspar, the latter of whom owned some sort of night club or brothel. His health was deteriorating rapidly, due no doubt to his lifestyle, when he met Baroness Marie Vetsera, at once a woman and still a little girl, ready to hero-worship and equally ready to fall in love.

Marie Larisch introduced them; having been his mistress she had now taken on the role of good friend, seeing fit to provide him with this ardent young girl who was prepared to worship him whatever the cost.

Their affair could not have lasted very long before the tragic end came. Rudolf had a preoccupation with suicide, and those closest to him became very afraid. It was Marie Larisch who regularly brought Marie Vetsera to be with him at Mayerling including that last terrible night.

'It is a long and harrowing story,' Karl finished, 'but I will only tell you that Rudolf shot the girl then eight hours later shot himself. My father told me that everybody at the court had been told that he had died of a heart attack and Marie

Vetsera had not been mentioned. The true story only emerged much later.

'Rudolf was granted a magnificent state funeral, but the fate of Marie Vetsera is considerably more tragic. Her uncles were summoned to collect her body from Mayerling and nearly forty-eight hours after her death her body was dressed up in a fur coat and hat to hide the head wound, was propped up by a pole down her back and walked to her carriage which would take her to the burial and the unmarked grave where Rudolf would never be allowed to join her.'

It was so hard on that warm sunlit afternoon to visualise that cold winter's night when Marie Vetsera's dressed-up corpse was taken over rough roads to the gloomy monastery where they could leave her.

Looking down at my tear-filled eyes Karl asked gently, 'Are you still in love with Vienna, *liebchen*, are you prepared to overlook her decadence, the fading brilliance, do you really only see her music and her laughter?'

I looked up at him helplessly and sweeping me into his arms he laughed. 'Go on believing in it, Alex. It will continue for some time yet, but what the end will be, who knows.'

'But this is your country, Karl. I would not like to feel this way about my country.'

'And yet you left it all behind you. If you found it so easy to do that, how can you still believe in it?'

'I don't know, I just do.'

'In spite of your bawdy King and his searching for pleasure?'

'Yes. It's not the King, Karl, it's the spirit of the people that matters. I hope nothing happens in my country to destroy that.'

He looked at me gravely then to my surprise he said,

'Tomorrow I must return to Vienna, Alex. These days have been wonderful for me, and for you too, I hope?'

'Oh yes, Karl, every moment. I'll never forget them.'

'I cannot tell you when I shall be in Grinzing again. The movements of my regiment are uncertain and in the near future I have a feeling we shall be expected to see service elsewhere.'

I nodded without speaking. He was looking at the hunting lodge but he was not really seeing it; his mind was on other things. Then, smiling down at me, he said, 'I'll see you before I leave Vienna, Alex, somehow or other I'll see you again even though I don't know at this moment when that will be. Trust me, *liebchen*.'

I smiled confidently. Of course I trusted him. I loved him.

It was only later as we drove up to the inn that he said, 'My sister is visiting Vienna when I return there. It is three years since I last saw her, so we shall have a family party to celebrate.'

It was the first time he had mentioned family to me and it gave me an opportunity to say, 'Where does she live if it is so long since you met?'

'She lives in Prague, but she will find Vienna more to her liking.'

'Why is that, do you think?'

'Like you, Alex, she remains loyal to the land of her birth.'

'Do you have other sisters, or a brother?'

'No. Sophia married a cousin and they have a son and daughter. It will be good to see them.'

'Will the celebrations be in Vienna?'

'Perhaps. Either in Vienna or in the country, where my parents prefer to live.'

Why did his words deflate me? Karl was not an ordinary soldier from ordinary people. He came from a family who had married their only daughter off to a relative; wasn't this what all noble families did, wasn't this why Zoltan Bartok had stayed away from Alicia? I had no doubt that Karl would come back to Grinzing if it was possible, but I had no real faith in our future together. He could be anybody; I was simply a girl who had been as ready to fall in love as poor Marie Vetsera, but she had been a baroness who moved in exalted circles. I was a mere foreigner who had found employment in a popular inn which visitors from Vienna found amusing and good value for the odd occasion.

I had wanted our last evening together to be perfect but now I felt there was a restraint between us, and yet it was entirely of my making. His eyes were unusually sombre as he held me in his arms to wish me farewell. 'Did my story of poor Marie Vetsera make you so unhappy, *liebchen*, that it is the reason why there have been very few smiles on that beautiful face this evening?' he asked.

'Perhaps, that and your leaving, Karl.'

'I did promise to come back, Alex.'

'I know.'

'You believe me, don't you?'

'I want to believe you.' Then in answer to his doubtful smile I laughed. 'Oh, Karl, of course I believe you. I shall count the days.'

'And you won't run away, you'll be here when I come back?'

'You know I will.'

Indeed. What would it take to make me shake the dust of Austria off my feet forever? Like Alicia I would hold my head up high. I would survive.

CHAPTER ELEVEN

THERE WERE MANY coy references to my handsome Hussar by the visitors to the Golden Pheasant, all of which I replied to with a sweet smile, and Herr Gruber muttered darkly, 'Him I can tolerate, as long as the other stays away.'

But he did not stay away. Within days after Karl departed he was back, standing in the gardens watching the inn, leaning against the bar in the evenings, a dark looming presence who robbed me of enjoyment even on those occasions when he chose to ignore me.

Once again Herr Gruber suggested that I should stay out of the public rooms and the unfairness of it made me very angry. Thus it was that on an evening when he made a point of asking me to dance I refused by saying I had letters to write and did not intend to remain in the inn. Catching hold of my arm he hissed, 'So you only dance with the Emperor's Hussars and with one of them in particular.'

'I do not have to ask your permission to dance with anybody,' I retorted.

He smiled a twisted sinister smile entirely without humour.

'No, you do not, but I could advise you to be more prudent, because I am in a position to make matters unpleasant for Captain von Winckler.'

'Why would you do that? He is not in your regiment.'

'I do not speak of the army, Fräulein. I speak of his family.'

'I do not know his family.'

'That is right, you do not know them, which is a good thing, I think. I would suggest you leave it like that.'

'Really, Colonel Bartok, I do not think you have any right to tell me who I should know, or who I should call my friends. Now will you please let go of my arm and allow me to go to my room.'

He released my arm but continued to stand with one hand against the wall on either side of me, and I could smell his breath and feel his body pressing me against the wall before his arms came round me and his mouth clamped down on mine.

He let me go so suddenly I would have fallen if I had not clutched desperately at a cupboard in the hallway. He was smiling, the most cruel cynical smile I had ever seen on anybody's face; I fled along the corridor towards my room followed by the sound of his laughter.

I did not go down to the public rooms again that night but sat instead in my room staring out of the window. It was a beautiful night with a full moon turning the gardens into an enchanting place, where lovers walked beneath the trees and waltz music floated on the summer breeze. I saw him leaving—there was no disguising his arrogant swagger—and it was only then I found the courage to leave my room.

'You are not dancing tonight?' Herr Gruber asked with a smile, and when I shook my head he said, 'Colonel Bartok was here, you were very sensible not to come down. He is supposed to be in the army, so why is he not with his regiment?'

Next day I decided to call upon Herr Windisch because I regarded him as a friend. Since his retirement he lived on the outskirts of Grinzing in a beautiful old timbered house that had once belonged to the village priest. I knew he was an avid gardener and that was where I hoped to find him. I knew very little about him, including whether he had a wife or children; if he had they never accompanied him to the inn, and I was unsure how he would view my visit to his house.

I need not have worried, for he received me most graciously, inviting me to join him in the garden where a servant brought refreshments out to us.

For a while we talked pleasantries about his garden, bright with shrubs and flowers, but eventually he said, 'You have not come here to discuss my garden, Alex. Something is troubling you. Are you not happy working for Herr Gruber? He is a somewhat morose man.'

'Oh yes, I am happy there. I love my work and the people I meet.'

'But there is something amiss, am I not right?'

'Yes. It is Colonel Bartok: he will not leave me alone.'

'And he is a very dangerous man. In you he sees Alicia, and you are very like her. Once he was in love with her, now he hates her, and he is intrigued by you. He wants to know more and is determined to find out.'

'You say he hates Alicia. Why is that? He was the one who walked out of her life.'

'True. But that is not how he sees it. His family found a

wife for him but his marriage was unhappy. I rather think he had expected a wife and Alicia; that she ended up marrying his uncle was something he has never forgiven her for.'

'But that is ridiculous.'

'Of course, but such was the way of things. His marriage fell apart, his family were furious with him, then his mother died and his Austrian relatives disowned him completely. The final straw came when Alicia married his mother's youngest brother and became the Countess Bruckner. In Vienna they live a life of luxury, close to the imperial family, and Alicia is beautiful and much courted. Whenever he hears of her it is like the twisting of a knife in his unforgiving heart.'

'I am very afraid of him and I don't know what I can do to avoid him.'

'And this handsome young Hussar has returned to his regiment and can offer you no protection, is that not so?'

'Yes.'

'But he will return to Grinzing one day, hasn't he said so?'

'Yes, but I know so little about him. I wish I knew more.'

He was looking at me with a gentle smile on his lips, his eyes were kind but I sensed in them a feeling of anxiety. After a few moments he said, 'You are troubled because you have learned something already about our intrigues in high places, how marriages are arranged, how families disintegrate because of them from the imperial family downward, and now you are in love with a handsome young man about whom you know very little. You have come to me to see if I can tell you more?'

'Can you, Herr Windisch?'

'I can try, Alex. I would not like you to suffer as I saw Alicia suffer. Your Hussar, then: an officer in the most prestigious regiment in Austria, so obviously from an aristocratic family, a young man who wears his uniform with pride and great presence, but when he returns to Vienna who are his family? When he is not with his regiment, or dancing attention on the Emperor, how does he spend his time, where does he live, who does he live with?'

I nodded wordlessly.

'When I saw you together I made it my business to make some enquiries about Captain von Winckler, very discreet enquiries you understand, and this is all I have been able to assemble. His father is Count Ferdinand von Winckler, a diplomat at the court of Vienna, his mother is Bavarian from the Wittelsbach family and therefore a distant relative, I think, to the Empress Elizabeth. Count Karl von Winckler is their only son.'

'You have managed to discover quite a lot about Karl in a very short space of time, Herr Windisch,' I murmured, and if there was bitterness in my voice I couldn't help it.

His voice was very kind as he said, 'Why should you worry, Alex? You are a young beautiful girl with all of life before you. This is a young light-hearted love affair that you are embarked upon, something you can look back upon when you are safely married to a nice respectable Englishman who adores you, something that will forever be a part of Vienna and waltz music, beautiful romantic Vienna that we may never see again.'

'Why do you say that, I wonder? Alicia said something similar. Why are you so sure that everything is going to change?'

'Well, nothing is forever. Empires can last too long; perhaps we all need to move on and make room for new things, or perhaps I am being pessimistic and in a hundred years, a thousand years, nothing will have changed.'

'And in the meantime what must I do about Colonel Bartok?'

'I suggest you keep away from the public rooms at the inn, but surely he must return to his regiment in Hungary. He seems to have been away too long already.'

'You have been very kind, Herr Windisch. It is nice that I have been able to talk with you.'

'You can talk to me anytime, Alex. I am your friend and I would like you to call me Ernst. That will mean we are truly friends.'

My talk with Ernst had made me feel happier and yet the problems had not gone away; now Karl too was another one to ponder over. For the first time since I left Stevenson Square I began to realise that I was living in a dream world of my own creation. It was the world of operetta, where country maids fell in love with princes against a background of lilting music, and I was not yet ready to face reality.

That night I sat in my bedroom window watching the gates but Zoltan Bartok did not come to the inn and I hoped and prayed that he had returned to Hungary. All the same I continued not venturing downstairs in the evenings until I felt confident that for the time being he would not be there.

I made up my mind that if Karl returned to Grinzing I would not be eager to rush into his arms. He did not write to me, and as the days passed my anger grew more and more. How could he even think he could simply appear on the doorstep and expect me to be waiting for him? I danced with other young men who came to the inn, but none of them had his charm or his handsome smiling face that had bewitched me so foolishly.

The summer was almost over and the leaves were falling on the cobbled paths. Dusk came early and lights streamed out from the windows along the street and in the gardens of the inn the lights in the trees seemed brighter since there were fewer leaves to hide them. Inside the inn pine logs were being laid in empty fireplaces and in the evenings when the fires were lit the sharp scent from them pervaded everywhere.

At the end of September Karl came back to Grinzing in the company of two of his brother officers. He greeted me as though he had never been away and I smiled, trying hard not to be angry with him for what I considered his neglect, particularly when he explained that they had been in attendance on the Emperor during his visit to St Petersburg.

'I have leave,' he explained with a disarming smile. 'Two whole weeks! Doesn't Gruber allow you to have holidays?'

'He's very kind. He allowed me days to go off with you in the spring. What would I do with holidays? I love it here.'

'But you are only seeing Grinzing, *liebchen*. You need to see Vienna. Come with me, a week in Vienna with the ballet and the opera, the palaces and the churches. Isn't that what you want, to get to know Vienna, isn't that why you came here?'

'Karl, it isn't possible.'

'You mean you don't want it to be possible?'

'I would love it to be possible. It just isn't, that's all.'

He smiled, so why did I have the distinct impression that the subject was far from closed? Later that evening saw him in earnest discussion with Herr Gruber, and as we danced the last waltz together he said disarmingly, 'Herr Gruber agrees with me, *liebchen*, that you should have a holiday and see something of Vienna. He'll speak to you tomorrow about it.'

'Oh, Karl, you had no right to mention it to him. I work here, I don't want him to think I'm craving for holidays all the time.'

'He doesn't, but he does agree that you work very hard, that he appreciates what you do and he is prepared to show his appreciation. Hear what he has to say in the morning.'

Herr Gruber was affable when I had expected him to be irritable. 'Captain von Winckler wishes to show you Vienna, Fräulein Alex,' he said with a wide smile, 'and I have told him you can go with him for one week. He is a very persuasive young man.'

'Are you quite sure that you are agreeable to me going, Herr Gruber?'

'But of course. You may not be able to think it, but I too was young once. I too liked the streets of Vienna and the cafés to be found there. With such a young man you will enjoy every moment. Just remember that you only have a week to see Vienna and sample every moment it has to offer.'

How my feet danced across the floor, how assiduously I counted my savings to see what sort of gown I could afford to buy for whatever joys Karl had in mind.

I wanted to ask questions. Where would we stay in Vienna, would he be with me or would we live separately and meet only for our excursions around the city?

The questions would not come until we arrived in Vienna and we stood at last in the foyer of a quite palatial hotel in the Ringstrasse. Then, in answer to my doubtful expression, he said lightly, 'You will like this hotel, *liebchen*, it is a good place from which to see the sights of Vienna. I have asked them to give you a room at the front. With a smile he added, 'I will see you every day but I am not staying here. What did you expect?'

'I didn't know.'

'My family home is in the Ringstrasse not far from here, but tonight I shall still be in my quarters at the barracks. I love you, *liebchen*. I have no designs on you, at least not until the time is right.'

In my luxurious bedroom I pondered his words.

That he was contemplating designs showed that that was all they would be. He had brought me to Vienna, but he had no thoughts of allowing me to meet his family; yet as the days passed it didn't matter. They were filled with enchantment as we wandered through the parks and streets, the heady excitement of the Prater Gardens and the awesome wonder of old churches.

My most exciting morning came when Karl refused to tell me where we were going as he hurried me through the city streets until at last we reached the Emperor's winter palace, the Hofburg, and smiling down at me he said, 'Today, *liebchen*, you are going to see something you will remember for the rest of your life.'

'You are taking me into the palace?' I asked.

'No, today we are going to the Spanish Riding School. Forget the ballet where men and women prance about the stage, today you will see the most meticulous and exquisite ballet you are ever likely to see.'

We were entering a vast hall lit by crystal chandeliers and it seemed that every seat was filled with expectant people; as we took our seats we looked down on an arena carpeted in rich crimson and I whispered, 'But there is no stage.'

He smiled, and at that moment the doors at the other end of the arena opened and through them came a procession of snow-white horses ridden by men wearing brown silk jackets, cream jodhpurs and Napoleon-style cocked hats.

Between the acts Karl told me that in all there were about sixty stallions but probably only two or three which could perform the most difficult items. The young horses turned white between the ages of four and eight and these less experienced horses were taught by the old riders, whereas the young riders were taught by the expert horses.

One charm of the performance was the silence. We could not hear the horses' hooves on the sanded carpet as stallion after stallion was asked to perform steps a ballerina might have found exacting. There were tears in my eyes as I watched those exquisite milk-white horses with their proud arched necks and delicately poised limbs, the delicate charm of the pas de deux and the faraway dedicated look of the riders.

How glad I was at the end of the performance that the valets who came to lead them away rewarded each of them with a tasty morsel for performing so well.

Karl looked down at me with a proud smile, asking, 'Well, what did you think of it, Alex? Have you anything in the whole of England to compare with that?'

'It was wonderful. I'll never forget it, never, it's been the most enchanting day of my life.'

'And it isn't nearly over, *liebchen*. We have three days left, three days to live and love and create memories that will last forever.'

I didn't ask myself at that moment if memories would be all I would ever have. As we drove along the Ringstrasse

Karl pointed out a very large house, larger indeed than the hotel where I was staying.

'That is my parents' house, *liebchen*, that is where I grew up, there and in the country near Ischl.'

'Ischl?'

'Yes, that is where the Archduchess Sophia had her summer palace, and it is very beautiful.'

There were so many questions I wanted to ask but pride stopped me. What had I to do with archduchesses and summer palaces, a middle-class English girl from the shires? Yet none of that had deterred Alicia.

'Is that where you will be spending the rest of your leave?' I asked innocently, and with a gentle smile he answered, 'I am leaving the barracks in the morning, my few duties there are almost done. I have two choices. I could go to the house we have passed, indeed my mother would like that, or I could be with you. What would you like me to do, Alex?'

I could feel my heart beating furiously, and I was well aware of my flaming face, but there was only one answer as I sat in the shelter of his arms. 'I want you to be with me, Karl,' I murmured.

'Then tomorrow, *liebchen*, I will give you a day even better than this one,' he said, his eyes bright with laughter.

'How can that be?'

'Tomorrow night I will take you to the opera house when everybody who is anybody in Vienna will be there. The Emperor, most of his court, all the aristocracy of Vienna, and the most lilting music you have ever heard. You shall dress up in your prettiest gown and people will look at you and ask themselves how have I been able to find someone so exquisite that she puts every other woman in the shade.'

'Oh Karl, that's ridiculous. Vienna will be blessed with hundreds of pretty women.'

'Aren't you interested in what we are about to see and hear?'

'Oh yes, I am. I have to confess I haven't seen many operas. My family were not terribly keen on them; my father preferred plays and my mother orchestral concerts.'

'But you have heard of Franz Lehar?'

'Yes, but doesn't he compose music for the operetta?'

'Yes, and tomorrow we are going to see *The Merry Widow* which all Europe is waltzing to. I am told the story is often silly, but the music so bewitching the world will be dancing to it forever.'

I do not know which excited me most, our night at the opera or what might come after, but Karl had said he would call for me to take me to the opera house and I had all day to see to my hair and decide what I should wear. I took out my new dress, which was made from heavy pale blue satin. It had a pretty bodice and large voluminous skirt and I stood back to admire it hanging outside the wardrobe door. When the chambermaid came in her face lit up with delight as gently she stroked the skirt, admiring the beauty of the dress and the narrow satin blue shoes that went with it.

'You will look very beautiful, Fräulein,' she exclaimed. 'I have dreamed of going to the opera dressed like that, and with such a handsome young Hussar to escort me.'

I laughed. 'Perhaps one day your dream may come true,' I said, but she only shook her head ruefully.

'Not for such as me, Fräulein, but I shall go to stand outside the opera house tonight to see them all arriving. I like to see the gowns and the jewels, the uniforms and the Emperor with his guests.'

'Is there no way you can make it come true?' I asked her, but she shook her head a little sadly.

'No, how could there be? I have no money, my family are poor, and I have no beauty like you. To make dreams come true there has to be a beginning, you know: beauty, riches, courage. I have little courage and neither of the others.'

'Oh but you have. Your face is very pretty. With clothes like you will see tonight even a very plain girl could be pretty and you are not plain.'

She laughed. 'And you, Fräulein, are very sweet and very kind. I wish you a very happy evening and a happy life.'

When she had gone I mulled over her words. I would have a happy evening, but what of the rest of my life? Karl had promised me music and laughter, love and excitement, but when it was over and had passed into limbo what would be left?

CHAPTER TWELVE

How could I not gaze in rapt admiration at Karl wearing his dress uniform, so handsome, tall and slender with his clothes impeccably correct? From all around us people smiled as we crossed the hotel foyer to where our car waited outside.

As we sat back in the darkness of the car he whispered, 'How beautiful you look, Alex. You make me so proud to be with you tonight. I have a gift for you.'

From the seat beside him he produced a long velvet-covered box and I stared down at it for several minutes while he urged, 'Open it, Alex, tell me if you like it.'

Against the velvet lining of the box the gold chain gleamed up at me but it was the dark blue sapphire stone sparkling with subtle blue lights that brought a gasp of admiration from me.

'Here, let me fasten it for you,' he said. 'I wasn't sure if you might prefer some other stone, but I remembered you said your dress was blue.'

'Oh Karl, it is beautiful, but it must have been terribly expensive.'

He laughed. 'Would you have preferred me to give you

something inexpensive? I can afford it, *liebchen*. A gift which has no value to the giver, when he can afford it, is hardly worth the giving.'

How I loved him! On that night we were two enchanted people living in an enchanting world with nothing but the here and now to concern us. So how could so much that was perfect vanish as though it had never existed?

This was how I had imagined it would be. The long sweeping staircase under the gleaming chandeliers, the exquisite gowns and sparkling jewels, the glamour of uniforms and shining orders over formal evening dress, and then as we sat watching the boxes filling up with dignitaries the Emperor was there surrounded by his retinue.

I had seen many pictures of Franz Joseph all over Vienna and Grinzing; now here he was in person accompanied by a large woman who chatted and smiled at him and I asked, 'Who is she?'

'Katherina Schratt, his mistress.'

'Will he ever marry her?'

'Oh no, but he has great affection for her. She has been in his life a great many years, even when the Empress Elizabeth was alive. I doubt if she minded, *liebchen*. The Empress spent her life touring Europe, and it was a well-known fact that she preferred Budapest to Vienna.'

Katherina Schratt had a sweet expression and she and the Emperor seemed to have plenty to say to each other. At that moment, however, people were entering the box next to the Emperor's and I gasped to see my Aunt Alicia taking her place there among a group of other people.

She looked incredibly beautiful in cream satin, with a flash of jewels round her neck and a jewelled tiara on her head. She was smiling and when the Emperor acknowledged their presence, the ladies curtsied, the men bowed their heads, then I was able to look more closely at the man taking his place beside her. He was tall and distinguished-looking. His hair was silver, and there was a decorated order against the sombre black of his evening dress.

Seeing my interest Karl murmured, 'Count and Countess Bruckner, and their friends.'

'You know them?'

'They are neighbours of ours in the Ringstrasse. The Bruckners are an old Austrian family from the region bordering on Hungary, and the Count's sister was married to a Hungarian, a marriage from all accounts not made in heaven.'

That was the moment the conductor took his stand and everybody in the house rose to the strains of the Austrian national anthem. The lights were dimmed, the overture was being played, and then the curtain rose on Lehar's enchanting operetta. It did not matter that the story was light-hearted and hardly in the tradition of grand opera; the tale of a rich widow and a dissolute count was set to the most magical music I had ever heard, coupled with glamorous gowns and enchanting hats. By the time the first act was over everybody in that vast audience was completely charmed and as we made our way to the various reception rooms everybody's joy in the evening was apparent.

I looked round for Alicia, feeling a great sense of relief that her party was at the other end of the room, and I took a seat in the shelter of a large palm.

'I have ordered champagne, *liebchen*. I asked them to put it on ice so I'll bring it to the table here.'

I was aware that round about us people were curious; smiles were exchanged, and I felt sure that Karl was well known in Vienna and there would be speculation as to my identity. I could see that he was being constantly involved in conversation on his way to the bar but I was happy to look around me, just as long as there was no danger that my aunt and her party might wander in our direction.

I looked up startled when a man's hand came down firmly on my shoulder and a voice hissed, 'I had not thought to find you in such salubrious surroundings, Fräulein Alex.'

I leapt to my feet with a little cry to find myself looking into the dark sardonic eyes of Zoltan Bartok.

'Who is the lucky man?' he sneered, and then Karl was there looking at him with haughty disdain while he handed me a glass of champagne. Turning to me the Hungarian said softly, 'You have done well, Fräulein, progressing from an obscure inn in Grinzing to the opera in Vienna. I hope Captain von Winckler will find your favours sufficiently appropriate.'

His expression was sinister, his voice sibilant and his smile the cruellest I had seen on a man's mouth. Without a second's hesitation I flung the glass of champagne into his face. I could see it rolling down on to his elegant uniform, staining its impeccable whiteness. I was aware of Karl's anger before he took hold of my arm and pulled me away. People all around us were staring, and I could only guess at the fury of the man we had turned our backs on; then above the silence that had descended on the room there was the sound of a shot. I was aware of Karl's hand clutching mine so fiercely that I cried out with the pain of it, then I felt him falling, pulling me down with him. I was aware of the dark red stain on his uniform and on the folds of my dress. Suddenly we were surrounded with people, hands pulling me away, Karl's brother officers surrounding his prostrate form. A sudden scuffle erupted at the end of the room coupled with angry shouts, and Zoltan Bartok was marched out.

I was being led away, but I wanted to stay with Karl: he needed me, and I had no idea how badly he had been hurt, but all my plaintive cries were being ignored as he was carried out. Then I found myself staring into Alicia's bewildered eyes and she was saying, 'Alex! Alex, what are you doing here?'

How could I believe that in less than half an hour I was sitting beside her in her box and on the stage was singing and movement, while the ridiculous story contin- ued and the music that I knew would live in my heart forever washed over those involved in the tragedy that had happened earlier where there had been such joy and companionship.

The rest of the evening passed as if in a dream. The wait in the foyer while the Emperor and his retinue left the opera house, the whisperings and the covert glances, then the silent ride through the city streets to the Ringstrasse and Alicia's house. All I was aware of was the glow from chandeliers, silent-footed servants who came to take our wraps, then Alicia was placing a glass of sherry in my shaking hands and she was saying, 'You will stay here tonight, Alex. We will talk in the morning.'

'But I can't,' I wailed. 'I have a room in a hotel, my clothes are there, I have to see Karl. I have to know if he is badly hurt. Please, Aunt Alicia, let me go to my hotel. I will tell you ev- erything in the morning.'

'You will stay here, Alex, and yes, you will tell me every-thing in the morning. Maria will take you to your room and something will be served to help you to sleep. I have to speak with Franz; he is bewildered by all this.'

I had no recourse but to do as she asked and meekly I followed Maria up the shallow staircase. I had no interest in the room I was shown into, noticing only that Maria was helping me undress and tears were rolling down my cheeks at the sight of the dried rust-coloured stain on the satin folds of my dress.

I was served hot milk and Maria stood beside the bed until I had drunk it all, then she was pulling up the covers around me and although I was convinced I would never sleep all too soon I could feel the events of the night slipping away.

I knew that it was morning by the sounds of traffic outside on the street, the clip-clop of horses' hooves, the pealing of church bells, the rattle of tramcars; then the events of the night before rushed back to me and I sat up with a little cry. How could I ever have slept when Karl might be dead? Why had I been prevented from staying with him, what was I doing here? Maria came in carrying a tray which she placed on the bed in front of me, and I whispered, 'What time is it?'

'It is ten o'clock, Fräulein. You will eat breakfast, please, and afterwards I am to take you downstairs. Countess Bruckner will see you then. She has said that I am to help you dress.'

'My clothes are at the hotel, Maria. I have nothing here,' I answered her.

'Your clothes were brought from the hotel this morning,

Fräulein, and they are in the wardrobe. The manager at the hotel has been told you will not be returning.'

'Maria, I have to know about Captain von Winckler. I have to go to Grinzing, I have work there.'

She stared at me for several seconds, then calmly she said, 'You will speak to the Countess, Fräulein, she can tell you what you want to know. Perhaps you will ring when you have eaten breakfast.'

I didn't answer. I didn't want breakfast, and I didn't need Maria's help. As soon as she had closed the door behind her I got out of bed and went to the wardrobe where all my dresses were hung, then opening the dressing-table drawer I found my other belongings inside it; it would seem nothing had been forgotten.

For the first time I looked curiously about the room. It was beautifully furnished with rich brocade curtains at the window and round the bed; a Chinese carpet woven with lotus flowers and bamboo leaves, exotic birds and peonies, covered the floor and the furniture was ornate with touches of gold. The door to the right led into a large bathroom where I washed quickly, anxious to see Alicia and listen to what she had to tell me.

I put on the dress and jacket I had travelled to Vienna in from Grinzing, confident that I would be returning there that morning, once I had been reassured by Alicia that Karl was in no danger.

Maria looked at me in some surprise when she saw my attire, and I said hurriedly, 'I'm sorry I didn't wait for you, Maria, but I am very anxious. Can we go downstairs now, please?'

She ushered me through the door and together we descended the staircase; for the first time I realised that the house was palatial, with its richly carved staircase, the marble floor beneath and the paintings of opulently clad men and women on the walls of the hall.

Maria smiled. 'Come with me, Fräulein, the Countess will see you in the morning room. She is quite alone.'

When she opened the door a small silken-coated dog rushed across the room to stand erect with his paws against my skirt and Alicia said, 'Come here, Max, we have no time for you this morning.'

She came forward and gently kissed me on both cheeks, then pointing to two chairs in the window she said, 'We will sit there. You can see into the garden, and we won't be disturbed. I want to know everything, Alex: why you are here, how you got here and how you came to be with Captain von Winckler at the opera last night.'

'Alicia, I have to know about Karl. Please tell me he isn't dead?'

'Franz has gone to the palace this morning. No doubt when he returns he will be able to tell you everything we need to know.'

'The palace? But why?'

'The Emperor has sent for him.'

'But what can that have to do with Karl? I just want to know that he is not badly hurt, and if I can see him.'

'Sit down, Alex. This is Vienna, where passions run high, where bitter Hungarians have no great love for their Austrian counterparts. It is not London, where officers would never shoot one another, or well-brought-up young ladies throw glasses of champagne into the faces of men who flirted with them. This is Vienna, waltzing to its doom. You did not believe me when I warned you of this, because you did not choose to believe me.'

I sat down weakly on the chair facing her, aware that she was looking at me with a strange expression in her violet eyes. The little dog had crept on to her knee where her hand gently caressed his soft fur and she said, 'I had thought Franz would be back before this. He went very early. Let us hope he has good news for you, Alex.'

'You knew it was Zoltan Bartok who shot him?' I asked.

'Yes. That is probably one reason why the Emperor has sent for Franz. He is the son of Franz's sister but they were estranged. Franz has not spoken to his nephew since his mother's funeral.'

'Because of you, Alicia?'

'Some of it, perhaps, but even before me he had no liking for Zoltan. He has lived a life of debauchery: women, drink, drugs. His wife had their marriage annulled, and looking back now I can hardly believe that I ever thought I was in love with him. How about you, Alex? Do you too think you are in love with a handsome young Hussar who wears the Emperor's uniform with such style and will never marry you?'

I stared at her out of wide anguished eyes. 'Why do you say that, how do you know?'

'So you do think you're in love with him, Alex. Well, Count Karl von Winckler will marry where his parents or his Emperor dictate. Love will not enter into it; love is transient, it is land and money which matters. With such families they are all that matter.'

I had no answer. What did I really know of aristocratic young Hussars except that my Hussar had been handsome and charming, and had said he loved me, needed to be with me.

I stood up in order to stare out of the window. Vienna basked under the warmth of the late summer sunshine and her streets were crowded with people who looked happy and at ease with life. I was impatient for Franz to come back with news of Karl. Franz was somebody in Vienna, so surely when Karl's family found out that I was a relative of his wife they would allow me to visit him. I had a great deal to learn at that moment.

It was mid-afternoon when Franz came back. We heard him speaking to one of the servants in the hall, and then he came into the room, his face grave; but then his was usually a face that gave little away.

Alicia had said she had letters to write and I had wondered who she wrote to. Not the family in England, but her daughter perhaps, or those friends she remembered occasionally from her schooldays. Now she looked up from where she was sitting at her bureau, saying, 'I expected you back ages ago. It must be very important for the Emperor to keep you so long.'

Without answering her immediately he went over to the wine cabinet and poured himself a drink, and I wanted to scream at him to tell me about Karl.

For several minutes he stood with the glass in his hand staring out of the window, while Alicia's exasperation grew, then turning to face her he said, 'We are leaving Vienna, Alicia, just as soon as it can be arranged.'

She stared at him in amazement. 'Leaving Vienna? But this is our home! How can we leave? What are you talking about?'

'The Emperor has commanded me to do so and I assumed his order to mean my wife and some of our servants.'

'But where are we going? To the country, is that it, just

when Vienna is coming to life with its concerts and balls, when people are coming back from the country to enjoy themselves? Franz, I won't go to the country. The Emperor has no right to ask it. I suppose it's because of Zoltan Bartok and the von Winckler family's antagonism after last night's trauma.'

'It may well be that has had some bearing on the situation, but it is more, much more.'

'And you have simply said yes, that we will go? Surely even the Emperor would expect you to speak to me about it. It is said he never made a move without the agreement of the Empress Elizabeth.'

'I am not the Emperor, Alicia, and you are not the Empress. It is my duty to do as I am ordered.'

'Even to bury ourselves in the country until he has a mind to order us back to Vienna.'

'We are not going to the country. We are going to St Petersburg.'

'St Petersburg! But why, I thought Count Karolyi was the Austrian Ambassador at the Court of St Petersburg.'

'He is being recalled, due to ill health, I believe.'

'You really believe that?'

'I have no reason to doubt it. There isn't much time. I have a great deal to do and we shall be expected to leave in about eight days.'

'But that's impossible! I have no clothes for Russia, and soon it will be the beginning of winter with all that snow and ice. I shall need to buy clothes, but I would prefer to buy them here.'

'I rather think the shops of St Petersburg will be better equipped to supply clothes for the Russian climate. However, you are aware of the circumstances, Alicia; I suggest you make your arrangements at the earliest possible moment.'

For the first time he appeared to notice me, and Alicia said sharply. 'And what about Alex? You have not said a word about Karl von Winckler, and all morning she's been waiting for you to tell her what is happening.'

Regarding me sombrely he said, 'Captain von Winckler is in the military hospital here in Vienna. He is not allowed visitors outside his immediate family and his condition is stable.'

'But he will be well again? Oh, please tell me he is going to be well.'

'His condition is not life-threatening now, Fräulein Alex, he will recover.'

'Thank God,' I breathed, and Alicia said sharply, 'And Zoltan Bartok, what news do you have of him?'

'He is in prison under constant guard. This will be the end of his military career, possibly the end of his life.'

'Why do you say that?'

'If they eventually release him what is there for him? He has few friends, if any, no family, his home has gone, sold to finance his extravagant way of life, and his future is a bleak and barren waste. In fact he has no future.'

'He is your sister's son, Franz, or doesn't that matter?'

'No. My sister was thrust into a marriage with a man she despised, she was unhappy in Budapest and her son was no comfort to her. The poor woman died lost and broken-hearted in a city she had little love for.'

'But surely it was your family too who were responsible for her marriage to Zoltan's father.'

'I agree. I made my anger very apparent over the years.'

'What are we to do about Alex?'

His expression was uncompromising to say the least. He had enough problems on his mind, and he did not want this strange girl who had appeared out of nowhere to add to them. He was staring at me haughtily and I was quick to say, 'You needn't worry about me. I have a job to go to—I shall go back to Grinzing and the inn.'

'Grinzing and the inn!'

'Yes, I work at the sort of job Alicia did. I am happy, I have friends there.'

For what seemed an eternity he and Alicia stared at each other, then adamantly he said, 'You cannot go back to Grinzing, Fräulein Alex. What occurred at the opera house last night will be common knowledge, and all in Grinzing will be aware of your part in it. Is it outside the realms of possibility that you can return to England and your family?'

'Yes, it is. One day I'll go back, one day when I can face them and show them that I've made something of my life, but it isn't yet. Alicia, please tell him I can't go home now. You couldn't go back, and you know I can't.'

'Was your home life so terrible that you have had to put miles between you?' Franz asked.

'No, my family were kind and decent and I loved them. The fault was in me; I had too much imagination, I wanted something else from life. I didn't deserve them.'

Alicia looked at him with a strange smile on her face. 'You see, Franz, Alex was like me, restless, and impatient, but unlike me she didn't run away for love or hurt anybody. Up to this moment the only person she has hurt has been herself.'

For what seemed like an eternity nobody spoke, then with

a little bow he said, 'Perhaps in St Petersburg, Fräulein Alex, you will find what you have been looking for.'

'I am to go with you?' I cried.

'What else is there?'

'Then will you please call me Alex. Fräulein Alex sounds so formal.'

He smiled, the first time I had seen him do so, and the smile on a face that always seemed so severe was unusually charming; then with a little bow he left us.

CHAPTER THIRTEEN

THE DAYS THAT followed sped past all too quickly. We shopped for things Alicia said we would need in the most expensive shops in Vienna, and when I remonstrated with her that I should spend my own money she merely laughed, saying, 'Alex, my husband is one of the richest men in Vienna. We cannot go to St Petersburg looking like poor relations, so we have to make a stand in the name of our own city.'

She was singularly uninterested in how we were getting there, but I asked a great many questions of Franz, who seemed surprised at my curiosity, eventually taking the trouble to describe our journey to me.

We were to travel through Poland and on to Russia by train, and when I confessed that I knew very little about St Petersburg he went to great lengths to explain that it was situated on the Gulf of Finland and was the Tsar's favourite city. I learned about the Russian court, the palaces and the churches, and the imperial dynasty that had ruled over the Russian people for centuries.

For what seemed an eternity I had yearned to visit Vienna and now too soon I was moving on to a city I had never even thought about.

So it was that early the next morning I took my final walk in the streets of Vienna. I visited the cathedral and the Hofburg, I stood enchanted at the sight of the Belvedere Palace and wished I could have seen the Schönbrunn, but time was short, and later in the afternoon I merely walked in the park with Alicia's dog Max.

I felt strangely lonely. I tried to imagine that Karl was beside me, smiling down at me, showing me the gardens and the lake, and it was while we were standing on the edge of the lake that Max greeted a lady standing next to us so that she reached down and patted his head.

'What a lovely little dog,' she exclaimed. 'Is he yours?'

'No, he belongs to my aunt.'

'You are not Austrian?' she asked.

'No. I am English.'

'Then you are on holiday?'

'Yes. I am leaving tomorrow.' I had no wish to tell my story to a complete stranger but we found ourselves walking out of the park together and towards the Ringstrasse.

'Do you live in this direction?' she asked.

'Yes, on the Ringstrasse, and you?'

'Yes, just there, the house on the corner. I am a visitor there.'

My heart gave a sudden lurch when I recognised the house as the one Karl had told me belonged to his family. This girl could be his sister, but I had to pose my questions very carefully.

'We had heard that Captain von Winckler had an accident the other evening at the opera house. Can you tell me if he has recovered?' I asked gently.

Smiling, she said, 'Oh, do you know Karl? But of course,

if you are neighbours. He is much better, but it was not an accident—some Hungarian officer deliberately shot him.'

'I'm sorry. But he is better?'

'He will be. I have come from the country to stay here until he is fully recovered, then we will visit my parents' house in Salzburg until it is time to rejoin his regiment.'

'I thought perhaps you were his sister.'

'Oh no, I am his fiancée, or at least I will be when he comes home.'

I was staring at her with wide anguished eyes, and now she too was staring at me curiously. Recovering my scattered senses I said hurriedly, 'I was just thinking how late it is. I promised to be home ages ago. I do hope your fiancé will soon be better, goodbye.'

I knew she was still staring as I ran along the pavement, pulling the little dog after me. I was trying to remember her face. She was tall and slender, not pretty, but she had a nice smile and kind brown eyes. I would have to tell Alicia; Alicia might know about her.

Alicia was not surprised. 'I've never heard of her, but then how could I? Of course we know the von Wincklers, but she is probably some aristocratic girl earmarked for Karl while she was still in the schoolroom. Isn't this what I warned you about, Alex?'

Now the days could not come quickly enough for our departure and early on that last morning I stood at my bedroom window watching a procession of servants leaving the house pulling a trolley containing a copious amount of luggage.

Although it was still autumn Alicia had insisted that we should wear something substantial for the journey, and consequently I was wearing a long beige woollen skirt and jacket. The effect was plain except for the sable collar at the neck of the jacket, hardly suitable wear for Vienna on that morning, but we were heading for colder weather as we journeyed northward through Poland and into Russia.

We travelled in some style. The train was luxurious by any standard and we were treated with the utmost deference by officials who obviously regarded us as people of some standing.

Franz said very little but seemed immersed in the documents he produced out of his briefcase. I would like to have spent some time in Warsaw but our time there was brief and as we journeyed onward the weather began to change.

Large black clouds coloured the sky and the sharp wind that had arisen blew roughly against the windows of the train.

'Not so soon,' Alicia grumbled. 'I thought at least we could expect some respite for another month or so.'

Franz merely looked up briefly before resuming his reading.

'Can you imagine it, Alex?' Alicia sighed. 'Snow everywhere before Christmas and all those balls and ballets we have been looking forward to having to be reached through streets piled high with snow.'

'It will be different,' I ventured.

She was in no mood to be placated. 'Well of course, horribly different. I remember reading *Anna Karenina* and not even a love affair of that dimension could relieve the monotony of that awful weather.'

'But it was wonderfully romantic, wasn't it?'

'And you are very young and happy to view the world through rose-coloured spectacles,' she said tartly.

I was never very sure how Franz regarded my presence in his life, whether it was as an intruder, a terrible nuisance, or someone who took away some of the strain of entertaining his fractious wife. I speculated romantically that he must adore her since he had not been afraid to marry an unknown English girl when there must have been so many women of his own station in life only too willing to be his wife.

With me he was polite but distant. He was a man who commanded instant respect and when I thought about Zoltan Bartok I could only feel that Alicia had been singularly fortunate to have Franz Bruckner as her husband.

As we travelled northward across the Russian steppes I could find nothing beautiful. The countryside was flat and sleet swept down obliterating any distant view we might have had. The meals we were served on the train were hardly imaginative and Alicia complained of their stodginess.

'Thank goodness we are taking our own servants with us,' she said feelingly, 'otherwise the pounds will simply pile on and I shall begin to resemble poor Katherina Schratt.'

'Katherina Schratt was a very beautiful woman when she first arrived at court,' Franz said drily. 'No doubt too many royal banquets have taken their toll.'

'That's exactly what I mean, Franz. Too much of this sort of food and the same sort of thing will happen to me.'

'I've seen pictures of the Empress Elizabeth,' I ventured. 'She was very beautiful. How can he compare his mistress with his wife?'

'I'm sure he doesn't,' Alicia said, smiling. 'The Empress

was away more than she was with him, so she laid the way wide open for Katherina. At the same time the poor man was devastated when she was assassinated.'

I was not sure if Franz had been listening to our conversation, but he had laid his papers aside and sat looking morosely through the window, and Alicia said, 'Franz does not like me to discuss the vagaries of the Habsburgs since I am still regarded as something of a foreigner, but then after all our own royal family with King Edward at its helm hardly merits close inspection. I can't begin to imagine what Granny or my mother would have had to say at his goings-on. Queen Victoria was so circumspect; boring perhaps, but circumspect.'

I was feeling vaguely uncomfortable. Alicia and myself were products of an English upper-middle-class family of no particular note, but Franz and his family had served the court of the Habsburgs for centuries. He was one of the old school with deep respect for his Emperor, even when he was no doubt all aware of the failings and scandals that surrounded them.

He consulted his watch, suggesting that we return to our compartment, and although it was only dawn when we arrived in St Petersburg I had not bargained for the escort of imperial guards that awaited us. There were people to assist our servants in handling our luggage, and others handing round hot drinks laced with vodka, then the guards surrounded us, marching with measured tread towards a procession of cars. From one of them two uniformed army officers stepped out to shake our hands.

It was evident they were officers of some high rank, taking command of the situation by ushering us into the first car.

The city streets we were driving through were narrow and badly lit, and my heart sank when I compared them to the beautiful thoroughfares of distant Vienna; then it began to change, the streets became broader, the buildings more palatial, and soon we were driving across a beautiful square where street lighting fell upon structures as beautiful as any I had ever seen.

My heart lifted. Could this be a city where I could learn to live again, where I could put behind me trauma and deception, desertion and despair?

When I stood at last in the place that was to be our new home I could feel that first sweet awareness that my heart could come alive again, that all men were not deceivers. I would prove that I could survive.

My trunks were unpacked and my clothes put away in the vast wardrobes. From my window I could look out across the square, to where the towers and domes of St Petersburg stood out sharply against the pink glow in the eastern sky. A log fire burned in the vast fireplace but already I had experienced a feeling of acute cold as we had walked from our car into the house, and shivering delicately Alicia had murmured, 'It can only get worse. The Russian winter is on its way.'

I never knew if Franz listened to her complaints since he retained his distant uncompromising attitude which seemed not to bother her in the slightest.

It did not take me long to feel the spell of St Petersburg, its incomparable palaces and art galleries, the exquisite performances of Russian ballet, and the ornamental concert halls where we listened to the great concertos and symphonies by Russian composers.

Vienna had been a city in love with itself, living life in three-quarter time, existing in an everlasting waltz, but St Petersburg had a grandeur that seemed to have been evolved from trauma, suffering and the extremities of the climate.

There was enchantment too. Long starlit nights and the sound of sleigh bells across the snow, church bells pealing from exquisite domes. In contrast were the long queues of silent people waiting in the snow outside the soup kitchens, and as they stood in the squares to see the arrival of their Tsar's guests for yet another function I sensed no joy in their stolid stares, only resignation and in some cases deep anger.

At the balls there were handsome young officers to dance with in plenty and as the months passed I told myself that I had forgotten Karl, that he was as much a part of my past as those family parties in distant England.

Alicia was enjoying herself hugely, oblivious to Franz standing in earnest conversation with serious senior officers or government officials.

'Does he never dance?' I once asked her, and with a laugh she said, 'Hardly ever, Alex, although when he does he dances like all Viennese men, excellently.'

'He seems content to discuss more important things with those men he surrounds himself with,' I answered her.

'Well of course, darling, they talk politics: which little Balkan king is going to fall out of line next, which princess would make the best marriage for which king's son, and bring him the richest dowry. In the end none of it will matter.'

'There seems to be so much poverty here,' I murmured. 'It

seems so unfair that there should be so much luxury and money for some and so little of it on those streets out there.'

'But since we can't do anything about it it's best we don't think about it,' she replied.

At that moment the Tsar and Tsarina, accompanied by their four daughters, swept down the staircase and before them the men bowed and the women curtsied.

After they had passed Alicia said, 'The Tsar is really quite a handsome man, but his wife is no great beauty.'

'The Grand Duchesses are all very pretty,' I replied.

'Yes, but the boy is sickly. I wonder which European thrones those girls will grace in the years to come?'

Talk of such things annoyed me. It seemed like a cattle market where instead of beasts men and women were being auctioned off to the highest bidder. Was that how Karl's fiancée had been found for him? Had she or he the most money, the bluest blood?

Alicia was saying, 'We'll have to find you a very handsome young nobleman, Alex, some young man destined for great things at the Russian court, and who you can invite back to Vienna to flaunt in front of your erstwhile lover.'

'I am not very interested in Russian noblemen, Alicia.'

'Then what do you want? You left home looking for adventure and romance; you thought you'd found it but it was an illusion. Life goes on, Alex, and believe me I shall be old and decrepit before I stop looking for the good things around the corner. Here is that nice young cavalry officer anxious to ask you to dance.'

He was charming, but he knew hardly any German and no English so consequently all we could do was smile at each other. Franz was still engrossed in his conversation with his cronies while Alicia was surrounded by a bevy of men and enjoying herself hugely.

It was several days later when I watched Alicia leaving the house in the company of a man in uniform. I had been walking her dog, and she waved to me gaily from the horse sleigh he was driving; as I entered the house I looked up to find Franz standing in the hall. I smiled but he seemed troubled and I wondered if his perturbed air had any connection with Alicia's departure. I was not left long in doubt, however.

'Did Alicia say where she was going?' he asked me.

'No. She was already in the carriage and driving away. Is something wrong?'

'There was trouble in one of the squares this morning. I hope her companion is aware of it.'

'What sort of trouble?'

He seemed reluctant to enlarge on it but seeing my anxiety he said. 'It is probably nothing,' and turned away to go into his study.

In the park that morning I had met people scurrying past me with their eyes on the ground and I had sensed an atmosphere in groups of people standing about, heated words, then silences at the passing of a stranger, a stranger who was dressed in furs and rich clothing they were unable to afford. Making up my mind I followed Franz into his study and he looked up at me curiously.

I told him what I had seen in the park and on the streets and he said evenly, 'There is always something and someone ready to cause trouble, Alex. Like I said, it is probably nothing.'

'Then why did you mention it? I've seen it everywhere, the poverty, the envy, the sadness. There was poverty in Vienna, in England too, but there was never the despair I've seen here. It feels like the rumbling of a volcano just waiting to erupt.'

He laid his pen down in front of him, and sat back in his chair, his face troubled, before he said, 'It is a cavalcade of inequality and calamities which have existed for centuries, peasants largely in revolt against a handful of nobles. The peasants are the miserable victims of a great injustice that gave to a handful of nobles all the colour of the world and to the rest nothing but hardship.

'The nobles think it can never change, while the peasants are waiting for the day.'

'And will it change, do you think?'

'Oh yes, but when or how I cannot say. Somewhere will emerge some man, or men, who will promise that this is the time. He will promise them the earth and they will believe him, and then out of bloodshed and terror the world will change, but if it will be for the better, who knows?'

'Are you afraid of it?'

'I should be, shouldn't I, Alex? Born into luxury and privilege, into an existence that breeds arrogance and obsessive pride, I should be afraid that one day those very peasants who I thought were nothing could come into my home and rob me of all I possess. But perhaps I'm too old, Alex, and realise that even if the world is changing we shall be unable to prevent it.'

'But could it happen in Vienna?'

'You think it could only happen here, that the rest of the world will be immune?'

'I don't know. I never saw despair in Vienna like the despair I have seen here. I never saw it in England.'

'And yet it was there. You did not see it, Alex, because you were cosseted in your neat gentle world with sufficient of the world's goods to make life comfortable for you. It was there, Alex, just as it was in Vienna.'

'You say those poor people have been waiting for centuries for things to improve. They could go on waiting forever.'

'Oh no. Read your history books, Alex. Over the years some man has from time to time taken control and changed the course of history. It is not always a good man, Alex; that is when we reach into the depths of hell and wrongs have to be righted.'

He smiled, that beautiful smile that illuminated the gravity of his face, and rising to his feet he said, 'Let us go into the salon and drink a glass of wine. It is not today that the world will be changing, and sufficient unto the day is the evil thereof, I think.'

I was happy that afternoon discussing the world and its troubles with Franz and I realised that I liked him. I appreciated his logical way of thinking, and the gentle humour behind it, and I wondered how much Alicia understood him.

Had she ever loved him, or was he simply the means to an end, just as her first husband had been made the means to spirit her away from England? They were two different sorts of men, but she had used them both, and as I talked to Franz that afternoon I found for the first time that I was able to think of Alicia shorn of her glamour and the admiration I had built around her.

Had I been so anxious to follow in her footsteps that I had failed to see her determined selfishness? I had made a heroine of her and wanted to be like her, but now I was uncertain. I still adored her, but not blindly; either Alicia was losing her appeal or I was growing up.

Franz and I dined alone that evening and I wondered how much he cared. It was almost midnight when Alicia arrived home, waltzing into the salon, her arms laden with flowers, her exquisite face alight with smiles. She kissed Franz on the top of his head. 'I hope you two have been enjoying your-selves,' she said lightly. 'Sergei insisted we drive into the country to see his sister; they have an enchanting place miles from anywhere.'

'You encountered no problems on your journey?' Franz asked.

'Problems, Franz, what sort of problems?'

'There was trouble in the city this morning, but obviously it didn't affect you.'

'No. Oh, there's always trouble somewhere or other in the city. Sergei says it's some young hot-heads, but the soldiers soon put them down.'

'You saw nothing?'

'No, of course not. Tomorrow there's the ballet—I'm so looking forward to that, I adore *Sleeping Beauty*, it's so romantic and we can look forward to that new man all St Petersburg is talking about. Well, I'm going to bed, it's been a long day. Goodnight, both of you.'

CHAPTER FOURTEEN

THE IMPERIAL FAMILY moved traditionally between Moscow, Yalta on the Black Sea and St Petersburg, but during their absence from the city life was quiet. It was only when they returned that the balls and grand occasions became imperative.

These were the times when Alicia became joyfully alive. Visits to the dressmaker's and the exclusive shops, the occasion to show off her jewels, the meetings with the friends she had acquired and who Franz referred to as the idle chatterers. They were the wives and daughters of senior officials at the court and most of them could speak German or English. From this selection I found two friends nearer my own age, and from them I learned a great deal about the scandals surrounding the court, even when they were not concerned with the Tsar's family itself.

My new friends were Olga Kinski and Paola Mitrovsky and although they were my age they had never set foot outside Russia. Their conversation was all about the Romanovs, the Grand Duchesses and their escorts, and beside them I felt strangely sophisticated. They were intrigued by my relationship with Franz and Alicia, and Alicia charmed them as she charmed everybody.

I remember that day in the early spring of 1914 when we walked in the park and all they could talk about was that the court was returning from Yalta and there would be the usual garden party to celebrate their return. They talked about the clothes they would wear, the young men they would meet, the coming to life of a city that had been strangely quiet during the bitterly cold winter.

There were so many times when I had to ask them to speak slowly and, laughing, Olga would say, 'Why don't you learn to speak Russian, Alex? You'll be here for some time.'

'Why do you say that?' I asked.

'Because you'll meet some handsome young officer who will fall in love with you and you'll never want to go back to Vienna.'

They were obsessed with love and they were both interested in the Habsburg court and the young men I had met there.

As they chatted away light-heartedly that afternoon I found myself thinking about Karl. Usually whenever I thought about him I thought about something else quickly so that his memory didn't linger, but somehow with their talk of love and handsome young officers his face intruded into my thoughts and Olga said, 'There is someone, isn't there, Alex? Why are you suddenly so silent? Who is he? Will he be waiting for you to return to Vienna?'

'There isn't anybody,' I answered shortly. 'How could there be when I've been here in St Petersburg for over two years?'

'But there was somebody?' she persisted.

'Yes, but not any more.'

'Tell us about him. Was he very handsome, was he rich?'

I laughed. 'Yes to both.'

'Then why is it over?'

So I romanticised about that night at the opera when one jealous lover shot another in front of the Emperor and all his court, and I could see their eyes grow round with the sheer excitement of it all. When the tale was told they pressed for more but all I could say was that there was no more, that there never would be.

I had been rash to tell them that story, because memories of Karl began to trouble my foolish heart. I was remembering dancing under the lights strung out in the trees in Grinzing, the charm of his smile, the haunting music of the waltz and promises that had proved worthless when the music stopped.

More than two years since I had last seen Karl and by this time he was probably married to the girl I had met in the park that afternoon. I had believed I had forgotten him, but the pain was as sharp as ever; would I be able to hide it if ever we met again?

One day we would go back to Vienna, one day I would look into his eyes and there would be nothing left. I was not to know that fate would not let go so lightly, that dreams and longings had to be paid for in one coin or another.

St Petersburg on a June morning was an enchanting place; the parks and gardens were gay with flowers, the sea sparkled and gleamed with sunlight and from early morning there had been an air of expectancy on the city streets. The imperial family were once more installed in the palace and every aristocrat in the city had been invited to the Tsar's garden party.

It was a morning like so many other mornings when Alicia received her hairdresser, her beauticians and her dressers, but when she offered their services to me I said I was quite able to manage on my own.

She had laughed at my independence.

'One day, Alex, when you marry a rich man who can afford to indulge you, take a leaf out of my book: have everything.'

When she surveyed the gown I had chosen to wear she looked at me critically and said, 'Why didn't you allow me to buy that cream one for you? You've had this one some time.'

'I know, but I've always liked it and I've always been told I look my best in blue.'

'I suspect your young Austrian count told you that,' she snapped.

'He didn't tell me he was a count, only that he was a captain in the Hussars.'

'Ah well, counts, barons, dukes, Austria has so many of them. Now tell me if I am going to convince our Russian friends that Vienna is superlative when it comes to fashion.'

She looked incredibly beautiful in her cream lace gown and large white hat with its sweeping ostrich plumes. This was the aunt who had coloured my youth, even when I had never really known what she looked like.

Somewhat tetchily she said, 'I hope Franz is going to be ready in time. There seems to be so much coming and going this morning, we might as well wait for him in the salon.'

She stood impatiently at the window watching the street, commenting on every passing carriage or motor, and I sensed her impatience, particularly when we heard the sound of passing footsteps outside the door and the abrupt closing of the front door.

'Really,' she said sharply. 'He never likes it when I'm only seconds late and yet he's been ensconced with people for over an hour and here we both are waiting for him. I've been so looking forward to this day after such a long dreary winter; if it was an occasion in Vienna he wouldn't be late.'

I felt vaguely uncomfortable. It seemed that a sudden silence had descended upon the house and all I was aware of was Alicia's annoyance and that the street outside was strangely empty; most of the Tsar's guests had passed us by. Still we waited until at long last Franz stood in the doorway wearing the velvet smoking jacket he favoured on a quiet evening at home.

Alicia stared at him in amazement before saying, 'Franz, do you know what time it is? And you're not even changed. Why aren't you ready? And who were all those people who came to the house, particularly this morning?'

He came in and closed the door behind him, looking first at Alicia, then at me. At last in a quiet voice he said, 'I suggest you sit down, Alicia. I have had some very grave news this morning from Vienna, and it will not be possible for us to attend the garden party.'

'Not attend! But we should be there now.'

'I am aware of it, but what I have to tell you is more important than any garden party.'

'Is it the Emperor?' Alicia cried. 'Has he had an accident, is he dead?'

'It is not the Emperor. This morning in Sarajevo the Archduke Franz Ferdinand and his wife were assassinated by a Serbian nationalist. I am ordered back to Vienna immediately.'

'But why? What can you do, what about the Tsar?'

'How can I tell at this stage what repercussions there might be? Obviously this terrible deed will not be allowed to go unpunished, but I have no means of knowing how Russia will react to it. Russia has always been on the side of Serbia and the Balkans. We shall learn nothing here about the full extent of this tragedy, which is why we must go back immediately to Vienna. My allegiance lies with Austria.'

'Then why were we sent here, if Austria and Russia have never been close?'

'What has happened this morning in Sarajevo will have altered many things. It could be far-reaching; nations will doubtless take sides. It does no good to remain here.'

'When do you propose we should leave?'

'I have told the servants to pack immediately and I suggest you and Alex do the same. I have asked for cars to be brought here early this evening so that we should get the last train out of St Petersburg to Warsaw.'

While we packed Alicia informed me that the Archduke was the heir to the Austrian throne since the suicide of the Emperor's only son, and that the wife who had died with him had never been truly accepted as suitable material to be called an archduchess. Instead their marriage had been morganatic and there had been many indignities heaped on the Archduke's wife.

It seemed to me that the more I heard about Vienna's aristocracy the more archaic it appeared. A nobleman could have a mistress who wasn't considered suitable material for matrimony, but when it came to a wife only the blue-blooded variety would suffice.

Complaining bitterly, Alicia said, 'This is all so ridiculous, expecting us to leave today. If we left next week, I'm sure we'd be in no danger here. Ever since we came everybody has been very nice to us; we've made friends, we've been popular. I'm sure Franz is panicking. Vienna always has to come first with Franz and if the Emperor told him to take a leap from the Prater Wheel I'm sure he would.'

'Franz is very worried,' I said quietly.

'Well of course, every time there is some sort of a crisis he feels his world is coming to an end; the Crown Prince's suicide, the Empress's assassination, then in just a few months life goes on as normal. Why is this time going to be any different?'

'Have you forgotten, Alicia, the time you warned me in England that the old imperial Vienna was dying, that the waltzing was going to stop?'

For several minutes she sat staring at me, then in a dull resigned voice she said, 'Perhaps it was easy to say that in England, Alex, when I was surrounded everywhere with so much that was familiar, when so much of my childhood remained. In Vienna it was all so volatile, glamour and tragedy merged so relentlessly. Very soon we shall see for ourselves how much this latest tragedy has altered the city.'

It was a journey taken largely in silence. Franz was preoccupied with his own tormenting thoughts and Alicia was petulant. There were frequent stops and starts as the ancient train lumbered across the steppes and I dozed fitfully to the sound of the engine and the clanking of swaying carriages.

Alicia took long rambles along the corridors to exercise her dog and conversation was minimal, so it was with the utmost relief that we changed trains in Warsaw and boarded the more salubrious express for Vienna.

I had expected to find the streets of Vienna sunk deep in misery but my first impression was that nothing had changed. Errand boys were still on the streets whistling cheerfully, people were going about their daily business and the sun was shining on the domes and spires of the fairy-tale city. By the time we arrived at the Ringstrasse the servants were already putting the house in order, as though we had never been away.

We saw little of Franz throughout the next few days and Alicia remarked caustically, 'To Franz his world is coming to an end, but the rest of Vienna is still waltzing.'

She entertained friends and they laughed and gossiped behind the closed door of the drawing room while I walked in the park with Max. From across the road I looked at the house which Karl's parents owned but it had an unlived-in air about it, and I learned from Alicia that a great many of the families who lived on the Ringstrasse were now at their country houses. She mentioned it casually, and I was glad that she seemed not to associate her comments with Karl.

These women that came to the house seemed unconcerned with the occurrence in Sarajevo. They talked about the opera, the ballet, the fun to be had at the Prater, and the threat of war was far from their minds. When I voiced my surprise to Alicia she laughed. 'Darling, of course there won't be a war. It will all blow over and be forgotten,' she said lightly.

It was several evenings later when Franz said, 'I think you should consider going to the country, Alicia. It will be pleasant there and a great many of our friends have left Vienna until matters are resolved.'

'Do you want to go to the country?' she asked.

'I shall need to stay in Vienna, but you will have company with Alex and she will like the house and the gardens. There is a life outside Vienna, my dear.'

'I can't understand any of it,' Alicia complained. 'It is the funeral tomorrow and Vienna is hardly in the doldrums. I supposed most of the crowned heads of Europe would be attending.'

'And so they are, yet it doesn't alter the fact that in Vienna there is great indifference. He was not a popular man, and in Budapest there is little attempt to hide the widespread relief at his death. He hated everything Magyar.'

'Then how can the Emperor even think about going to war to avenge their assassination? It seems that here nobody really cares.'

'Terrorism should not be appeased, Alicia, it should be destroyed wherever it is found.'

At least on the day of the funeral Vienna turned off its music and the streets were lined with darkly clad people paying their respects, either for the deaths of Franz Ferdinand and his wife or in honour of the rows of powerful uniformed figures who followed the cortège.

In the days after the funeral I sensed a deep lethargy in Franz. Conversation round the dining table was minimal and Alicia seemed unnaturally irritable. Every morning she leafed anxiously through the letters the servants placed beside her breakfast plate and seeing my curiosity she said, 'I'm waiting to hear from someone, Alex. I thought she would have written by now.'

She did not say who the someone was and I didn't ask. There were so many aspects of Alicia's life I was unfamiliar with.

Then one morning she whooped with glee as she picked out the envelope she had been waiting for. There were several pages which she read eagerly, then looking up she said, 'This is wonderful news, Alex. I was so sure Violet wouldn't let me down.'

'Violet?' I enquired.

'Why yes, I told you about Violet in England. She's the American lady I travelled Europe with; we spent wonderful months together.'

'But you said you'd lost touch, that you never heard from her.'

'That was then, Alex. We did lose touch, but when I became Countess Bruckner I wrote to tell her and as time went on we resumed our friendship. The Americans didn't want our royal family, they were glad to be rid of them, but they have never lost their fascination for anything royal or remotely upper crust. Violet will adore introducing her Countess friend to all and sundry! Titles of any description are serious business in America, darling. They have no aristocracy, only money. Violet will give us a wonderful time.'

'Us?'

'Why yes, darling. You shall come with me, you'd hate the country. Whole days spent hunting in the forests and banquets every evening when we eat too much and drink too much. We shall go to America instead and spend time with Violet in California.'

'What about Franz?'

For several seconds she stared at me blankly, then she said, 'Alex, Franz will be here in Vienna poring over whatever plans the Emperor has for revenge on the Serbs, then in a few months after they've been suitably chastened things will get back to normal and we shall come home. Doesn't that seem the most sensible thing in the world to you?'

'How will you get there?'

'From France or Germany. It doesn't really matter as long as we travel as quickly as possible. Now do look through your wardrobe, darling, and start putting aside the things you'll need.'

Her enthusiasm over the next few days was unremitting. She seemed unconcerned with Franz's gravity and lethargy and he made no effort to dissuade her from visiting America. He showed no interest, and when I remarked to Alicia that he seemed far from well she merely said, 'Alex, Franz is showing his displeasure in the only way he knows, by looking thoroughly miserable. As soon as we're out of the house and out of his life he'll enjoy the peace and quiet and his involvement with his silly old war.'

In two days we would be leaving. Our trunks were packed, and over dinner Franz announced quietly that the Emperor was prepared to wage war against Serbia over the death of the heir to the Austrian throne.

'Then it's just as well that we shall be out of the country,' Alicia said lightly. 'By the time we return it will all be over, and Vienna will be back to normal.'

'I too believe it is just as well that you are leaving immediately,' Franz replied. 'In a very short space of time the whole of Europe could be involved.'

'Why should the whole of Europe be interested in the death of two Austrians? People have been assassinated before, the history of Europe has been built around such happenings. This one will be no different from the last.'

'And I am telling you, Alicia, that this time the hounds of war will be released throughout the civilised world. Germany will come in on the side of Austria, that much has been agreed, but Russia is pledged to support Serbia and the Balkans. Already there are murmurings in France and England, who have little love for Germany or its Emperor, not even when he is Queen Victoria's grandson. The rest of the British royal family utterly despise him.'

Flippantly Alicia said, 'At least the Americans will have the good sense to stay out of it, and they're far enough away.'

I felt irritated by her frivolity, so I could only guess how much it angered Franz. After he had left the dining table she said, 'Two days, Alex, two days and we're far enough away from all this talk of war.'

'We are not Americans, Alicia, we're English. We should be concerned if England comes into the conflict.'

'Don't be pompous, darling. Of course we're concerned, but there is nothing we can do about it. I haven't been English for years, and you were happy to turn your back on your country.'

It was true, but at that moment I felt no sort of satisfaction with the choice I had made. Was I going to spend the rest of my life running blindly into a mad future with little thought for the people I had left behind? Ever since I had known about Alicia I had wanted to be like her; she had been my idol, all I aspired to, and now I wondered what was wrong with me. I found myself questioning her reasoning, disagreeing with many of the things she said, resenting her indifference to a world staggering on the edge of a great catastrophe.

On the morning we were due to leave for Bremerhaven I went into Franz's study to say goodbye and found him sitting at his desk with his head in his hands, and there was such an air of despondency about him I paused on the threshold feeling that my entrance was an intrusion into something indescribably tragic.

After several minutes he raised his head and our eyes met; at that moment I felt as if a dark impenetrable cloud hovered between us, a cloud filled with fear and uncertainty and in my foolish young heart was born a conviction more profound than any I had ever experienced. I could not go to America with Alicia. Whatever the years would do to me, this was where I must stay until the fates decided otherwise.

CHAPTER FIFTEEN

I LEFT THE ROOM without speaking, closing the door quietly behind me, and then Alicia was there saying, 'Is Franz alone in there, Alex? I must say goodbye to him and reassure him that we'll be back before he's had time to miss us. The car is here, Alex, and they've taken my luggage. They'll be taking yours any time.'

I went quickly into the hall where two men were already handling my trunk and putting forward a restraining hand I said, 'No, please leave them, I'm not going.'

The man stared at me uncertainly and I said, 'I've changed my mind. Countess Bruckner will be back in a moment.'

He shrugged his shoulders and walked out of the house towards the car waiting outside, and then Alicia was saying, 'Goodness, Alex, where are they? These cases should be in the car by now.'

'Alicia, I'm not going. I've changed my mind,' I said more confidently than I felt.

She stared at me in amazement, then taking hold of my arm she drew me inside the room. 'Alex! What is this? We were looking forward to it, and we are coming back; it is only for a few weeks at the most. What do you hope to achieve by staying on here?'

'I don't know. I just know that I can't go with you.'

At that moment her eyes were angry, her whole expression one of disbelief, then suddenly it changed and almost sadly she said, 'You wanted to be like me didn't you, Alex, you wanted to act like me and think like me but now you've realised that you're not really like me at all. To be like me, Alex, you have to be ruthless and selfish, you have to be free to run whenever your life crumbles, but you can only run so far. After that, my dear, you are a slave to the conventions you have sworn your life to. It will always be like that, Alex, so only ever be yourself.'

Sadly she reached out and embraced me. I could smell her perfume, feel the silken texture of her hair, the softness of the furs around her shoulders; then she was running away from me and I stood at the window until the car passed out of sight. She didn't turn to wave, and I sat down weakly on the nearest chair feeling like an empty shell. I did not hear the door open; I was unaware that Franz had come into the room until he touched me lightly on the arm. I looked up into his eyes, and was met with his grave sweet smile and his voice saying, 'Why didn't you go with her, Alex?'

'I don't know. I thought I could go, and then I suddenly felt that the life I was leaving was more important than the life I would be going to. I shouldn't really be here, Franz. My home is in England where my family live and perhaps now is the time to return there.'

'Perhaps. But first spend some time in the country. Our war could soon be over, with luck it will never really begin, but if it does at least you will be safe there and God willing it may never be allowed to spread.'

'Franz, you look ill. Have you seen a doctor?'

'It is nothing, I just worry about the future, all the meetings with the Emperor, all his worries piling up on so many shoulders. Poor old man—he has never deserved the tragedies that have troubled his life. One day, Alex, when all this is behind us you will dance at the Emperor's ball, I promise you.'

I smiled. 'And you will introduce me as your little niece from England and Alicia will be back and all will be well again.'

He smiled, but in his eyes I found no reassurance that he believed in fairy tales.

'Keep your luggage packed,' he advised me. 'Before the end of the week I will see that you are taken to the country. Maria will go with you, and there are servants at the hunting lodge. Have you never driven in the Vienna Woods, Alex?'

At that moment I could feel tears stinging my eyes when I thought about those long romantic rides into the Vienna Woods with Karl, the low charm of his voice, the laughter in his blue eyes, and something else that I had thought was love.

There was just one visit I had to make before I left for the country and that was to Grinzing. I asked the driver to stop here on our journey to the hunting lodge and as I walked along the wide street lined with inns and coffee houses I felt that I had never been away.

It was a warm sunlit morning in the second week of July and from every doorway music poured. The linden trees were lush with greenery, blossoms bloomed in inn gardens and window boxes were gay with geraniums. Children played in the street and people were going about their business as though there could never be any hint of darker things to come.

At the doorway of the Golden Pheasant Herr Gruber was in earnest conversation with one of the gardeners and then his wife was there carrying two steins filled with foaming lager. I had no plans for calling at the Golden Pheasant but it was my intention to see Herr Windisch. I felt I owed him many explanations as an old friend to both me and Alicia.

As I waked up the path to his house my heart was filled with a strange sort of nostalgia. I had been happy in Grinzing until fate ordered it otherwise; now it seemed my entire future lay hidden beneath a mountain of uncertainties.

His initial surprise was followed by his customary charm and I was invited into the comfort of his living room where a plump countrywoman produced refreshments and he sat back in his chair regarding me with a grave smile. At last he said softly, 'So, Alex, you have not been able to forget Grinzing.'

'No. I am on my way to the country, so I thought I should come to see you. Grinzing was not out of our way.'

'Are you alone?'

'Yes. Franz, Count Bruckner, is staying in Vienna but he thought I should go to the hunting lodge.'

'And Alicia?'

'She is on her way to America.'

The expression on his face did not change, and I had the impression that my words had not surprised him.

'When I was last in Vienna I made enquiries regarding Count Bruckner and I was informed that he was in

St Petersburg; indeed the house in the Ringstrasse seemed devoid of life. I suppose he was recalled when the heir to the throne was assassinated.'

'Yes. We had to come back immediately. That afternoon we were to have attended the Tsar's garden party, but instead we were ordered home.'

'And the funeral has taken place in Vienna and the city is now back to normal?'

'I was surprised to find Vienna very normal. It was only on the day of the funeral that Vienna seemed to accept what had happened.'

'Of course. The Viennese are better able to cope with gaiety than tragedy, even when there has been so much of it.'

'I wanted to come back to Grinzing but my aunt and her husband told me it wouldn't be possible. Herr Gruber, and everybody else for that matter, would be aware of what happened in Vienna and I no longer had any place here. It seemed so terribly unfair. I had done nothing wrong and yet I was having to pay a price. That night at the opera was so wonderful it was terrible that it ended the way it did. The shooting has never been referred to since. It might never have happened and I do not know anything about Karl or Colonel Bartok.'

'It interested me to make enquiries, Alex. Colonel Bartok died in prison; some say it was suicide by poison, and that he was helped to his death by a brother officer who smuggled poison into the prison for him. He had no future, he had lived a dissolute life. I am sure Count Bruckner has been made aware of his death, since Bartok's mother was the Count's sister.'

'I didn't know. I was never told, and my aunt said Franz had little regard for his nephew.'

For several long minutes there was silence, then gently Herr Windisch said, 'You do not care about Bartok, Alex. Your thoughts are for Karl von Winckler, and I suppose you have not been told anything of him either.'

'No, nothing.'

'Then from what I have heard I may be able to enlighten you. Captain von Winckler spent several weeks in hospital. The bullet lodged in his spine fortunately missing his heart, and eventually he recovered after spending some time in the country before rejoining his regiment. I have never seen him in Grinzing although many of his friends have been here.'

I sat silently staring through the window. There were so many things I wanted to ask him but they seemed pointless and I hated the treacherous tears that flooded my eyes and rolled slowly down my cheeks.

Gently he leaned forward and covered my hand with his. 'You will forget him, Alex, and you will learn to live and love again. You should know that last October Karl von Winckler married his Salzburg cousin Valerie Redlich. I have no doubt it was an arranged marriage, as so many of them are with the aristocracy. One day he will be the head of his family; his father has been an invalid for many years and is not expected to live long.'

'How easily it all falls into place,' I murmured.

'Yes. No thoughts are concerned with love. A man and his desires are unimportant when it comes to family pride; it matters only that the blood be the right colour and that money and land are there.'

'He didn't know anything about me. I never told him about Alicia, but it wouldn't have made any difference, would it?'

He smiled sadly. 'I doubt it. A beautiful English girl with a love of adventure, with no title and only the money she had worked for. There was great consternation among the aristocracy when Count Bruckner married the beautiful Alicia, but Bruckner didn't care and Alicia knew how to charm the people who mattered, even the Emperor himself. And now, Alex, you will go to the country and wait as we are all waiting to see what will happen. In the end, perhaps, titles will count for nothing, since there will be nothing left.'

'You think there will be war?'

'I cannot believe that the Emperor will allow his nephew's death to go unpunished and other countries will take sides. In the end thrones might topple and those very people who are now so concerned with their status will find themselves exiles, struggling to hold on to whatever status they can salvage.'

His expression was kind and in a small voice I said, 'And I shall go home to England and beg my family's forgiveness. I shall find peace and gentleness, I shall learn to be grateful for all the things I threw away so lightly when I was young and foolish. But before then we really don't know what is in store for us.'

'No, Alex, which perhaps is just as well. One day you may come back to Grinzing, you will listen to the waltzes and dance in our cafés, and the memories will stay with you long after the waltz comes to an end.'

I thought about our meeting sitting before a log fire in the vast living room of the hunting lodge that evening. The servants had welcomed me graciously, they had fed me and showed me over the lodge, and now I was alone, looking round the room at the heads of deer and stags mounted on the walls, at deep-piled exotic rugs laid across the stone floor and suits of old armour in dimly lit alcoves.

I could not imagine Alicia living in this place. Alicia belonged to sophisticated town houses and ballrooms, to expensive fashion houses and gatherings where there were scandal and laughter. In her new life in America would she think about us, would even the rumblings of war persuade her to come home?

During the day I walked in the woods and listened to the birdsong. It was beautiful and lonely and every day I asked myself how long it could last. Then Franz came and I could tell by the gravity of his face that he had no good news to impart.

The Serbs had rejected the Emperor's ultimatum that they should suppress the nationalist movement which had resulted in the assassination of the heir to the Austro-Hungarian Empire and in his beloved villa at Bad Ischl his generals were urging that war was inevitable.

War was declared on Serbia on the twenty-eighth of July and Franz had gathered the servants together to tell them the news. They received it stoically; some of the young maidservants wept, though the men betrayed little emotion, but after they returned to their duties he turned his attention to me.

'Perhaps now you should return to England, Alex, while there is yet time,' he said gravely.

I knew that he was right. This was not my country, and had no place in his life now that his wife had elected to visit America. And yet something lingered in my expression that caused him to say, 'The war will escalate. There are rumbling all over Europe and the Russians are already mobilising their armies behind the long frontier from the Baltic to the Black Sea.'

'You think England will become involved?' I asked anxiously.

'I believe so, but you still have time to return there. They are already saying in England that all over Europe the lights are going out. I have to go to Vienna today; I will see that you are brought back within the next few days.'

'You will send someone for me?'

'Yes, there are people living in their country houses who must get back. I will ask them to call for you. Be ready to leave immediately.'

So I packed my belongings and spent my days staring through the windows. I felt I was living in a cocoon and that outside the world was crumbling and time was catapulting us into an unknown chaos.

I had just eaten my evening meal two days later when one of the servants informed me that a gentleman had arrived to take me back to Vienna. A large staff car stood in front of the house and beside it I could see the solitary figure of an officer standing rigidly holding the door of the car open, but when I looked up I gasped with astonishment at Karl eyeing me with uncompromising hauteur. The smile was wiped immediately from my face and he took his place by me in the car without a word.

I hated every mile of that journey with him sitting like a marble statue; my nervous question about his health was met with the stilted reply that he was perfectly well.

There was so much unspoken anger between us I felt unable to ask any more of the questions trembling on my lips. Instead the journey was taken in resentful silence and he deposited me at last in Vienna with the briefest of bows and the coldest of expressions.

I wept long and bitterly that night. I wanted to go home, to get away from Vienna at the earliest opportunity, but fate decreed otherwise. Hours later Franz informed me that Germany had invaded Luxembourg and Belgium.

On the third of August she declared war on France. Great Britain entered the war on the side of France and now it would appear all of Europe was involved, so any hope I had of returning to England was a forlorn one.

'I cannot stay here,' I said helplessly. 'This is not my home and why should you be burdened with me? I need to find some sort of work. Surely there must be something I can do, and perhaps I can find somewhere to live.'

'Alex, there is no need for you to feel this way. There will be work, the hospitals will be crying out for help in one form or another, but as for somewhere to live I have no objections to your staying here. Your aunt did not marry a man who is indifferent to compassion.'

'I'll try not to be a nuisance, Franz, and I am truly sorry for any problems I have caused you.'

He smiled gently, that sudden sweet smile that seemed so much more attractive on a face that lit up so seldom.

'Who brought you here from the country, Alex?' he asked suddenly.

'Captain von Winckler,' I answered shortly.

He raised his eyebrows and was quick to say, 'I asked for

an officer returning to Vienna to escort you, Alex. I did not personally request Captain von Winckler. You were not happy about the journey?'

I shook my head and the tears, unbidden, rolled slowly down my cheeks. 'We didn't speak, he was so terribly angry. I wanted to ask him why, in fact there were many things I wanted to ask him, but it wasn't possible. When we were sent immediately to St Petersburg I wrote long letters to him to the house in the Ringstrasse. He never replied to any of them. I thought he could be dead.'

'What did you say in your letters?'

'I told him about Aunt Alicia and you. I told him I had never really known her, but it wasn't easy to explain.'

'He probably never received your letters,' he said drily.

'But why?'

'Alex, the von Wincklers have always married their Salzburg cousins and Karl was to be no exception. That he should be involved with an English girl would be something they couldn't countenance, particularly an English girl related to Countess Bruckner, who all Vienna knew had once been involved with Zoltan Bartok.'

'None of that was my fault, Franz.'

'Of course not, but Zoltan Bartok was responsible for shooting Karl in the opera house.'

I stared at him helplessly. Of course. Karl had been seriously wounded and we had been sent away to St Petersburg so as not to complicate matters when he recovered, if he recovered. Now he was married to his Salzburg cousin and I was expendable.

There was so much bitterness in my heart at that moment

that I heard Franz through a haze of self-pity and then suddenly the meaning of his words hit me like a sledgehammer. 'Forget his anger, Alex, forget love and every other emotion you felt for him. In the months and years to come there will be greater things at stake than the ending of a love affair.'

I looked at him fearfully and he went on in a low unemotional voice. 'Think instead, Alex, that war will bring great sadness and death to many people across the whole of Europe. Crowns will totter, even empires may slide into oblivion. What is the littleness of love against all that?'

I knew that he was right, and yet my foolish heart was only able to remember that day when Karl had promised me so much. There were many other days to remember, music we had waltzed to, tunes that would live in my heart whenever I heard them played. He was angry with me, and I hated him for making me love him. I was still young enough to be selfish in the face of adversity.

Winter came early to Vienna and already the Austro-Hungarian armies were suffering disastrous campaigns in the south and the east. Hospitals were hastily set up in crumbling mansions throughout the city and in the country outside Vienna, and in one of these I found work. Carmelite nuns acted as nurses and the rest of us scrubbed floors and rolled bandages. We attended to provisions and did every menial task imaginable so that I tramped home exhausted and made the decision that I would find somewhere to live nearer the hospital.

It was a deserted farmhouse with a crumbling roof, from which the inhabitants had long since fled. I chopped wood to burn in the enormous stone fireplace and I learned to cook on the ancient stove in pots so heavy I could barely lift them.

There had been terrible casualties inflicted on the Austro-Hungarian troops faced with the success of the Russian advance in Galicia and the hospital was filled with new arrivals. It seemed incredible that Christmas was only days away and we were decorating trees brought in from the forest to cheer the men recovering all too slowly from their injuries.

It was on a morning when snow piled up outside the windows and I was tottering uncertainly on a stepladder endeavouring to hang a bauble on one of the branches of a tree when I looked down to see Karl staring up at me. I would have fallen if he hadn't grasped my arm to prevent it.

I stood beside him shaking nervously, afraid of the anger I had seen on his face the last time we had met, but instead as our eyes met and locked the anger had gone, and in its place was desperately intense yearning. The next moment I was clasped in his arms and his voice was murmuring my name; then he was kissing me and I was kissing him back with all the passion I was capable of. Only the advent of one of the nursing sisters forced us apart. Her expression was stern, but neither of us cared, and when she had left the room bristling with annoyance Karl said, 'Alex, I have to see you alone. We must talk—do you ever get away from this place?'

'Yes, but it will be later tonight.'

'It doesn't matter how late. Some of my men are in here and more are expected tomorrow. After that I have to return to the front, so we haven't much time.'

'I live in an old farm about a mile up the road. It's falling to pieces round my ears but I spend so much time here by the time I get home I'm too exhausted to care. Will you visit me there?'

'I'll be there, *liebchen*, get there as soon as you can. Do you have transport?'

'I can find something. You will come?'

'I promise, Alex, nothing this war can do to me will keep me away.'

CHAPTER SIXTEEN

ONE OF THE FORESTRY men took me home in his disreputable old cart pulled by his equally disreputable mule, who was not averse to stopping when he felt like it so that together we had to tug on his harness while offering carrots to tempt him to continue.

Inside the house I lit the lamps and put a match to the pine logs. Outside in the snow there were no sounds, but inside the ticking of the clock was depressing since it merely emphasised the desperate passing of time.

The urgent neighing of a horse disturbed the silence and hurrying to the door I could see Karl tethering his horse to a post. Then he was at the door and I was in his arms.

Suddenly we were like children, drinking Hungarian wine, sitting in front of the fire with the flames lighting up the room and dancing on the ceiling, and even though love was urgent we had to talk.

He had learned from Franz of the conspiracies his own family had used to make sure we didn't meet again. There had to be nothing to interfere with his betrothal to Valerie his cousin, and even the Emperor himself had sanctioned our removal to distant St Petersburg.

He had never received any of the letters I had written to him, and had merely learned that the Bruckners had taken me with them to St Petersburg and that I was obviously unconcerned about his recovery.

'Karl, how could you think that?' I cried. 'As if I would go away without a word! What is it about your society that demands so much and condemns without proof?' He smiled sadly, and I said softly, 'And now you have a wife, Karl. Do you love her?'

'No. I like her, she is my cousin, we were good friends as children, but I have never loved her. I never thought I would.'

'But you married her.'

'Yes. I had lost you and it was expected of me. You don't understand that, do you, Alex, and yet Vienna is where you wanted to be in spite of our deplorable eccentricities. Why did you never tell me that you were related to the Bruckners?'

So I told him all I knew about Alicia, and when it was told I realised how little it was.

And now Karl was saying, 'Count Bruckner tells me his wife is in America. Why didn't you go with her?'

'I was unhappy that she could leave Franz when he was far from well, but that was not really the reason. Perhaps I hoped that one day I might see you again, however impossible our future together might be.'

His expression was bleak as he stared steadily into the fire. We had no life together, but we had love that was urgent and desperate. Once, my foolish heart had believed that love would lead to something permanent, to a life together; now all we had was the passion of the moment and as we consummated our desire with the sound of the blizzard beating on the rotting windows it seemed singularly unimportant that this was all there would ever be.

We lay at last with all passion spent and I had to ask him, 'When do you have to leave?'

'I'm not sure. Some time in the morning after the new contingent have arrived.'

'Will I ever see you again?'

'Yes, Alex. I have to see you. I can't let it end like this.'

'We don't know how long the war will last or how many changes there'll be.'

'No. It could well be that everything we've believed in across the years will come to an end: empires, dynasties. If I'm alive, Alex, I'll find you wherever you are. If I fail to do that you will know that I didn't make it. And what will you do?'

'Go home to England and make my peace with my family. They are good people who will forgive me even when I don't deserve it.'

There were times over the next few months when Karl was able to visit. He came to see his men who were in hospital, either recovering or desperately wounded, and he came to see me. I never knew when it would be, only that they were snatched moments of ecstasy in the midst of adversity.

He came with news of terrible losses to the Russian army and now Romania too had entered the war on the side of Italy and France. I learned little of how the war was affecting England, but Germany was strong on the side of Austria and

Hungary and when I listened to the cheers echoing in the corridors of the hospital whenever the German army proved victorious I was the only one who kept silent. How was it possible to cheer on an army that was at war with England?

There are so many days long passed into limbo, but I remember one afternoon when Karl pounded on my door, entering the farm with laughter on his lips and bringing with him a sudden flurry of snow. It was just before Christmas; the war had been on fifteen months and showed few signs that it would ever end. He came with a small fir tree under his arm and a box filled with cones that we spent the afternoon painting to hang on the tree. We laughed like happy children, drinking wine and trying hard to behave as if there was no war.

We looked up in surprise at the sound of sleigh bells and then sharp knocks on the front door. I could only think that they had sent somebody to fetch me from the hospital but when I opened the door it was Franz standing there smiling and shaking the snow from his greatcoat.

The two men looked at each other across the room, then Karl came forward, holding out his hand, and Franz said evenly, 'I came to visit a friend in the area and felt I should see you also, Alex. Is this where you live?'

'Yes. I was lucky to find it, even though the wind whistles down the chimneys and the windows are ill fitting. Please will you join us in a glass of wine?'

Franz accepted the wine and took the chair Karl pulled forward for him. Suddenly the conversation was stilted as the two men discussed the losses on the Russian front, the advent of the Ottoman Empire on the side of Austria and Romania

on the side of Italy and France; neither of them mentioned
England. I found myself wondering which man would outstay
the other, and in the end it was Karl who said stiffly, 'I must
go. I am not expecting an easy journey.'

He bowed over my hand and more rigidly to Franz, then he
was gone and I clenched my hands together to stop myself
running after him into the snow. Even so I stood at the window
to watch him mount his horse and ride swiftly along the road,
then I turned to find Franz watching me with an expression I
could not read. At last he said, 'Captain von Winckler is fortunate to be able to absent himself from his men at such a time.'

'He came with men who were injured and to enquire about
others,' I replied tersely.

'And is he able to visit you often, Alex?'

'How can he? He comes occasionally and I am pleased to
see him. Captain von Winckler is an old friend.'

His eyes were not unkind as he said, 'You know that while
we were in St Petersburg he married his cousin?'

'Yes, I know.'

'And it does not matter?'

'Of course it matters. It seems to me that everybody con-
spired to keep us apart. Karl accused me of being
secretive about you and Alicia, but you know it wasn't like
that. Save for that wretched evening at the opera house he
need never have known about you at all.'

'But you expected more of him, Alex, and if there had been
more it was inevitable that he would find out about us.'

I was silent. Of course he was right and there was
nothing to say.

'And you are in love with him all over again and I suppose

he has told you he is in love with you. He probably is—you are a beautiful spirited girl, but where do you think it will lead?'

I looked at him helplessly. I had no thoughts on where it would lead. We lived for the day; how could any of us know if there would be more? In some impatience I said, 'You don't like him, do you?'

'Oh yes, I like him well enough. Karl von Winckler is an aristocrat with an impeccable record for bravery, honesty and decency, but he is also the son of a family related to the Emperor himself, a family who laid down rules for their son when he was a child, rules that must not be broken. He has already complied with one of them, that he marry his Salzburg cousin. I am sure that if he survives this war there are others he will obey implicitly.'

'Are you telling me that I don't figure in any one of them?'

'That is so.'

But I was remembering the passion we had shared, his words of tenderness, the warmth of his smile, the urgency of our love, and when my eyes looked up Franz was watching me with a strange intensity, well aware where my thoughts had been.

'You think I should not see him again?' I murmured.

'My dear child, how can I tell you to do the impossible? But I know more about the intrigues and complexities of those people close to the imperial court than you are ever likely to. Perhaps I should tell you the story of Mayerling.'

'I already know it, Karl told me.'

'And what did you think?'

'I thought it was terrible.'

'Yes, it was. I was there that night they walked Marie Vetsera's body out of the hunting lodge with a stiff pole propping up her spine and two of her uncles holding her tightly. No stigma must fall on Crown Prince Rudolf, so that poor infatuated girl had to be blamed for everything.'

'You think such a fate might be in store for me?'

Almost wearily he said, 'No, Alex. I think, I hope, that in the end you will be strong. You will tell yourself that you are not like poor Marie Vetsera, you are an English girl going home to sanity.'

He rose to his feet and started to shrug himself into his coat.

'Do you have to go?' I asked him. 'Couldn't you stay to eat dinner with me?'

'No, it isn't possible. I have to get back to Vienna tonight if I can, although the tracks were pretty well hopeless this morning.'

'Have you heard from Alicia?'

He raised his eyebrows and smiled. 'I did not expect to hear from her, not in war-torn Europe where countries that once were friends are now bitter enemies, and where Alicia will not set foot until we have had the sense to resolve our difficulties. She thinks she is safe in America, but I wonder.'

'You think America will come into the war?'

'It is possible. There is something between America and Great Britain that still matters. It could be a common language, but more than that it is based on ancestry, the way they think.'

'But when the war is over—it can't go on forever, one day it must be over—she'll come back, won't she, Franz? You are her husband, after all.'

'And that matters in Alicia's scheme of things, do you think?'

'Oh yes, surely it must.'

He kissed me gently on both cheeks then with a wry smile he said, 'Hold on to your illusions, Alex, even when they let you down again and again. They may not always do so, but they make you a better person.'

I watched him trudging towards his sleigh, then he was gone and the sound of sleigh bells echoed long after the snow obscured him from view. I heaped pine logs on the fire because the room felt suddenly cold, either because of the open door or the fact that I now seemed alone and friendless.

Franz had stirred many doubts and uncertainties in me about Karl and in my innermost heart I believed they could be true. I loved him, but what would the littleness of love matter when faced with more important things?

Winter came early in 1916 with snow flurries brought in on threatening clouds from the east, and in late September it was cold with icy winds and sharp showers of hail. At the hospital there was dysentery so that if the men did not succumb to their wounds they died from that terrible epidemic.

There were days when we heard of successes and others when the news was of disasters, and then the mother superior received instructions that the hospital was to close and we were to return to Vienna where large town houses would be turned into hospitals and nursing homes.

I received this information with mixed emotions. Vienna was civilisation, and what we had now was wretchedness, but always the hope remained that one day Karl might be there, however briefly. It was not to be, and in Vienna Franz insisted that I take up my room at the house in the Ringstrasse.

The Emperor remained at Schönbrunn where he celebrated his victories by addressing throngs of people from the balcony in the company of Katherina Schratt and members of his family. Then in Vienna the bitter weather and shortage of food was ignored and at the opera house grand concerts were organised to listen to the music of Johann Strauss. Franz was insistent I should accompany him to one of these occasions, making me dress up in my best attire and lending me Alicia's tiara and diamond necklace with long glittering earrings to complete the picture.

We sat in the opulent box looking down on an array of bejewelled women and elderly men still sporting glamorous uniforms and silken orders. There were very few younger men in the audience beyond those recovering from war wounds but the evening reminded me compellingly of that other far-off night when I had sat with Karl gazing enraptured at a scene I had only ever dreamed about.

I looked up at the box opposite where a woman was regarding us through her lorgnettes and then I felt suddenly sick when I recognised the woman sitting next to her as the one I had met in the park: Karl's wife.

Flustered, I turned my head only to meet Franz's subtle gaze. In an even voice he said, 'It was inevitable that the von Winckler family would be here, Alex. The Countess would hardly allow a war to interfere with her social arrangements.'

'She knows who I am,' I murmured.

'An incident several years ago, that is all. You know that the lady with her is Karl's wife, Valerie?'

'Yes.'

'You have seen her before?'

'Yes, I met her long ago. She was visiting Vienna, before Karl married her.'

His hand covered mine very gently and with a brief smile he said, 'Forget the past, Alex. We are here to enjoy the music.'

And the music was the best that Vienna had to offer. Lilting waltzes and lively polkas, brisk regimental marches and haunting operettas; we were treated to them all, and during the interval I went with Franz into the anterooms where I had once encountered Zoltan Bartok. Again I met the cool haughty stare from Karl's mother, then the woman standing besides her smiled and came forward to speak to me.

'How nice to meet you again,' she said. 'You remember we met in the park?'

I smiled. 'Yes, I do remember. It was some time ago.'

'Yes. We've been living in the country—my mother-in-law prefers it.'

I felt that my smile was stiff and I was glad that Franz joined us, calm and urbane, ready with conversation. 'Good evening,' he said easily. 'Does this mean that you are return-ing to live in Vienna?'

'I would like to. I keep hoping Karl will be able to visit us here.'

'How long since you have seen him?'

'Not since our wedding in Salzburg. He is active on the Eastern front so it is difficult. One day the news is good, then it is terrible. Oh, I do wish this dreadful war could be over. Do you have a husband or a friend in the war?' she asked me.

'No, but I am English. My country is at war with Germany.'

For several seconds she stared at me, then with a little smile she said, 'Of course,' and I realised that she knew I was the girl Karl had been with on the night he was shot. With another brief smile she rejoined her party, and we made our way back to the box. Franz said gently, 'That was not easy for you, Alex. Something inside you must have wanted to cry out that you had seen Karl, that he was your lover, that whether she was his wife or not you were the woman he loved.'

I didn't answer and the music played on. In future whenever waltz music was played would I always be transported back to glamour and forbidden love?

It was hard to imagine that most of Europe was at war as we drove through the streets of Vienna just before midnight that night. The ground was covered with a light peppering of snow but a full moon shone down on a city strangely untouched by the traumas surrounding us. As we entered the house a servant came forward to take my wrap and Franz said with a smile, 'Are you joining me in a drink?'

'No thank you, Franz. I am rather tired and I have to be at the hospital very early in the morning.'

'Of course, then I'll say goodnight.'

In spite of my excuse that I was tired sleep was a long time in coming. My thoughts were all on Stevenson Square. I could see my father tying up his dahlias in the garden and my mother chatting with Aunt May about some new item she had bought in the shops. I could hear Mrs Pearson scolding Polly about some quite insignificant thing she had omitted to do and, when I looked through the window at the sleeping city, all I could remember was the square with its pristine houses and the sort of life that went on behind the lace curtains at the front windows. What would life be like now in England? Would there still be church bells on Sunday and the procession of children accompanied by their parents sauntering round the square, or would there be food shortages as here, and an increasing toll of tragedies for many people? What changes to the people I knew and loved? So many large houses in Vienna were now serving as hospitals and although it was just as tiring to work in them, at least I was no longer subjected to the ancient farmhouse with its smoking chimneys and cracked walls.

Those very same things had now become mementoes of the nights I had spent with Karl. We had laughed at smoking chimneys and the wind that whistled through the broken window frames. One day Karl would go home to luxury; he would make love to his wife in a sumptuous bedroom surrounded by wealth and status. How would he remember the love we had shared in surroundings that were dilapidated and shabby, unless the day came when he could smile at such foolishness?

I remembered his face, the low charm of his voice, the warmth of his gaze, but when I thought about his words they became more and more unbelievable.

He had promised a future together, but I couldn't believe in it. He had sworn to love me as long as life lasted, but love was transient. There were more important things than love, like honour and family, country and position, and the more I thought about it the more I believed in its stupidity.

As I trudged through the streets of Vienna on my way to and from the hospital even Vienna seemed alien with passers-by immersed in their private traumas, their shoulders hunched against the bitter wind, their feet sliding along pavements icy with sleet. This was reality: not the empty palaces and haunting waltz music, not the pride in an empire that had lasted too long, but the distant sound of gunfire and the increasing mountain of casualties.

In 1916 the world was accustomed to calamities, but Vienna was ill prepared for the death of her Emperor.

CHAPTER SEVENTEEN

THE OLD GENTLEMAN, as he was often referred to, died only one long corridor away from the room in which he had been born eighty-six years earlier. It was the twenty-first of November, a day of blustery snow showers and high winds, and over all Vienna there seemed to be an atmosphere of weariness and apathy.

Every day brought tidings of death to families in the city and as the third winter of war tightened its grip on a hungry people the loss of the Emperor was just another calamity to add to all the others.

His loyal subjects filed out to Schönbrunn where for three days his body lay in simple state, then on the Monday after his death they stood silently in streets covered with snow as eight black horses with trim black plumes between their ears hauled the massive funeral hearse into Vienna to rest, in full magnificence, in the Hofburg chapel.

A peacetime funeral would have brought in all the crowned heads of Europe but only Germany's ruler, Wilhelm II, came to Vienna for the funeral on the thirtieth of November. The army was heavily engaged on three battle-fronts and apart from the Life Guards detailed to escort the hearse there was only a single battalion of infantry in the city.

I stood in the company of sad-faced mourners near the opera house to watch the funeral procession on its way to St Stephen's cathedral where the Emperor's body was to receive its final blessing before it was deposited in the imperial vault. Three kings had now joined the procession: Ludwig III of Bavaria, Frederick Augustus of Saxony and Ferdinand of Bulgaria, but in my memory it will always be Vienna's elderly statesmen who demonstrated the most grief. I thought about Franz over the last few days, sunk in misery, trying to accept that the reign of Franz Joseph was at an end and an era of Europe's history was drawing to its close. An old man standing beside me said mournfully, 'It is hard to remember any other sovereign at the head of affairs in Vienna.'

Brought up in the golden age of peace and prosperity Franz sank ever further into a deep depression and as I trudged through the streets of the city I became more and more aware that splendour and romance had gone forever. Music was still played in the inns of Grinzing but the tunes were wearying and filled with a strange nostalgia for days that had gone, and Franz had little or no conversation over the dining table.

One evening he looked up with a sad smile, saying, 'I regret I am a poor companion, Alex. Are there no young people with whom you could spend an evening?'

I shook my head. 'My colleagues are happy to get back to their homes when their shifts have finished. I am very tired.'

'There is no young man, perhaps?'

'No.'

'You never hear from Karl?'

'No. I should forget him. His parents and his wife are here in Vienna. He will come back to his wife, not to me.'

'You are sure about that?'

'Yes.'

It was several days later when I met Karl's wife in the Ringstrasse on my way home from the hospital. She paused with a half-smile and I would have moved on but she fell into step beside me and seemed disposed to chat.

'I see you often walking past the house,' she began. 'Where do you go every day?'

'I work at one of the hospitals.'

'You are a nurse?'

'No. I help out in other ways—there is a lot to do.'

'Yes, of course. I help my mother-in-law with her charities. I knit garments and gloves for the soldiers, but perhaps I too should have looked for hospital work. Will you remain here when the war is over?'

Did I imagine it or was there vague anxiety in her question? I was quick to reassure her. 'There is nothing in Vienna for me. I shall go home to England.'

The war moved on to its inevitable end and the future of Europe was irretrievably changed. America had come into the war on the side of Britain and France in 1917 and although they had suffered enormous casualties in the war they emerged victorious. The German Emperor was sent into exile, Russia was facing revolution, royal families moved into exile and new republics were emerging.

On the eleventh of November 1918 the Viennese Emperor

Charles renounced all participation in the affairs of state so that Austria and Hungary too became republics and when Franz returned to the house later that day he seemed suddenly to have become an old man. The country and the life he had loved were no more; it was as though a giant shutter had come down on his world, obscuring all that he had lived for.

'I shall leave Vienna,' he told me briefly. 'I intend to live in the country, where the life of a country gentleman is all that will be required of me.'

'But Alicia will not like that, Franz. She loves Vienna,' I couldn't help remarking.

'She loved the old Vienna, which she often said would not outlive Franz Joseph. Besides, Alex, you have a trusting expectation that she will return here.'

'But she must return now that the war is over, she is your wife.'

His smile was infinitely sad. 'I have no such faith, Alex, but what will you do? One day Vienna will rise from its ashes; she will learn to waltz again, the devastation you see now will be magnificently rebuilt. We still have our palaces, our opera house, our traditions, they do not easily die, but they are not your traditions and it is time for you to go home.'

I knew he was right, but fate had yet one more card to play.

Very early in the morning two days later I was awakened by urgent knocking on my bedroom door and I went to open it with some anxiety. Helmut, Franz's manservant, stood there, his face filled with foreboding. 'It is the master, Fräulein Alex. I cannot rouse him, he is very ill.'

The doctor was immediately sent for and I watched him shaking his head sadly. 'Count Bruckner has suffered a stroke,' he informed us. 'It is a severe one, he may not come out of it.'

Three days later he was dead, and this time there was another funeral to attend at which I was the only relative, although I was surrounded by people who had respected him. We returned to the luxury of the house in the Ringstrasse and I was filled with such utter desolation I went immediately to my bedroom and burst into floods of tears.

Later that evening Helmut informed me I had a visitor and I recognised the man standing in the hall below me as Franz's lawyer. He smiled, and I indicated that we enter the drawing room where Helmut served coffee and Herr Adler made an attempt at polite conversation.

After Helmut had removed the trays he leaned forward with a smile to say, 'Count Bruckner left his affairs in my hands, Fräulein. We were old friends; he had implicit faith that I would carry out his wishes to the best of my ability. He was a rich man, but obviously much of his money has vanished because of the war. Even so he has been astute enough to leave sufficient to take care of several legacies.

'He has left money for Helmut and other of his servants, and he has left money for you, Fräulein Faversham.'

I stared at him in amazement, and he smiled.

'He came to see me; he said he owed you a debt of gratitude for the years you elected to stay with him, for the love you had for Vienna, and with this money he wishes you to return to England and make a new life for yourself there.'

'But there is my aunt. Surely he has thought about Alicia?'

His smile was cynical, the smile of a man with few illusions about the woman on both our minds.

'He has heard nothing from Countess Bruckner for over four years. Hardly surprising, you might say, when she was residing in America and America was at war with Germany, who was our ally. The war has been over two weeks, but there has been no word from Countess Bruckner. Enquiries about her whereabouts are in motion but up to now I have nothing to report.'

'Surely she must come back to Vienna now that the war is over.'

He shrugged his shoulders and I realised that whatever thoughts he had about Alicia he would keep to himself.

'May I be permitted to ring for your butler, Fräulein?' he asked.

When Helmut answered the call the lawyer said, 'I need the key to the safe, Helmut. Can you give it to me?'

Helmut nodded, and in a few minutes returned to hand it over.

He left us and I watched him sorting through the documents then selecting one of them he said with a smile, 'This is pertaining to you, Fräulein. Count Bruckner has bequeathed to you the sum of twenty thousand pounds which you will be at liberty to transfer to an English bank now that the war is over.'

'But that really isn't fair. That money should surely belong to my aunt when she returns from America.'

'If and when Countess Bruckner returns here she will find that her husband has left her very well provided for; this legacy to you was his wish and I have been appointed to see that his wishes are carried out.'

I stared at him open-mouthed. I was rich, and it was too much. What had I done to deserve it?

Seeing my doubt he said gently, 'You need not feel embarrassed by this, Fräulein Faversham—Franz knew what he was about. Now there is also the question of jewellery. He wishes you to receive one of Countess Bruckner's diamond rings and a bracelet. He has left the choice to you.

'These were gifts from Franz to his wife, his wishes on the matter are very explicit.'

I was careful to choose a simple plain gold bracelet when so many of them were heavy with jewels, their colours shimmering against the dark velvet they lay on, and when the sheen of diamonds seemed cold and so much like the icicles that hung from every tree. If Alicia came back to claim her jewellery she would not be able to say that I had robbed her of the most expensive.

I wanted to leave Vienna before Christmas, although I doubted I could arrange that so soon. Much of the magic had gone, but Christmas in the old Vienna had been a time of enchantment. The city would try hard to recapture all that had been lost, but I did not want to be here to yearn after the glamour that had gone; I needed to go home to rekindle a past I had thrown away. Even so Herr Adler came constantly to the house to discuss Franz's affairs and still he had no news of Alicia's whereabouts.

He had traced her living with her American friend in California as late as October 1916, then they had moved to San Francisco and all knowledge of their whereabouts after that had been lost.

'Surely she must come back?' I insisted.

He shrugged his shoulders. 'I will go on trying, of course,' he said. 'Is it likely that she would go to England?'

'I don't think so. In all these long years after she left she showed no interest in returning there to live.'

'But you, Fräulein, you will go back there?'

'Yes, and soon. Surely you do not need me to stay on here?'

'Of course. Say your farewells to Vienna, Fräulein, and to the friends you have made here. When are you intending to travel?'

'I was hoping to go before Christmas but I don't think it is practical. Early in the New Year I expect.'

'And will you be spending Christmas here in this house?'

'No.' I had a sudden inspiration. 'I shall go to Grinzing. I can stay at one of the inns, I know people there.'

'Very wise. Perhaps in Grinzing something will have remained of the old days.'

I took only a small suitcase with me to the inn I found in Grinzing. It was not the Golden Pheasant but a small unpretentious inn at the opposite end of the main street. As I unpacked in my tiny bedroom overlooking the woods I was thinking of my meeting with Valerie von Winckler in the park the day before.

I was sitting at a table in the small café at the edge of the lake watching the skaters and I had not seen her until she came to sit at the table opposite me. Her expression was kind, her voice unsure. 'I hear you are soon to leave Vienna, Alex. Are you going home to England?' she asked.

'Who told you?' I asked curiously.

'We heard that Count Bruckner's house might soon be on the market so I assumed you would not be staying here.'

'No.'

'Does that mean that Countess Bruckner is not coming back to Vienna?'

'I don't know. I believe Herr Adler is making enquiries.'

'Yes, of course. You are leaving before Christmas then?'

'No. I am going to Grinzing for a few days, because I have friends there I wish to see.'

I wanted to ask about Karl, I wanted her to go, but she was not being unpleasant, and I sensed in her a genuine desire to be friendly. She was not one of the people who had regarded me in stony silence from the next box at the opera, but she was Karl's wife and for that reason alone I wanted her to move on.

At last she rose to her feet and stood for a moment looking down at me; our eyes met and she smiled. 'I hope you have a happy Christmas in Grinzing, Alex, and that you have a good journey home to England. Not all your memories of Vienna will be sad.'

With some anger I could feel the sharp sting of tears in my eyes before they rolled down my cheeks, and brushing them impatiently aside I smiled tremulously. 'You are very kind, Valerie, thank you for your good wishes. I hope that you too have a very happy Christmas.'

She smiled and walked away, and my eyes followed her tall slender figure walking slowly along the margin of the lake. How strange it was that the only person to wish me a happy Christmas was the wife of the man I loved. Surely she could not know that we had been lovers? Yet there had been something in her expression that spoke of sympathy.

I should have known that Grinzing would put on a show. Fairy lights shone from the branches of the linden trees, music poured out of every door, and in every window efforts had been made to decorate as in the old style, as if there had never been a war, as if old imperial Vienna was still alive and flourishing.

I was invited to dine at the Golden Pheasant by Herr Windisch, and even the innkeeper and his wife were all smiles and welcoming. My escort was kind and charming but it was not the old Grinzing in spite of the decorations and the waltz and zither music. The dancers were the residents of Grinzing instead of handsome young men in uniform with beautiful girls hanging on their arms. It was too soon to recapture what had been, and looking in my eyes Herr Windisch said almost sadly, 'Perhaps it was wrong to come back and expect every-thing to be the same. It can never be the same, Alex. One day, perhaps, not the old people remembering, but a new young people, not trying to recapture what has gone, but willing to find something new.'

I stayed on in Grinzing until New Year's Eve. I was not looking forward to it but I had nothing better to do. I decided I would eat dinner at the inn then simply stroll along the street, recapture old memories, and retire early. New Year's Eve would be no better than Christmas; people would try, but as I had realised, it was too soon.

In some ways it was as I remembered it, with Strauss and Lehar wafting from every open door, and laughter, however strained, but when I walked through the garden of the Golden Pheasant I was unprepared for the man who came out of the shadows to meet me. Then I was staring up into Karl's intent handsome face before he swept me into his arms.

At last he released me and I murmured, 'Karl, how did you know I was here? Are you alone, why are you here yourself?'

He drew me inside the door and we found a table away from the dancers, where the music was less strident and more haunting. Holding my hands across the table he said, 'Valerie told me she had spoken to you in the park; she said you would be here.'

I stared at him in amazement. 'She knew you would come here?'

He nodded. 'I had to see you, Alex, I couldn't let you return home to England as though nothing had meant anything. I didn't want you to think that.'

'But she's your wife, Karl. Why should she care about me?'

'She is also my friend, *liebchen*. When we were children we spent long hours in the fields around Salzburg, or in the Vienna Woods together. I comforted her when she fell from her swing, she comforted me when my dog died. It was the innocent friendship of children before the real world took so much of it away. I am still her friend, and she knows that I am unhappy. When we were children we did not know that older, perhaps wiser, people would plan that one day we should marry; those old wise heads could not begin to think that one of us or even both of us might look elsewhere. So, Alex, what might have happened if I had not taken you to the opera that night and fate had not played into their hands?'

'Nothing would have happened, Karl. You would still have married Valerie. The old order wouldn't have changed to accommodate a starry-eyed English girl who asked too much and dreamt so unwisely.'

'I shall never forget you, *liebchen*.'

'And I shall never forget you, Karl.'

'What will it be like in England? I have never been there.'

'I don't suppose it will have changed very much.'

'Will there be snow on the mountains?'

I smiled. 'There aren't any mountains like those here where the snow still lingers in the summertime, and where I am going there are only gentle hills and wooded valleys.'

'What a pity that I never saw it for myself.'

Our meeting was tender but gentle but the passion that had consumed us both was somehow missing. I loved him but he was no longer mine. It seemed on that night that what I felt for Karl was bigger than love: it was a burning desire for his well-being. Although I was going out of his life I was leaving him with a woman who had shown me kindness and consideration and I desperately wanted them to be happy together.

In some strange way my thoughts reached out to him, and covering my hand with his he said gently, 'I hope you too meet someone, *liebchen*, some nice Englishman who will make you happy and fulfilled. Do you remember the Englishman on the train? He didn't entirely approve of you and me getting along so well together.'

'No. Englishmen expect their women to be a little off-putting, and to regard all foreigners with a certain suspicion.'

'We disappointed him, then?'

'I'm afraid so.'

We laughed at the memory of the Englishman's obvious disapproval, then over the music we heard the ringing of bells from every steeple around and Karl stood up and drew me to my feet. 'Happy New Year, *liebchen*,' he said, holding me in his arms. 'Nineteen nineteen, a new beginning, a new world. Will it be as good as the old one, do you think?'

I didn't know. Empires had gone, republics had been born; in Russia there was revolution and I was returning to a country I had somehow lost but hoped desperately to regain.

We stood together while all around us there was laughter and music and Karl said, 'I will walk with you to your inn, Alex, then I must return to Vienna.'

'You are going to Vienna tonight?'

'Yes. Today is New Year's Day. Have you forgotten how importantly we always regarded it? The Emperor has gone, but today there will still be Strauss at the Hofburg and the Belvedere, the men will wear their uniforms, the women their jewels, and they will try to believe that old imperial Vienna still lives.'

CHAPTER EIGHTEEN

ALTHOUGH I HAD a cabin on the cross-Channel ferry from St Malo I was unable to sleep. It was not a rough crossing but there was fog and the dismal sound of the foghorn coupled with numerous anxieties kept me awake and dawn found me on deck staring at a grey glassy sea and swirling mist.

I could see the lights of Dover only dimly through the gloom and my fellow passengers were gathering around me, their expressions no doubt as miserable as my own. By the time we had disembarked it had started to rain and as I boarded the boat train for London I was only too aware of damp clothing and a feeling of acute chill.

A woman sitting opposite said wearily, 'I never slept a wink. That wretched foghorn kept me awake all night. Have you come far?'

'From Vienna.'

'Really.'

I thought it was possible she had never even heard of Vienna; at least her tone had been uninterested, and if I had said I had come from Mars she couldn't have been more unconcerned. Almost peevishly she said, 'I hope this train isn't going to be late in London, I have people waiting for me.'

The compartment was filling up by this time and I felt relieved that the man sitting next to her was claiming her attention.

I had decided to stay overnight in London before journeying home and it was a relief to change into dry clothing and the comfort of my hotel bedroom. How strange it seemed to hear English spoken all around me and newspaper boys whistling down the street, to see London buses and taxis and a great many men still wearing khaki uniform. I was even more surprised when the waiter apologised that there was so little choice on the menu, and when I stared at him he hastened to tell me that London had still not quite got back to normal. There were still food shortages and other problems to overcome before life picked up its pattern.

I would have given anything not to have been on that train taking me home, not because I didn't want to see my family again, but because I was terrified of their rejection. It was nine long years since I had waited in the hallway for the taxi that would take me away, nine years of living a different life in another country, but that wasn't really the problem. It was the way I had gone that troubled me most. I saw it now as something callous and ungrateful, the action of an uncaring daughter towards parents who had loved her and given her the best they had.

Now I was afraid of how they would receive me. Would it be with a remembered warmth or would they have long since discarded me as someone of no account?

As I stepped down from the train a pale watery sun was struggling to shine through and people all around me were hurrying with bent heads against the sharp wind that swept along the platform. I too kept my head down, but for a different reason. On that afternoon I did not want to meet anybody from the past, anybody who could spread the news that Alex Faversham had come home.

It was all as I remembered it. The double-decker red trams standing outside the station, the large railway hotel on the corner, the parish church spire over the rooftops; as I sat back in the taxi nostalgia tugged at my heartstrings and I was a girl again running along the pavements on my way home from school.

There was activity in the town hall square and seeing my interest the taxi driver said, 'They're putting up a cenotaph for them that were killed in't war, right over there, miss, near the art gallery.'

'Were there very many people killed?' I asked.

'There were. There'll be a good few names on it when it's finished. Any of your folk in it, miss?'

'I don't know, I've been away.'

'Well, I were too young to go. Me Dad was injured on the Somme and I reckon he'll never be the same again.'

'I'm sorry.'

'Terrible it were. All them rat-infested trenches and wholesale slaughter. Anyway we made 'em get rid o' that wretched Kaiser and a whole lot of others 'ave gone the same way. I reckon it's goin' to be a different world wi' all them republics. What do you say, miss?'

'You're probably right. It will be a different world.'

'A better world too, miss, don't ye reckon?'

How could any of us be sure? It seemed to me that over all Europe the lights that had gone out were only just being relit, and the wind of change that was sweeping across long-established dynasties was about to replace them with something new and brittle, something so fragile that it could not last.

He turned his head to look at me for a brief moment when I had not replied, then with a grin he said, 'I take it you don't agree with me, miss.'

'Perhaps it's too soon,' I said with a smile. 'Has anything else changed in the town?'

'Well, Stevenson Square doesn't change although some o' them 'ouses could do wi' a coat o' paint. Nothin' much got done durin' the war ye know, now I reckon there'll be plenty o' work in the decoratin' trade. 'Ere we are, miss, doesn't look very different, does it?'

It could have been that afternoon nine years ago and as we drew up to the front of the house I looked up at the white-painted door where the brass knocker stood out brilliantly and the sun shone on windows that were clean and bright. As I paid the taxi driver then stood hesitantly looking up at the house I half expected to see my grandmother standing in the window and Mrs Pearson opening the door for me, then as I walked up to the door the agonising fears came back. Who would come to the door, how would they receive me, what had the years done to them?

I was unprepared for the stranger who answered my knock and stood regarding me curiously, a very young housemaid wearing a frilly cap and apron.

'Is Mrs Faversham in?' I asked.

'Mrs Faversham?'

'Yes. My parents lived here. Have they moved?'

She continued to stare and then from the back of the hall came Mrs Pearson's voice saying sharply, 'It's freezing in here, Lucy, what are ye doing with that door open?'

I had never thought to be pleased to hear Mrs Pearson's voice, sharp and hectoring, and yet on this occasion it filled me with relief that at least there was something that hadn't changed.

Lucy retreated behind the door and then Mrs Pearson was there staring at me with wide incredulous eyes and hardly changed at all since the last time I had seen her. Her face was still plump and florid, her expression hardly welcoming as she said, 'Well! Well!'

I looked at her helplessly and turning to Lucy she said, 'Go in the kitchen and put the kettle on. You'd best come into the house, Miss Alex. I suppose yer expectin' to find that nothin's changed.'

I followed her into the drawing room and after closing the door she said, 'How long has it been, Miss Alex?'

'Nine years, Mrs Pearson.'

'Aye, all of that.'

'My mother is out?'

'Your mother and father don't live here any more. They live in Devonshire in your grandmother's house, and your sister and her husband live here.'

'Della?'

'No. Miss Ruth and her husband.'

'Is my grandmother not well, that my parents are living with her?'

'Your grandmother died two years ago. Nine years is a long

time, Miss Alex, a great many things can happen. We've had a war, you know. It was terrible, though from the looks of you you probably escaped that.'

Stung to retort I said, 'How can you tell that from the looks of me, Mrs Pearson? I agree that the war was terrible; I would have had to be living on another planet to escape it.'

'Aye, well, you were allus ready with an answer, I'll say that for you.'

'Does my sister Della still live across the square?'

'No, they've moved into Sir John's house. Sir John died and his lady wife went to live with her sister in Berkshire. Miss Della's husband has gone into Parliament, MP he is, and highly thought of. Your sister Ruth'll tell ye about all the changes. I must go and see if Lucy's managin' in the kitchen, she's not up to much.'

'What happened to Polly?'

'She got married and moved away, Miss Alex. I suppose you *are* still Miss Alex?'

'Yes, Mrs Pearson, that is one of the things that hasn't changed.'

After favouring me with a long hard look she left me and I was able at last to look round the room. The furniture was still Grandmother's apart from one or two modern introductions, which I suspected had come from Ruth, in the shape of vases and photographs.

There were a great many of them and I felt a sense of relief to see the old family photograph on top of the piano. At least I had not been cut off but sat in the midst of them with the family dog on my knees.

At that moment Lucy arrived pushing a tea trolley, shortly

followed by Mrs Pearson who quickly dismissed the maid and started to pour the tea. I was about to hear something of the distress I had caused to my family and Mrs Pearson had spent so many years in the employment of the Faversham family she felt she had every right to admonish me.

'Whatever made ye do it, Miss Alex?' she began. 'Your mother was desolate, it made her very ill. It was Miss Alicia all over again but at least we all knew she'd gone off with a man, whereas none of us knew where you'd gone or who with.

'Your grandmother said it could be some man you'd met when you stayed with her, but your father said it wasn't possible, you'd only been with her a couple of weeks. Mrs Roper said it was likely you'd answered one of those adverts in a magazine, just like her own daughter had done.'

'I have to talk to Ruth, then I shall go to Devon to see my parents, I'll telephone them this evening.'

'You're going to give them a shock. They thought they'd never see you again, just as they've never seen Miss Alicia.'

'Alicia left without a letter. I did tell them I loved them, I would never forget them and I would come back one day.'

'You also said you'd write often and tell them where you were living. You never wrote, Miss Alex. Can you begin to realise how your mother waited and waited for those letters that never came?'

'I do realise it, Mrs Pearson. I wanted to write but there were many reasons why it wasn't easy, then during the war it was impossible.'

'I said to your mother, she's gone to America, that's where she'll be, and them not in the war. When it's all over she'll come back, and then the Americans came into the war and she was upset all over again thinking of you out there.'

'Was it very terrible in England, Mrs Pearson? Did anybody I know get killed?'

'Your cousin Edith's husband got killed on the Somme, devastated she was, and your Aunt May's youngest, Master Simeon, was wounded in Flanders.'

'Is he better?' I asked anxiously.

'Well he'll allus have a limp, shrapnel they say, but he's back at the works and both him and his brother are married to very nice young ladies.'

'I'm so glad, and Aunt May?'

She sniffed. 'She married Mr Stedman and moved into his house on the Crescent. Your Aunt Jane did a lot for the war effort, Red Cross and the like, but Mrs Stedman was more of a one for entertaining American officers from the base nearby, and British officers from the barracks.'

I couldn't help smiling. Aunt Jane's worthy efforts would hardly be able to compete with Aunt May's welcoming home fires, and seeing my smile Mrs Pearson snapped, 'I know you and your Aunt May allus got along, but I used to say to Polly after ye'd gone, two of a kind they were, Miss Alex and Mrs William. Your father maintained he'd bred another Miss Alicia.'

I didn't answer; instead I got up from my chair and walked over to the window.

'The square seems very much the same, Mrs Pearson. Are the same people living here?'

'Most of them. After you left there was a lot of gossip and for a time your mother kept herself to herself, then it all died down. There were more important things to think about. Did anybody see you arriving?'

'I don't know, the square seemed very quiet.'

'And of course you've changed. You're a woman, and in some ways very different from the girl I remember.'

'How, Mrs Pearson? How am I different?'

'Well, there's an air about you, a sort of elegance. You were allus such a tomboy, you ran and danced when you should have walked, but lookin' at you now you're like something out of them magazines your sister Della used to bring round.'

I had an air. It was an air Vienna had created in me; no doubt it would die slowly with the years, but it was still a part of imperial balls and impossible operettas.

'Will my sister be home soon?' I asked her.

'She'll be picking Miss Sally up at her school.'

'Gracious, I'd forgotten Sally. What is she like these days? She was little more than a baby the last time I saw her.'

'She's not a baby now, she's growing up and she's taken to the piano just like her mother.'

'I'm so glad. They had such hopes for Ruth.'

'I'm sure Miss Ruth'll want you to stay here so I'll see about a room for you. She'll not be long afore she's back.'

Sitting in front of the fire I heard the front door open, then the sound of voices in the hall and I knew Mrs Pearson was preparing my sister for the surprise that awaited her.

As we stared at each other across the room my first reaction was that she looked older. She was wearing a brown skirt and woollen sweater in pale blue and it seemed like something she might have worn in the past that I only vaguely remembered. Standing facing her on the hearthrug in pale silver grey with the sheen of furs round my throat and wearing elegant high-heeled suede shoes, it was I who felt overdressed and unreal.

With a cry of delight she rushed across the room and enveloped me in her arms, then she was bringing Sally forward, a pretty brown-haired girl so very like Ruth as a schoolgirl.

'Alex, you look wonderful,' Ruth enthused. 'That outfit must have cost a fortune, where did you manage to buy it so soon after the war?'

'I've had it for ages. It isn't new, I simply managed to bring back everything out of my wardrobe.'

'Brought back? But where were you?'

'I have such a lot to tell you. Mrs Pearson has been filling me in but I have to ask if I can telephone Mother and stay here tonight. It's impossible to get down to Devon until the morning.'

'Of course, you must stay here, at least for a few days. Mother will understand if you tell her you'll be arriving at the weekend.'

I smiled ruefully. 'I have to go tomorrow, Ruth. I'll come back here if you'll have me, but please understand I've hurt them so much that I can't afford not to go immediately.'

She nodded. 'I suppose so, but we do have this evening. You can tell me all about your adventures and then Paul will be home around six. He'll bombard you with questions.'

'Do you hate me very much for what I did to you all?' I had to ask her.

'I thought I hated you, Alex. Mother was so upset, Father too, and Grandmother insisted on blaming herself for everything. She thought you'd met somebody in Devon; she said you'd been secretive, not wanting to go to places with her, going off on your own.'

After all the years that had passed guilt was consuming me again. How could I ever have thought that I could simply come back and forget the past and ask my family to forget it also?

There were tears in my eyes when I looked at her, and my voice trembled with emotion as I said, 'What I did to you all was terrible, Ruth. I wanted to write but I couldn't. I thought Father would try to trace me and I didn't want to come home before I was ready. There was so much I wanted to see, wanted to do.'

'Did Mrs Pearson tell you about Della?'

'Yes. They're living at the Hall, and John is an MP.'

'It's all very grand. Edith's husband was killed during the war. She's very bitter and Aunt Jane gets so impatient with her. She says she should be well over it by this time, but Edith is like an utter recluse.'

'And Simeon was wounded?'

'Yes, but he's recovered very well. Aunt May remarried, did Mrs Pearson tell you that?'

'Yes, among other things.'

Ruth laughed. 'You know how Aunt May always provided the town with plenty of scandal. A great many things have changed, Alex, but some things stay the same. What happened to you during the war?'

'I'll tell you later. Just now I would like to get out of this coat and unpack a small case. Are you quite sure you don't mind having me for one night?'

'I'd be horrified if you moved out. Oh Alex, I want to know so much! While you settle in I'll telephone Mother. I think it's better if I prepare her, don't you? You can speak to her later.'

When we moved out into the hall Mrs Pearson came out of the kitchen to say she'd put me in the guest room at the front of the house, and seeing my surprise she said with something approaching malice, 'Well you are a guest now, Miss Alex. Miss Sally's in your old room.'

While I unpacked I could hear Ruth's voice downstairs on the telephone. It was a conversation that seemed to be going on forever, and in the end Sally opened my door and asked me to go downstairs quickly. Grandma wished to speak to me at once.

My mother's voice was filled with emotion, alternating between questions and tears, and I too was tearful to be hearing her after so many years, the relief in it, the hunger and the joy. Then I was talking to my father and his voice too was filled with questions interspersed with relief.

Throughout our evening meal, and long after, Paul and Ruth asked me about my time away and my replies filled them with amazement although I was careful not to tell them everything. I told them about Emily and our travels in Europe, then I spoke to them about Vienna, my work in Grinzing, the waltzes and the operettas, the palaces and domes, the Spanish Riding School and the snow-white stallions performing on a velvet carpet, the joyous atmosphere of the Prater. I told them about the beautiful Vienna Woods and the sadness of Mayerling but I did not tell them about Alicia and Franz, I did not speak of Zoltan Bartok or Karl. That part of Vienna must be locked away in my heart forever.

Paul was naturally curious about the war years. 'Why didn't you come home when you knew that war was inevitable, Alex?' he asked. 'England was at war with Germany.

'But not with Austria, Paul. Germany invaded the Low Countries and that brought France and England into the war against Germany. There is more, much more, but too much to tell you in one evening.'

Would any of them understand that while England was at war I was working in a hospital in Austria? It was something that had been thrust upon me and always at the back of my mind was Alicia. I had to keep her out of it.

I slept badly that cold winter's night in my old home. My mind was obsessed with what they had told me about the years I had been away and I desperately wanted the hours to fly quickly so that I could meet my parents again.

CHAPTER NINETEEN

I WAS AFRAID and I was apprehensive, but there was no anger, no recriminations, only intense and utter relief that the daughter they had presumed lost forever had miraculously returned to them.

My mother was still the beautiful woman I remembered but the lines of care on her face made me feel that it was I who had helped to put them there. I had sorrowful thoughts for the grandmother I would never see again, and it was many days before we were able to talk about the years we had lost; even then in my own ears my reasons for leaving them seemed selfish beyond words.

My father asked few questions although when they were alone together I feel convinced my mother filled him in on all my adventures. I told her about Emily and our time together in Italy and France, then I told her about Emily's meeting with an old friend and that they returned to England together. After that I had to tell her about Vienna, but nothing of Aunt Alicia or Karl, nothing of Zoltan Bartok or Franz, so all I could mention was my work there in Grinzing and later in the hospital during the war. I longed to describe

St Petersburg and the glamour of imperial Vienna, but that would have meant Alicia and the family's old antagonism towards her was still there, would always be there.

Life took up a familiar pattern of walks in the country, church on Sundays, visits to the theatre and the cinema; I was introduced to the friends my parents had made in the vicinity. They were people like themselves, with daughters like me and sons who asked me to dance and play tennis, and once again I was plagued with uncertainty. This was not how I wanted to live my life and for the first time my mother became aware of my restlessness.

One day she surprised me by asking, 'Have you not thought to get in touch with your friend Emily, Alex? Didn't you say she lived in Devon?'

'Well yes, in a small village along the coast, but it's years since we met. I wrote to her often during those early times in Austria, but then the war came and it wasn't possible to send letters.'

'There's nothing to prevent you visiting her home. I'm sure she'd be happy to see you.'

'It's been nine years, Mother. Maybe she isn't there now,' I pointed out.

'Well, you won't know, dear, unless you take the trouble to find out,' she said with the utmost conviction.

So on a spring morning bright with sunshine I ventured back to Witherington and my first thoughts were that nothing had changed from the stone church standing proudly at the top of the High Street to the row of cottages leading up to it.

I paused at the gate to stare uncertainly at Emily's house

surrounded by its garden gay with pansies. It seemed unchanged but even as I waited a boy came from behind the
house trundling a bicycle. He was about fourteen years old
with a shock of blond hair and seeing me standing there he
smiled and came towards the gate.

'Does Miss Parsons still live here?' I ventured.

He shook his head. 'No, we live here. We've lived here for
seven years.'

'Oh, I am sorry. It's years since I saw Miss Parsons. We
lost touch—I don't suppose you know where she is living
now?'

'Me mum might know, come in and I'll ask her.'

I followed him up the path and opening the front door he
called out, 'Mum, there's a lady here asking for Miss Parsons.'

A woman came from the back of the house hurriedly
wiping her hands on a pot towel. She smiled, apologising that
she was in the midst of baking, and I too apologised for interrupting her morning's work.

'We bought this house from Miss Parsons seven years
ago,' she explained. 'Didn't she write to tell you she was
moving?'

'I was living abroad. Her letter may have gone astray.'

'Do come in, I've got her address somewhere. I'll make
you a cup of tea while I find it.'

'I don't want to trouble you.'

'You're not. Come into the parlour because the kitchen's
in a bit of a mess right now.'

The parlour was not as Emily's had been with its pretty
chintzes and watercolours. It was far more modern and untidy
but when I stood at the window and looked across the garden

almost expected Flora to come bustling out of the kitchen trundling her tea trolley. Instead the new occupant came in carrying a tray and with a bright smile on her face said, 'I've found it, I knew I had it somewhere. We bought this house from Miss Emily when she went to live in Exeter.'

'Did you know her well?' I asked.

'Oh yes. I was brought up in this village and went to the local school and to the church when her father was the vicar. I always loved this house even when I only dreamed I'd live here. I never thought she'd leave it.'

'Why did she?'

'There is a lot you don't know, love. She got married. I never thought she would although all the village knew she was sweet on Edward Danson as a girl. I think it was her father who put an end to it. He was a good man but very demanding, and she'd never have left him to get married, so Edward Danson married somebody else, a friend of hers, and they moved to Exeter. His first wife died and he met Miss Emily again; this time there was no father to put a stop to it. All the village was delighted for her.'

'So they moved into Edward's house.'

'No. They had a new property built on the outskirts of Exeter. I watched her wedding! All the village was there, the church was full, and she looked so pretty in pale blue. When I was a young girl we used to come here and sit in the garden watching Miss Emily paint her watercolours, she was very good.'

'I know, I watched her painting in Italy.'

'Really. You were in Italy together, then?'

'Yes, we had a wonderful time.'

'We all heard she'd gone off travelling and we thought she

was so brave. She could never have done it when the old man was alive.'

We were interrupted by the boy's head appearing round the door, asking pertly, 'When's dinner ready, Mother? I've got a football match this afternoon.'

'I really must be going,' I said quickly. 'Thank you so much for the tea and the address. I do hope I haven't held you up too much.'

'Of course you haven't, I've been glad of a chat. Go and set the table, Anthony, I'll be back when I've seen this young lady out of the house. Dinner'll be on time.'

He grinned at me cheekily, and as I left her at the front door she said, 'Him and his football, my life revolves round it. If you get to visit Miss Emily do remember us to her. Tell her the Bramptons have been asking about her.'

Mrs Brampton had written Emily's new address down for me as well as her telephone number, and Mother was insistent that I should telephone her that same evening. When I prevaricated she said, 'Alex, she'll be delighted to hear from you. You had marvellous times together; I'm sure over the years she's often wondered how you were faring. I'd very much like to meet her.'

I would have liked my parents to meet Emily but Mother was unaware of the lies I had told to make it appear that I was free to travel with her. How could I suddenly introduce parents to Emily, who had thought they'd been miles away, the father who was a seaman and a mother who sailed the seven seas with him?

There was no mistaking the joy in Emily's voice when I telephoned her, however, and she was insistent that I visit her very

oon and gave instructions on how to find them. Coupled with
my parents' encouragement I agreed to visit her the next day.

I had known that Emily's house would be charming and
strangely reminiscent of the Old Vicarage with its large
garden and mellow stone. Emily and Edward greeted me en-
thusiastically and the nine years between seemed to slip away
so that it might have been yesterday when we strolled together
along the shores of Lake Maggiore.

They showed me round their house with great pride and
they were so happy as the time passed that much of my foreboding passed also. I had a lot to explain, a lot to atone for,
and later as I shamefully admitted the many lies I had told to
persuade Emily to take me on her travels I was unprepared
for her reaction.

'I always thought you hadn't told me the whole truth,
Alex,' she said. 'How could you do that to your parents? It
must have been terrible for them.'

'Yes, it was. I am ashamed, but I'm home now and I shall
never in my life behave that way towards them again.'

She smiled. 'So, how are you spending your time, your
life? Where do you go from here?'

I looked at her helplessly. 'I don't know. Nothing I'm
doing is enough. I'd do things differently, I'm probably older
and wiser, but I'm still crying for the moon.'

'And the aunt you invented in Vienna, did she ever exist?'

'Yes, Emily, that at least was true.' So I told her about Alicia
and Franz, about St Petersburg and Vienna, but nothing about
Karl. There were so many hidden corners in my life, I believed
would never be able to tell the entire truth to anybody.

I spent a happy day with them and promised that I would

invite them to visit my parents. 'A new start, Emily,' I said quickly. 'I have told Mother that we must not speak of the past and she has agreed. Do you promise too?'

Smiling, she was quick to agree, and it was only later when she left me to speak to a friend on the telephone that I picked up a magazine lying on the table near my chair and saw it was the same magazine that had contained Emily's advertisement for a travelling companion. When she returned and saw me looking through it she said, 'I enjoy looking through the pages asking for all sorts of people. It reminds me of my own search for somebody like-minded. There's one in there that interests me because I know the lady making the request.'

'Surely you're not thinking of applying?' I said with a smile.

'No indeed, but I was intrigued. It's on page twenty-seven—see what you think of it.'

I turned to the page mentioned and she came to point out the advertisement, enhanced by capital letters and surrounded with a border.

It was strangely outdated for this new decade and Emily said, 'It is the sort of request only that particular lady could have made. I doubt if she is geared to modern thinking or modern living.'

GENTLEWOMAN TO ACT AS COMPANION TO YOUNG LADY RECENTLY BEREAVED IN THE WAR. MUST BE INTELLIGENT, INTERESTED IN READING, LITERATURE, OPERA, BALLET AND THE THEATRE. PLEASE APPLY TO THE HON. MRS LAVINIA GRAEHME-BURROWS, GRANTHAM HALL, NEAR SIDMOUTH, DEVONSHIRE.

* * *

I looked up and Emily said, 'I knew her when I lived in the village. She attended the church when Father was the vicar. She was always very grand; she was a widow, her second husband had been the second son of an earl and she had one daughter she despaired of and one son. The son was all he should be, but the daughter married a wastrel who ran through her money and deserted her. I believe she died in France but she left a daughter, Miss Stephanie, whom Mrs Graehme-Burrows brought up. This I think is the young lady who is requiring a companion.'

'But why, if she is young and well connected?'

'I rather lost touch with the old lady after Father died. She didn't care for the new vicar and found another church nearer the Hall, but news gets around. Apparently Miss Stephanie was a bit of a handful. The family took her in hand and when she was seventeen they found a husband for her, an army man, eighteen years her senior. Unfortunately he was killed in the war and so at a very early age Miss Stephanie is a widow and possibly a problem.'

I handed the magazine back with a smile saying, 'I can't think of what sort of a woman they'll be looking for. Surely the girl should be allowed to get on with her own life? It's long overdue.'

'The position doesn't appeal to you, Alex?'

I laughed. 'Oh Emily, Mrs whatever-she's-called won't be looking for somebody like me. I'd be guaranteed to lead anybody astray.'

'I doubt if Miss Stephanie would need much leading unless widowhood has changed her out of all recognition. The thing intrigues me. The war has been over some time, Miss

Stephanie has been bereaved at least four years and I doubt if there was much love in her arranged marriage anyway. Take the magazine, Alex. I've finished with it, and your mother might find it interesting.'

'Emily, you will come to see us soon? I'll arrange with Mother to telephone you and I'm so very glad that you're happy with Edward and I love your house—it's everything I thought it would be.'

That night I talked about Emily and Edward and their house over our evening meal and Mother said with a smile, 'I really thought you'd gone off with some quite terrible person, Alex, either a man or some silly girl you'd met, certainly not anybody like Emily. Now we're both looking forward to meeting her.'

That night I introduced Mother to the magazine Emily had given me and we laughed together at the notices requesting governesses, companions for the elderly and the sick, cooks and housekeepers; I told her the story Emily had told me about the lady requiring a companion for her granddaughter.

'That's terribly sad,' Mother said. 'How awful that a husband was found for her at such an early age and that she should lose him. Now it seems that they are endeavouring to arrange her life all over again.'

I am not sure when the moment was born in me but as I read the advertisement again in my bedroom I began to feel close to Miss Stephanie, a girl a little younger than myself, a girl whose life had been planned for her probably entirely against her will in order that she behaved herself and conformed to the standards a lofty family had expected from her

What sort of a woman would apply for the position and what sort of a woman would they want? Probably somebody stiff and starchy, somebody very proper, somebody as unlike me as chalk from cheese.

When I joked about it to Mother I was unprepared for her reaction. 'Why should you think you're unsuitable for something like this, Alex? You've had a good education, you come from a decent family background and Hall or no Hall one can't really ask for anything more respectable than Stevenson Square.'

'Oh Mother, you're not seriously thinking I could apply for anything like this?'

'Of course not, dear, but don't run yourself down so. They'd be very fortunate indeed to find anybody like you.'

'So you are suggesting that I should apply,' I said in some surprise.

'Of course not,' she was quick to say again, and then reflectively, 'but you do seem strangely restless, Alex. All this must seem terribly dull to you after Vienna and your travels abroad. Somehow I get the feeling that you're not entirely happy.'

'Why would you think that, Mother?'

'Because you go to dances and parties with some very nice young men, yet none of them are what you want. I always have the feeling that you're looking for other things, but what things I can't imagine.'

I put my arms around her to reassure her, saying, 'Mother, I'm home now, and if I ever get the urge to travel again you'll

be the first to know, as well as exactly where I'm going and
with whom.'

All the same, in spite of my reassurances she was right. I
was restless; there was more to life than the afternoons on the
tennis court and the band concerts in the park, more than the
tea dances and evenings at the theatre where it was difficult
to avoid the admiration in the eyes of several young men, in
particular Jason Green, the son of a local councillor and the
owner of a new two-seater car.

My parents were pleased about the friendship, and Jason was
nice, but always at the back of my mind was Karl, Karl in the
uniform of imperial Vienna, waltz music and crystal chandeliers lighting up some grand staircase. Why couldn't I forget him
as he had probably forgotten me, why wasn't what I had now
enough? Why this desperate need to search for more?

Emily and Edward came for dinner and my relieved parents
liked them immensely. Later in the evening when Edward and
Father played snooker Mother told Emily that I had been a
little more than interested in the magazine she had given me
and Mrs Graehme-Burrows' request for a companion for her
granddaughter.

Emily smiled. 'You're not really interested are you
Alex?' she asked.

'Not really. I just felt rather sorry for her, that's all. Besides
I'm not the sort of person she will be looking for.'

Emily's face was thoughtful. 'You could be just the sort
of person she needs, Alex: young, enthusiastic about life, but
intelligent about it too. Her grandmother was domineering,
just as my father was, which is why they were so friendly with

each other. He recognised himself in the old lady; she wanted her daughter and her granddaughter to be like me, acquiescent and docile.'

'And that is how she will want her granddaughter's companion to be.'

'But her granddaughter is a married woman. What will she want?'

'Oh well, it's no use talking about it, I suppose. I am not going to apply.'

'You're sure?' Mother asked with a little smile.

'Yes, quite sure. I'm happy here. Why would I want to live in some large hall near Sidmouth?'

'But Stephanie doesn't live in Sidmouth,' Emily said quickly. 'She lives in London, much to her grandmother's disgust, and visits her only when she has a mind to it. I can't think why her grandmother is so anxious to interfere with her life unless she feels it's becoming too bohemian.'

'Oh dear,' Mother said feelingly. 'Then we certainly don't want Alex involved.' Meeting Emily's gaze she was quick to go on. 'We've had our fair share of bohemian activity in our family already, with my husband's youngest sister who went off to marry a merchant seaman; none of us have seen top nor tail of her since, and then there's my sister-in-law who ran the gamut of every widower in the town until she remarried. Of course Alex went off into the blue, and even before that she was accused of dancing when she should have walked.

'I can't think why my daughter is so obsessed with having little to do in her life. You were happy to stay at home and entertain your father's guests and make friends in your village, but whatever Alex does doesn't seem enough, Emily.'

'Girls are becoming more outgoing,' Emily said gently. 'One of these days they'll be in the professions and I suppose we were born too soon. For Alex it could all begin to change now.'

'There still isn't very much apart from nursing, teaching, serving in some shop or other, secretarial work and office work but even then men are given precedence. I do wish Alex would see this and resign herself to a good life within the family.'

I was glad when they changed the subject; over the next few days I intended to think seriously about moving on, but this time with my parents' full approval.

CHAPTER TWENTY

THE MORE I thought about that application in the magazine the more it intrigued me so that in the end I decided to apply. Mother was troubled. Father was exasperated and Emily agreed to act as my sponsor should I be considered.

'Don't worry, Mother,' I assured her. 'I'll be considered too young, I won't hear any more beyond an acknowledgment. I'll still be here to torment you for many years.'

'Oh my dear, I do hope not. You'll meet some very nice young man and what is wrong with Jason Green? He is evidently very fond of you and he does come from a very good background.'

I shook my head dolefully and Mother said, 'I never hankered after anything beyond finding a nice husband and raising a family. It's what girls did in my day.'

'I know Mother, but this isn't your day, is it?'

'Della and Ruth are happy enough. Della's letters are filled with the good times they are having, going here there and everywhere, and both your sisters are content looking after their husbands and their homes.'

It was no use. She would never understand, and in my

father's cynical expression I could only see the comparison he made between me and Alicia.

The letter came inviting me to an interview two weeks later and both Mother and Emily advised caution.

'She can be a very autocratic woman,' Emily said. 'What sort of person is she looking for? Stephanie too could be a problem. She's a widow, so why should her grandmother still be directing her life?'

I had to admit that I had had similar thoughts on the subject.

Father offered to drive me to the Hall but I said I would prefer to take a taxi from the station. It was something I had to do entirely on my own.

The Hall was a huge house surrounded by formal gardens and a vast parkland. A tall grey-haired man opened the door to me wearing the uniform of a butler and as he grandly escorted me inside I was overwhelmed by its splendour.

'Mrs Graehme-Burrows will receive you in the morning room,' he informed me and indicated that I should follow him.

I waited behind him while he knocked on the door and announced me; then he stepped aside and I was looking across the room at a lady sitting in a large chair at the window, indicating unsmilingly that I should take the seat opposite. A small Yorkshire terrier came busily to inspect me before she called him to her side.

She was exactly as Emily had described her: a handsome woman with fine dark eyes and immaculately coiffed grey hair. I waited while she put on her glasses to give me a closer inspection, then she said, 'You're very young. I expected someone older.'

'I did give you my age in my application, Mrs Graehme Burrows.'

'Did you? Yes, I suppose you did.'

I waited while she read through my letter. I had taken particular care that morning to wear my severest clothes, a navy blue dress with a white organza collar and a navy blue boater. I was even wearing my old spectacles that had once been prescribed for me when I had an eye infection and which were more or less plain glass.

Before I had left the house I had reassured myself that I looked every inch the sort of dull but respectable young woman she would be looking for; now as she frowned over my letter I was becoming far less sure.

'You say in your letter that you travelled abroad with Miss Emily Parsons. I heard that she was travelling abroad after her father died and I doubt if her father would have approved. He was always most protective of her.' Then looking at me sharply she said, 'And with somebody so young. Where exactly did you travel to in Europe?'

'France and Italy. We went to all the wonderful places we could find, we visited the museums and the opera. It was a marvellous time for us.'

'What makes you think you would be suitable to accompany my granddaughter to these places?'

'It is for you to tell me if you think I am suitable, ma'am. I can only tell you about my previous experience. If you are looking for something else then I must apologise for wasting your time.'

For the first time I detected a gleam of real interest in her eyes and there was a half-smile on her lips when she said, 'At least you have a tongue in your head. My granddaughter can be difficult. She married very young, her husband was killed during the war and she insists on keeping the house in London when I would prefer her to be here with me. She is twenty-five years old, self-opinionated and she thinks that being a woman who has been married, however briefly, gives her the right to do exactly as she pleases.

'She has money. Her husband left her a good sum but it is in trust until she is thirty and better able to spend it wisely. Consequently she is still largely dependent on me. She is extravagant and spends freely on the wrong sort of clothes and the wrong sort of entertainment, and I am unsure about the sort of company she keeps. I have interviewed six women, none of whom was suitable; not from my point of view, from hers. This morning she is out riding in the park and refused to stay in the house to meet you.'

'Then it would seem I have had a wasted journey,' I said dismally.

'Not necessarily. You are the youngest person I have interviewed, so she might conceivably view you with more interest.'

'Is she likely to be back soon?'

'She will be curious, curious and difficult. After you have met my granddaughter you may think twice about taking on this position.'

We stared at each other solemnly, then in a lighter voice she said, 'I am not exactly giving you much encouragement, am I? But my granddaughter troubles me. I feel sure Emily Parsons wouldn't have praised you so highly if she hadn't thought you worthy of such praise. We will now see what Stephanie has to say.'

For some time we sat in silence until she suddenly said, 'I have two grandchildren. Stephanie is my daughter's child and Andrew is my son's child. Andrew is all I could desire of a grandson. He received a first-class degree at Oxford and has a position in the Foreign Office. At the moment he is in Rome. When he comes home three months from now I hope he will spend some time with Stephanie.'

'Live with her, do you mean?'

'Oh no. Andrew has a flat in London, but he could perhaps introduce her to the opera and good music instead of these good-time parties she seems to favour.'

I was beginning to feel sorry for Stephanie, a young widow coerced into marriage with a much older man, however impressive his status. I felt sure she believed a little fun was long overdue.

Once more Mrs Graehme-Burrows relapsed into silence and then we heard the loud closing of a door and footsteps crossing the hall. Then the door was flung open and I looked up to see a girl standing in the doorway wearing immaculate riding attire and brandishing a whip. She looked at me without expression, without a smile or even a welcoming nod of her head, and sharply her grandmother said, 'This is Miss Alexandra Faversham, Stephanie. It would have been polite for you to have stayed in to greet her.'

'She was your guest, Grandmother.'

'Invited on your behalf,' her grandmother snapped.

With a decidedly sulky expression she advanced into the room and took the chair opposite the older woman.

'I do so hate the smell of horseflesh in my sitting room, Stephanie, as I have told you before. Why don't you go upstairs and change, then we will have tea and you can talk to Miss Faversham.'

'Does that mean that I am to have Miss Faversham, then?'

'You did say all the others were too old. At least you can't say that in this case.'

Stephanie jumped to her feet and made for the door, and her grandmother picked up a letter that had been lying on the small table beside her chair. 'This is from Andrew,' she called. 'He will be back in England in just under three months and I intend to ask him to keep an eye on you. Andrew will know the sort of places you should go to, the sort of amusements you should indulge yourself with and the sort of company you should keep.'

Without a word Stephanie slammed the door behind her and her grandmother sighed.

'You see, Miss Faversham, you are not going to have an easy ride. Are you quite sure it is within your capabilities?'

'I will try.'

She smiled. 'Andrew will be a great help. His name is Andrew Falkener. His father and Stephanie's mother were the children of my first husband. I have been married twice. Stephanie is so like her mother and she gave me a great deal of trouble, whereas my son was more responsible and Andrew is very much like him. Do you have brothers and sisters?'

'I have two sisters. Both of them are married and older than I.'

'I see. We will talk some more about your family background with Stephanie. She tells me she intends to return to London at the end of the week. Would that present any problem for you?'

'No, although I shall have to return to my parents' home to pack. Will you require me to come back here?'

'I don't know what plans she has made; we shall have to ask her.'

When she rejoined us Stephanie was in no mood to be cooperative.

'She needn't come back here. Perhaps you will make your own way to my house in London, Miss Faversham. Or would you prefer me to call you Alexandra?'

'Most people call me Alex.'

'Then I shall call you Alex. It's much less of a mouthful.'

'Why can't you return to London together?' her grandmother asked. 'It seems far more sensible that way.'

'Because, Granny, I'm given a lift back to London in Terry Marsden's new two-seater. He wants to show it off, and we're returning to London on the same day.'

Her grandmother frowned. 'I don't want you to see too much of the Marsden boy. His parents are far from happy with him. The war has been over some considerable time and he still hasn't found himself a proper job. I know he did very well in the war, that sort of thing suited him, but since it ended all he's done is speed about in fast cars and go off to race meetings.'

'Nobody complained about Terry when he was getting himself shot at, and decorated. Surely he and people like him are entitled to have a little fun?'

'Andrew hasn't behaved like that and he too went to war and did very well.'

'Oh, Andrew, Granny! Whatever Andrew does is better

than anyone can match. I know he did well in the war and in your eyes he can do no wrong, but I like Terry. We have fun together and he's always the perfect gentleman. I'll give Alex instructions on how to find me in London.'

And that is how it was and all the way home I knew there would have to be more secrecy. How could I tell my parents that my reception had been less than welcoming, that Stephanie Vanburgh was a rude objectionable girl and that I was exchanging a life of privileged normality for something I could conceivably hate?

Instead I told them that my welcome had been charming, that Stephanie and I would become great friends and that I was looking forward to living in London.

Once more I was moving on from people I loved and friends I had made, from tea dances and a nice young man who obviously liked me very much and had great hopes that there might be more.

Emily was not deceived.

'I can hardly recognise the portrait you have painted compared with the people I remember, Alex,' she said rather sadly. 'At least not unless they've changed considerably.'

'I agree that Stephanie did seem spoiled and rather silly, but I can only do my best with her. Her grandmother was really quite nice. She talked about her grandson Andrew, and she told me she had been married twice.'

'Yes. Her first husband, Alec Falkener, was very nice. I never knew her second husband; they spent a lot of time abroad and they were only married a few years when he died quite suddenly.'

'She seemed very proud of her grandson. Did you meet him?'

'Oh yes. A very nice young man, clever, with a good position at the Foreign Office, totally different from Stephanie. Honestly, Alex, I'm not at all happy about things. I wish I'd never shown you that magazine.'

I laughed, more light-heartedly than I felt. 'Do stop worrying, Emily, I'm looking forward to living in London. I'll write often and let you know how I'm making out.'

I looked at myself in the mirror and decided I had to change and the first thing was to get my hair restyled. I was remembering Stephanie's bobbed hair and skirts considerably shorter than my own. I remembered her ridiculous high heels and long painted fingernails, and I realised that ahead of me was a new life, one the war years had created with a new generation that had seen the old world crumbling in a storm of death and gunfire.

Now they were clutching at life with a desperate fervour to shut out what had gone before and embrace with foolish optimism an unknown future.

My mother deplored my blonde bobbed hair. 'But you had such pretty hair, Alex! What a pity to have had it cut short when you were always so pretty.'

So I didn't show her my new short dresses with their fringed skirts and low necklines, or the towering heels on my new shoes. I was optimistic in thinking I would be invited to Stephanie's parties; maybe she would keep me severely in my place as a paid companion, but strangely enough it was Mother was said, 'Didn't the opera come into your conversation? You'll need to pack something suitable for such an occasion.'

Mother had no conception of what might be expected of a paid companion, but even so I decided to include one of my grander dresses in my suitcase. Perhaps Stephanie's cousin could be relied upon to escort us to the opera, and as I folded the wild silk gown I reflected that Stephanie Vanburgh was in for a good number of surprises. She would be expecting the plain girl in good sensible clothes and wearing glasses that did her no favours; either I was about to astound her or displease her, but at least I would soon know how my future would be resolved.

Stephanie did nothing to welcome me. When I arrived at her house in London I found a large lady cleaning the brass door knocker who said, 'If you're wantin' Mrs Vanburgh, miss, she's just gone out. Milly'll see to ye.'

Milly was summoned and proved to be a pretty pert young housemaid who regarded me and my suitcase with some curiosity.

'The missus didn't tell me we were expecting guests,' she said.

'I'm Miss Faversham and she was expecting me this morning.'

'I only saw her for a few minutes when I took in her morning tea, then she went out. You'd best come in, miss. I'm not sure where she'll want to put you.'

I smiled at her sympathetically. 'Does she often do things like this to you?' I said gently.

'Oh, miss, all the time. She was out gallivanting last night, and I never heard what time she came in. I'll put you in the side bedroom. If it's not right she'll change you around.'

'Thank you, Milly.'

She made no effort to help me with my suitcase and I received a sympathetic look from the woman now mopping the front steps.

The room she showed me into was pretty with flowered chintz at the window and on the bed; there was a plain green carpet on the floor and a large wardrobe and dressing table.

'Mrs Vanburgh has her own bathroom but there's one next door, miss. Would you like a cup o' tea?'

'I would love one. I've come all the way from Devon and I had breakfast very early.'

'When you've unpacked, if you'll go into the drawing room I'll bring you one in. Just ring the bell over the fireplace.'

After she had gone I sat down weakly on the bed to contemplate what I might expect from the future. Obviously I was not a welcome guest and as the day wore on depression started to set in. For one thing I was hungry. Milly had provided me with cups of tea and biscuits but she seemed not to know when she could expect her mistress back or when dinner would be on the table.

I could hear rain pattering on the window and Milly came in to add coal to the fire and draw the curtains. Anxiously I looked at the clock. It was just after five; Mrs Purvis, the cleaner, had gone home, Milly I found in the kitchen sitting at the table with a magazine in front of her and there was crockery in the sink which told me that she at least had eaten.

'I don't know what to do. I need a meal, so perhaps I should go out. Is there a café or something nearby?'

'Oh no, miss, it's very residential round 'ere, you'd 'ave

to go on the High Street. I'm sure Mrs Vanburgh'll be in soon, she's nearly allus in afore six.'

'But where does she go?'

'To the hairdresser's, to the shops, to meet friends for a gossip. She'll remember that you're comin' today, I'm sure.'

Miserably I walked upstairs and sat on my bed. Surely there was food in the kitchen but Milly had offered no suggestions and the hunger pains were increasing. I went to stare out of the window and realised for the first time how much like Stevenson Square it was, a large square lined with tall trees and imposing Georgian house, its pavements lashed with rain.

Just then a taxi drew up in front of the house and a woman jumped out and ran lightly up to the house. Miss Stephanie had come home.

I was unsure whether to go downstairs or wait in my bedroom but after a few moments I heard voices downstairs and then my bedroom door was flung open unceremoniously and Stephanie Vanburgh stood in the doorway with a bright smile on her face and absolutely no contrition.

'I'd forgotten that it was today when you were coming,' she said. 'I'm glad Milly looked after you. I was at a party last night and it was early this morning when I got in. I'm sure you'll understand why I forgot. Have you eaten?'

'I had tea and biscuits.'

She laughed. 'I have a few friends dropping in this evening and I've asked caterers to come in. If you don't want to join us Milly will bring you something up here.'

'I would really like something now. Apart from breakfast, tea and biscuits is all I have had to eat today,' I said firmly.

'Very well, I'll ask Milly to rustle something up for you.

I really don't mind if you don't join us; you won't know anybody and you could be very bored. We'll have a long talk in the morning to decide where we go from here. You'll probably be glad of an early night.'

So that was it. Milly served me a lacklustre meal that did little to assuage my hunger, and as I lay in bed all I could hear was the sound of laughter and loud music from downstairs so that sleep was a long time coming. Not for the first time in my life I asked myself why I seemed to have given up the substance for the shadow.

CHAPTER TWENTY-ONE

I PULLED BACK the curtains to reveal a pale wintery sun illuminating the square and a boy delivering newspapers came whistling cheerfully along the pavement. I looked down to see that Milly had opened the front door and was taking the newspaper from the boy, who grinned at her cheekily.

There were no other sounds from within the house and I suspected that Stephanie would not be an early riser. I went down into the kitchen. Milly looked up from where she was making toast, asking, 'Would ye like it served in the breakfast room, miss? I can do bacon and egg if you'd like some.'

'No thank you, Milly, just toast and I'll eat it in here with you. Did the party go on some time? I fell asleep eventually.'

She smiled. 'They used to keep me awake but not any more, I reckon I'm used to 'em now.'

'How long have you worked for Mrs Vanburgh, Milly?'

'Nigh on four years. I worked for another family across the way but they had a cook, right martinet she were, said I was harum-scarum and'd never learn so when I heard Mrs Vanburgh was lookin' out for somebody I came here.'

'And have you been happy here?'

'Oh yes, most o' the time. She's easy goin' and 'ardly ever in. O' course I have to look after her guests when she throws a party and that's pretty often, but I knows how to serve the right drinks and I tries to look the part.'

'Have you always been in service?'

'Yes, miss. I left school at twelve at the end o' the war and there wasn't much for girls, was there. I'd like to 'ave gone into a shop but I was never as clever as me sister. She works in one o' the big shops in the West End, she's prettier than me, and she talks proper but she gets so mad at me sometimes.'

'Why is that?'

'Well, she knows 'ow to dress and she can buy clothes at a discount, but Mrs Vanburgh gives me things, things she's got tired of, and I likes to flaunt 'em in front o' me sister and it makes 'er furious.'

'I'm sure it does.'

'I reckon you'll be comin' in for her clothes now, miss, bein' 'er companion, like.'

'Oh no, Milly, I can assure you I am in no need of Mrs Vanburgh's clothes. I have my own.'

'But I doubt you'll 'ave the sort o' clothes necessary for the things she likes to do, miss, and you're only her paid companion, after all.'

'I know, but I do have a little money put by, enough to buy decent clothes anyway.'

She looked uncertainly at my plain beige skirt and cream silk blouse. They had been expensive country clothes but Milly's mind was on party frocks and dancing shoes. To change the subject I said, 'Doesn't Mrs Vanburgh eat breakfast?'

'Only when 'er grandmother's visitin', which isn't very often.'

'Doesn't she have other guests?'

She grinned at me slyly. 'Only Mr Gantry and occasionally Mr Marsden, who's an old friend, she tells me.'

From the look on Milly's face I was reluctant to speculate on the relationship with Mr Gantry and as if suspecting my thoughts she said quickly, 'I reckon she's very fond o' Mr Gantry and he is very good-lookin'. Do you 'ave a gentleman friend, Miss Faversham?'

'Not a very close one at the moment.'

She blushed. 'Well I 'ave two: Bob, who's a window cleaner, and Alec, who's a policeman. Nothin' serious, but they took me to the circus in the summer.'

'Both of them?'

'They both asked me and I couldn't decide which to go with, so we all three went.'

I laughed. I had no great hopes of my new employment but Milly at least would be a distraction.

'What time do you suppose Mrs Vanburgh will be up?' I asked.

She shrugged her shoulders. 'Can't tell, miss. Why don't ye take a walk out? It's not a bad mornin' and it's nice in the park.'

'Yes I might do that, Milly. If Mrs Vanburgh comes down will you tell her I won't be long, because we really do have to talk.'

She was right about the morning. It was fresh and cold but there were children playing in the park and wildfowl splashing about in the lake. All around me were the imposing buildings of London and as I stared at them memories of Vienna

came rushing back to me; tears filled my eyes and rolled un-
checked down my cheeks.

For months I had shut out all thoughts of Vienna and a past
that seemed singularly remote, but this morning they
suddenly felt strangely more powerful than they should have.
Angrily I told myself that it was over, that I was recalling a
romantic dream in the heart and mind of a romantic girl, but
I did not want the past to haunt me forever. One day it would
have to go, never to return.

Milly met me in the hall when I returned to the house, whispering, 'She's in the drawing room, miss, and she's bin askin'
for you.'

So hurriedly I took off my outdoor clothing and went to
learn something of what to expect from my future. I found
Stephanie stretched out on a sofa in front of the fire with a
magazine in her hands and a petulant expression on her face.

'Where have you been? I thought you didn't know people
in London.'

'I've been walking in the park.'

'We have to talk, Alex. I'm not really sure what to do with
you.'

I took the seat opposite her but didn't answer, and after a
few seconds she said, 'You are my grandmother's idea. I
don't require a watchdog and I do have my own life to lead.
I really don't mind your being here, but I'm sure you will
agree that we should go our separate ways.'

'Your grandmother is paying me to be your companion, to
accompany you to concerts and exhibitions, to encourage you
to enjoy music and literature. Isn't that what you thought
too?'

'Yes, it's what she wants, but it's not what I want.'

'Then I am getting my pay under false pretences.'

'Why should it worry you? You are free to do exactly what you want and go where you want. My grandmother doesn't need to know anything about us, and when she visits then we can simply pretend otherwise. Of course she'll get Andrew to look us up and no doubt she'll ask him to take us to the opera, but he needn't know any different either.'

'What you are saying is that we both lie to your grand-mother. Doesn't that strike you as being very dishonest?'

'No, it doesn't. She's always interfered in my life. She did the same with my mother; I agreed to marry Henry to get away from her but then when he died there I was back in her clutches again. Did you never want to live your own life, get away from people who were trying to run it for you?'

'Yes I did, and I am very ashamed at the way I did it. I'm sure your grandmother is only trying to do the best for you.'

'Henry was domineering. He called me his child bride, because I was seventeen and he was thirty. My grandmother thought he'd be good for me, teach me common sense and decorum. Well, he didn't have time, he was killed in the war and I can't even get the money he left me until I'm thirty.'

'How can you afford to live in this house and spend money the way you do, then?'

'The house is mine and he left enough to pay for its upkeep. It's the bulk of the money I can't get my hands on. So what do you say, Alex? Let me live my life and you go to your stuffy museums and boring concerts. You'll meet people like yourself, make new friends, and you can treat this place like a first-class hotel. I shan't mind.'

'But I shall mind very much, Stephanie. I promised your grandmother that I would try to be your friend and companion and I intend to keep that promise.'

She stared at me angrily. 'You won't like the sort of parties I enjoy, or the sort of people I'm with.'

'How do you know?'

'Probably by the way you dress, like a schoolmarm. I had a teacher who looked like you: plain clothes and spectacles, but at least you've had your hair styled—I suppose that's something.'

'So where do we go from here?'

'Tonight I'm going to a nightclub with friends. You won't like it but you can come with us. After tonight I doubt you'll want to come with us again. If you haven't the right dress you can borrow one of mine, since we're about the same size, although you are a little taller. The dresses I have are short, so they'll be far shorter on you.'

'I don't think I shall need to borrow from you, Stephanie. I would like to think I have the appropriate apparel.'

Her expression did little to agree with me; however with a brief shrug of her shoulders she said, 'The nightclub is a favourite of ours and is very expensive. We are a crowd of girls and young men who have all known each other for some time, but I'm not sure if any of the young men will be to your taste.'

She got up from the sofa and swept towards the door. I could cheerfully have shaken her; she was spoilt and rude, but today was not the day to remonstrate with her. There would be a better time, I told myself.

She gave me no further information about the evening

ahead of us and she was out of the house for most of the afternoon. I heard her come in and go straight up to her bedroom so I too decided to get ready for the evening ahead.

I stared doubtfully at my new dress, which had been ridiculously expensive. It lay on my bed, a confection of turquoise wild silk, shorter than usual, with a tiered skirt of which the last tier was a fringe of heavy silk threads. It was only when I stood at last in front of the long cheval mirror that I became fully aware of the transformation from a well-brought-up country girl to a modern city flapper.

From my blonde bobbed head to the gold high-heeled dancing slippers on my feet I was a totally new and manufactured woman, far removed from that other me in a more gracious, less brittle world.

I waited in the drawing room for Stephanie to put in an appearance, unsure of how she was going to welcome the new me, and indeed when she stood in the doorway staring at me in comical astonishment I was unprepared for her laughter and her sudden rush across the room to take me in her arms.

'Alex, you're gorgeous! Why did you put on such ugly clothes? Why the spectacles and the long skirts, why the prim and proper you when you're so beautiful?'

'Your grandmother would never have engaged me looking like this,' I replied doubtfully.

She trilled with laughter. 'Of course not. I'd have wanted you and she'd have thought I was mad. Now here you are looking like this and we're going to have such fun. The men will all fall in love with you, but you have to promise not to flirt with mine, although you're welcome to the others.'

'And who is yours?'

'His name is Roger Gantry. I'm absolutely mad about him and he about me, I hope.'

'Have you known him long?'

'Long enough. I met him during the war at some regimental thing I went to with Henry. My cousin Andrew was his commanding officer but that night Henry got stuck with his cronies and it left me free to dance with other men. Roger was attentive, Andrew was critical, Henry never noticed and it's gone on from there.'

'Even when you were married.'

'Especially because I was married. Henry was stodgy and proper; Roger was audacious and full of life. He took me to nightclubs and dances after Henry went to France, then Roger too went away and I didn't see him until after the war. Then Henry was dead and I thought providence had brought him back into my life.'

'But you're not sure if he feels the same way about you, are you, Stephanie?'

'Why do you say that? I have other friends who express their doubts, and my grandmother is particularly against it, but why you, Alex? You're new on the scene.'

'I sensed it. Does your grandmother know him?'

'Heavens no. He wouldn't be her choice. If ever I marry again she'd like it to be somebody like Andrew: solid, dependable, and solvent.'

'And Roger isn't?'

'He's mad about cars and horses, and he's talking about going abroad, tea-planting or some such ridiculous notion.'

'And would you go with him?'

'I'd go to the moon with him if he asked me. I'll have

enough money for both of us, but will he want to wait until I'm thirty?'

'He will if he loves you.'

'I suppose so. Have you ever been in love, Alex? You're a couple of years older than me. Did you never meet a man you wanted to marry?'

'Yes. I met somebody once, but it was abroad. He was Austrian and I'm English, and it would never have worked out.'

'Why ever not?'

'Well, for one thing the war came. One day if you're interested I'll tell you a little about it but not tonight, there isn't time.'

Indeed at that moment we heard the sound of laughter from outside the house and then the pealing of the front bell and Stephanie said, 'They're here, have you a wrap?'

'Yes, a silk one.'

'You won't be nearly warm enough with that. Borrow one of mine—I'll ask Milly to bring it in.'

The guests were largely Stephanie's age, a bevy of young pretty girls, similarly attired, and young men in evening dress, charming and cheerful. There was a lot of laughter followed by warm embraces and I was being introduced as Stephanie's friend Alex Faversham from the country.

Milly served drinks, then in no time we were driving through the city streets in three small fast cars and I sat in the back of one of them with a young man's arm around my shoulders, wearing Stephanie's blue velvet wrap edged with arctic fox.

The nightclub was well patronised by groups of men and girls of a similar age. The wine flowed freely, the air was filled with sounds of merriment and of saxophones and I reflected somewhat sadly that it had taken a war to change everything so dramatically. From waltz music to the stridency of jazz music, from elegance and gracious surroundings to this noisy desperation for enjoyment the new world called living.

The girl standing next to me said, 'Stephanie's in a mood, look at her face.'

Indeed Stephanie's expression was one of acute misery and the girl said, 'He said he was coming, I heard him promise faithfully that he'd be here, but one never knows with Roger. I'd send him packing, but she won't; she's mad about him.'

'Do you know him well?'

'He's one of the crowd. The more she shows she's crazy about him the more he behaves like this.'

'Then he really isn't worth bothering with, is he?'

'If you two are friends have a word in her ear. She might listen to you—she won't listen to us.'

'I doubt if she'd paying attention to me.'

'Oh well, she's in for a fall. He'll not commit himself to anybody until he's certain she's got money, and Stephanie has it coming, but it's some time off.'

'He knows that, does he?'

'Heavens, yes. He'll have made very sure about that.'

Just then two young men approached to invite us to dance, dancing that stayed on one spot because there wasn't room for anything else.

Stephanie had little conversation on the way home and immediately we reached the house she pranced up to the front door with barely a smile for the boy driving the car or his companion.

The evening had degenerated into a disaster and now like

a spoilt child she was poking at the dying fire and grumbling, 'Heavens, but it's cold in here. I really don't think Milly's up to things; I'm going to have to find somebody else.'

'It's after three in the morning,' I said.

Without answering she allowed her wrap to fall on to the floor and moved over to the drinks cabinet.

'Drink?' she asked.

'No, thank you. What is wrong, Stephanie?'

'Why should there be anything wrong?'

'You haven't exactly been the life and soul of the party, have you, so there must be a reason.'

She poured herself a drink and stood regarding me with stormy eyes. 'If you must know, it's Roger Gantry. He promised faithfully that he would join us this evening and he didn't come.'

'And that matters very much?'

'Well, of course. How can he be in love with me when he breaks so many promises?'

'Why are you still in love with him when he does that?'

'Oh, it's not altogether his fault. He does love me but he needs money more. His family won't help him out and my money is all tied up the way Henry left it.'

'It's probably well invested and likely to make more.'

'What do you know about it? If you knew anything about money you'd hardly be a paid companion, would you?'

She was in no mood to listen to any argument and I was sorely tempted to slap her.

'I'm going to bed,' I said evenly. 'Thank you for the loan of your wrap and I'll see you for breakfast.'

'A real companion would be anxious to listen to my problems and help if she could.'

'Stephanie, I will listen to your problems even though I doubt you would take any advice from me, but not at this time in the morning and not when you are so angry. Perhaps there was a good reason why Mr Gantry couldn't come. At least he should be allowed to explain.'

'How many explanations am I expected to listen to?'

'That is something only you can decide. Goodnight, Stephanie.'

Sleep was a long time in coming. I did not have to put up with Stephanie and her tantrums; Emily had warned me about her and with my usual optimism and carelessness I had disregarded everything she had said. Now I had only myself to blame. What would tomorrow bring? I asked myself dismally.

CHAPTER TWENTY-TWO

I WAS EATING breakfast alone when I heard her come downstairs but instead of joining me I heard the slamming of the front door. Next moment Milly's face appeared round the door and she said, 'She's gone out, miss, and she's 'ad no breakfast.'

'Perhaps she's gone to post a letter,' I ventured.

'Oh no, miss, she's all dressed up. I reckon she's meeting somebody.'

'Well there's nothing we can do, Milly.'

'The more I stays 'ere the more I thinks I've made a mistake,' she moaned. 'What about you, miss?'

'Perhaps.'

'I reckon I should 'ave worked 'arder at school to make somethin' of meself. I thinks now I would 'ave bin all right in a shop.'

'But you might not have met a nice window cleaner or policeman,' I said with a smile.

'There'd a bin other pebbles on the beach though—p'raps a nice winder dresser or shop assistant.'

'Things will get better, Milly. She had a disappointment last night that upset her a bit, that's all.'

'I expect it was 'im, Mr Gantry. They'll be off each other for a week or two then it'll all blow over and she'll be smilin' again. It never lasts.'

In my heart I had to agree with her, but what of the rest of my day? Did I go out or stay in and wait for her return? Did I suggest some sort of venture into the art galleries her grandmother had been hoping for, a suggestion I felt sure would be received with scant enthusiasm?

I ate a solitary lunch and was preparing to go out when there was a ring at the front door and seconds later Milly came in to announce that Mr Gantry was here to see Mrs Vanburgh.

There was nothing else for it but to invite him in and I saw immediately the sort of charm he would have for Stephanie. He was tall and good-looking, with a disarming smile that seemed to tell me he had been anxious to meet me all morning.

'I'm so sorry Mrs Vanburgh is out,' I said quickly, 'and I have no idea when she will be back.'

'Then we should get to know each other,' he said easily. 'I met Dolly Ewart this morning and she told me Stephanie had a friend staying with her. I feel absolutely terrible that I didn't join you last night but something cropped up that I simply couldn't get out of. I'm sure Stephanie'll understand after I've explained.'

'Would you like tea, Mr Gantry, or perhaps something stronger?'

'Oh no, tea will be fine. You are from the country, I believe. Would that be Devon?'

'Yes.'

'I've met Stephanie's grandmother who lives in Devon, briefly, rather a formidable lady. Is she also a relative of yours?'

'No. We have met but I do not know her well.'

'Apparently I missed a delightful evening last night, but I'm sure there will be many others. Are you staying in London for some time?'

'Perhaps. I have no plans to leave at the moment.'

'Well, we must give you a very good time, we have all the ingredients for it. You didn't tell me your name.'

'No, I'm sorry, it's Alex Faversham.'

'As in Alexandra?'

'Yes.'

'It's a favourite with me, and such a pity to shorten it, don't you think.'

'I've always been Alex to the family, Mr Gantry. I'm used to it.'

'Please call me Roger. I'm sure we're going to be great friends.'

I smiled without comment and he went on, 'What do you two girls intend to do together in London? Shops, I suppose, and afternoon tea dances—they are very popular.'

'That rather surprises me. I would have thought most young men would be busy with their occupations.'

'True, but there are ways and means. So many of us are only just beginning to find something suitable after serving in the armed forces. I was in the army for almost four years, and I don't want to clutch at straws, as I'm sure you'll understand.'

'We intend to visit the theatre, and hopefully some of the art galleries here. I do not know London very well.'

He laughed. 'The theatre certainly, Stephanie knows the

sort of thing she likes, but I hardly think art galleries would
be to her taste. You are going to be very good for her, Alex.'

'I hope so.'

'Any other rewarding venues in mind?'

'The opera perhaps.'

This time he threw back his head and laughed, and faced
with my surprised expression he said quickly, 'I am sorry, you
evidently enjoy the opera.'

'I believe Stephanie's cousin is inviting us to accompany him
to the opera one evening, but I'm not sure when that is to be.'

'Andrew Falkener?'

'Yes. I gather he was your commanding officer.'

'He was, but no, I can't say I really know him well. Apart
from winning the war we would have had little in common.'

'I have never met him either.'

'He's a nice enough chap. Done very well in the Foreign
Office, but then he has the right background. His father was
a brigadier and his grandfather a general, I believe.' He consulted his watch. 'I'm going to have to leave you, my dear; it
doesn't look as if Stephanie's in a hurry to get home and I do
have another appointment. Please tell her I'll be in touch very
soon and that I am very sorry to have missed her.'

I accompanied him to the front door and he was halfway
down the path when a taxi drew up at the front gate and
Stephanie stepped out of it.

I did not wait to see how they greeted each other but went
into the kitchen carrying the tea tray with me. Milly took it from
me with a mischievous smile and for want of something better
to do I sat at the kitchen table while she busied herself at the sink.

'I suppose it'll all be on again and she'll forgive 'im,' she said.

'I don't know, Milly.'

''E's good lookin', I'll say that for 'im, but where's it goin'? 'E'll 'ave a good excuse and that's for sure.'

We heard the sound of the front door closing, then the kitchen door opened and Stephanie beamed at us. The dour face of the evening before was now wreathed in smiles and she trilled, 'I've been shopping. Do come and look at what I've bought.'

Her purchases were spread out across the drawing-room floor and it was obvious she had consoled herself by spending a great deal of money.

She laughed at the evident dismay on my face. 'I know what you're thinking, that I've been too extravagant and when am I going to wear all these things, but I assure you I will. I've been with the girls and we've loads of things lined up: parties, and there are some new shows coming to town that we all want to see. I expect they'll invite you.'

'Stephanie, that isn't why I'm here. Besides, I don't have the clothes or the money for the things you're talking about.'

'Don't worry about that, the men will pay for us.'

'I thought you said most of them were short of money.'

'Yes, for marriage perhaps, but not for enjoying themselves.'

'And have you forgiven Mr Gantry?'

'Oh yes, poor darling. He's staying with his Aunt Maud in Highgate. The old girl is rich and she dotes on him, but unfortunately she calls the tune and he has to be there when she needs him. Last night she wasn't well and he couldn't get away.'

'Doesn't he have a place of his own?'

'He did have, but keeping it up was terribly expensive and when she told him he could move in with her it solved a lot of problems.'

'And created others, I expect.'

'Well yes, but with luck the end will justify the means.'

'I'll help you carry these upstairs,' I said. 'I'm not surprised your husband rationed you for money.'

She laughed. 'Oh well, thirty isn't too far away. I'm glad he didn't make it forty.'

Together we collected her parcels and she said, 'Tomorrow we're going to Maisie Leadbetter's do in Belgravia. If you haven't anything suitable I can lend you one of mine—one or two of them might recognise it but don't worry about that.'

After we had deposited the parcels on her bed I turned to her.

'Stephanie, I'm not being fair to your grandmother. This really isn't why she engaged me, to dance all night at one party after the next. When I suggest art galleries and museums you're not interested, and yet that surely is why I'm here, to put a little bit of culture back into your life.'

'If you're so interested in art galleries, you go. Granny won't know any different.'

There was no reasoning with her and as she set about hanging her new purchases in the wardrobe she took out a short silk dress. It was black heavy georgette, unadorned and sophisticated, and with a little chuckle she said, 'Henry liked me in black. He said it made me look more grown-up but I hated it and I've never worn it since he died. It will suit you beautifully with your blonde hair, you can have it if you like.'

I looked at her doubtfully. I did not need Stephanie's clothes. Franz had made me a rich woman and my family was more than affluent; it seemed to me at that moment that all my life had been a deception, and one of my making.

* * *

The next few weeks consisted of a merry-go-round that turned incessantly in a world hungering for the years it had lost. Young men who had seen the horrors of war and girls who had watched them walk blindly into torment; now life had to be lived, however aimless, however confusing.

It seemed that the wailing of saxophones would never stop. I heard it in my dreams, in every waking moment, and it seemed that there was too much laughter; or was it simply me with too many memories?

I was something of a mystery to some of those young men, Stephanie's friend they'd only just heard of. They talked among themselves: where had I come from; did I have any money; and a good many of them flirted with me while several would have preferred something more serious.

Stephanie was amused.

'Most of them are younger sons,' she said, smiling. 'They're looking for some rich girl their mothers would approve of. If you tell them Granny's paid you to be my companion they'll disappear like a summer storm.'

Her words annoyed me, but I also realised the truth of them. Roger Gantry was showing her every attention and she was happy to bask in his more than obvious adulation. I was well aware that he asked questions about me and was cynical enough to wonder to myself if he thought I was worth cultivating.

The bombshell fell at the breakfast table several weeks later. 'Oh, no,' Stephanie cried, staring down at the letter in her hand. 'Why does she have to spoil everything, just when we were enjoying ourselves?'

I looked at her angry face and decided to wait.

'My grandmother is coming to London! Here, read her letter.'

Her grandmother had been experiencing hearing problems and was coming up to London to see a specialist. She would prefer to stay with Stephanie rather than in some hotel and she expected to be in London for just over a week.

I handed the letter back and Stephanie said peevishly, 'She's done this before. She always has a very good excuse for coming here but she spoils everything. We have to go to the theatre, some boring play or other, and take tea with people she knew years ago. We have so many things lined up, Alex! What am I going to say to Roger? She doesn't like him so he won't be able to call and it is my house, after all.'

'It's only a week, Stephanie.'

'It's a week when we have things we want to do, places we want to go. What about you? You'll have to wear those silly glasses and get back into those country clothes.'

'I always looked forward to seeing my grandmother. Don't you have any affection for her?'

'Some, I suppose, but perhaps your grandmother wasn't an interfering martinet like mine. Henry always got along with her; he talked the way she talked and she thought he'd change me and make me more responsible. I'm sure she regarded it as a great inconvenience when he was killed during the war.'

Her bad mood continued for most of the day, and there were long telephone calls to a great many of her friends and one very long impassioned one to Roger Gantry.

He appeared in the early evening; I could hear their voices, hers tearful, his reasoning, and then without a word they went out together.

I told Milly about the advent of Mrs Graehme-Burrows and

her expression said it all. It would seem Stephanie was not the only one who was not looking forward to the old lady's visit.

Her first words to me when we sat down to afternoon tea on the day of her arrival were, 'You've had your hair cut. I thought you had very pretty hair, I don't much like this new-fangled boy's look. I preferred yours long, Stephanie, and this new style is so unfeminine.'

'It's far more fashionable, Granny,' Stephanie answered.

'Like too-short skirts and ridiculous spiky heels,' the old lady snapped. 'When you get to my age your feet won't be fit for anything and you'll probably need surgery to put them right.'

We were relieved that first night when she decided to go to bed early. I did not take her complaints too seriously, but Stephanie had very little humour about her grandmother.

She informed us the next day that her grandson was return-ing from Italy within the next two weeks. 'I shall ask Andrew to escort you to the opera. I've written to him so I'm sure he'll be in touch as soon as he returns to London.'

'Does it have to be the opera, Granny?' Stephanie asked. 'Why can't it be one of the new musicals? Surely Andrew will ask which we prefer.'

'No doubt he will—it is I who have asked him to take you to the opera. Andrew likes music; he's cultured and educated. I wish you were more like him.'

I was beginning to think that Andrew might be something of a prig and that I would not warm to him. Besides, what would he think of my role in his cousin's life? Aware of my anxiety, the old lady said, 'I have told Andrew that you are here, Alex, and I have told him why. You will be invited to accompany him along with Stephanie and both of you must wear something appropriate for the occasion.'

I was as pleased as Stephanie when the week came to an end, but not for the same reasons. I was hating the spectacles and the governess look I was expected to wear and I was wishing I'd listened to Emily's misgivings and the doubts of my parents.

We saw the old lady off at the station and listened to more of her strictures then with lighter hearts we ate afternoon tea at the Waldorf before returning to the house. Off went the spectacles and the blouse and skirt and we heard the sound of Milly singing in the kitchen, something she hadn't done for days.

We were back to tea dances and parties, back to brittle conversation and the wailing of saxophones.

It seemed to me that there was some sort of secrecy in Stephanie's dealings with Roger Gantry. They were always whispering together in quiet corners and there was a great deal of amusement among her friends.

She was out of the house the afternoon her cousin Andrew Falkener telephoned and it was left to me to speak to him. He had a nice voice, clipped and low-pitched, and when I explained that Stephanie was out he said, 'Am I speaking to Miss Faversham? My grandmother explained the situation to me.'

'Yes, this is Alex Faversham.'

'My grandmother has suggested that I escort you both to the opera, but before I do so I thought I should ask a few questions. Do you enjoy the opera, Miss Faversham?'

'Very much, but I haven't seen a great many of them.'

'Unfortunately Stephanie prefers something lighter, and I

don't want to have to drag her screaming to something she positively hates.'

'No, I'm sure you don't, Mr Falkener.'

'Have you any suggestions?'

'She has talked about several musicals and revues, but then they wouldn't satisfy her grandmother.'

He laughed. 'No indeed, and we don't want to cheat her, do we? Perhaps I should call to see her within these next few days and we can talk about it together. Do please tell her that I telephoned and that I will be in touch later in the week.'

He sounded reasonable and agreeable and I tried to put a face to him: somebody rather grave with a distinct charm, a man who could be kind, a man who would know how to deal with Stephanie.

More and more I was worried about Stephanie. I had thought we were becoming friends; now she had become wary of me and I sensed there were many things going on in her life that she was keeping from me.

One minute she seemed desolate, the next she was emotional; each day her moods swung from one extreme to the other and behind it all I suspected Roger Gantry was the cause.

CHAPTER TWENTY-THREE

STEPHANIE RECEIVED THE news of her cousin's telephone call with poor grace.

'This is all Grandmother's doing,' she wailed. 'She knows I don't like the opera! Why must she interfere, and just when we were having such a good time?'

'Don't you think it would be very ungracious of you to sulk about it? After all it's not as though Mr Falkener is spending every evening with you—it's just the one occasion.'

'Did he say how long he was to be in London for?'

'No. He said he would either telephone or call to see you.'

'I should wear your glasses and your prim and proper dress; if Andrew has a choice I'm sure it would lean to some woman who is something of a blue stocking.'

'He sounded very nice.'

'Some of my friends think he's quite dishy in a remote sort of way, although I doubt if he'd give any one of them a second glance.'

I made up my mind that I would be out when Andrew Falkener paid a visit. I had kept up some sort of pretence for her grandmother, but I didn't see why I should have to do so for her cousin. Consequently I made an excuse to go to the shops, and in spite of her protests I stayed out until I felt sure he would have departed.

'What an age you've been,' she complained. 'You should have been here to back me up. Isn't that what Granny's paying you for?'

'She is paying me for a great deal that I am unable to do because you are objecting to it. There really is no need for me to accompany you and Mr Falkener to the opera.'

'We're not going to the opera, we're going to the ballet instead. I must say Andrew is showing some sympathy. We shall have to dress up; I'm not even sure if I have anything for the grand occasion but Granny said everybody makes an effort for the opera and the ballet.'

'Perhaps you'd like to see if I have anything suitable? You can borrow anything you like.'

'Don't be silly, Alex. If I'm not likely to have anything, you're even less likely.'

'What are we going to see?'

'*The Nutcracker*. I've seen it before, many years ago, when I desperately wanted dancing lessons. I fancied myself as a ballerina, but Granny thought marriage would suit me better.'

'Are you quite sure I am to be invited?'

'Quite sure, he's had his instructions from Granny.'

It was an evening I was not looking forward to and as I surveyed myself in the long mirror in my bedroom I began to have doubts.

The dress I had chosen was one I had worn for the ballet in St Petersburg a great many years ago, but it was graceful and beautiful and perhaps even now there was a place for it in modern London.

Stephanie stared at me in amazement. She was wearing a long evening dress that she had probably had a good many years but even so it lacked the glamour of the one I had no doubt worn for a far grander occasion.

'Gracious me,' she said. 'You look like some duchess. Where on earth did you get a dress like that from?'

'I've had it a long time, from another life.'

'What a dark horse you are, Alex! I'll need to know a lot more about you and that dress, but not now, there goes the bell.'

I knew him instantly. The last time I had seen him was years before when he collected his luggage prior to leaving the train at Salzburg. There was no sign that he remembered me as he took my hand in a firm grip and smiled his greeting.

His dark hair was silvered at the temples, although the face was the same, a cool serious face, with grey searching eyes. But his smile was warm and Stephanie was saying airily, 'Doesn't Alex look very grand? I can't hold a candle to her.'

'You both look very nice,' he said. 'I suppose Grandmother advised you to dress up.'

'Of course, we have to do justice to you and the ballet. I'm so glad it wasn't the opera, Andrew. Everybody always dies in opera.'

He smiled. 'I hope next week to take you both to experience the vitality of *Carmen*. That is one opera I think you might enjoy.'

'Oh Andrew, not another one! Somebody will die in that.'

'Yes, but there is more to *Carmen* than death. Are you ready, girls? The taxi is waiting.'

* * *

In spite of Stephanie's sulky expression I was enraptured by the music and the wonderful dancing but, much more than that, by the atmosphere of elegantly clad women and men in evening dress. I was reminded of that other opera house in far-off Vienna; only the uniforms were missing and if I closed my eyes it was possible to imagine the Austrian national anthem as the Emperor took his place in the royal box.

After the performance Andrew entertained us to supper in a most exclusive restaurant and it was only when he finally deposited us on the front doorstep that Stephanie asked, 'How long are you staying in London, Andrew?'

'A couple of weeks, then I am going to stay with the parents in Devonshire.'

'Then you'll be able to report to Granny that you've done your duty nobly and that will be the end to it.'

He merely smiled, ignoring the waspishness behind her words, and as he saw us inside the house he said briefly, 'I'll be in touch. Goodnight, girls.'

Inside the house Stephanie said, 'It could have been worse, I suppose, one ballet and one opera. Andrew will have done his duty and then he can conveniently forget about us.'

Irritated by her attitude I snapped, 'Doesn't it occur to you that you should be grateful, Stephanie? The ballet was wonderful and your cousin was gallant and very generous. Why can't you be grateful for once?'

'Because I would have preferred to be with Roger. Tonight wasn't my favourite kind of evening.'

Nothing I might have said would have made any difference. Stephanie was obdurate in her defiance and it stemmed from things in her past that I had no conception of. A girl pushed into marriage, a girl whose mother had been less than perfect and a grandmother who had in the end despaired of both of them.

'You can please yourself what you do about tomorrow,' she said from halfway up the stairs. 'I'm meeting Roger for lunch and then we're going to some place to watch a polo match.'

'And you'll enjoy that better than *The Nutcracker*?'

'I'll be with Roger—with him I'd enjoy a revolution.'

It was easy at that moment to forget the joy I had found in the evening at the ballet. All the restless urges of my life came to plague me as I struggled to go to sleep. Would I ever be content to be happy with normality? Why did I always need more? I felt that Stephanie was a disaster waiting to happen.

I saw hardly anything of her during the next week. It was I who spoke to Andrew on the telephone, and when I informed him yet another time that she was out of the house he said, 'I understood my grandmother to say you were her companion and yet you are rarely together. What sort of commitment do you actually have to my cousin?'

Stung by his criticism I said sharply, 'I think commitment works both ways. Stephanie has made it very clear she needs her own way to be with her chosen friends, not friends who have been selected for her.'

'Perhaps you and I should have a quiet word together,' he said evenly. 'My grandmother should be told if you have difficulties. After all it is she who seems to want to fashion Stephanie's life for her.'

'Yes, you are right, and I really do need to speak to somebody. I am rather less than happy with what is going on.'

'Then I suggest we meet somewhere where we can talk,

over lunch perhaps. I am free tomorrow. Shall we say one o'clock at Claridges?'

'Yes, Mr Falkener, I will be there.'

'There is really no need to continue calling me Mr Falkener, Alex. I am not here to criticise you or disagree with you. I have known Stephanie a long time and I know what you are up against, I would really like to help you.'

I badly needed a friend. I did not need this job for the money, but at the same time I had embarked on a mission and I did not want to fail.

It was not difficult to pour out my woes to Andrew.

He listened to me quietly while I told him the story of my time with his cousin since the first day we met and at the end he said, 'Surely my grandmother told you you would not have an easy ride.'

'Yes, she did, but it has been far worse than anything I anticipated. She has invited me to meet her friends, go with her to the sort of things she enjoys, but I am concerned about her friendship with Roger Gantry. She is obsessed by him, and I'm not sure where it is going.'

'I know Gantry. He was under my command during the war; he was a good officer, but there were some unsavoury stories about certain aspects of his life. His family don't have much to do with him apart from an elderly maiden aunt who keeps him supplied with money and I'm not sure what sort of job he has had since he left the army.'

'I don't really think he has one; apparently he is searching for something.'

'Do you think it is serious with Stephanie?'

'On her part, yes. On his I'm not sure.'

'Her husband has left her well provided for but she can't touch any of it until she's thirty, a wise precaution I think. However I can understand your concern about Stephanie and your part in it.'

'What was her husband like?'

'Henry? Far too old for her, although he was a decent man. Why on earth he wanted to marry a woman young enough to be his daughter I can't imagine, but my grandmother had a hand in it. She and Henry were friends. She probably thought he'd be good for Stephanie, but my parents thought it was a ridiculous suggestion and so did I.'

'Your parents live near Mrs Graehme-Burrows?'

'About twenty-five miles away. My mother doesn't particularly get on with her, nor my father for that matter, but she's an old lady so I put up with her foibles, largely from a distance, I'm glad to say.'

'What do you think I should do?'

'About your job, do you mean?'

'Yes. I'm not being allowed to do the job your grandmother is paying me for, and I have the strangest feeling that disaster is imminent and I feel helpless to do anything about it.'

'Disaster?'

'Oh, I know it sounds ridiculous but I've learned to believe that life doesn't always play fair. Even when things seem to be going well there's usually something devious waiting round the corner.'

He smiled. 'Was it Vienna that disappointed you, Alex?'

My eyes opened wide and I gasped, 'You knew, you knew all the time?'

'No, actually I didn't. I didn't recognise you at first, but it was your enthusiasm at the ballet that reminded me of that young girl with her anticipated joy in a city she had yet to experience.'

'I was thrilled to be going there, but I thought you seemed very disapproving.'

He laughed. 'I thought you were perhaps too eager, too sure that everything was going to be perfect. And was it?'

'Oh yes. I loved Vienna, everything about it: the music, the waltzes, the glamour. But you went to Salzburg. Why was it preferable to Vienna?'

'I went to the Mozart Festival. I found it more real; I had the strangest feeling when I was in Vienna that somehow or other it was doomed.'

I stared at him uncertainly. I was remembering Alicia's words and her thoughts on an empire that was dying: all those vital laughing people waltzing their way to catastrophe yet so very sure that they were invincible, and then the sudden swift end to it all.

'Didn't you feel it, Alex, or is it that you don't even want to see it, even now?'

'Surely it can't all be lost. Vienna will come back, won't she?'

'Oh, she'll come back, but what has gone can never be retrieved. It will be a different Vienna and one too close to Germany for comfort. Germany has so many wants and aspirations we shall all know about them sooner or later.'

Andrew Falkener knew more than I about the state of the world, but in a lighter vein he said, 'We still are not much nearer to deciding what we might do about Stephanie.'

'No, and I am very concerned. I wanted to be her friend and I wanted to please your grandmother but I'm afraid I have done neither of these things.'

'Hardly your fault.'

'Perhaps not, but ...'

'You are concerned, and yet some young women might be very happy to dance the night away at a nightclub or party. In fact it is doubtful if a woman of Stephanie's age would be remotely concerned that she was not doing the job she was supposed to be doing.'

'You think I'm making problems when there aren't any?'

'No. Stephanie's always been a problem. We'll meet for the opera then I'll create an opportunity to talk to her. She won't thank me for it but I'll try to make her see that the situation is worrying you. I'll do what I can, Alex.'

In the days that followed the only time we met was over breakfast and then Stephanie had little conversation beyond saying that she was meeting such and such a friend and that I was free to amuse myself.

I never saw her in the evenings because she came back to the house very late and even Milly said, 'She's never in, Miss Alex, and I 'ates to 'ave to ask 'er for me wages. She 'asn't paid me for two whole weeks.'

'I'll remind her, Milly. I can let you have some money.'

'Oh no, miss. She's done this before, and she'll see me right when she remembers.'

On the morning we were due to go to the opera she arrived at the breakfast table in her dressing gown, her face pale and wan without its usual make-up, and when I stared at her curiously she sniffed into her handkerchief and dabbed at her eyes.

'I don't feel at all well,' she said mournfully. 'I shall go back to bed.'

'I think you should do that, Stephanie. I hope you'll be feeling much better for the opera this evening.'

'Oh of course, there's that wretched opera. If I'm not well enough to go you'll have to go without me, that's all.'

Why did I think she was play-acting, that she was looking for an excuse, any excuse, not to go to the opera? I watched her tottering to the door like some pitiful tragedienne.

'Would you like me to call the doctor?' I asked her.

'No, I shall go to my room and rest. I don't want you or Milly to keep coming in to see how I am—I simply want to be left alone, and I don't want anything to drink, or eat.'

'But we can't ignore you, Stephanie,' I protested.

'Milly's my servant and you're my paid companion so you will both obey my instructions,' she snapped, and I was appalled at the vindictive expression on her face.

'I shall have to speak to you before this evening. Your cousin will expect an explanation,' I ventured.

'If I'm well enough to go I'll go, if not then I won't go, it's as simple as that.'

I heard her talking to Milly and several minutes later Milly's head appeared round the door and she said, 'She's gone back to bed, miss, she says we 'aven't to call the doctor and she doesn't want either of us to disturb 'er.'

'I know, Milly. Has she done this before?'

'No, but there's somethin' afoot. I doubt she'll be goin' to the opera.'

'I don't think so either, but what can we do? We can't leave her alone all day.'

'I thinks we should, Miss Alex. I've 'ad the sharp end of her tongue all too offen and I intend to do as I'm told. Like she says she'll no doubt see you later in the day. Maybe Mr Falkener'll sort 'er out.'

Inwardly I agreed with her but at the same time it seemed remarkably unkind to leave her alone if she was as ill as she said she was.

Why didn't I believe her? The pinched face and dark circles round her eyes looked more to do with eye make-up, I thought, than with sickness.

It was mid-afternoon when she came downstairs wearing her dressing gown and the same expression, with drooping shoulders and unsteady gait. She stated adamantly that she was far too ill to attend the opera and asked me to make her apologies to her cousin.

Her cousin listened to my apologies on her behalf with a cynical smile. He didn't believe them either and when I voiced my distress that she hadn't wanted either food or company he said, 'There's nothing you can do, Alex. You can't make her eat if she doesn't want anything and if you carry out her instructions she has only herself to blame.'

So I went with Andrew to the opera and enjoyed every moment of it; at the same time behind my enjoyment lay concern about what I would find on my return to the house.

CHAPTER TWENTY-FOUR

IT HAD BEEN a wonderful evening and I thanked Andrew warmly as I bade him goodnight outside the front door. He smiled, saying, 'I wouldn't worry too much about Stephanie, Alex. It didn't surprise me in the least that she cried off the opera, and I think you'll find she's fully recovered in the morning.'

'I think I should call in to see her but she insisted that we left her alone.'

'Then that is what you should do. She surely can't quarrel with you for obeying her instructions.'

He smiled again and waited until I had entered the house before going to his taxi. The rooms were in darkness and I found myself tiptoeing about the house so as not to disturb the overpowering silence. It felt cold in the hall and only in the kitchen did a fire burn low in the grate. I suspected that Milly was either out with her men friends or asleep in her room.

I paused outside Stephanie's bedroom door for several minutes but there was no sound from inside and although my conscience was troubling me I had to agree with Andrew that she should not be disturbed.

I lay for a long time thinking about the evening I had just spent, the music and the dancing, the vitality of the story as well as its pathos, and I thought about Andrew Falkener. I liked him; there was a calm serenity about him, and I liked his good-looking gravity that was such a change from the giggling exuberance of the young men I had grown accustomed to recently.

Somehow the Andrew I had come to know seemed far removed from the young man I had seen leaving the train at Salzburg. Then he had hardly registered beyond his English reserve; my foolish heart had been too enraptured with the prospect of Vienna and my dashing Hussar.

It was barely light when I heard a knocking on my door and then Milly was shaking me, her voice shrill with emotion. I struggled to sit up, staring at her distraught expression while I tried to understand what she was saying.

'Milly, calm down,' I protested. 'What is the matter? I can't understand what you're saying.'

'She's gone miss.' The bed's in a mess and the suitcases aren't in the cupboards. All 'er clothes 'ave gone, she must 'ave done it when we were out last night.'

I hurried into my dressing gown and went with Milly to Stephanie's room. The curtains were still drawn but the covers on the bed and been thrown back and the wardrobe doors were open, revealing that there was nothing inside except for one or two garments she had evidently not wanted to take with her.

She had taken all her shoes and the drawers in the dressing table and the tallboy were empty of underwear. I stared at Milly blankly and she whispered, 'Where can she be, miss? I wish I'd looked in 'er room last night but she told me to go out. She said I 'adn't to disturb 'er when I got back in, and I 'ad to do as I was told.'

'Yes, of course you had. What time did you get in?'

'Around ten-thirty, miss. I'd bin with Joe to the music hall—I told 'im I didn't want to be too late in case she changed 'er mind and wanted somethin' to eat.'

'Well, I wasn't late, Milly. I shall have to tell Mr Falkener but we'll have coffee first. It's only six o'clock now and I don't want to disturb him so early.'

Breakfast was a silent meal with both of us deep in thought. It was Milly who broke the silence by saying, 'Will she be comin' back, miss? Or if she doesn't, what am I to do about the 'ouse?'

'We'll wait to see what Mr Falkener has to say, I think, Milly. Are you quite sure she hasn't left a note?'

'I've searched the 'ouse, miss, but there's nothin'.'

'Do you know if she had a passport?'

'Oh yes, miss. She'd been abroad, she talked about it, afore the war that is.'

'Then it looks as if she's taken her passport with her—the drawers in her room were empty.'

'I can't be expected to stay on 'ere, Miss Alex. This isn't my 'ouse and I need to find work. Mrs Vanburgh owes me money.'

'You mean she hasn't paid you?'

'Not for three weeks. She's done it afore but she's allus remembered. This time she won't be 'ere, will she?'

'You'll find other work, Milly, I'm sure of it.'

'Well, I won't be gettin' a reference from 'er, will I?'

'I'm sure Mr Falkener will help you. I thought you would like shop work.'

'Oh I would, miss, but I've no experience and that's what they'll be lookin' for. There's a nice confectioner's round the corner from me mam's and they're quite often lookin' for help, but I doubt if they'd take me on.'

'Why don't you try? Talk to your sister. She'd help you, I'm sure.'

Milly's expression was entirely unconvinced, and after a few seconds she said, 'I'd best get busy cleaning her bedroom and starting on the rest of the 'ouse. I need to do something to take me mind off things.'

'You've only had coffee, Milly, and nothing to eat.'

'No, I couldn't eat a thing. There's bacon and eggs in the larder if you wants something.'

I didn't, and I sat alone in the kitchen listening to the sounds from above until I decided to get dressed and think about telephoning Andrew around nine o'clock.

I could picture his expression, feel his annoyance, and behind it was his grandmother. I was certain she would blame me, accuse me of not doing my duty, taking her money under false pretences. I had done a great many stupid things in my life but surely this must be the most stupid of all.

After the initial surprise Andrew's voice was brusque. 'I'll come round to the house this morning,' he said. 'You'll be there?'

'Of course.'

'Then I'll see you around ten-thirty.'

I heard Milly talking to somebody in the hall; I recognised Mrs Purvis's voice and then Milly was showing her into the morning room. Her face was red and truculent, and brandishing an envelope she said, 'I've 'ad a letter this mornin' to say she won't be needin' me any more. What's it all about?'

I explained as briefly as I could and watched while she sat down heavily in the nearest chair.

'Ye mean she's not comin' back?' she asked.

'You know as much as I do, Mrs Purvis.'

'Well, she's no right to be sackin' me like this. She owes me for last week and I needs the money.'

'I'm sure you do, but Mrs Vanburgh's cousin is coming to see me and I'm sure he'll be able to help us.'

'Aye, well, me 'usband'll 'ave somethin' to say about it. Six years I've bin comin' 'ere and it's taken 'er all 'er time to bid me good mornin'.'

'Then why did you stay, Mrs Purvis?'

'We needed the money and it was easy. She was out most o' the time and if I'd only done 'alf of what I should 'ave done she'd never 'ave noticed. Now I'll 'ave to look round for somethin' else.'

'I'm sure you'll find something. I'll help in any way I can but I don't suppose a reference from me will help very much.'

'Well no, miss, you were a servant just like me.'

I saw no point in contradicting her, and after a few moments she rose from her chair and stalked out of the room. I heard her addressing a few words to Milly and then the slamming of the door.

Milly's face said it all. 'She wrote to Mrs Purvis, miss. Why couldn't she 'ave written to us, or at least to you?'

'Too dangerous, Milly—we were perhaps in a better position to stop her.'

We heard the opening of the hall door and Milly said, 'This must be Mr Falkener, miss. Shall I make coffee for you?'

'Oh, yes please, that would be nice.'

Andrew smiled briefly at her as she left the room, and then he was looking at me searchingly before he took the seat opposite. 'Now tell me all about it,' he commanded.

So from the trauma of her lethargy to the morning we found her gone I told him everything, including her letter to Mrs Purvis and the money she owed Milly.

'And does she owe you anything, Alex?' he asked.

'No, your grandmother pays my money into the bank. I'm very much afraid I shall be expected to return most of that.'

'Has she never hinted that she might be doing something like this? And who do you suppose she has gone with?'

'I can only guess that it's Roger Gantry.'

He sat without speaking for several minutes then he said, 'Like I told you I know Gantry. He was an officer under my command during the war—as an officer he was good, as a man I found him brash, over-confident and pretty unscrupulous. He lived in London with his aunt, I believe?'

'Yes, his Aunt Maud.'

'Mrs Maud Hemsley. She'd been a widow for many years, a very rich widow from all appearances, and she doted on Roger. He kept her very warm when he was on leave, and moved in with her after the war. I think perhaps I should call upon Mrs Hemsley.'

Milly came in with the coffee and addressing her Andrew said, 'I believe Mrs Vanburgh owes you money, Milly. If you tell me how much I will pay you.'

'But I can't take it from you, sir. Will she pay you back?'

'Let me worry about that. How many weeks?'

'There's three weeks, sir.'

'And what will you do now?'

'I'll 'ave to find other work; I can't stay on 'ere. What'll 'appen to the 'ouse?'

'It's too early to say, Milly. Think about yourself. When I get back I'll give you the money my cousin owes you.'

'What about Mrs Purvis, sir?'

'Mrs Purvis?'

'Yes, she did the rough work. Mrs Vanburgh wrote to tell 'er she wouldn't be needed any more. She owes 'er money, at least that's what Mrs Purvis says.'

'Let me have Mrs Purvis's address and I'll contact her. Now I'm going to see Mrs Hemsley; when I have any news I'll call back.' Milly left us and Andrew said, 'What are you going to do, Alex?'

'I shall have to see your grandmother and I intend to leave here as soon as possible. I shall need to pack my things and get away at the beginning of the week.'

'Don't do anything in a hurry. Wait until I've listened to what Gantry's aunt has to say. When you do decide to leave I'll drive you to my grandmother's.'

'That is kind of you, Andrew, but it really isn't necessary. It's a long drive to Devon.'

'My parents live in Devon, not very far from my grandmother, and I'm due for some leave. I was intending to visit them quite soon. I'll leave you now and let you know later if I have anything to tell you.'

How slowly the hours ticked by. Milly and I ate a light lunch but neither of us was very hungry.

'Why don't you go out?' I asked her. 'Take a walk in the park or visit the shops.'

'I think I'll go round to me mum's, miss. I feels she should know what's happenin' to me, and it's so awful just waitin'.'

'I know, Milly.'

'What will you do, miss?'

'Do some packing, wait for Mr Falkener to either telephone or call. I'll see you later.'

How silent and empty the house felt after she had gone. Folding and packing my clothes kept me occupied for a time but then when I could do no more I wandered aimlessly around the house wondering what would Stephanie do with it, the furniture, the ornaments, some of them valuable. Surely she must come back if only to sort matters out at home.

I was relieved to hear Milly coming through the front door around five o'clock and immediately her first question was, ''Ave ye 'eard from Mr Falkener, miss?'

'No Milly, not yet. Have you been to your mother's?'

'No. I decided against it. I walked in the park, I just felt I wanted to be on me own and I thought you'd want me to get back fairly soon.'

'That was kind of you. Perhaps we should have something to eat, although I have to confess I'm not very hungry.'

'Nor me, but we can't go to pieces because Mrs Vanburgh's done this to us. I'll make some sandwiches.'

We ate them at the kitchen table waiting anxiously for news from Andrew. It was early evening when he came and immediately he apologised that it was so late. 'Mrs Hemsley was distraught. She also had her solicitor calling and we couldn't really talk until he had left.

'I'll tell you all that I know, Alex. It isn't very much. Mrs Hemsley didn't actually know he had left the house until lunchtime today when she found a letter left by him on the hall table. She was accustomed to his comings and goings and never knew when he was in or out. The letter told her he had the chance of employment overseas and he was taking it, he also told her that Stephanie Vanburgh was travelling with him. She learned he had taken all the money he could lay his hands on as well as all the old lady's jewellery.

'He told her in his letter that he hoped in time to return the money, but it will be too late for the jewellery.

'That, I think, has caused the old lady the most distress. Her jewellery was important to her. It came from her husband and from her parents; it can never be replaced and no doubt Roger Gantry will sell it as quickly as possible.'

'How could he do this to an old lady who has been so good to him?' I cried.

'I doubt if Roger Gantry has much of a conscience. He and Stephanie are two of a kind, but what sort of a life they will build together is debatable.'

'The safe in Stephanie's bedroom is open and there is nothing in it. I suppose she does have some money, as well as the house and its contents.'

'I don't know anything about her circumstances, but no doubt my grandmother will know more. I'll call for you in the morning around ten, we'll lock up the house, deposit Milly at her mother's and then we'll drive down to Devonshire. There's nothing else to be done here.'

'No. Oh, Andrew, I want it all to be over and done with! I want to see your grandmother and then I want to go home. I swear I'll never in my life do anything so foolish again.'

'As foolish as what?'

There was a half-smile on his face and in some desperation I cried, 'As foolish as leaving home thinking the grass would be greener on the other side. Twice I've done it, and twice it hasn't been at all what I'd thought it would be. Now I just want to put it all behind me and face mediocrity.'

'Alex, forgive me, but I don't think you'll ever face mediocrity. I think there's something in you that will continue to search for adventure; I just hope you'll find it, that's all.'

I stood at the front door while he drove away, then I went into the kitchen to tell Milly.

'I never liked 'im,' she said angrily. ''E was allus smilin', and too nice. What an awful thing to do to that old lady. I 'aven't got much jewellery but I'd 'ate anybody to pinch it.'

'We'll take you home in the morning, Milly. Mr Falkener is driving me to Devon and we're calling to see his grandmother. She'll want some explanations from me, I'm sure.'

'That she will, miss. I wouldn't like to be in your shoes.'

I smiled ruefully. 'No, and I'm on my own. I don't think Mr Falkener can do anything to help me—he probably thinks I'm as irresponsible as she evidently will.'

'I'm going to cook dinner, miss. We've 'ardly eaten a thing today and there's food in the 'ouse, at least she didn't take that with 'er. There's lamb cutlets and vegetables, and a fruit pie. We'll 'ave a banquet. She owes us somethin'.'

'And we'll eat it in the dining room, and put flowers on the table.'

'I couldn't do that, miss.'

'Oh yes, you can, Milly. There's claret in the cabinet and we'll sit in front of a roaring fire and count our blessings.'

'Do we 'ave any, Miss Alex?'

'Of course we do. We both have family and homes to go to. We're young, and you have two nice gentleman friends who will give you every support, I'm sure.'

'I don't know about that. I shan't be livin' 'ere any more.'

'If they care enough they'll find you wherever you are; if they don't they're not worth bothering with and you'll find somebody else. Think about that job in the confectioner's— I'll give you a reference and so will Mr Falkener.'

'Will 'e, do you think?'

'I'm sure he will. I'll tell them Mrs Vanburgh is overseas but she has asked me to write on her behalf. Surely she wouldn't begrudge you a good reference, Milly?'

'I'm not so sure about that, not after what she's done to me. I'll start to get dinner. Will you be settin' the table, Miss Alex?'

So Milly and I dined in style and if our laughter was a little bit hysterical who could have blamed us?

CHAPTER TWENTY-FIVE

OUR JOURNEY TO Devon was taken largely in silence, not an oppressive one but rather the silence between two people who had other things on their minds.

I had said goodbye to a tearful Milly, who had waved us off from her mother's front door. I was aware that Andrew had given her the money Stephanie had owed her, plus something extra which had earned her astonished gratitude. He had also given her money for Mrs Purvis; now we were on our way to his grandmother's house and I was becoming increasingly afraid of my reception.

It was a warm day in September with the countryside looking its best, from rocky tors to shimmering sea edged by red cliffs. I was wishing I could have enjoyed it truthfully instead of longing to be far enough away.

Occasionally Andrew commented on different villages we were passing through and over lunch he said, 'Try not to worry, Alex; you have nothing to reproach yourself for. That you were with Stephanie at all was a ridiculous situation.'

I silently agreed with him, but at the same time I had only myself to blame. Why couldn't I have been content to live my life like other women lived theirs, instead of forever searching for something different?

At last we were driving through the tall iron gates towards the mellow stone house in the distance and breathlessly I asked, 'Does your grandmother know about Stephanie or have we to break that news to her?'

'She knows some of it but not all.'

'How much does she know?'

'That she's gone off with Gantry, that she's left her London home and taken most things of a personal nature with her. She knows nothing of Gantry's behaviour towards his aunt and nothing of Stephanie's behaviour towards you.'

'She's going to blame me for some of it, I'm sure.'

He covered my hand with his for a brief moment, saying, 'Try not to jump to conclusions, Alex. Tell her the truth and don't let her manner upset you.'

But her manner did upset me, from her cold arrogant expression to the terseness of our greeting.

'Sit down, both of you,' she commanded.

Only I sat facing her while Andrew went to the window where he stood looking out across the gardens, almost as if he wanted no further part in the proceedings.

'Well,' she demanded. 'What have you to say for yourself?'

'What do you want me to say, Mrs Graehme-Burrows?'

'I appointed you to look after my granddaughter by being a good friend, advising her on what was right and wrong, encouraging her to develop an interest in culture, instead of which she has gone off into the blue with a young man of doubtful reputation. Didn't you know what was going on? Couldn't you foresee what was happening in her life?'

'I knew she cared very much for Roger Gantry and I also knew she cared nothing for what you call culture. Did you really expect me to be able to change her mind, or stop her caring for him?'

'Did you even try?'

'Of course I tried, but I knew I was failing. Long before I entered her life she knew what she wanted to do with it.'

'But you were supposed to be her friend, show her the error of her ways, lead by your example. Obviously your example only encouraged her to make a terrible mistake.'

'If you really think that, Mrs Graehme-Burrows, nothing is going to alter your opinion.'

'I should have decided on somebody older, more responsible, more able to be a good influence on my granddaughter.'

'You told me that you had already interviewed several older women and Stephanie had refused to meet them.'

'That is true, but she shouldn't have been given a choice. I feel I have wasted a great deal of money to no avail.'

'I am prepared to refund any money you think you have wasted on me, ma'am, particularly over the last three months when I rarely saw her.'

'How can a girl in your position do that?'

'You don't really know anything about my position, Mrs Graehme-Burrows. I applied for the job because I felt it might be a challenge, not because I needed the money. I would like you to tell me how much I am in your debt.'

'Really! What do you think about this, Andrew? You've said very little.'

'I was waiting for an opportunity, Grandmother,' he replied, leaving his place at the window to take the chair next to mine. 'Whenever was there a time when you didn't despair of Stephanie, her moods, her rebellion, her attitudes? You arranged a marriage for her to a man old enough to be her father. Perhaps he might have been good for her if he'd lived, but unfortunately he didn't and her marriage and his death only increased her rebellion.

'Do you really think Alex could have prevented her running off with Roger Gantry?'

'She should have known something was going on.'

'But could she have stopped it? Between them they planned it very well.'

'Why do you say that?'

'She knew we were going to the opera, to which she had obviously been invited. She sent her servant out of the house, pretended to be unwell and insisted that in no way was she to be disturbed. She left no note, and took everything she could possibly carry with her.'

'Are you quite sure she's gone with that man?'

'He's left his aunt's house where he's been living for some time. He's also taken his belongings plus the old lady's jewellery and as much money as he could lay his hands on.'

'You're sure about this?'

'Absolutely. His aunt was obviously very distressed. In his note to her he said he was going abroad where he's been offered some sort of employment and that Stephanie was going with him. How much money they have between them and how long it will last I can't imagine.'

'Didn't he say where they were going?'

'No. I suppose she can sell the house?'

'I've already heard from her solicitor since I am in charge

of her money, thanks to Henry. As you know she can't get her hands on it until she's thirty, and she can't sell the house or get rid of any of its contents until then either. I don't think she was aware of that.'

'So, what they are travelling with is all they have?'

'Yes.'

'It seems that you and Henry between you have made a thorough job of keeping her well reined in.'

'Andrew, it was necessary. Her mother caused me untold heartache. She died abroad, in poverty, and I didn't want her daughter taking after her. Perhaps if there'd been no war and Henry could have had the chance to mould her into the sort of woman he wanted none of this would have happened.'

'And perhaps that would have been too easy.'

'Perhaps if you'd taken more interest in her, Andrew…but then you were always away.'

'Don't throw the onus on me, Grandmother. Stephanie and I were cousins, never friends, never close. My father was never close to his sister, it seems we were that sort of family.'

I sat listening to them wishing I was miles away. I thought about my own family, my squabbles with Della, my desertion of them, the disapproval of Aunt May, but none of it had been like this. Then I thought about Alicia, and I wished I knew what had become of her.

I was snapped suddenly out of my old memories by Mrs Graehme-Burrows voice asking, 'And what do you propose to do now, Miss Faversham?'

'I shall go home to my parents' house. Mr Falkener has kindly said he will drive me there, but please allow me to re-imburse you for the salary I have received and not earned.'

'And have you tell your parents and Emily Parsons in particular that I have taken money from you? No indeed. Let it serve as a lesson to you, young lady, not to embark upon any more such hare-brained enterprises.'

'I'm sure you're right.'

'And what about you, Andrew? Do I take it you are spending some time with your parents?'

'Yes, I'm on leave for some time. When I go away again I rather think it will be to the Far East.'

'Why not somewhere civilised like Rome or Paris? Why this urge to visit places I've never heard of?'

'I go where I'm sent, Grandmother. The choice is seldom mine.'

'Oh well, have it your own way. Goodbye, Miss Faversham; I don't suppose we shall meet again. I'm sorry for my granddaughter's stupidity and your problems with her.'

She did not offer me her hand and I turned away while Andrew dutifully kissed her cheek and followed me out.

In the car he merely smiled ruefully, saying, 'Well, it's over, Alex. Now you can decide what you're going to tell your family and try to put these last few months behind you.'

I introduced Andrew to my parents and Mother insisted on entertaining him to tea. I knew her questions to me would come later but she and Andrew chatted easily together; he talked about his family home and his mother's penchant for filling much of her time with local musicians and the concerts they organised.

'But that's wonderful,' Mother enthused. 'My middle daughter was good with music and we hoped she'd make a career out of it but she got married instead.'

'Then you'd probably enjoy Mother's concerts,' he said with a smile.

'I'm sure we would. We try to get to the theatre or anywhere else where there's good music to be heard.'

'Then I'll ask Mother to send you an invitation to her next concert. I hope you'll come with them, Alex,' he said to me.

'Thank you, and thank you so much for bringing me home. You've been very kind; I'm sorry it couldn't have ended differently.'

'Indeed. I hope we'll meet again.'

He smiled and raised his hand as he drove away; then I returned to the house.

Mother looked at me anxiously and I knew that explanations for my return home would have to come.

'What a nice man,' she said gently. 'Emily said he was totally unlike his cousin. I've no doubt you'll tell us everything when you feel like it, Alex.'

Over the days that followed I told them about my days in Stephanie's house, the trauma of her leaving and the feeling that somehow I had failed her, but Mother would have none of it. 'She must have been a nightmare. Of course none of it was your fault, never for a moment think that it was.'

So now I was back to living the life of a well-brought-up woman with adequate means who was also the daughter of the house. How I envied the girls who did not have my advantages! I watched them setting out to their shops and offices and I thought how much fun they were getting out of life. The girl who stamped my books at the library had a man friend who waited for her at the bus stop every evening; the girl who styled my hair chatted about dance halls and saving up for summer holidays; but it seemed to me that all I had was mediocrity.

My mother and father sensed my restlessness and Mother said, 'I don't understand you, Alex. You have a lovely home, enough money and friends. Most of those young women who go out to work would change places with you tomorrow.'

It was true I had friends but the young men who had admired me were puzzled by me. None of them wanted a woman who was dissatisfied with what they had to offer.

The advent of Aunt May and her husband brightened up the house and everybody in it. She hadn't changed; she was still the same effervescent woman who basked in the smiles of a patient, admiring, reserved husband. She talked about their foreign travels, their parties and their regular visits to friends they had made. She talked about Aunt Jane, who apparently remained as caustic as ever, and Della, who constantly vied with her on the social scene.

'I wish she'd have children,' Mother complained. 'I'm sure John would like children. There are the title and the family home to think about, and she's getting older. Children are not easy when you have them late in life.'

'Oh, there's plenty of time,' Aunt May trilled. 'They're having the good fun now. After all, look at Ruth: she's always put her daughter first and they never seem to do very much.'

She was interested in me and my future, and one day when we were out shopping she said slyly, 'I don't suppose anybody really knows what you did in those years we never heard from you, Alex, but I can't think they were uneventful.'

'No, Aunt May, they weren't. The war was terrible for all of us.'

'War, Alex! But you were out of the country.'

How was it possible to explain to Aunt May? Her history was minimal; any mention of Vienna and she would immediately think of balls and glamour, much as I once had when I was a schoolgirl. Now I had seen two Viennas and the glamour and tragedy were very much intermingled.

On the sixth day she departed with much kissing and embracing and after she'd gone Mother said, 'She'll never change. Not even a terrible war and everything that went with it changed her.'

Emily had been amused by her—she was everything Emily was not—but for a week I felt that Aunt May had enriched our lives by her sheer normality.

Two days later a letter arrived from Andrew with an invitation to his mother's musical evening. He said if my father didn't wish to drive there he was prepared to drive over for us and Mother cried, 'That really is so kind of him, Alex. I'm sure your father will wish to go, and besides, he likes driving. I wonder what we're expected to wear for an occasion such as that.'

The invitation was a quite splendid gold-embossed one and Mother thought we should do justice to it by dressing up.

We arrived in the company of a line of other vehicles and ahead of us stood the house, in the centre of considerable parkland, with a vast conservatory where the concert was to be held. I was glad we were wearing evening apparel when I viewed what other women had on; at the house Andrew stood with his parents to greet their guests.

My first thought was that at least his grandmother was not in evidence, and his mother greeted me with a warm smile, saying, 'I've heard quite a lot about you, Alex, you poor child. What a time you must have had with Stephanie.'

I smiled, then Andrew was taking us to our seats saying, 'I'll see you all at the interval. There's a buffet laid out in the hall; we'll meet there.'

The artistes consisted of some well-known performers and some who were local but with great aspirations. The music was lovely, the atmosphere congenial and as the evening progressed I relaxed and became able to enjoy it. Andrew joined us at the interval and stayed to eat with us.

'You're very kind, Andrew. Won't you need to circulate, though?' I ventured.

'Yes, in a little while, but I'm so glad you came. What have you been doing with yourself since our last meeting?'

In a few short words I told him, and at the end he laughed. 'I can see you're not exactly filled with enthusiasm for your life as it is at the moment, Alex. Do you ride?'

I stared at him. 'I can ride, but I'm no expert. I haven't a horse of my own but I did ride in Austria and before that as a young girl.'

'Then why don't you ride with me? The countryside round here is very beautiful and we have one or two good mounts in the stables. Before you leave this evening we'll decide on a date and I'll drive over for you.'

'Thank you, Andrew. I shall look forward to it.'

I did look forward to it, and I enjoyed the day. We rode our horses across the short cliff-top grass and his mother entertained us to lunch and afternoon tea. I found both his parents charming, and with a twinkle in her eye his mother said, 'I expect you found my mother-in-law particularly intimidating?'

'I'm afraid so.'

'And how did you find Stephanie?'

'Difficult. In many ways I felt sorry for her and there were some good times when we could laugh together and enjoy each other's company. I felt she'd been a child too long and a woman too soon.'

'Yes. My mother-in-law never understood either her daughter or Stephanie. She thought marriage to an older man would help her to grow up. It didn't, and neither did the idea of finding a ready-made friend for her.'

'No. I don't think an older woman would have been the answer either. There were so many problems in her mind, so many insecurities. I was helpless to deal with them and every day I worry about her. How she is coping, where is she, and will it last with Roger Gantry?'

Her smile was sad and looking across the table to where Andrew was chatting with his father she said, 'Andrew holds out little hope that she will be happy with Roger Gantry. He knew him during the war, and Stephanie herself is her own worst enemy.'

'It is nice for you to have Andrew home?'

'It certainly is. He is away most of the time and we miss him.'

'And the next time it could be the Far East?'

'It seems so. He's spent time in India and Malaya and he loved it out there. I'd rather it was Europe but one never knows. Have you travelled much, Alex?'

'Only in Europe.'

'Ah well, there is much to see there. Andrew speaks well of Italy and Austria; he adores music and it seemed those two countries could offer a great deal.'

I liked her. She was a beautiful woman with wise searching eyes and I would have loved to know what she really thought of me. Did she approve of his friendship with a girl who had been able to do so little for his cousin?

CHAPTER TWENTY-SIX

DURING THE SHORT early days of winter I saw a great deal of Andrew as we rode our horses and took long walks into the country. We went into Exeter and explored the book shops around the cathedral and I felt a happiness and contentment I seemed never to have known before.

It was not the all-consuming passion I had felt for Karl: that belonged to a youth burdened with insecurity and a burning desire to do something with my life. With Andrew it was a calm and gentle closeness more allied to friendship than love, but as Christmas approached I began to feel a terrible unhappiness that in the New Year he would be leaving for his new posting overseas.

Ruth desperately wanted us to go home for Christmas—we had always thought of Stevenson Square as home—and my parents had come round to thinking it was a good idea for us all to be together. When mother saw that I was uncertain she asked gently, 'It's Andrew, isn't it, Alex? You don't want to leave him.'

'Oh, Mother, Andrew and I are simply friends, but when he goes away after Christmas I'll probably never see him again.'

'Would he like to come with us, do you think?'

'No, he'll want to be with his parents. After all it may be a while before he next visits them.'

'You're going to be awfully lonely here on your own when we've gone back home.'

'I know. Let me think about it, Mother.'

So one afternoon I told Andrew what my family had decided to do over Christmas and he said, 'Will you be going with them, Alex?'

'I don't know.'

'If you are so uncertain what else will you do?'

'Stay here, I suppose.'

We were riding our horses back to the stables, and suddenly he reached over and took hold of my hand. 'You needn't be alone, Alex. Spend Christmas with me at Heatherlea—my parents will make you very welcome.'

'Andrew, they've both been very kind to me, but really there's no need for this. I'm sure your parents will have many things planned, and they'll want to spend time with you alone before you go away.'

'My parents are accustomed to my comings and goings. My mother had half expected me to spend Christmas in London; that I might change my mind she'll regard as a bonus.'

'But to invite me?'

'Yes, that too will please her. She's grown very fond of you, Alex. I rather think both my parents had despaired of me. Now there's you and they would both like there to be more.'

I was aware of my racing heart and that he was looking at me with questioning grey eyes as we reined our horses to a standstill on the hillside.

This was a man who did not make airy conversation: he

was trained in diplomacy, not given to rash promises or ideas that had not been carefully thought out. He smiled at my obvious embarrassment, then lightly he said, 'Think about it. You would enjoy Christmas at Heatherlea.'

And I did think about it all the way back to the stables. I thought about my sister Della's husband, who had been the first man I thought I was in love with. A young girl's foolish romantic dream; now I couldn't even remember what he looked like. I recalled all those other young men who had danced with me and taken me to the tennis clubs. Young men who had been nice enough but who hardly filled my heart with euphoria. Then I thought about Karl—but I must not think of Karl. Karl was poetry and music, the sort of enchantment that belonged to a vanished fairy tale.

My mind went back to that first brief meeting I had had with Andrew years before on the train to Vienna. A young Englishman, faintly disapproving of a fellow countrywoman with her head in the clouds. I had not known that old Andrew and the Andrew I had come to know I liked. Surely it was possible for so much liking to grow into love?

He helped me down from my horse and held me momentarily in his arms, then releasing me he said, 'You need to think about us, Alex. I've taken you by surprise?'

'A little, Andrew. Are you quite sure your mother will want me for Christmas?'

He laughed. 'Quite sure, why don't we ask her?'

'You ask her. I should feel so awfully foolish if I saw her hesitate.'

'Very well, I'll give you her answer tomorrow, but I can assure you it will be in the affirmative.'

'And how about your grandmother? She'll hardly be in agreement with the arrangement.'

'My grandmother will have her say and she will be disregarded by my parents and by me. We are fond of the old lady to a certain extent but in no way will she be allowed to dictate my life as she has with Stephanie. I think even my grandmother would admit that she's never had to find fault with my judgement, or so she's always said.'

That evening his mother telephoned to say they would be delighted if I joined them for Christmas. She also went on to say that she was pleased Andrew and I seemed so happy together.

For the first time my parents seemed content with the way my life was heading. They both liked Andrew, and Mother said, 'He's very nice, Alex. Does this really mean that you might have a future together?'

'Would you like that, Mother?'

'Oh yes, dear, we would. We'd be awfully sad that once again you'd be going away from us, but at least you'd be with a man we both like, a man who would take care of you.'

Father had never put his anxieties into words—he had left it to my mother to do that—but this time he said, 'I hope that you wouldn't simply be marrying Andrew to put some more adventure into your life. There could be dangers as well as excitement.'

'Of course not, Daddy. I would never use Andrew in that way. I shall love seeing more of the world but I shall also be a good wife and helpmate in any way I can.'

'Well, the family are going to be surprised once again by you. Do we tell them or is it too soon?'

'Tell them that I have a man friend, tell them something about him, but the rest can keep until after Christmas.'

I watched them depart in the early morning. Mother was a little tearful, since she would really have liked me to travel with them, but in the early afternoon Andrew came for me and as we drove to his parents' home I thought of it as to a whole new start in my life.

'By the way,' Andrew said, 'Grandmother will be with us for Christmas.'

'Oh dear. How will she receive me, do you think?'

'With courtesy, I am sure. Mother has put her in the picture, and she will be aware that nothing she can say will alter anything.'

I believed him; all the same I was wishing she wouldn't be there.

Mrs Graehme-Burrows greeted me cordially enough but there was no real warmth in her attitude. I felt sure that she regarded me as something of an adventuress and with a certain astonishment that her beloved grandson hadn't shown the common sense she had credited him with.

His parents were warm and welcoming, and apart from the times when we sat down to meals Andrew and I contrived to be alone together.

Snow didn't come until New Year's Eve so that only Andrew and I walked to the church through a flurry of snow, wrapped up against the cold and wearing boots well able to cope with the icy paths. Then he held me in his arms at midnight whispering, 'Happy New Year, darling. Are you ready to face a whole new world in a new land with me?'

I knew that this was what I wanted. Something steady and dependable, a man from my own world, not a romantic dream figure from the world of operetta, but a man for the new, grown-up me.

Over the next few days we made our plans. We would be married quietly at the end of January because Andrew had been informed by the Foreign Office that he would be expected to sail out to India in early February to take up his appointment in Delhi. Only his grandmother offered a dissenting note.

'I don't see all this necessity to rush into things,' she said acidly. 'You've only known each other a few months, and starting your married life in a strange country, practically strangers, isn't a good idea in my estimation.'

'It isn't a strange country to me, Grandmother,' Andrew said reasonably. 'I've spent years in India and Alex will enjoy the life there.'

'Oh, nobody listens to me any more, but what do you really know about each other? What do you know about Alex's family, Andrew?'

'What do you really know about Alex, Grandmother?' Andrew prevaricated.

'I know that I deemed her to be respectable, and that Emily Parsons had found her so, but from my memories of Emily Parsons she was an unworldly sheltered girl who was unqualified to judge people outside the village where she'd spent all her life.'

'You're saying she should have gone more carefully into Alex's credentials,' he said with a smile.

'Yes. So, it appears, should I have done.'

'Well, you did me a very good turn, Grandmother, because

through your incompetence I found the woman I want to spend the rest of my life with. I hope you're going to attend our wedding.'

'I'm not sure. I hate travelling about in January at my age. If you'd waited a while, until the summer at least, you'd have had more time to get to know each other.'

'With me in India and Alex in Devon, do you mean?'

'Have it your own way. I can see nothing I say is going to make the slightest difference. I would have thought you'd spend a little time seeing what you can find out about Roger Gantry and my granddaughter.'

'Hire a private detective, is that the idea? Or pull strings at the Foreign Office? Grandmother, I haven't any idea where they are, and I have no right to intrude on Stephanie's life. If this is what she wants, then we should accept it and let them get on with it.'

'Hardly an attitude I expected from you, Andrew.'

'Perhaps you expect too much of me. Stephanie was the black sheep and I was the golden boy, but none of us is all bad and I certainly am not all good.'

'It pleased me to think so, Andrew. I'm not sure about attending your wedding. How many people are you expecting to be there?'

'I'm not sure just now. As well as her parents Alex has two sisters and two aunts with their husbands; I'll leave that part of it to her. Here there's just Mother and Father, you and a few close friends. We want a fairly quiet wedding because there really isn't all that much time.'

She smiled, that sceptical smile that I found all too disconcerting.

On the way home Andrew said, 'I hope your father doesn't think I've pushed things along too quickly. I really should have asked his permission to marry you first.'

'I'm sure you'll find him entirely co-operative,' I said with a smile. And so he was. He liked Andrew and my mother was quite ecstatic, as was Emily when I telephoned her with the news.

'How did his grandmother take it?' she asked.

'Like I expected her to take it, Emily, none too well. I'm not the girl she would have chosen for Andrew.'

'My dear Alex, I don't think the girl she would have chosen for Andrew really exists. I've never met a perfect human being, have you?'

'Emily, you and Edward will come to our wedding, won't you?'

'Oh yes, of course we will. I'm so glad to be invited.'

How quickly the days of January sped by. We heard that my sisters and their husbands would be coming, as would Aunt May and her husband and also Aunt Jane and Uncle Alec, and I decided to ask Ruth if she would allow Sally to be my bridesmaid. She informed me that Sally was thrilled and couldn't stop talking about it.

Della and her husband elected to stay at the best hotel in Torbay along with Aunt Jane and Uncle Alec. Edith, their daughter, declined the invitation and Mother said, 'It's understandable, dear, she lost her husband during the war. I can't think that attending somebody else's wedding is something she's ready for just yet.'

Aunt May and her husband, and Ruth and her family, elected to stay with us and Aunt May was the first one to say,

'He's very nice, Alex, good-looking and obviously a gentleman. I used to wonder about the sort of man you'd settle down with.'

I laughed. 'What did you expect, Aunt May?'

'Oh, somebody frivolous, then later somebody romantically handsome and quite unsuitable. You've learned a bit of sense, darling. I didn't learn much myself until I was older.'

'Are you saying marrying Uncle William was a mistake?'

'Oh no, Alex. He was a lovely man but you have to admit we never had much in common. I played the field after he died. I was determined I wouldn't rush into anything and in the end I got Henry and we're so right for each other.'

Ruth too was happy about Andrew. 'He's very nice, Alex. It'll be interesting to see what Della thinks when we get together next Sunday.'

Aunt Jane was her usual uncluttered self, somebody who had hardly changed since my schooldays in her clothes, her hairstyle, her manner: treating Aunt May to her usual disdainful expression, apologising for Edith's non-appearance.

Then there was Della and her husband. I could not believe that I had once considered myself in love with John Thornham. He had changed more than any of them, become incredibly pompous and put on considerable weight. He greeted me with hearty affection, saying, 'Well, well, young Alex. You're looking very beautiful and I hear you've captured a very eligible young fella.'

'You'll meet him presently—he's coming to dinner with his parents.'

We had elected to eat dinner at the hotel where Della and the others were staying, largely because Mother felt unable to cope with the number, and because this was the hotel where we would be holding our wedding reception.

Dinner was a pleasant civilised meal where our two families met for the first time. Andrew sat next to Della and she laid herself out to be charming as only Della could be; across the table Aunt May winked knowingly at her efforts.

Sally was enjoying herself hugely and together we had spent an enjoyable afternoon trying on the dresses we would wear for the wedding. She had chosen pink, which she said was her favourite colour, and white gardenias for her hair and bouquet.

Mother was unsure about my selection. 'I did so want to see you in lashings of lace and tulle like the other two,' she said almost sadly. 'After all, you are the youngest. I'm not too sure about this wild silk gown in cream, which is more suitable for a garden party or a dance than a wedding.'

'Andrew tells me there'll be plenty of garden parties in Delhi, Mother, and wedding dresses do shriek at you that that is what they are when you see them at balls.'

'I know, dear, but you could have had it altered, perhaps even dyed a pastel colour. However if this is what you want you should be allowed to have it. What about your hair?'

'A hat, Mother, this one. I thought it was beautiful, fit for a garden party with its sweeping brim and lovely feathers.'

Again she wasn't sure, but I knew what I wanted and when I viewed the result in the dressmaker's room I felt happy with my choice.

When I went into the ladies' room at the hotel Della was quick to follow me.

'How on earth have you managed to capture him?' she

said, sitting down beside me where she started to touch up her make-up. 'He's quite charming, good family too. I've been telling him that John is an MP and that we're living in his grandfather's house which is quite a showplace.'

'I was sure you would,' I murmured.

'Well, we have to keep our end up. Aunt May told us his grandmother was a total snob and a bit about your stay in London with that granddaughter of hers.'

'Trust Aunt May to put you in the picture.'

She laughed. 'By the time you're married the old girl will have been put well and truly into the picture that the Faversham family can hold their own with anybody.'

'What had Andrew to say about all your credentials?'

'Nothing, but I'm sure he was duly impressed. John's hoping to go out to India on a trade delegation next year and I could go with him. I suppose we could look you up if we get to Delhi.'

'Do you want to go to India?'

'I shan't get paid for but there's nothing wrong with taking advantage of what's on offer. We're not exactly paupers; John can afford it. John's decided to give you a cheque as a wedding present; after all you'll not be wanting to take things out there.'

'Things?'

'You know, the sort of things people give for wedding presents. Cutlery and china, no doubt you'll have it all there.'

'Yes, I'm sure we shall.'

'Are you wanting children?'

I stared at her in surprise. 'We haven't talked about it but yes, I think we would like children.'

'I've never been the maternal sort and I'm thirty-six next birthday. You're not getting any younger either, Alex, so if I were you I'd have them sooner rather than later.'

'You're not intending having children then, Della?'

'There's the house to think about. It's been in the family for years. And there's the title: who do we hand it on to?'

'Are there cousins?'

'I believe so, but I've never met them because they've spent their lives in the Far East. A bit like your Andrew, really. It's something we have to think about, and Aunt Jane is very intrusive about things.'

'I'm glad you and John managed to come for the wedding, Della. We haven't been together much as a family, have we?'

'No, and you are the one who opted out. What a silly, hare-brained thing to have done. Don't you regret it?'

'Not for a moment. I shall never regret it; when I'm old and creaking with rheumatism I shall remember it and tell my grandchildren about it.'

'Is there much to tell?'

'I think so.'

'Then why not tell it now?'

'Oh no. It's for a time when the world seems less rosy, a little greyer, a little less enchanting. Then perhaps I'll be able to charm it with the story of my life.'

CHAPTER TWENTY-SEVEN

EVEN AUNT JANE seemed to enjoy my wedding, but with her usual asperity she said, 'I'm so glad you didn't go in for all that frothy white stuff. Edith had that and look what good it did her, a widow at thirty.'

Aunt May raised her eyes heavenward and Ruth discovered the courage to say, 'There are an awful lot of young widows around, Aunt Jane. Edith isn't alone in that.'

Andrew's grandmother permitted herself to smile and look agreeable, particularly when she realised she was being introduced to a baronet and his wife, and someone who was also a Member of Parliament. It would seem I was not quite the social climber she had thought me to be, and I saw that she was being especially nice to Emily and Edward.

Mother came into my room while I was changing for our journey into London, and there were tears in her eyes as she embraced me.

'You looked so beautiful, Alex,' she said gently. 'I can see why you chose to wear that dress; it will be far more useful to you than a traditional one would have been. I think everybody has enjoyed themselves, even Aunt Jane.'

I smiled. 'Yes, and Andrew's grandmother. Did she have anything to say to you and Dad?'

'She said she'd enjoyed the ceremony and was very pleased that Andrew now had a wife to take on his travels.'

'She actually said that!'

'And she thought you looked very beautiful and thanked us for a lovely day.'

When I later told Andrew he merely smiled. 'I told you she would come round, darling,' he said.

'But not until she'd met the blue-blooded ones in my family; until then she'd thought me an absolute adventuress.'

He laughed. 'We are all aware that Grandmother is something of a snob. She never worried me, Alex, and now apparently we have her blessing.'

'Hasn't she heard a word from Stephanie?'

'No. Not one word since she moved away. I think it is very worrying for her but there's nothing we can do.'

We were to stay in Andrew's flat in London for four days so that he could spend time at the Foreign Office before we sailed out to India the following week. We were sailing on the *Empress of India* to Bombay and while Andrew was at the office I shopped in London for last-minute things I thought I might need.

I was happy. I had discovered in Andrew a passion I had not thought he possessed. He was a wonderful lover, a kind and generous man, and if I thought about the past at all it was not the warm joy of it that I was remembering.

I did think about it though. The biting winds straight from the Baltic that swept across the fields straight into that old farmhouse that had been our Eden. The snow that lay heavy on the

ground, the wind that came through every crack in the doors
and windows, the long ecstatic nights and then in the morning
the tears while I watched Karl riding away into the storm.

How civilised was this new life in a London looking
forward to spring, with the prospect of a sea voyage to an
exotic land; and yet the past was not quite done with me yet.

It was one morning while I shopped in Mayfair that I was
hailed by a woman's voice calling, 'Alex, is that you? I
thought I recognised you.'

I turned to see a woman hurrying across the street with a
bright smile on her face and I recognised her immediately as
one of Stephanie's friends, one of the crowd she liked to
carouse with.

'I'm so glad to see you,' she enthused. 'Can't we go somewhere and have coffee?'

I would have preferred to go on my way but I did not want
to appear ungracious so we went into a small coffee lounge
that seemed reasonably quiet and almost at once she said,
'You've heard from Stephanie, of course?'

'No, not a word.'

'But you were living in the same house. Wasn't her cousin
escorting you both to concerts or the opera?'

'She went without a word, and there has been no commu-
nication from her.'

'So where are you living now?'

'In London for the next few days, then I'm going out to
India. I'm simply shopping around for last-minute things.'

'You're going to India on your own?'

'No, with my husband.'

'I didn't realise you were married.'

'It's pretty recent.'

'But your husband's English.'

'Yes, of course.'

'You know she's gone off with Roger Gantry, don't you? She was mad about him, but we all thought it was pretty one-sided. After all Roger has played the field with a good many of the girls.'

'Apparently it was Stephanie he was really fond of.'

'It was her money, Alex.'

'But you know her money was left in trust until she's thirty.'

'Well, there's a few years to go, but I did hear he's had money from the old aunt he lived with. I don't suppose that will last forever but he'll probably be looking for a job.'

'Yes, I should think that is likely.'

'We were all stunned when we realised they'd both gone off without a word. I tried telephoning her house hoping that you would be there, but there was never any reply and then the line simply went dead and I realised it must have been cut off.'

'Yes, that is what would have happened.'

'But the house is still there. There's no for sale sign up and no sign of any servants.'

'No, I believe not.'

'Don't you have any idea what is happening, Alex?'

'No, I don't. I thought you and your friends would know more than I. After all, haven't you all been friends some considerable time?'

'Not really. Stephanie enjoyed the crowd and the partying but she never told us very much about herself although we knew she'd been married to an army officer much older than herself. He was killed during the war, you know, and she was a very merry widow indeed.'

I smiled, deciding to say nothing.

'Doesn't she have a grandmother in the country? I know she was always a little put out when she decided to visit.'

'Yes, her grandmother lives in Devon.'

'Well, doesn't she hear anything?'

'I really have no idea.'

I couldn't for the life of me remember her name although we had been in each other's company several times. There had been so many of them, all of a pattern, all intent on living every moment to the full until the stars paled. That had been Stephanie's life too, and now my companion was seeming a little frustrated that I could tell her so little.

'I'll give you my address, Alex, so that if you hear anything about Stephanie you can contact me.'

'Have you forgotten I shall no longer be in the country? And I'm hardly likely to hear anything in India, unless they've arrived there, of course; however India is a big country.'

'I suppose so. I was so pleased to see you this morning, and now you've been able to tell me absolutely nothing.'

'I know, I'm sorry.'

'Oh well, enjoy your stay in India. Will you be there some time?'

'I think so.'

'Your husband will be working out there?'

'Yes. He works for the Foreign Office.'

'Wasn't that where Stephanie's cousin worked?'

'Yes. I must be leaving you now—I have so much to do and not really enough time to do it in. I enjoyed those parties;

it is a pity I can't help you more with Stephanie's where-abouts.'

'Yes it is. We're all a bit miffed about it. What is the use of having friends when you just sail out into the blue and not tell them a thing.'

'I know. I'm sure when she's settled she'll write to you. I do have to go now. It's been nice seeing you again, goodbye.'

'Which way are you going?'

'I've finished my shopping and I'm going back to the flat now so I'm looking for a taxi.'

'Oh well, I still have shopping to do. 'Bye.'

When I told Andrew of our meeting he merely said, 'There was nothing you could tell her, Alex. You were right to be so reticent.'

How thrilled I was to be boarding that beautiful ship at Southampton, to see the crowds of people waiting for her to sail, and the brass band waiting to play for her departure.

Our cabin was spacious and beautiful and the man who escorted us there was attentive in showing us where to find everything. I sat on the bed hugging my knees, my eyes shining with delight, and Andrew laughed.

'You're enjoying all this?'

'Oh yes, it's wonderful. I've loved the travelling I've done but I never thought in my wildest dreams to be sailing out to a new life in India on a liner like this one. I'd like to be on deck when she sails.'

'We will be. You'll hear the music, it's usually "Auld Lang Syne", and you'll see the fluttering handkerchieves and the streamers.'

At that moment the steward arrived carrying a huge bunch of red and pink carnations and taking them from him Andrew looked at the card before handing them to me. 'They're from my parents, Alex.'

The steward said with a broad smile, 'There's more sir, I couldn't carry them all.'

He arrived next with a large bouquet of red roses from my parents, and, wonder of wonders, a basket of freesias from Mrs Graehme-Burrows. Andrew laughed at my expression, saying, 'Didn't I tell you, the old lady's come round and welcomed you to the fold.'

I was truly happy that moment, There were no dark clouds to cast a pall over my life, when always in the past whenever I had thought I was happy, there had been doubts and uncertainties to shadow the future.

I read the cards attached to the flowers with tears in my eyes; neither of us had any means of knowing how long it would be before we saw our families again.

We stood on the deck surrounded by fellow passengers until the last strains of the band died away; now the great ship was steaming down Southampton Water guided by her attentive tugs, and ahead of us stretched the Solent and the future.

Our dining companions were genial and pleasant and although on the first evening we did not dress for dinner there was an air of liveliness around us. The officer sitting at our table was quick to tell us of all the entertainment the ship had to offer and looking across to the captain's table he said with a smile, 'There's a party of Americans on board. We like to do our American cousins proud, and our English passengers are happy to put up with it.'

'You mean they're all on the captain's table?' the man sitting opposite asked.

'All of them. They come from California and they're sailing out to Bombay, then after a few days to the Far East. Great travellers, the Americans. They seem to put no time limits on their journeys overseas.'

We could hear their laughter, their English which was not our English, and one of our party said somewhat dourly, 'I suppose they've money to burn, but they're good at splashing it around.'

The officer smiled. 'They are also warm-hearted and friendly, at least the ones I have met have been. After a few days at sea we'll all know one another much better and let the good times roll.'

I suppose travellers everywhere talked about themselves; they were quick to ask where we were headed and anxious to tell us their stories. Only Andrew was a diplomat; the others were visiting families in the army or businessmen travelling for their various companies.

The days passed quickly. There was so much to do, from painting classes to ballroom classes, and every night there was dancing in the ship's ballroom; if we wanted something more classical there was that too.

I wore my wedding dress for the captain's cocktail party and it was just right for the occasion. When Andrew elected to play bridge I spent time in the ship's library and it seemed there was always something to please most people. I made a friend of an older lady sitting at our table who informed me her son was an army officer and they were heading for Calcutta where he was stationed.

Somewhat plaintively she said, 'He's been away from home much of his life. This journey is a one-off for us; we decided to spend some of our money to stay in Calcutta several weeks.'

'Is your son married?' I asked her.

'Oh yes. He was married three years ago to a girl he's known out there for some time. We haven't met her. Her father's in the army too.'

'He married out in India?'

'Yes, there was trouble there and he couldn't get leave to come home. We've had photographs and letters, but we're both looking forward to seeing them.'

'Do they have children?'

'Not yet. We're hoping for grandchildren but we're also hoping he'll be coming home. He's been in India such a long time.'

'I do hope so.'

'What about you, dear, will you like living in Delhi?'

'I believe I will. Andrew's been out here before so he knows about the life here, and he tells me I'll enjoy it.'

'I don't suppose it will be anything like army life, but my son tells me it's not all a bed of roses. There is trouble somewhere most of the time and some Indians are unhappy under British rule.'

'No, Andrew has also told me about that. I suppose it's understandable.'

I felt sure she suspected me of wearing rose-coloured glasses, seeing only the glamour and none of the problems, and it seemed that all my life I'd been anxious to do this. One day I would come down to earth, one day when my still-dancing feet had learned to walk.

In the meantime there were nights when we danced away the hours, and days when we wandered first through the streets of Gibraltar and then Alexandria, and I who had only known Italy and Austria was excited and enchanted with all that I saw. Andrew was the perfect guide. He'd seen it all before but he was kind enough to see it through my eyes and love it as I was loving it.

He told me that the Americans were great bridge players and the men spent most of their time at the bridge tables, but the ladies were seen having lessons on the dance floor or learning to cook Eastern dishes laid on by the ship's chefs.

From where I sat in the restaurant I did not have a good view of them. The men were jovial, the women beautifully dressed and seemed to have a lot to talk about, but with typical British reserve the British passengers kept themselves to themselves; yet whenever we met up with the Americans there was great camaraderie between us all and no antipathy.

Andrew played bridge one afternoon with one of them and he told me they came from the wealthy part of California, and were all great friends back home, members of the same clubs and churches.

I had told him a little about Aunt Alicia and was surprised one day when he said, 'Didn't you say the missing aunt had gone to America, Alex?'

'Yes, but I don't know where. I don't expect I'll ever see her again.'

'But she was married to an Austrian, wasn't she? Won't she have gone back there?'

'If she ever did she would find that her husband had died. There would be nothing for her in Vienna.'

'Are you telling me that she left you with her husband in Vienna? Why didn't you go with her?'

How I was wishing that I wasn't expected to answer these questions. I shouldn't have told him half a story, but then what else could I have done without telling him about Karl and a forbidden love that should never have been?

Gathering my thoughts together I said, 'I stayed with Franz because he was ill, because I didn't think she should have left him. He was a kind man who didn't deserve to be treated like that.'

'But your aunt wasn't Austrian, Alex. I suppose when the war came she felt she had no place there.'

'I thought wives should stay with their husbands regardless of their nationality. It seems to me that Alicia always did what she wanted regardless of who she hurt on the way. I idolised her when I was a young girl. She was the mystery that I wanted to solve, the one nobody was allowed to speak about, and when I did meet her she was very beautiful and I could understand why she'd run away from mediocrity in search of something more exciting.'

'Just a little bit like yourself, Alex?' he said with a wry smile.

'Perhaps, except that although I admired her I didn't always understand her or agree with her.'

'You must tell me more about her one of these days.'

'There's very little to tell. I knew her hardly at all because there was so much of Alicia I never understood, and when she went out of my life I think it was for good.'

How wrong I was in that supposition.

Two days later I walked into the library and stared straight into her eyes, and with that disarming smile and the lilt in her voice that was unchanged she said, 'Alex, if I visited the moon I would expect to find you coming towards me. What is happening to you now?'

I simply stood staring at her, unable to speak. She was still beautiful, still exquisitely dressed, and she said, 'Come and sit over here with me. We'll chat and then we'll have tea together. Are you alone?'

'I am now.'

'And later?'

'I am with my husband.'

She laughed. 'Well, well, we have a great deal to talk about. I would like to meet this husband of yours.'

CHAPTER TWENTY-EIGHT

STILL BEMUSED BY our meeting I did not realise for some time that Alicia was asking all the questions and I was learning nothing about her. Pulling my scattered wits together I said at last, 'You're not telling me anything about you, Alicia. Did you go back to Vienna?'

'Well of course, when it was possible after the war. I went to the house in the Ringstrasse and found it shuttered up, then I went to the hunting lodge and spoke with the servants. They told me of Franz's death and I went to see his lawyer.'

'And what did he tell you?'

'That Franz had died and you were with him but had since returned to England. I collected my jewellery and the money Franz had left for me. He was generous to you, Alex.'

'Yes, he was, and I told him he needn't be. I had a family to go back to however badly I had treated them, but he was insistent I should have a sum of money, and some of your jewellery. I chose a ring and a gold bracelet.'

'I was very fond of that bracelet, Alex. You showed good taste.'

'You can have them both back, Alicia. I thought you would

never return to Austria and it was Franz's wish that I take something. My husband is generous; I have my own jewellery.'

'Tell me about your husband. Is he handsome, rich, charming? What does he do?'

'He's a diplomat. We are on our way to Bombay where I think we're expected to stay for some considerable time.'

'How did you meet him?'

I was not going to tell her, so instead I said, 'His parents live in Devon like mine. You probably don't know that Grandmother died while I was away and my parents are living in her house. My sister Ruth and her husband and daughter are living in Stevenson Square.'

'At least they've kept it in the family,' she said drily. 'I'm sorry about Mother, though she was getting on of course.'

'Yes.'

'And the rest of them? Jane and Alec, and wasn't there May? I didn't know her.'

'Aunt Jane and Uncle Alec are well. Their daughter lost her husband during the war. Aunt May has married again. My sister Della is married to Aunt Jane's nephew, which I think you already knew. Now they're living in the Hall and John is a Member of Parliament.'

'And that's all.'

'That's all.'

'I want to know more about your husband. What is he called?'

'Andrew Falkener.'

'When shall I meet him?'

'Soon, I'm sure. Until a few moments ago I didn't even know you were on board. Who are you with?'

'With my husband. He's an American, name of Jefferson

Carsdale. We live in Santa Monica and we're on a tour to Malaya and one or two other places.'

'You met him in America?'

'Yes, when I was still married to Franz. I joined my old friend in California, at her invitation. She was thrilled to show me around, a European Countess with status and money. Unfortunately for Violet, Jefferson preferred me to her and for the second time that was the end of our friendship.

'I told them both that I had to return to Austria; she thought he would forget me, but he didn't. He bombarded me with letters, then he came looking for me. The rest is easy to see.'

'So when you knew that Franz was dead you went back to America?'

'Of course, darling. Europe was a hotbed of unfortunate people who had lost their identities, their countries and their titles. Austria was a republic, all the glamour had gone and at least in America we were far enough away from your troubles.'

'And you found Jefferson waiting for you.'

'More than that. I wired him from the ship, he was waiting for me in New York.'

'And Violet?'

'She's living in Miami. We do correspond now and again so she's evidently forgiven me. After all I didn't deliberately go out to capture Jefferson, it just happened.'

'Do you never see your daughter?'

'No, and I never hear from her. I think about her, and there are times when I want to hear from her, but I realise now it will never happen. And what about you and your Austrian Hussar? Did you ever see him during the war?'

'Yes, I saw him.'

'And?'

'He married his cousin, as had always been his family's intention.'

'Didn't I try to tell you so, Alex?'

'You did. I wonder if he's happy.'

'I saw a lot of arranged marriages when I lived in Vienna, between people of the same class, people who had known each other a long, long time. It worked. Of course there were the inevitable mistresses and affairs, but the marriages stayed together. It was that sort of society.'

I didn't speak, but I could feel her watching me, and after a few moments she said, 'You know, that one moment of weakness when I made myself return to the house in Stevenson Square opened up so many wounds. What a pity that you didn't stay a little longer in the library that day so that I could have knocked on the door, received no answer and walked away.'

'You mean you would rather not have met me?'

'You have to admit I didn't expect you to turn up in Vienna, to meet you in the opera house where a young officer was shot because of you.'

'I know, it was terrible.'

'But we did enjoy St Petersburg, didn't we, Alex? I've entertained my American friends with the story so many times: those wild sweeping steppes and the blinding snow that swirled down from them. The balls at the palace and the garden parties, all the wonderful excitement to be found there.'

'And the terrible ending, Alicia. The Tsar and his family massacred and the advent of Communism.'

'But we saw that coming too. All those sad poor people

with nothing to hope for, with all the money in the world in the hands of a few people while they had nothing. I suppose in time things might get back to normal; at least the war's over and, even though the glamour's gone, somebody sane might come around to seeing the need for change.'

'So you're not likely to be setting foot in Europe again?'

'Not in the conceivable future, darling. I like America, it's bold and it's brash but it's safe. Like I said, we're far enough away from all Europe's disasters and I doubt if it'll be tempted into another world war.'

She looked across the room and following her gaze I saw that Andrew was walking towards us. Alicia said, 'So this is your husband, Alex! Very nice, very English. You couldn't have done better.'

I introduced them, and his surprise was very evident.

'I don't suppose Alex has told you very much about me. I'm the aunt the family wished to forget.'

He smiled. 'Actually, she has. I know that she always wished she could meet you, that you spent time together in Austria and Russia and that you'd lost contact. How did you discover each other on board?'

'I saw Alex walking into the ship's library just now and I couldn't believe it was her. I thought, what is it about Alex that I can never be free of her?'

'But you still thought you had to speak to her?'

'I was curious. What was she doing on a ship sailing out to Bombay? You know I sailed all over the world with my first husband. Was she following in my footsteps?'

He smiled, that cool English smile that said very little, and, a little disconcerted, Alicia said, 'How did you two meet?'

'We met in London,' Andrew replied, 'We are both fond of music, and my parents live in Devon, as do Alex's.'

'And did you have a big wedding with all the trimmings?'

'No, just our two families and we had to come away from Devon almost immediately after. Tea's being served, Alex. I was wondering it you would like some. Perhaps you'll join us, Alicia?'

'Thank you, Andrew. I suggested tea to Alex just now, but I really must look for my husband. No doubt we'll meet again before we reach our destination.'

'You're staying in India?'

'For only a few days, and then we're heading out to Malaya. I suppose you know that too?'

'Yes. You'll find it very interesting—there's a lot to see.'

We walked out of the library together and then holding out her hand she took hold of Andrew's saying, 'It's so nice to meet you and to know that Alex is happy.'

Then she put her arms round me and gently kissed my cheek.

I could tell that Andrew was bemused by our meeting but it was only when we were sitting in the ship's lounge over afternoon tea that he said, 'I've seen her sitting at the captain's table with the Americans. Is one of them her husband?'

So I told him what she had told me and with a wry smile he said, 'It would seem your Aunt Alicia is a lady destined to fall on her feet. She's a beautiful woman; I can understand why you wanted to meet her.'

'It was the mystery surrounding her that fascinated me. The pictures that were incomplete, where someone had been cut off, the hushed whispers when the women were together the fact that my grandfather hated her name to be mentioned that nobody would ever talk about her. I thought, What can she have ever done to deserve this resentment?'

'And then you met her, and you liked her?'

'Oh yes. I thought she was beautiful, charming, and she talked so plaintively about the past. I saw the tears in her eyes. I didn't go out of my way to meet her in Vienna; it just happened, and afterwards she insisted that I go to live with them. We went to St Petersburg, then Franz was very ill when we got back to Vienna. The war was upon us and Alicia said she was going to America. I couldn't leave him.'

'Or was there somebody else you couldn't leave, Alex?'

I could feel the warm blood colouring my face, and he was looking at me searchingly. Seeing my confusion he said gently, 'It's all right. Neither of us are children and neither of us have talked much about our lives before we met. You're a warm beautiful woman; there must have been someone.'

I didn't answer him immediately. The tea lounge was busy as waiters moved between the tables and music played, and Andrew waited patiently to hear if I had anything to say. At last I looked up to see that his eyes were kind, encouraging, and I said, 'Yes, I did love somebody once, but it wouldn't have worked out. It was impossible.'

'Why?'

'He was an officer in the Emperor's Hussars; he came from a very noble family who expected him to marry his cousin, which he did. There was no future for us together, so after the war I came home.'

'But there was more, wasn't there?'

'Oh Andrew, I shouldn't be telling you all this, and you shouldn't be asking me. We're husband and wife, we've only been married for a short while. Why do we have to talk about the past, why can't we simply forget about it and move away?'

'Because the past has a nasty habit of resurfacing and secrets are better brought out into the open.'

'Does that mean that you have no secrets yourself?'

'I was in love once with a girl I met at Cambridge, the sister of my friend. I took her to May balls and thought we were destined to spend the rest of our lives together.'

'She married somebody else?'

'No. She was sailing to America when the Germans sank the ship she was on. She was taking her mother out to stay with her sister. They both died.'

'Oh, that's terrible! And you've never forgotten her, have you?'

'You don't forget people, Alex, you simply come to understand that it was good while it lasted. Then it is over and none of it is ever coming back.'

'You no longer love her?'

'I was twenty-four and in the army serving in Flanders when she died. I'm now thirty-four. Growing up was thrust upon us; we learned about death and we accepted it. I loved Marcia then; now I love you. Can you say the same thing?'

'I haven't thought about Karl for years. I loved him and I lost him, and now we have each other. I want so much for us to be happy. When I was a young girl I know I was often compared to Alicia, not to my face, but when they talked to each other, but I know in my heart I'm not really like her at all. I've often been rebellious, seemingly uncaring, too silly for words perhaps, but I have grown up, and when we left S Petersburg and I saw Alicia leave for America I knew then there was a great difference between us. She didn't care enough and I cared too much.'

He reached out to cover my hand across the table, and he smiled. 'We'll never speak of it again, darling,' he said gently.

'No. I don't want to think about the past, Andrew; it wasn't all happy. I want our life together to be better than that. Do you understand?'

'Of course. We'll consign Vienna to history, as well as all those other things that caused us pain. A whole new beginning, Alex.'

'Oh yes. What a pity there isn't champagne, we could have drunk to that.'

I had believed I could never talk to Andrew about the past, and even now I couldn't tell him everything, but I felt that much of it had been laid to rest and we would be able to move on confidently into our future together.

During the next few days Alicia introduced us to her husband, who said heartily, 'Another beauty in the family,' placing his arm round my shoulders while Andrew merely smiled.

We arrived at Bombay in the early morning and while we waited to disembark Alicia came towards us alone. She embraced me and shook hands with Andrew, but her face was reflective and as she turned away she smiled almost sadly.

'I don't suppose we shall ever meet again, Alex,' she said gently. 'I shall be at the other side of the world and you will be here. I shall think of you, though. I did often think of you, you know, when I left Vienna. I knew you thought I was being unkind both to you and Franz, but that was me. I have no illusions about the way I am.'

'I never told the family that we had met; I didn't think you would want me to.'

'No. They consigned me to history a long time ago and rightly so. Do you think that there has to be some kind of retribution for the things we do wrong in our lives? Up to now I've escaped remarkably well, but there are moments when I think I can't really have got away with it.'

'I went back to face it and I felt better for it.'

'I could never have gone back—there must be a coward in me somewhere.'

My last sight of her was standing with her friends watching Andrew and me walking towards the train that would take us to Delhi. They all raised their hands and waved and then we were being escorted to our compartment and our luggage was being brought on board. It was a luxurious train by any standards but on the platform there were crowds of people waiting to see if there was room for them, either in the corridors or even on top of the train. It was my first sight of an India where the British could travel in great style while the natives took second place.

'Is it always like this?' I asked Andrew.

He merely smiled, saying, 'This is a different world from the one you've lived in. You will find much to admire and glory in but you will find other things to unsettle you. Always try to remember that we've done our best, and it hasn't been easy.'

'But you like India, don't you, Andrew?'

'Oh yes. I love her sunshine and her pageantry, her architecture and her history. There's a magic about India you'll never forget, but there's a darker side to her: the resentment of a people unable to call their country their own, different religions, different histories, different ideals. The longer I've been here the harder I've found it to get answers but one day there have to be some, although how long we have to wait for them is anybody's guess.'

I was looking at him doubtfully, and with a smile he said, 'You're going to love so much of it, Alex, the soirées and the garden parties, the balls and the pageantry. Even the darker side I mentioned will have a fascination you'll never forget.'

As we journeyed on through the night towards our destination I thought about his words. I had craved for adventure, longed for excitement in my life, but never in my wildest dreams had I expected to be with my new husband on a voyage across India.

There was so much to do, so much to see, that thinking was something I had to put off until later, but my first impression was that I was going to love this new country and the bungalow that was to be our new home with its garden and shuttered rooms, the luxury of its silken cushions and ornaments in jade and ivory. Servants pandered to our every wish with shy smiles and silent courtesy.

In the days that followed I wrote long letters home to tell them that India was wonderful, that this was something I had been waiting for all my life.

I could imagine Mother's wistful smile at the words of a daughter who had spent her life crying for the moon.

CHAPTER TWENTY-NINE

THE TIME PASSED quickly until in the end I was left wondering where the hours went. There was so much to do, so much to see, and I was loving every moment of it: the soirées and the polo matches, and balls and the sheer exuberance of its strangeness.

We spent a wonderful holiday living on a houseboat on a lake in Kashmir, and rode our mules along the slopes of the Himalayas in Nepal. I looked with awe at the sheer beauty of the Taj Mahal, and the painted elephants carrying exotic brides to their weddings with Indian princes. They would provide me with memories that would last forever, and then I had my own happiness to savour. My son Adrian was born eighteen months after we arrived in Delhi and as we rejoiced in our new child I thought only of the future for all of us.

He was a happy, uncomplicated baby, and an ayah was found for him whom we all loved. Her name was Julaba; she was seventeen years old and she idolised the baby and cared for him tenderly. I was hoping Andrew could get some leave so that we could travel home to introduce him to the family, but there always arose some reason or other why we couldn't manage it.

He would say, 'Don't worry, darling, we will get home one of these days. Just at the moment it isn't convenient, that's all.'

It was one evening at a ball at the Viceroy's palace that I noticed him talking very earnestly to an Indian Army officer he had greeted earlier in the evening. I had not seen him before, but they seemed to have a great deal to say to each other and I thought that Andrew looked more than a little concerned. When he joined me he said, 'Sorry about that, but I haven't seen Ericson since just after the war. He was under my command on the Somme; I didn't realise he'd decided to stay in the army. He's been out here some years, Calcutta and the frontier.'

'It all seemed very serious.'

'It was. He knew Roger Gantry, and a few weeks ago he took some leave in Kuala Lumpur and ran into him.'

'Was Stephanie with him?'

'No, he was alone, drinking heavily and a bit dissipated.'

'What was he doing in Malaya?'

'Ericson said he'd been living in Australia and other places, didn't seem to have any sort of job and was thinking about going back to England if he could get enough money together.'

'But what about Stephanie, didn't he mention her at all?'

'No. Ericson knew Stephanie, but of course he didn't know she'd gone off with Gantry so I told him a little of the story. He didn't seem to think there was a woman figuring in Gantry's life at the moment, at least nobody meaningful.'

'I wonder what has happened, where she is and who she is with.'

'I'll try to get hold of some answers. Somebody in Kuala Lumpur might manage to find out something for me.'

'It's worrying you, Andrew.'

'I never really liked Stephanie very much but she is my cousin and I do feel a certain responsibility. At least I'd like to know what has happened to her.'

Nothing came of Andrew's questions and then to our joy he was to be allowed leave; I was so excited to be going home thoughts of Stephanie were momentarily forgotten.

Once again we were sailing on the *Empress of India* and while we waited for her to arrive from the Far East we spent time pleasurably in Bombay.

Adrian had bid a tearful farewell to his ayah, who promised to be waiting for him when he returned, and Andrew said, 'It would have been nice to bring her with us but her family wouldn't have liked it. To work for us here is one thing, to travel outside India with us is another.'

The ship brought back many memories, of Alicia and the Americans, and as we waited at the ship's rail for the moment when she sailed Andrew said with a sharp catch in his breath, 'That's Gantry, look there, walking along the quayside. He's coming to board the ship.'

A native walked behind him pushing his luggage, and the man Andrew said was Gantry was totally unlike the suave, impeccably clothed Gantry I remembered. This man was swarthy, sloppily dressed and much fatter. He walked unsteadily up the gangway and Andrew said testily, 'I don't suppose he's travelling first class, but I've got to see him; something's very wrong somewhere.'

So after dinner that evening he said as soon as we'd

finished eating, 'I'll see if I can get hold of him. Will you be in the cabin?'

'Either there or in one of the lounges. I'll put Adrian to bed, and come up here when he's gone to sleep.'

'I have to see him, Alex. You do see that, darling?'

'Of course, I'm as anxious as you are.'

I was waiting for him in the lounge while I listened to the ship's orchestra, and as soon as I saw his face I noted the concern in it.

'I only managed to speak to him for a few minutes. He was pretty well oiled but he's promised to sober up and meet me later this evening. I think we should meet him in one of the quieter lounges.'

'Will he be able to do that?'

'Yes, I've explained to one of the officers. Perhaps you'd like to come with me.'

We had almost given him up, and then we saw him standing at the door explaining to one of the waiters that we were waiting for him.

This was a man who had lived in the decadent aftermath of the war, a young man who had asked too much and offered too little.

He had put weight on and his face was grey and drawn, his eyes puffy, his mannerisms uneasy. All the same he smiled at me almost flippantly, saying, 'So we meet again, Alex. I'm surprised you want to speak to me; we certainly upset your apple cart when we moved out of London.'

Andrew ordered drinks to the table and Roger said, 'Are you two an item, then?'

'Yes, we've been married several years, but this is our first real leave,' Andrew explained. 'We have a small son, and we thought it was time the family met him.'

'I don't know what I'm doing going back to England. There's nothing for me there, but there's nothing for me in the Far East either.'

'What have you done since you left London?' Andrew asked.

'We went out to Australia, where I had the offer of a job in the outback. It worked for a time, then it all went wrong.'

'Why was that?'

He permitted himself a bleak smile before answering. 'Stephanie hated the outback. She wanted life: the shops, the theatres; she wanted to go to Sydney but there was no work for me in Sydney. The money was dwindling, including the money I'd got for the old lady's jewellery, and then we had another blow. Stephanie tried to sell the house in London but she couldn't until she was thirty, three years to go, and we were desperate. Her grandmother refused to help; my old aunt didn't want to know me and things just went from bad to worse.

'Stephanie wanted more and more, but when I couldn't give it to her she found other men who would. I was drinking like a fish—it couldn't go on.'

'She left you?'

'Oh yes, she left me. God knows where she went. I've only heard rumours about her, nothing concrete, and she's made no effort to look for me, but then that was Stephanie. I always knew what I was taking on.'

'Then why did you do it?' Andrew asked.

'Several reasons. Her style, her thirst for life, and most of all her inheritance. She said there'd be enough money, but her husband was an acute old devil to tie it up like that; he evidently understood her more than I did.'

'You have absolutely no idea where she is now?'

'None whatsoever.'

'I do feel some concern for her,' Andrew said calmly. 'I know her faults all too well, and we've never been close, but my grandmother has always worried about her.'

'If I were you I would consign Stephanie to the devil: she'll either survive intact or come to a sticky end.'

'What will you do in England?'

'See if the old lady's still alive. If she is she might conceivably take me back; if she's died her money'll have gone elsewhere. Either way it's a leap in the dark.'

'Couldn't you get a job?'

'What sort of job? I'm not the kind of chap who studied for a profession. I went straight from the schoolroom into the army, where a good school ensured I got a commission, but not even my education can help me now.'

'You could think of joining the army again, I suppose.'

He stared at Andrew with narrowed eyes, then after a few minutes he said, 'That's a thought, anyway. Somewhere in the world there's bound to be mayhem, somewhere they could be looking for somebody like me: a chap with no roots, no ties. My war record wasn't bad.'

'You were a good officer, Gantry. It's a pity you haven't tried to do more with your life,' Andrew said reflectively.

'Blame your cousin Stephanie for that. With the right sort of woman it might have been very different.'

Our meeting with Roger Gantry disturbed me strangely because of the sad vacancy in his eyes, the feeling that there was nothing in the future for him, the flippancy that covered an ocean of despair. I knew the meeting had affected Andrew in a similar manner.

We did not see him again on the ship although Andrew asked him if he would like to dine with us one evening. He refused on the grounds that he hadn't anything suitable to wear and the last we saw of him he was walking down the gangway towards the waiting porters. He didn't look up at the people still on deck and, although I had never really liked him, at that moment I felt sorry for him, for a life that promised nothing.

How easily life fell into place now that we were home in England. I was surprised how Andrew's grandmother had aged in just a few years; she was troubled with arthritis and incredibly forgetful, and yet she received us with something like the old authority I remembered so well.

She didn't mention Stephanie and I think Andrew was relieved when she didn't. The things Roger Gantry had told us could hardly have been conveyed to the old lady.

Adrian was made much of by Andrew's parents and mine, but I was more than surprised when Mother said, 'We're thinking we might go back to the Midlands, Alex, because we're missing Sally growing up and the others. They come to see us whenever they can but they're so tied up with one thing or another, and our roots are there, after all.'

'Father's roots are there, Mother; yours never were.'

'Perhaps not, but we lived there most of our married life. You and Andrew are abroad and likely to remain so for some time; we've talked about it and really feel it would be for the best.'

'It was so nice to think both our families were in Devon.'

'I know, dear. But when you come on leave it will be nice for you to see the old town.'

'Where will you live?'

'There are some very nice properties going up all over the place, or we might even look at one of the houses for sale in Stevenson Square.'

'They're awfully big.'

'Well yes, but we could cope.'

We visited Emily and Edward and when I voiced my anxiety about my parents returning to the Midlands Emily said with a little smile, 'I shouldn't worry. Your sisters are there and you will be far away.'

I offered no more objections to their leaving, and when our leave was up we returned to India with the feeling that when we next set foot in England many things would have changed.

Adrian would be ready for school, an English school, and if we went back to India we would be going without him. I knew his grandparents would care for him during school holidays but it seemed to me that the people who carried the white man's burden were asked to make too many sacrifices in the name of Empire. When I said as much to Andrew he replied, 'I don't intend to remain in India until my retirement, Alex. Perhaps somewhere in Europe would make a nice change.'

'That would be wonderful, but where?'

He laughed. 'There are various possibilities: Italy, France.' Then with a wry smile he added, 'Austria.'

I wouldn't think about it. I didn't want to go to Austria with Andrew. Austria was something to forget, and with it all the terrible trauma that was still haunting me if I would let it.

* * *

We found an English tutor for Adrian until he was six and then Andrew decided he should go home to England and prep school. I knew that he was planning all sorts of things but I decided to ask no questions until matters were finalised.

It was spring when he told me we were going home and would not be returning to India. A replacement for him was coming out from the Foreign Office and we would have several weeks' leave to sort ourselves out, then he would know where we were to go from there.

I didn't really care. I was looking forward to seeing the family, to an English spring and gentleness, cricket matches and tennis parties, musical evenings and gossip over the teacups, church spires across the hedgerows and summer meadows.

So for the first few weeks of our leave I visited the family. My parents had found a house they liked not too far from Stevenson Square and although I had once been terribly anxious to get away now I was enjoying meeting old friends, seeing old sights, reviving old memories.

Girls I had been at school with were anxious to hear about my life and even when I had to admit that theirs seemed uneventful by comparison we had warmth and laughter to enjoy and of course there was Aunt May, always to be relied upon to keep us amused.

Cousin Edith was plain and eaten up with a strange sort of bitterness. Other women had lost their husbands during the war; Stephanie had jumped on the bandwagon and a merry-go-round that never stopped, but Edith spent all her time at church.

Aunt May said, 'It wouldn't surprise me if she becomes a nun. She's obsessed with religion.'

'But she used not to be like that,' I said sadly.

'Oh I don't know. Her mother was always breathing down her neck to be different, and that boy she married was cut in the same mould.'

I tried to see as much of Edith as I could but she saw in me some sort of rebel who didn't deserve a good husband or a happy life.

I saw little of Della and John; on numerous occasions they needed to be away from home and their house was just something they stayed in when necessary and moved out of as often as possible.

Back in Devon we spent long weeks with Andrew's parents. Andrew had to be in London much of the time but he came home at weekends; I was loving helping his mother with her musical interests and the very large garden.

With a wry smile Andrew said, 'Do you propose to visit my grandmother, Alex?'

'I feel I should, but I'm not too sure that she will want me to.'

'I think she will. I would if I were you.'

So one golden morning in midsummer I drove with Adrian, who was on holiday from his school, to her house only a few miles away. The lanes were bright with flowers and tall leafy trees, the sea was calm and blue beneath the bright red cliffs and over it all was a gentle mellow peace.

She received us in her pristine drawing room where she sat in the window with her small dog beside her chair and I did have the distinct impression that she was pleased to see us.

Adrian was a friendly pleasant boy who showed her pictures he had painted and when he went out into the garden with the dog she turned to me with a smile saying, 'He's so much like Andrew was as a boy. He's doing well at school?'

'Yes, his reports are very good.'

'And I'm so glad you're not going back to India—it's too far away. Where will it be this time?'

'I'm not sure yet.'

She sat for several minutes looking down at the rug that covered her knees in spite of the warmth of the morning, and then, raising her head, she smiled. 'You seem to have made my grandson very happy, Alex. I've been a silly woman in many ways. I wanted the moon for him, for both of them, but with Stephanie it all went wrong. I worry about her, wonder where she is, what she's doing with her life. Do you think we'll ever know?'

'Perhaps one day she'll come back.'

Andrew had purposely not told her about our meeting with Roger Gantry because he thought it would worry her too much.

'The less she knows about Stephanie the better,' he had said evenly.

'Well, she'll have her money now, and that for the sale of the London house,' she commented glumly. 'She'll run through it like water unless she's changed out of all recognition and he'll help her to spend it, I've no doubt.'

When I left her that afternoon I suspected that she would continue to worry about Stephanie until the end of her days.

CHAPTER THIRTY

IT WAS MID-SEPTEMBER and Adrian was back at his school. We were busy packing what we would need for our next posting and Andrew kept me in suspense until the last moment, which told me it was somewhere I could get excited about. Indeed the sheer joy of it made me think I was the luckiest woman alive when he told me at last that we were to go to Rome.

My mother-in-law had gone to one of her usual Tuesday afternoon choir meetings and I was busy in the garden cutting down her dahlias. All summer they had bloomed profusely, large and small gay velvety flowers, but now they were past their best.

I was so engrossed with my work that I did not see the car coming up the drive until it was almost at the house. Then I looked at it curiously. We did not usually have callers on a Tuesday because everybody in the vicinity knew my mother-in-law would be out, and this car was one I hadn't seen before. It was a low-slung sports model in bright red, and stepping out of it was a tall slender woman wearing a bright scarf round her head and incredibly ornate sunglasses.

Her eyes swept over the garden but instead of approaching the house she walked towards me. Clutching my pruning shears I went to meet her and it was only when I was within feet of her that I gasped with surprise. It was Stephanie.

She was laughing, then in the next breath she said, 'Gracious me, Alex Faversham. What are you doing here?'

'I'm living here at the moment. How are you, Stephanie?'

The words were banal, stupid even, but at that moment I couldn't think of anything else to say.

'I'm well enough. Why are you living here?'

'I've been married to Andrew for some considerable time.'

'Living here with his mother?'

'Actually no, we've been in India for some years. We're on leave at the moment.'

'You have done well for yourself, I must say. My paid companion, and now my cousin's wife! I wonder what my snooty grandmother had to say about that.'

'Have you been to see her?'

'Not yet, that's something I have to think about.'

'She's quite well, a little frailer perhaps, but otherwise she has all her faculties. She's worried about you a lot over the years.'

'Of course, she must have done. Is Andrew at home?'

'No, he's in London. Andrew's father is at the golf club and his mother's at church for choir practice.'

'Heavens yes, I do remember those musical soirées of hers. Can we go in the house? I'm dying for a cup of coffee or something stronger.'

'Certainly. Excuse me while I get out of these things and get rid of the shears.'

I felt inadequate to handle this blasé self-assured woman while wearing my gardening clothes smeared with loam and the expression on her face was one of cynical amusement.

I washed and changed hurriedly, but at least now I felt ready to meet her on her own ground.

She was standing looking through the window, and in those first few moments I knew that she was the vulnerable one and I was the invincible one. She turned and motioning to the sofa I said, 'Do sit down, Stephanie. I've asked them to bring coffee; would you like a drink, a glass of sherry perhaps?'

'Civilised but no, I prefer a G and T.'

So while I helped her to the drink she took her place on the sofa, looking round the room casually and then saying, 'I always liked this room. My aunt had good taste, better than Grandmother.'

I smiled, and she went on, 'Are you living here indefinitely?'

'No. We're going to live in Rome and we're looking forward to it.'

'Heavens yes, so would I. How did you come to marry Andrew?'

'You did throw us together, didn't you? The opera, the days when you couldn't be bothered to see him or go anywhere with us; then when you left he was there to sort things out.'

'He didn't sort things out enough. I couldn't sell the house, so it had to stay there to rot until I was thirty.'

'That had nothing to do with Andrew; your husband made those decisions.'

'My husband with any help Grandmother gave him.

Neither of them trusted me to handle my own life.' She laughed. 'I'd like to have been a fly on the wall that morning you all realised I'd gone. It must have been worth watching.'

'It wasn't very pleasant. Andrew dealt with paying the servants.'

'I was sure he would, but you'd been paid by my grand-mother, Alex. Did she ask for it back?'

'I offered, but she didn't accept it.'

'Kind of her. And she really accepted you?'

'Stephanie, I didn't have to be a paid companion and there's nothing wrong with being that either. I did my best with you and it wasn't easy. I was never the sort of girl who wanted to spend my days gossiping over the teacups and when I did cut loose I tried very hard to make a success of it. You were my failure and I'm sorry, but please don't gloat about it; it was your fault, not mine.'

She smiled. 'Aren't you interested in what I've been up to since we last met?'

'I'm very interested. You went away with Roger Gantry, and I remember that you were very much in love with him.'

'Love! Well yes, I suppose I was at the time. We're not together now, haven't been for ages.'

'So where did it all go wrong?'

'Money, Alex. We didn't have enough of it. He pawned his aunt's jewellery and that kept us solvent for a time, then he got a job in Australia and I hated every moment of it. We lived in some weird shanty town in the outback, a place of wooden shacks and bushland, where the men congregated in the bars although the women were kept out of them. I was bored to tears and Roger changed. Then I found out about the house:

I couldn't sell it, I had to wait three long years until I was thirty, and the money Roger was earning wasn't enough. In any case he was capable of spending all that on himself.'

She was talking with staccato nervousness, her thin hands plucking on the silk of her skirt, and for the first time I was really seeing her face with its lines of dissolution, the heavy make-up that was unable to disguise the puffiness of her eyes and greying of her skin.

She looked up and gently I said, 'You left him?'

'Yes. I had to, or I'd have gone mad. I never let him get his hands on my jewellery so when I got to Sydney I sold it. It was jewellery my husband had bought me, plus some my mother had left me, and I got quite a bit of money for it, enough to set me up in a flat in Sydney and give me time to look around.'

'You didn't think of coming home?'

'To what? Grandmother's sulks and strictures, everybody's amusement because my life had gone haywire? No thanks. I had to make a new life. I got a job in a bar. I'd never worked before but I learned how to pour drinks, chat the men up, flirt with the boss and I met Algy Grantham. He was English, some aristocratic family's younger son who his family had been anxious to get rid of by sending him abroad somewhere. We got along. We went to race meetings and parties, we lived it up and we got by on the money his family sent out to him. It wasn't destined to last, of course, and when he was ordered home I stayed on in Sydney and met somebody else.'

I didn't prompt her but waited patiently while she sat frowning, her thoughts on a past she was finding unpleasant, almost as if she could no longer believe in it. At last she shrugged her shoulders and went on with her story.

'He was half French, half Tunisian. Good looking, dubious, but there was a certain excitement about him. He could make money gambling, he was good at that; and for a time it worked. Then of course he had bad times and he became violent and angry, with me and with life, and I left him. He started to look for me all over Sydney and I became frightened. That's when I decided to get out of Australia so I went to Hong Kong, where I met Lucian. I married him.'

'So you have a husband, Stephanie?'

'Of sorts. He's a lot older than me, another Henry if you like, but I'd come to realise that perhaps my grandmother'd been right in marrying me off to a man older than myself. Lucian's old, rich and doesn't really care what I do as long as I see him regularly and don't cause any scandal. He's Jewish, his daughters don't like me so we never meet, and he goes off to stay with them in America whenever he gets the chance. His health isn't good, you see.'

'You live together?'

'In a way. I have a home with him, but I like to move around a bit and Lucian's very bad with arthritis so the only place he wants to go to is America. I never go there with him. While he visits them I go to Europe, Spain or Italy. If you invite me to visit you in Rome I could conceivably take you up on that.'

She was audacious, a girl without conscience or much compassion, but as before I was finding her to be strangely entertaining. There was a disturbing restlessness about her. She didn't like herself very much and yet that compelling insecurity was arousing my sympathy again. Could there have been more to Stephanie, could the people who had known her have failed to find the real woman beneath the façade of flippancy?

'Where are you staying now?' I asked her.

'I booked into some hotel in Torquay, not being sure how the family would receive me. Besides, I like it better. I'm there until Sunday. Will Andrew be home at the weekend?'

'Yes, and he would like to see you, Stephanie.'

'I'll call to see Granny and I'll see my aunt and uncle, then once again I'll disappear into the blue and you can all forget about me.'

'You sold the house in London then?'

'Yes. Lucian said I should have got more for it but that's the Jew in him; I wasn't unhappy with the price but it was soon spent. I say, why don't we go out for lunch? That's unless you've something else on this afternoon.'

'You can have lunch here. Andrew's mother won't be home until later but she will want to see you.'

She laughed. 'Don't be too sure. She always thought I was a brat, the worst sort of brat. No, we'll go out for lunch, some nice country inn. I don't suppose anybody will recognise me but it doesn't matter if they do.'

So we drove in Stephanie's car to a place Andrew and I liked on the outskirts of Sidmouth and as we talked the years dropped away and I was listening to the old Stephanie whirling round to the sound of saxophones as she talked about the men she had met and discarded. At the end she said, 'It wasn't always like that, Alex, some of them ditched me. I haven't told you about them.'

I left my mother-in-law and Stephanie alone later in the afternoon. Mrs Falkener had been disconcerted by her visit, at first uncertain about how she should receive her, but in the end Stephanie's lack of sensitivity overcame her misgivings.

Before she left we showed her photographs of Adrian and she said, 'I thought Andrew would never get married. He was sweet on that girl years ago and it seemed he'd never really met anybody else. I'll never have children; but then I'm no good with kids, I'm too much of one myself.'

When she'd gone Andrew's mother said, 'What a hotchpot she's made of her life. I shudder to think how much of it she's going to tell her grandmother. I hope not all of it.'

She came once more to the house on Saturday morning and I left her and Andrew together so that they could talk. She left without seeing me but Andrew said she had invited us to dine with her that evening providing we didn't talk about old times.

We kept the conversation light, but it was Stephanie herself who said, 'Granny still doesn't approve of me, my husband, my way of life, my past. She made it very clear. I don't think I'll visit her again, but I'll come to her funeral. You'll invite me, Andrew?'

'Of course. I hope you will see her, Stephanie—she's old and you've caused her a great deal of problems. You can surely overcome your rancour for one or two brief visits.'

'I can, but can she?'

She came to the front of the hotel to see us drive away and then Andrew said quietly, 'She'll never change. It was something that was born in her like her mother before her. Now do you want to know what is in store for us?'

'Oh yes, when are we going to Rome?'

'George Stevenson is coming home in October and I'm taking his place. He's having heart problems and his wife' had enough of living abroad, so we'll have time to get settled in before Christmas.'

'What about Adrian?'

'We'll have my parents and Adrian for Christmas; they'd like that, I'm sure. They'll want to come home for the New Year, because Mother always has so much on with her music then.'

'I suppose so.'

'And we'll take a holiday, just a couple of weeks, it's all planned.'

'A holiday? In late December? But where?'

'Austria.'

It was as though I had been expecting it: a past that would not let go, a price to be paid.

I had not realised that Andrew had been waiting for me to say something, and with a smile he said, 'You're not curious, Alex? Don't you want to know why I've suddenly decided we should spend the New Year in Vienna?'

'Well yes, why?'

'You know I had good friends in Salzburg. I spent quite a lot of time with them across the years, going to Mozart concerts and other festivals; we kept in touch and they're now living in Vienna. We'll have a lot to talk about, and you'll have a lot of catching up to do.'

'Why do you say that? I don't know anybody in Vienna now.'

'But you told me you had friends in Grinzing. Surely you'd like to see them again; besides, don't you want to see if some of the old Vienna still lingers? I'm sure you do.'

I was quiet for the rest of the drive home, my thoughts in turmoil. Of course I wanted to go back to Vienna. I wanted to see her palaces and her thoroughfares; I wanted to listen to the music in the Hofburg palace and watch the exquisite cavorting of the snow-white horses under the crystal chandeliers. I wanted to walk into the opera house again and follow the train of people up the long staircase to listen to music I had craved for in all the years since, but in Vienna there could be danger: to my heart, to my future.

It was ridiculous. I was not the girl who had waltzed starry-eyed under the lanterns on a cold Christmas night or loved desperately and despairingly to the sound of distant gunfire.

This was a new me, a wife and mother who was happy with her life, not a woman wanting to capture a past that had gone forever, taking old and punishing dreams with it.

I made myself chat normally, but inside I was churning up with anxiety. Suppose in the new Vienna I suddenly found myself looking across a crowded room into eyes that were steely blue in a face I had loved desperately. Would those same eyes look into mine without recognition, or with a re-membered pain?

I wouldn't think about it; there was too much to do in the weeks leading up to Christmas. A new home, a new land. I loved Rome with its history and its vitality. Then Andrew's parents came out to us for Christmas bringing Adrian, who was growing tall and who loved every moment of life in the ancient city.

'Why go to Vienna when so much is happening in Rome?' Andrew's father asked one evening.

'A little bit of many things,' Andrew replied seriously. 'You think Rome is enchantingly gay, don't you, but under-neath it all there is another Rome I wasn't exactly prepared for.'

'What do you mean, dear?' his mother asked. 'I've always loved Rome and nothing's changed for me.'

'Good, then we won't talk about it.'

'No, I'd like to talk about it,' his father objected. 'Is it that Mussolini fellow who's making himself felt?'

Andrew smiled. 'Yes, everywhere one goes, even tonight when everybody is happily looking forward to Christmas. Look over there at that column of young boys, Mussolini's boys strutting like peacocks across the square, oblivious to the Christmas lights, oblivious to people wanting to celebrate Christmas in the old way. That is St Peter's Square, but they are more concerned with slogans and marching than with why we are here and that this is Christmas Eve.'

'You think we're in for trouble.'

'Perhaps, I'm not sure. Certainly not tonight at any rate.'

It was much later when we were alone that I said, 'Andrew, what was all that you and your father were talking about earlier?'

'Nothing to worry about, darling.'

'I've seen your face when you've watched those boys marching in the streets. You're not happy about it, are you?'

'No.'

'Is that why we're going to Vienna, to get away from it?'

'On the contrary, we're going to Vienna to see if they are being similarly troubled.'

'Not with Mussolini's fascists, surely.'

'No, Alex, with Hitler's youth.'

CHAPTER THIRTY-ONE

HOW STRANGE THE tricks that fate plays upon us. I was only half looking forward to our days in Vienna; I wanted to go and yet much of me was haunted by memories. Two days before we were due to leave we received news that utterly devastated me.

My father had suffered a heart attack and on New Year's morning he died. It was the worst possible start to the year 1936, and only days later we stood in the churchyard in my home town huddled round his graveside.

It was a raw blustery day when grey skies hung low over the stone church with its square tower and flurries of snow swept down on to the paths lined with people who had known him and the family. Men who had worked for him, men he had known through business and leisure, friends over many years, and I looked up with tear-filled eyes at the leafless branches of the trees waving helplessly in the wind.

I was glad now that Mother had elected to return to the Midlands where most of the family still lived, but I was finding difficulty in accepting that my father, who had always seemed so robust and strong, was dead. I had never known him have a day's illness; he'd often laughed and joked with others that he was the healthiest man he knew.

Because Father had been such a public figure Mother had decided we should eat lunch at the large hotel where I had once been entertained by Alicia, and as we stood at the head of the stairs to meet those who had attended his funeral I found myself remembering that meeting. I had no appetite, but Andrew whispered, 'You must eat something, Alex. It's a very cold morning and if your father was here he would say the same.'

Going back to my roots wasn't easy for a woman who had rebelled so fearlessly against them, and as always Della didn't make it easy for me.

'You were always his favourite, Alex,' she said dourly, 'and you went out of his life for nine long years.'

'I know. I'm sorry for that.'

'I never even remember him being ill. That he should die so quickly was awful.'

'Better than a long sickbed,' Aunt May said philosophically.

'Perhaps so; all the same it's so hard for Mother. Are you staying on with her for a while, Alex?' Della asked, but almost immediately Ruth was there saying, 'I've told Mother she can come to stay with us until she's feeling better. Didn't it occur to you, Della?'

'Of course, but you know John, here there and everywhere. His time's never his own, and it spills over on to me.'

Andrew joined us and after listening to the conversation he said, 'Stay on for as long as you like to comfort your mother and talk about old times with people you know here.'

In the event Mother wouldn't hear of it.

'The reason I moved up here was to be with people I've known most of my married life. Your place is with Andrew, wherever he has to be.'

'Oh Mother, we've missed so much, all of it my fault. Now I feel I should stay on with you for a time.'

'And I say no, you should not, darling. Return to Rome with Andrew, and perhaps in the summer I'll feel like visiting you when Adrian is at home from school.'

'That would be wonderful. Promise you'll do that.'

'I'll certainly think about it. Has Della been getting at you? If she has, don't take any notice. Some of that old resentment still lingers with Della, although it's quite ridiculous.'

'You're staying with Ruth for a few days?'

'She insisted but I really would rather have gone home. Mrs Pearson is coming to live with me, so we'll be two old widows together, getting a little more cantankerous and crotchety every day.'

I smiled. 'You'll never be crotchety, Mother. Mrs Pearson was always thus.'

'Well, she's all for moving into something smaller than Stevenson Square. Her one sister died so she's nobody close and she's been with us many years.'

'I'm glad she'll be with you.'

Mrs Pearson was still unsure about whether I was fit to be a member of the family. She regarded Andrew as if she couldn't quite believe in him, a gentleman, with nice manners and a well-bred appearance: hardly the sort of man she had thought the young Alex would have captured.

'Are you staying on?' Della asked again sharply.

'No,' Mother said quickly. 'I am insisting that Alex returns to Rome with Andrew.' Then turning to me she said, 'When will that be, dear?'

Andrew answered for me. 'I have to get back there by Monday so we shall probably leave London on Saturday. It'll give us time to get settled in to the New Year.'

'Heavens, yes,' Mother said with a sigh. 'It is a new year, isn't it. It hasn't been a good start; I wonder what the rest of the year will do to us.'

'You can stay with us tonight,' Della said grudgingly. 'I'd rather like Andrew to see the Hall. It's quite a show-place, Andrew.'

'So I believe,' Andrew answered.

'It was my father's place, the family's place,' Aunt Jane said feelingly. 'I'm glad John hasn't bothered to make many changes.'

Aunt May's eyes were raised heavenwards and all I could think of was that nothing ever changed.

So we stayed with Della and John and Andrew was treated to a tour of the house as well as the grounds, in spite of the icy wind and the flurries of snow.

It looked so beautiful as we surveyed it at last from the windows while behind us a huge log fire burned in the grate and in the corner of the room still stood the decorated Christmas tree.

Della surveyed it ruefully, saying, 'I should have taken it down immediately but everything happened so quickly. Mother always said it was unlucky to take the decorations down before Twelfth Night, but I reckon we'd already had our bad luck.'

I never felt truly comfortable with John. He was pompous and his entire conversation revolved around politics and what sort of future he expected to have at Westminster. I couldn't really have said how Andrew viewed him. They spoke pleasantly together, but no real camaraderie developed and I doubted if either Della or John spared us a second thought after we had left the house.

How could we not be aware that Europe was changing? The Fascist youths on the city streets were proclaiming loudly that there would be a new Rome to rival Julius Caesar's, and we all thought they were brash and stupid, braggarts only fit to be laughed at.

We heard about the Maginot Line and the Siegried Line and sophisticated women chatting over their coffee cups thought how silly it all was. Surely the world was not mad enough to go to war again; it was too soon after the last one. Hadn't we learned anything from that? But no one listened to ordinary normal people when there were too many men with ambitions and deep-seated scores to settle in their hearts.

I was happy in Rome. I loved the vitality and the life that pulsed through the city streets and squares, the lingering ambience of an ancient city that had seen so much history and drama. Nothing would change it, any more than London or Paris would change, and then I thought about Vienna and a way of life that vanished as if in a dream, taking with it an empire that they had thought was forever.

The summer was over and already autumn leaves were falling in the Borghese gardens. Somehow or other there seemed a strange sadness, indefinable yet increasingly potent. People seemed more sombre as they went about their daily tasks; laughter was more forced, men pored over their newspapers at pavement cafés and women's smiles failed to hide the anxieties in their eyes.

Andrew betrayed nothing and if he was worried at the news that came to us daily he said very little. He spent more time in his office, and when we were entertained in the homes of his colleagues and friends the conversation between the men was thoughtful and profound, accompanied by expressions that were grave and serious.

Whenever I questioned him he merely smiled his slow sweet smile, saying, 'Nothing to worry about, darling. You married a diplomat; there's always something somewhere to cause concern.'

'So you *are* concerned about something?'

'Perhaps, but nothing you need worry about, Alex. We should think of taking a holiday, something to cheer us up. I'll write to my friend in Vienna to ask him if the offer of a few days with them is still open.'

But that was the last I heard about it.

In the summer Mother had come with Adrian to spend the whole of August with us. We did all the things everybody does in Rome. We went to the Colosseum and St Peter's, we went to the catacombs and drove along the Appian Way and Adrian was vastly intrigued by the sight of columns of young Italians in uniform marching along the city streets.

'Are they soldiers or just students?' he asked me.

'I rather think they are would-be soldiers.'

'We have an Officers Training Corps at the school, and I'd like to join it one day.'

'Oh Adrian, why?' I asked plaintively. 'You surely don't want a career in the army.'

'Not particularly, but if there's ever a war it means I'd get a commission.'

'But there isn't going to be a war. Whoever has talked to you about a war?'

That was the moment I saw Andrew very clearly in Adrian. The reticence, the quick desire to change the subject so that it would not worry me.

In the last few days of August Andrew had managed to take a few days' holiday and we went to the coast near Genoa; for the first time in months I felt the beauty and the peace of Italy. When the holiday was over and we saw them off at the station Mother said feelingly, 'Come to us soon, Alex, just for a few days if that's all you can manage.'

I promised but I had no means of knowing when that would be. As we drove back from the station Andrew said gently, 'Your mother's looking well, Alex. They're very fond of each other.'

'Yes. It's been a funny sort of year; it started so badly with Father's death and somehow or other it's still unsettled.'

'Unsettled?'

'Why yes. Surely you must feel it.'

He didn't answer, but his expression was sombre. The English newspapers were filled with the scandal of England's new King Edward and his American lover, as well as the over powering ambitions of the German dictator and Mussolini.

'What do you think the King will do?' I asked him.

He shrugged his shoulders. 'What will he be allowed to do?' he answered philosophically.

'Suppose he wishes to marry her?'

He shook his head. 'Not possible, he doesn't have that power. The constitution, Parliament and the people would be against it.'

'He's very popular.'

'When the crunch comes I rather think his popularity will be disregarded.'

'But if they love each other?'

'My dear girl, he's the King. A great many men made the ultimate sacrifice during the war and I rather think this is one sacrifice they might have expected of him.'

But the King didn't make it and by the end of the year England had a new monarch. Kings would come and go, Andrew assured me, but Great Britain would survive.

At that moment he ignored the sterner things that troubled him, things more important in a changing world than the King's desire to follow his heart.

We went home for Christmas and in the bosom of our respective families the old magic of the season helped us temporarily to forget the troubled world. Andrew's mother as always was busy with her musical circle and the choirs she had assembled for the Christmas period. Then we went north to spend time with my family and see in the New Year with them.

Back in Italy life took up its pattern and the old anxieties resurfaced.

Just before Easter I had a long letter from Emily and although we had corresponded often this letter was so filled with excitement that I could imagine her writing it, her face alive with delight, she had so much to tell me.

They had decided to travel in Europe in the autumn. *It seems so long since we were there, Alex,* she wrote. *We've been spending so much time making the house and garden to our liking and we've been taking holidays at home. Now we've got the bug again and you'll be interested to know that we've decided on Austria.*

I know how much you loved Vienna. Well, we're going to the Tyrol, Salzburg and then Vienna for a whole week in September. We hope to go to the opera and other unmissable events. I do wish you could be with us for a few days; you would know what we should see.

I passed her letter across the table so that Andrew could read it and he said with a smile, 'Will she be looking for your Vienna, do you think?'

'I expect so, but that's long gone.'

'Why don't you join them while they're in Vienna? You know it well; you could show them all the things they need to see and as I'm fixed at the moment I really don't see any chance of getting leave.'

'What about your friends in Vienna?'

'I know, I said I'd write to them, but I saw little prospect of getting away so I didn't bother. One day we will go to see them, but why don't you accept Emily's invitation and recapture a few memories?'

'Oh Andrew, I don't know. I would really like to have gone there with you. Being on my own wouldn't be the same.'

He smiled gently. 'You'd be with Emily and Edward. You could spend time with them, or stay longer if you wish. You could go to Grinzing; there must be people you knew there who you might like to see again.'

I didn't speak. Was Andrew really so sure of me? Was he so complacent that he was unafraid of the resurfacing of old passions? Twenty years was a long time: another life, another world.

'I'll have to think about it,' I said, putting her letter back in its envelope.

'What needs thinking about, darling?' he said evenly. 'Find out where they are staying in Vienna and I'll book in for you. Stay for a few weeks, visit Grinzing and the Vienna Woods, see the new Vienna.'

'And if I hate it?'

'You won't. Not all of it will have gone—use your imagination, people it with people you remember. I wonder if your aunt ever went back there with her American husband.'

I stared at him in surprise. 'I don't know. Surely she wouldn't.'

'From the short time I knew her I wouldn't think she had much conscience about the past. She never showed much anxiety about leaving it.'

He was right. If Alicia wanted to go there she wouldn't hesitate.

Andrew got up from the breakfast table and bent down to kiss my cheek. 'Think about what I've said,' he urged me. 'It makes sense.'

I thought about little else for days, and then I wrote to

Emily and swiftly received a reply filled with so much delight at the prospect of seeing me in Vienna that it seemed to me I was being catapulted headlong into the past.

CHAPTER THIRTY-TWO

FROM THE FIRST moment I stepped into that train it was a journey of nostalgia, but this time I was not sharing a compartment with two young men, one of them gay and handsome, the other serious and rather grave.

Now my companions were four elderly people who occupied their journey by either sleeping or eating. They had enormous parcels of food and there was no conversation between us since two of them were German and the other two Italian.

They chattered away in their own languages and although we exchanged smiles they had heard me speaking in English to Andrew as he placed my suitcases on the rack above me and obviously thought I wouldn't be able to converse with any of them.

The journey northwards through Italy to Milan where I was to change trains passed reasonably quickly. I read the magazines I had brought with me, ate in the dining car and as I waited on the platform for the train to arrive for Vienna I looked around me with interest at the people waiting to board it with me.

There were no dashing young men in Hussar uniforms,

no sparkling young Fräuleins in velvet and furs, only serious travellers waiting impatiently for a train that was running a little late. At last I was on board and this time my compartment was to be shared with an elderly cleric and a young couple obviously in love and probably newly married.

This was my real journey into the past, but it was not until I caught my first sight of snow-capped mountains and deep blue lakes that I knew for certain that at least this was a panorama only providence could change.

I was glad when the young couple moved out to go to the dining car; their embraces had become an embarrassment. Had I really forgotten what it was like to be young? The cleric smiled at me, addressing me in English. 'Ah, what it is to be young, lady, and in love.'

I smiled. 'Yes, one forgets.'

'But you are still young, madam, do not tell me that you have forgotten so soon.'

I laughed. 'Perhaps not entirely.'

The young couple left us at Salzburg and we were joined by a severe-looking monocled man in officer's uniform, not a uniform I could ever remember seeing before.

He took his place in the corner, favouring us with a brief nod before opening up his newspaper and burying himself behind it.

The train started on its journey towards Vienna and the cleric sat back with his eyes closed while I looked through the windows in an endeavour to recapture what I could remember of that other journey.

After a while the train slowed considerably before coming

to a halt and the officer looked up with some annoyance, saying, 'Not another delay! The train was late in arriving at Salzburg.'

Angrily he opened the window allowing a drift of dust to waft into the department, then quickly closing it again he said, 'They're working on the line. I hope it isn't for long because I have an engagement for this evening. Something will have to be done about the railway system, and something will be done.'

I had thought I had forgotten my German but I understood him perfectly. Now, addressing me in English, the cleric said, 'Have you too an engagement in Vienna, madam?'

'I'm meeting friends from England who have been touring Austria and will be in Vienna for a week.'

'That is nice, and will you know what they should see?'

'Yes, I lived in Vienna for several years.'

'You lived in Vienna,' the officer said in a surprised voice. 'Why was that?'

'I had relatives there; I worked there.'

'So you speak German?'

'Yes. I thought I had forgotten most of it, but I understood what you were saying perfectly.'

'Is this the first time you have been back?' he asked curiously. 'Yes.'

'Then you will find it changed. The old order is gone and Europe is waking up to better things. You will find Vienna more vibrant, less eaten up with its ridiculous waltz music and cloying sentimentality.'

I didn't speak and the cleric said gently, 'I am an old man; the pace of life is a little fast for me.'

'But you do agree, do you not, that better times are ahead? When we have finally put the past to bed we can progress with the future, which will be very exciting, I can assure you.'

After a few minutes the priest rose to his feet and to me said, 'Would you care to join me for a meal, madam? Or do you prefer to eat alone?'

'Oh no, I would like to join you.'

The officer was looking at us coldly, and after a few seconds he said, 'I shall eat later.'

In the dining car the priest said gently, 'Too much of our military friend would exhaust me. In Vienna we are seeing more and more of them.'

When I looked at him curiously he said with a wry smile, 'German officers. When you were last in Vienna you would find the ballrooms full of young Hussars and soldiers from other regiments. Now the only uniforms we see are German uniforms.'

'He spoke of changes. Are they the ones who will be making the changes, then?'

He shrugged his shoulders. 'I believe so, and he is sure so.'

'I have been living in Rome; there are changes too in Italy.'

'Ah yes. It is better not to say very much. Who knows nowadays who might be listening?'

I was hoping to find that some of the old Vienna still lingers. I have talked about Vienna to my friends for such a long time; made them see how I loved her, made them want to come here, and now that they are coming they could be bitterly disappointed.'

'Take them to the old places and let them see how it was, the Hofburg and the Schönbrunn, the Prater gardens and the opera house, the parks and the Vienna Woods. So much of it is left, and when you show them tell them how it used to be with the uniforms and the jewels, the music and the pageantry. If they have any imagination at all they will understand.'

After we returned to our compartment the cleric fell asleep in his corner and after a while the German officer said, 'So madam, you are spending some time in Vienna?'

'Yes, a week, perhaps a little longer.'

'And how long are your friends here?'

'I'm not sure.'

'When your friends have gone home I should be happy to show you Vienna, madam.'

'Thank you. You are very kind, but I know the city very well, and I shall not be staying on after my friends leave.'

'*Ach so*, we have to be polite to our English cousins, you understand.'

'Thank you, sir.'

The rest of the journey was taken in silence. The officer opened up his briefcase and became absorbed in what he found in there. I closed my eyes and leaned back against my corner while the priest slept on. It was only when I became aware of movement in the passage outside that I opened my eyes and found that in the distance I could see the towers and domes of Vienna shining golden in the late afternoon sunshine, and I realised that we were almost there.

The officer was on his feet gathering his belongings together, then he was lifting my case down, saying, 'Is this all your luggage, madam?'

'Yes, enough I think for the time I shall be here.'

'You will need a porter. I will get one for you.'

'You are very kind. Thank you.'

'And efficient, madam, we German officers are well known for our efficiency.'

'I'm sure you are.'

He surely was. He helped both the priest and me with our luggage, he found a porter for us and then raising his right arm in a Nazi salute he bade us good afternoon.

As he strode away from us the priest laughed, saying, 'Now you know how changes are going to be made, madam: real efficiency, enough to shake us out of our slothful Austrian ways and make us see what we have been missing all these years.'

I laughed. I liked him, his humour, the cynicism in eyes that saw too much and saw it clearly, and taking hold of his outstretched hand I said, 'It has been nice travelling with you. Please, no more changes. Cherish what you have.'

I watched him walking away towards the taxi rank, a small plump man in his dusty grey garb, his head now covered with his flat cleric's hat. As he got into his cab he turned once and raised his hand in farewell.

The streets around the station were filled with people intent on getting home from their shops and offices and as we drove through the streets I was unable to recall the last time I had been here. It seemed to me that the streets had been less crowded, the traffic not so intense; but then when had I ever been on these same streets at this hour before?

Emily had given me the address of the hotel where they were staying and I found it to be a large stone building in a vast cobbled square close to the cathedral. It had an old-fash- ioned ambience about it, and I felt sure it had been chosen by the touring agency as one reflecting the old Vienna, from its marble foyer and staircase to the potted palms and flowers, as well as the courtesy of the men and women behind the reception desk in their immaculate uniforms.

I was shown into my bedroom by a uniformed man and hotel maid who were quick to point out every amenity, including a quite delightful bathroom and large windows overlooking the square. They informed me that dinner was served at eight o'clock and a table with my friends had been reserved for me. I knew that they were not due to arrive until the morning so I was aware that I would be dining alone.

One look around the dining room that evening confirmed what I had already thought. The guests were without exception foreign tourists and the hotel was doing its best to recreate the old Vienna for their enjoyment. The small orchestra played music from *The Merry Widow* and other operettas, and only people like me who remembered the old city in its days of empire would see the difference.

Gone were the uniforms, the large *The Merry Widow* hats and the tiaras, the long sweeping gowns and feathered fans. Now the gowns were circumspect, much like the one I was wearing; the men wore dinner jackets and one or two of them lounge suits. I wondered if it was only I who regretted the change.

If my fellow guests were disappointed they didn't show it. They laughed, chatted and enjoyed the music, and after dinner in the hotel lounges the orchestra entertained us to more of the same.

I waited in the foyer the next morning for Emily's coach to arrive from the station and then they were there, her sweet

face looking round with great expectancy like a small inqui-
sitive bird while Edward indicated where the porters could
find their luggage.

I hurried out into the square; when she saw me her face lit up
with a bright smile and Edward came forward to kiss my cheek.

She was chatting merrily away as we walked into the hotel
and turning to a couple nearby she said, 'This is the Alex I've
been telling you so much about. She knows Vienna well so I
know she's going to be a wonderful guide about the city.'

The couple smiled politely, and Emily went on, 'I've been
so looking forward to meeting you here, Alex. Will you be
able to stay with us the whole time we're here?'

'Yes, of course.'

'From here we're going on to Budapest. Just think of it,
when you and I were in Europe Vienna and Budapest seemed
like a dream and now it is really happening.'

'Have you any idea what you want to see specifically, Emily?'

'Oh, everything. Particularly the Spanish Riding School at
the Hofburg and the palaces.'

So in the days that followed I took them to the Schönbrunn
palace, the Belvedere and the Hofburg palaces, and around
every corner, across every cobbled square, history tugged at
my heartstrings and as we walked through the parks and along
the Ringstrasse I half expected to see Karl striding towards me,
his eyes alight with laughter, his hands outstretched to greet
me.

The house in the Ringstrasse where I had lived with Franz
had a new door knocker and one day I saw a woman walking
through the front door holding a small boy by the hand. It
seemed strange to find children in Franz's house: Franz who

had always seemed so reserved and out of touch with everything beyond the narrow circle he moved in.

Further along the Ringstrasse Karl's house was as I remembered it, a typical Viennese mansion, and although we passed it several times I saw no sign of servants or anybody else.

Our visit to the Spanish Riding School was an unqualified success and I watched the joy on their faces as they followed the intricate movements of the beautiful stallions performing their balletic steps.

'I'll never forget them, never,' Emily enthused. 'Oh, I'm so glad we came, I really do understand now, Alex, why you had to come here. Haven't you seen people you knew then?'

'No Emily, it was a long time ago.'

'I suppose so, dear, and people move away, don't they?'

'Perhaps in Grinzing I'll find people I knew before. When you and Edward have left I'll go there.'

'Our tour guides are taking us to Grinzing on the night before we leave; I'm sure you could come with us. It is our last evening, and if it isn't possible then of course we don't go.'

'But you must go. Grinzing is lovely, and you'll hear the music and visit the inns there. You mustn't think of staying behind.'

In the event I was invited to go with them and half of me was looking forward to it while the other half was dreading it.

Grinzing hadn't changed, outwardly at any rate. Lights still shone in the trees and music poured out of every inn doorway. I should have known that we would not be visiting the Golden Pheasant but were taken instead to an inn specially reserved for visitors to the city, where two men and two women sang the music of operettas to us and later music played by a gypsy band took over and a group of Romany dancers entertained us.

The tourists had loved every minute of it, and once I too would have loved it, but not now.

They were due to leave for Budapest after lunch and in the morning we visited the opera house where we were allowed to see inside. For me it was peopled with ghosts. I could picture the Emperor surrounded by his courtiers taking his place in the royal box, his plump smiling mistress by his side, and Franz, haughty, unsmiling, Alicia too, flirting coyly with the men who had adored her, her enchanting beautiful face oblivious to the man sitting beside her who was paying her little attention.

Memories of that other night were there too and I was seeing Zoltan's cynical eyes staring down at me, his smile cruel, and Karl lying at my feet with his blood staining my gown.

I was gasping suddenly for breath, feeling a sudden frightening urge to get out of the building and into the sunshine, then I was aware of people staring down at me and arms were lifting me up to carry me to a couch in the foyer.

I was dimly aware of voices, of the ministrations of several people, and a liquid being poured down my throat. I heard Emily's voice saying, 'I do hope she's going to be all right. What is the matter with her?' Then a man's voice said reassuringly, 'Just a faint, madam, it is very hot in here. She'll be perfectly well in a moment or two.'

I had never fainted in my life before and had never been prone to such weaknesses. Now I was aware that people were staring at me curiously and Emily and Edward were looking

at me with the utmost consternation. Pulling myself upright
I said quickly, 'I am so sorry. I really don't know what came
over me—it must have been the heat. I've never done anything
so stupid before.'

'We're taking you back to the hotel, Alex. Are you sure you
feel well enough?'

'Of course, Emily, please don't fuss. I'm fine.'

'Then we'll get a taxi, and do rest up this afternoon after
we've gone. We feel so responsible; it's all this sightseeing.
You should have said if you were feeling tired.'

'It's the heat, nothing to do with sightseeing. I hope it
hasn't spoiled your last morning in Vienna.'

'Of course not, and this evening we're going to telephone
you from Budapest just to make sure you're better.'

I felt a fool. Had I been so eaten up with the past that I was
allowing it to take over my life? The sooner I left Vienna the
happier I would be.

In all the years since I had left Vienna I had only ever
thought of Karl and the glamour of a remembered past. Now
today of all days I had suddenly remembered eyes that were
cruel and an act of depravity that had ended what I had
believed was my happiness with the man I loved.

CHAPTER THIRTY-THREE

IT SEEMED STRANGE to be alone now that Emily and Edward had left, visiting the shops, the intimacy of the coffee houses, walking in the park, strolling across the squares; I felt I was marking time. We had been unable to get seats for the opera during Emily's visit and now I didn't feel like going there on my own.

I despised myself for fainting during that morning visit. If anger and hatred could do that to me, how much more disturbing would love be.

I decided to go to Grinzing, make enquiries about the people I had known there and then think about returning to Italy.

It was one of those golden mornings in late September when late summer roses still bloomed in the gardens and the leaves were just beginning to turn on the linden trees. It was pleasantly warm, too early for the cold winds from the Baltic to descend on Vienna, and as I walked down the main street of the village the years dropped away and I could even think it was the old Grinzing from the whistling of the post boys and the smiles I received from passers-by.

I paused for a moment at the gates to the Golden Pheasant.

then prompted by the smile from a girl placing check table-cloths on the tables in the garden I went inside. I walked around the garden before entering the inn. I remembered Karl and his friends standing in the doorway, I even remembered Zoltan Bartok and his dark cynicism, but the sun was shining and unlike at the opera house the trauma had not been so intense.

In the lobby of the inn a young man sat at the desk and looking up with a smile said, 'May I help you?'

'It is many years since I was in Grinzing. Do Herr Gruber and his wife still live here?'

I had spoken to him in German but he answered me in English and when I raised my eyes in surprise he said, 'I did not think you were Austrian, lady, but no, the Grubers have not been here for many years. Frau Gruber died and he did not wish to stay on here without her.'

'I am sorry. Is he still in the village?'

'Alas no. He lives in Linz with his niece and her husband.'

'Thank you. I didn't think he would still be here, but I had to try.'

I turned to walk away and he asked, 'Is it possible that I can help with other people you knew?'

'Perhaps you can. I knew Herr Windisch, who had a house at the edge of the village. He came here almost every night—is he still living in the area?'

'Ah yes, madam, he has not been here for some time but I see his servant shopping in the village for him so he is still with us.'

'Thank you so much; I'll go there now, I hope he's well enough to see me.'

It might have been yesterday. The lawns in front of his

house where smooth and green and flowers still bloomed profusely in the garden. He was sitting on the terrace in what was his favourite place, and the click of the gate closing behind me did not rouse him from his slumber. Indeed I was now close enough to touch him gently on his shoulder and when he opened his eyes he stared at me without recognition for several seconds and I said gently, 'Herr Windisch— Ernst—I'm sorry to disturb you. I'm afraid you don't remember me.'

He reached into his pocket for his spectacles, and then after a moment his face broke into a smile and he said, 'Alexandra, forgive me. It is my eyesight that is failing, not my memory. So you have come back to us.'

'For a short while, yes. How are you?'

'Well enough for my age. I am eighty-one, hardly a young man, but I manage. Now come and sit here; I will ring the bell and my servant will bring us some refreshment.'

He asked many questions so I talked about Andrew and Adrian, about our time in India and now in Italy, and a little of England after the war years. Then he talked to me of Austria saying sadly, 'The republic has not been a success, Alexandra; it has been a disaster, but things will be changing and I'm not sure if the changes are the ones we need or want.'

'What sort of changes?'

'The German dictator is an Austrian, so I rather think it will be Germany who will bring them about, and there will be very little we can do.'

I didn't speak. I was suddenly thinking of the German officer who had travelled with us into Vienna; I was remembering his authority, his singular efficiency and his contempt for a country he had described as some sort of Ruritanian operetta awash with the sentimentality of waltz music and little else.

'Are you telling me you will have no say in how your country is governed?' I asked him.

Instead of answering my question he said, 'And what about Rome? I remember going there when I was still a young man, so much history, so many years of it, and yet that too faded. The glory that was Rome is no more, I fear.'

'But a certain Italian dictator is very anxious to resurrect it.'

'Ah yes, a desire to carve up the world. And will the rest of the world allow it, do you think?'

'I don't know. My husband is troubled by it all; it is his job to be troubled. I rather think he was glad for me to get away if only for a short time.'

'But to get away here?'

I smiled. 'I've been with English friends who were visiting Vienna. I haven't been lonely.'

'And who of your old friends have you seen?'

'You are the only one.'

'Well, Frau Gruber died and he is living with his niece in Linz.'

'I know, they told me at the inn.'

'You have seen no old friends in Vienna?'

'No. I've looked at the house where I lived in the Ringstrasse but nothing is the same, none of the people living there are the same.'

'And yet I think the von Wincklers still have their house in the Ringstrasse, although I hear the Countess prefers the country house in the woods.'

'Do you ever see him, or his wife?'

'They came here one evening to a concert given by the opera house.'

'Do they have children?'

'I believe so, a boy and a girl.'

'I'm so glad. I hope they are happy.'

'At least as happy as you have been, Alexandra?'

'Yes, of course. And I have been happy, Ernst. It was time to move on.'

'Then you must go home, or at least back to Rome, my dear. It would be a mistake, I think, to stray among the moments that have fled.'

'I have no intentions of doing that. In any case there is little danger that Karl von Winckler and I will ever meet again. We live in different worlds.'

He smiled. 'Perhaps you always did.'

He shivered, and I suddenly realised that a chill wind was blowing across the garden. Ruefully he said, 'Soon now the winter winds will sweep in and we shall feel the snow in them and there will be weeks, months of it before spring comes again to Vienna.'

All the way back to Vienna I thought about our meeting. I did not think that we would ever meet again. He would be locked away with the rest of my memories and perhaps only resurrected when I too was old and memories were all I had left.

As I sat in the hotel lounge that evening listening to the music of Lehar I made up my mind that I would return to Italy after the weekend. I had three days to recapture my favourite places in the city, three days to see once more the spectacle provided by the Lippizaner stallions at the Hofburg, visit the cathedral of St Stephen, rekindle my memories of the Schönbrunn palace.

I spent most of my last morning packing away things I would no longer need, and yet it seemed a sin to spend the time indoors when outside the sun was shining and the streets of the city were filled with people going about their daily business. There was a vibrancy about Vienna this morning.

It was pleasantly warm and I walked across the square towards the park. I did not even look along the road towards Karl's house; I simply strolled along the paths edged with late roses towards the lake. Then suddenly I saw them, a procession of young men walking with military precision in their uniforms, each one wearing an armband displaying a swastika, singing some sort of marching song in loud enthusiastic voices.

I stood still on the path while on the grass a man had paused to watch them also, his entire stance proclaiming arrogant contempt and disapproval. They passed, and he looked at me. He didn't recognise me, even though my heart was racing like a wild thing, then he turned away.

I waited without moving, my hands clenched against my breast, then suddenly he turned round, his face incredulous, and walking quickly towards me he cried, 'Alex, is it really you?'

He took my hands, staring intensely into my face, and I couldn't speak. He was no longer in uniform, but the sun shone golden on his hair now that he had removed his hat, and the face that I had loved was still the same: handsome, filled with vitality. While he held me close in his arms all I could think of was why on my last day in Vienna fate had allowed us to meet.

In the first few breathless moments I told him that it was my last day in Vienna; immediately he said, 'Then tonight we must have dinner together. We have so much to talk about.'

So I told him where I was staying and he arranged to call for me at eight o'clock; when I returned to my room I took out of my case the evening dress I hadn't thought I would wear here again.

'This is a new restaurant I am taking you to, Alex,' he told me when he fetched me. 'Many of the old ones are no more, and this has a good reputation.'

I was glad it was to be a new venue because too much nostalgia was a dangerous thing. The restaurant was charming, typically Viennese, and the food was good. A Magyar orchestra played gypsy music and a violinist played haunting Hungarian melodies as he passed from table to table.

How strange it was to dine with Karl and talk about Andrew and my son, and how diffident he was about his own marriage and family until in the end I said, 'You've said very little about your own life, Karl, but you've listened very patiently to my story.'

'But you knew about mine, Alex. I had to discover yours. Do you have to go home tomorrow? Is your husband expecting you?'

'I was going to telephone him this evening. I haven't told them at the hotel that I was leaving.'

'Then why go tomorrow, why not stay on? At least we should have some time together.'

'Oh Karl, I don't know. We're two different people; why open old wounds?'

'Think instead that we are healing old wounds. We're two old friends who used to be lovers and who have met again after many years.'

Friends! With all passion spent, to fear no more the heat of the sun.

We walked through the city squares where a full moon illuminated domes and towers, and small eerily lit alleyways led on to cobbled squares that shone gloriously under the night sky.

As he parted with me at the hotel he held both my hands in his and his smile was cajoling. 'Stay a little longer, Alex tomorrow we could drive into the woods and capture some of the magic we once knew. We could go to Mayerling. It's going to be a beautiful day and nothing in the Vienna Woods has changed.'

In the end I said, 'I'll stay on for a few days, but it can't be for long.'

Mayerling, he had said, that hunting lodge which was now a convent, but where tragedy had struck one more blow at an empire that was already crumbling; I could not go to Mayerling without thinking of Crown Prince Rudolf and poor Marie Vetsera.

I had been a fool to stay. The old magic was still with me as we drove through the Vienna Woods and the years had not eliminated the old Alex as we talked together, danced together, even enjoyed the more prosaic pleasures of the Prater gardens where the young people of Vienna strolled with their arms round each other until the stars paled. I felt young again, young and possibly foolish, but we laughed often, and

I liked to think that our laughter was joyous and without bitterness.

I was glad that Karl had not invited me to go to the opera house with him; there were too many traumas attached to it. But when I told him of my stupid fainting episode he said gently, 'So not even *Die Fledermaus* will tempt you, *liebchen*?'

It was madness to allow old traumas to affect the present. If Karl could face it I should be able to face it also, and so I told him I would enjoy *Die Fledermaus*. It would be the highlight of my return to Vienna.

People still dressed up for the opera, but it was not the old glamour I remembered. All the same some of the old magic was still there and as we walked up the staircase people were smiling at us and their greetings did not appear to be embarrassing Karl in the slightest.

As we took our place in the box I thought curiously: does he often visit the opera house, or dine in restaurants with women other than his wife? Then another thought took hold of me. Would any of these people remember that I was the same woman who had been his companion on that terrible night?

The operetta was a joy, a souvenir to be treasured in a more sombre though madder world, and as we drove back to my hotel Karl said, 'Aren't you glad you went, *liebchen*?' and I admitted that it had been one of the happiest evenings of my life.

'There will be many more,' he promised, and it was then I told myself firmly that my days in Vienna were numbered.

'I have to think about going back to Rome, Karl,' I told him. 'I have to think about Andrew, and you have to think about your wife and family. Our time together has been charming, but it isn't meant to last.'

'So, when are you thinking you might leave?'

'After the weekend. Monday or Tuesday at the latest.'

'So soon.'

'I'm afraid so.'

'Then all we have is two more days. Tomorrow we will go to Grinzing, eat lunch at the Golden Pheasant, then drive out to the woods. Perhaps tomorrow evening you will dine with me at my house in the Ringstrasse.'

'I don't know, Karl. Why there, why not some restaurant?'

'Because it is Saturday evening and the restaurants will be crowded and noisy. I want us to dine where it is quiet, where we can talk, just the two of us. You will like my house, *liebchen*. It is charming; it will remind you of the house you shared with Franz Bruckner.'

'I'm not sure that I want to be reminded. The only memories I have of the place are Alicia's desertion and then Franz's death.'

'There are no unhappy memories in my house. I grew up in it; it was a happy household even if my mother was very grand and my father very stern. My sister and I had good times here. My family used to enjoy it, but now they prefer the country.'

I would like to have asked questions. He so seldom mentioned his family; at first I thought it was because he would embarrass me by talking about them, but then I began to think he felt aloof from them.

'So, will you dine with me tomorrow, Alex?'

'Yes, of course.'

'We'll spend the entire day together and talk about what we'll do on your last day.'

My last day! I was aware of the dangers, but this was a new confident me, a me that was unafraid of old passions.

In the hotel lounge the orchestra was still playing for the people sitting there but I walked towards the lift. Somehow or other I had had enough of waltz music for one evening. I should telephone Andrew, tell him I was leaving for Italy on Monday morning.

I tried several times to reach him but on each occasion I was informed that he was out until in the end I thought it could wait until tomorrow.

In later years when I tried to remember that last day with Karl I found that memories were elusive. The check tableclothes were on the tables set out in the garden of the Golden Pheasant, the usual music floated out of every doorway and people were enjoying themselves. It was only when we were leaving Grinzing that a group of youths came into the garden and started to sing their new songs of bravado.

Karl rose to his feet with an angry frown, saying, 'We must go, Alex, I don't want to listen to this.'

They saw our discomfort and they were amused by it. They were the new brave world; we belonged to the old and the old to them should be finished and dead. Their laughter followed us out of the inn and as we drove away. I remember that I was increasingly aware of his silence, the silence of anger and disbelief that he was unable to do anything about it.

Our last beautiful day was spoilt before it had even started. It should have been an omen that there was more to come.

I returned to the hotel to change for dinner and Karl came for me in the early evening.

I had known the house would be reminiscent of Franz's house from its shallow curving staircase to the pictures of old Austrian royalty on the walls.

Over the fireplace hung a huge picture of the Empress Elizabeth sitting sidesaddle on her stallion, beautiful, elegant, and then another one of her in a ballgown painted at Schönbrunn. Karl escorted me round the house with pride, the complete aristocrat, and as I listened to him the pitiful history of our doomed love came back to torture my foolish heart.

CHAPTER THIRTY-FOUR

WE DINED AND we talked. We were waited on by soft-footed servants and I found Otto, Karl's butler, occasionally eyeing me curiously and with a gentle irony.

I was certain how the evening would end and it seemed inevitable. This was surely what it was all about, not simply old sights and old memories; it was a love affair that had never completely finished. I wanted Karl to make love to me and then I would return to my world and he would return to his. How much more subtle were the machinations of fate.

We were sitting in front of a warm fire; his arms were around me, our kisses were passionate and loving, and only dimly I heard the shrilling of a telephone from somewhere outside the room. Then Otto was there, a gentle smile of apology on his face saying, 'Countess Winckler is on the telephone, sir. Would you prefer to take it in the library?'

Karl made his excuses and a few seconds later I heard the sharp closing of the library door. That was the moment I came to my senses.

I shouldn't be here. This was all I had ever been, a mistress, and this was all there could ever be, a love affair. Twenty years before he would not have been allowed to marry me, and now he was speaking to his wife on the telephone and I had a husband and a son who for the last few days I had forgotten.

I looked round the room with something like panic. I had to leave, get out of this house and out of his life. Hunting feverishly in my handbag I found my diary and after tearing out a page I wrote a brief note simply to say goodbye, and to thank him for the few days we had enjoyed. Then I folded it and left it in front of the clock on the mantelpiece.

I stood trembling for several minutes outside the door, from where I could hear his voice from further down the hall. I hurried towards the front door and then Otto was there eyeing me with some surprise; I said hurriedly, 'Otto, I have to go. Would you get my wrap for me?'

'But Count von Winckler will not be long, madam, just a few minutes, no more.'

'I know, but I have left a note for him. Please, I must go now.'

I could have wept at the sympathy in his eyes, at the concern he showed as he handed me my wrap and opened the door for me. It was raining, fine drizzling rain, and Otto said quickly, 'Stay here, madam, and I will get a taxi for you.'

'No, Otto, it doesn't matter. My hotel is near—I'll walk.' Before he could say another word I was running down the steps.

I could feel the gentle rain on my face and the dampness of the wrap round my shoulders, and as I hurried at last across the square towards the hotel my feet too were damp from the puddles that had formed on the cobbles.

In the hotel foyer I shook the drops of water from my wrap; people were staring at me curiously, a woman in evening dress who appeared to have been walking in the rain.

I went to the desk to pick up my room key and there the receptionist smiled at me saying, 'Madam, you have a visitor. He is in the bar; I will tell him you are here.'

I stared at him in amazement. What visitor could I have? Not Karl, there would not have been time—and then Andrew was there and I was sobbing into his arms.

'What is this?' he was saying gently. 'And why are you so wet?'

'Oh Andrew,' I murmured, 'why didn't you tell me you were coming?'

'I wanted to surprise you. Besides, I wasn't sure I could manage it until yesterday. Where have you been in the rain?'

'Can I go upstairs so that I can get out of these damp clothes?'

'Of course. I'll wait for you in the bar, then you can tell me what I've been missing.'

'I had planned on leaving on Monday, Andrew. I've already packed most of my things.'

'I know. I told them I was your husband so they allowed me to put my case in the room. We'll talk later, darling.'

So we sat in the hotel lounge and talked. We listened to music and I thanked providence for whatever modicum of common sense I had been able to muster. Without that intrusive telephone call the outcome would have been very different and I was still trembling with fear at how close to catastrophe I had been.

'Why were you walking in the rain?' Andrew asked. 'You had obviously dressed for the occasion, whatever it was.'

'I had dinner with a friend: someone I had known when I lived with my aunt, a neighbour.'

'Didn't they think to get a taxi for you, Alex?'

'Yes, of course they did, but it is Saturday evening, and I said I wanted to get back. It wasn't far.'

'And what of Vienna, darling? I suppose you've found it very different.'

'The old glamour has gone but the city is still the same. Emily and Edward loved it. I showed them all I thought they should see.'

'Of course, how are Emily and Edward?'

'Very well, they left to go to Budapest.'

'So what did you do on your own?'

'I went to Grinzing where I saw Herr Windisch but the Grubers are no longer there. It was full of tourists like Emily and Edward. We went to the Spanish Riding School and that is still wonderful. How long can you stay, Andrew?'

'A few days, no more. For those days we'll try to forget the mess Europe is in, because we'll have to face it soon enough.'

So we went to the Hofburg to see the stallions and we went to the opera to see *The Magic Flute*; on our last morning as we walked in the park my heart raced furiously when I saw Karl walking towards us along the path. He raised his hat and paused, and I introduced them.

Karl said evenly, 'I knew Alex briefly when she lived in the Ringstrasse, a long time ago.'

Andrew smiled. 'Yes, this is a journey of nostalgia for her.'

'Are you here for some time?'

'No, we are leaving this afternoon.'

At that moment we saw them marching towards us along the path and we stepped to one side to allow them to pass. Young enthusiastic boys in uniform they were proud of, the swastika armbands proclaiming their allegiance to a new and frightening regime; looking up at the faces of the two men I was with I recognised the same look of hostility. An Austrian and an Englishman, unknown to each other, but both of them filled with resentment at a world that was changing.

Karl raised his hat and smiled. 'Enjoy the rest of your stay,' he said evenly. Then he was gone and as I watched him striding away I knew I would never see him again.

As we continued our walk and sat at last in the little café garden to drink our coffee Andrew said, 'Count von Winckler was unimpressed with that little procession, Alex.'

'You too, Andrew.'

'Yes. I suppose he remembers a very different Vienna.'

'He was an officer in the Emperor's Hussars.'

He nodded and I was glad he asked no more questions. He did not remember Karl—their meeting on the train had been brief—but strangely he had remembered meeting me. There was always something surprising in Andrew, a something hidden by an English reserve that intrigued me.

We left Vienna in the early afternoon and as we waited on the platform for the train to arrive a man wearing uniform marched towards us and I suddenly recognised the German officer who had recently shared my compartment on the way to Vienna.

He stared at us, wished us good morning, and marched

past, and Andrew said with a smile, 'Another friend of yours, Alex?'

'No, he was on the train the day I arrived. He joined it at Salzburg.'

'He evidently had important business in Vienna.'

'He helped me and a priest with our luggage and assured us of his efficiency. He also offered to show me Vienna if I was in need of an escort.'

Andrew smiled. 'And you agreed, of course.'

'You know I didn't. I probably know Vienna as well as he does.'

There were many times on that train journey when I found Andrew deep in thought. His mind was on other things, things that troubled him, and it was not until we were driving through the streets of Rome that he said evenly, 'Rome looks much the same, and yet like Vienna it has changed.'

'I suppose so. I love it, though. I love its vitality and its history.'

'I wouldn't get too attached to it, darling. I have a feeling that we shall not be here long.'

I stared at him in surprise. 'You mean we're leaving?'

'Nothing definite as yet, but I do feel it's on the cards.'

'But will we be going home, or somewhere else?'

'I don't know. It's just a presentiment I have at the moment. I've had them before and they rarely let me down.'

His words troubled me. I was happy in Rome; at the same time I would be happy to go home, but I knew that Andrew's work would not allow us to stay there for a long period. Where would we end up next, I wondered?

* * *

Life picked up its pattern. With friends I shopped in the city and drank wine in the outdoor cafés that lined the squares of the city and as the weeks wore on we were more and more made aware of the marching feet of young Italian fascists. Like the boys I had seen in Vienna their eyes were bold and confident of a new and promising future.

It was one evening when we dined at a restaurant high up in the hills overlooking Rome that Andrew said calmly, 'Make the most of the next few days, Alex. We shall be leaving Rome at the end of the week.'

'Where are we going?'

'Back to England for the time being.'

'And then where?'

'I don't know. I shall be informed when we arrive in London. You'll be able to spend some time with your mother, and we'll see something of Adrian, darling. You'll enjoy that.'

'Of course I will, but I wonder if I'll ever get accustomed to constantly moving on, just when we've got established.'

'We never get established. We're birds of passage, but the next time might be different.'

'How can it possibly be different?'

'I just have a feeling about it, trust me.'

So Andrew stayed in London and I went to stay with my mother, who received me with tears in her eyes. Mrs Pearson said shortly, 'How long is it for this time, Miss Alex?'

She never called me Mrs Falkener, always Miss Alex, and then I was back again wiping my shoes on the mat in the hall, hearing her voice advising me to put on my slippers and not to talk to strangers when I walked home across the park.

'She still treats me like a child,' I grumbled, and Mother

merely laughed, saying, 'You won't change her, Alex, but do you really want to?'

'I suppose not. It wouldn't be the same, would it?'

We talked about my time in Vienna with Emily and Edward, and about the marching boys there and in Rome. Mother said fearfully, 'People everywhere are talking about trouble. Surely there isn't going to be another war, and yet all we ever hear about in the news is that man Hitler ranting and raving somewhere or other, and that other one in Italy.'

'Don't worry, Mother, I'm sure they'll not affect us.'

So why didn't I believe in my assurances? Maybe it was Andrew's reticence, his normal conversation that hid so much that made his thoughtful silences seem more profound.

We spent time with Adrian in the Lake District and one day he astonished me by saying, 'If there's a war, Mother, I think I shall join the navy.'

Andrew said sharply, 'What is this talk of war? In any case, Adrian, you're far too young to even think about joining any of the services.'

'Well, war or no war, that's what I'd like to do. I'd like to go to Dartmouth Naval College; I really don't fancy anything else.'

'You'll change your mind a dozen times before you embark on any profession,' Andrew said, and I was surprised how irritable he seemed at Adrian's persistence.

His headmaster assured us that he was a bright and competent boy who was doing well at school but Andrew said, 'He's talking about a career in the navy. Why do you suppose that is?'

The headmaster smiled. 'There's all this talk about

trouble in Europe and how it might affect us. The boys are naturally interested. We don't hide them from the world: they see the newspapers, they have access to the radio, they go home for holidays and listen to their parents talking about things. I'm sure we all hope nothing dire is going to happen.'

I felt sure that his worries stemmed from other matters he felt unable to discuss and I had learned not to ask questions. Andrew would tell me what I needed to know when the time was right.

I heard more about the state of the world from Della's husband than from Andrew. As a Member of Parliament he enjoyed holding forth about a good many things his constituents were not privy to, and this annoyed Andrew intensely.

'He shouldn't be discussing these things in his position,' he grumbled. 'I suppose he's simply showing off.'

I laughed. 'Of course, and Della encourages him, she always has.'

I knew that Andrew preferred to spend time with Ruth and her husband. Sally was at university now and we saw little of her but Ruth and I had never had any trouble in picking up our old closeness.

We went south to stay with Andrew's parents and there again they were concerned about the feet marching across Europe. Then we had Neville Chamberlain returning from Munich to reassure us that there would be peace in our time.

There was much relief on the faces of people I met in the streets and the shops, yet I saw no relief on the face of my husband, only a cynical detachment. When I remarked on it he said evenly, 'If everything is so wonderful, Alex, then why are we preparing everywhere for war?' It was true, from air raid shelters to the distribution of gas masks.

One evening on his return from London he said, 'We're moving on. I received my posting this morning; we're leaving at the end of the month.'

'Where to this time?' I asked.

'Washington, and I think Adrian should come with us. He can go to school in America. They speak our language; he will like it there.'

'But he's doing so well at school. How long are we expecting to stay there?'

'I don't know, but it could be some time. We'll drive up to see him over the weekend.'

I was unsure how Adrian would view our move to America, or how he would take to coming with us, but I needn't have worried. He thought it a wonderful idea; with all the optimism of youth he viewed his future with great enthusiasm and for the moment at least all his ambitions to join the Royal Navy were put on hold.

Andrew's parents and my mother were rather less enthusiastic about our leaving, and one morning I drove over to see Andrew's grandmother.

She seemed to have aged considerably since our last meeting, but her mind was as bright as ever; only her arthritis was troubling her. Whatever hostility she had felt towards me had long since gone and in its place was the sort of friendship reserved for a trusted member of the family.

We talked about our move to America, of which she disapproved, and then we spoke of Stephanie, a subject which must have been constantly on her mind.

'She comes to see me when she wants something,' she said bitterly. 'She's supposed to have a husband but she's always short of money. Heaven knows what she spends it on.'

'But she lives with her husband, surely?'

'She doesn't talk about him, and I don't ask.'

'Where is she living?'

'She tells me they're living in Andover but I can't place any credence in anything she says.'

'I'd like to see her before we leave. Do you have her telephone number?'

'I have neither her address nor her telephone number. If she visits before you leave I'll ask her to call and see you, but that's the best I can do.'

I promised that both Andrew and I would say goodbye before we left, but that evening when I relayed to Andrew what she had told me about Stephanie he said, 'Why is she short of money? She eventually got her husband's inheritance and she was able to sell the house in London.'

'I don't know. I can only tell you what your grandmother told me.' I concealed the fact that I knew Stephanie had spent the money from her house.

He shrugged his shoulders. Andrew and Stephanie were hardly likely to be on the same wavelength.

CHAPTER THIRTY-FIVE

The days were hectic: long telephone calls home, farewells to be said and endless packing, since we had no means of knowing how long we would be in America. Then we went to collect Adrian from his school.

He said goodbye to his teachers and his friends, but his face was alive with excitement and I was remembering what it was like to be young, not to be plagued with nostalgia, to look forward avidly. He was thrilled to be sailing on the *Queen Mary*, and we heard no more for the time being about his wish to join the navy. There would be no war, we would be in America, and to Adrian the future was rosy.

Andrew and I took Adrian to visit Andrew's grandmother and she received us warmly and with a great deal of advice as to how we should conduct ourselves in America. 'Be very British,' she advised us. 'They couldn't wait to get rid of us, but they still like us. Thank goodness we're still good friends.'

On the day before we were due to leave I saw from the window of the living room a low rakish sports car coming up the drive and I knew immediately it could only be Stephanie.

She strolled across the lawn, looking up at the house, then turned to look towards the sea. In spite of the car and the fashionable attire she seemed suddenly like a woman surrounded by a great loneliness. I went to the door to meet her and she smiled a smile that said, Don't concern yourself about me; I'm my own woman; I don't need advice from anybody.

In the drawing room she sprawled on the sofa in front of the fire looking round her at the room she had been familiar with since childhood.

'You haven't changed anything, Alex,' she said finally.

'Of course not. It isn't my house.'

'And how is Andrew? Is he here?'

'Yes, he's out with Adrian at the moment, shopping for last-minute things.'

'Why shop here? There'll be more to buy in America.'

'Perhaps, but they must both feel the need to get things here.'

'So, how was Rome?'

'I liked it there, but of course things were changing.'

'There's going to be a war, you know. You'll be well out of it.'

'Why are you so sure?'

'That peace in our time didn't fool me, Alex. Hitler said it to get rid of him, and now we're rushing round like mad to make up for lost time. Don't say you haven't noticed it too.'

'Yes. All the same I hope it doesn't happen.'

'It could be like the last time, all those young officers looking for a spot of romance before they go off to face the enemy, and I'm still young enough to enjoy the experience. I was in my teens the last time we went to war; I'm considerably more sophisticated now.'

'How is your husband, Stephanie?'

Her smile was entirely cynical.

'I don't see much of him, darling. Like I told you before, Lucian and I have little in common but we stay together.'

'You live in Andover, I believe.'

'Lucian lives in Andover. I spend most of my time in London. London's expensive—I've got a flat there and I get help from Grandmother. I suppose she's told Andrew that.'

'Her money won't last forever, Stephanie.'

'I know, if she can no longer give it to me then I'll have to cut my losses and go home to Lucian.'

I was becoming annoyed with her. This was the old Stephanie, thinking that the world and people should revolve around her, and I wanted her to go. Stephanie on the other hand showed no signs of going.

'I would like a drink, Alex. G and T, I think, unless you prefer tea. My aunt is out, I take it?'

'Yes, she'll be back around five.'

'I'm not anxious to see her; she never approved of me.'

I went to the cabinet to get the drinks and she came over to watch me pour it.

'A little more gin, darling, I hate it wishy-washy.'

She took the glass and went back to her seat.

'I suppose you're happy with Andrew,' she said, fixing me with her bright probing stare.

'Yes I am. He's a nice kind man, and we have a nice son.'

'There's something terribly bland about the word "nice", Alex. Can't you make it sound a little more exciting?'

'I'm happy in my marriage, Stephanie. I love them both; life has been very good to me.'

Suddenly she was bored. She didn't want to hear about how life had been good to me, she wanted to hear that there were troubling undercurrents in my marriage, that it was not as perfect as I was pretending it was, and my irritation with her grew.

For want of something to talk about I said, 'I suppose you're still in touch with all your old friends?'

'Not really. Some of them got married to each other, some of them moved away. None of them really rallied round after Roger. I'm in with a new crowd now, just as exciting.'

'Have you never seen Roger since you parted from him?'

'No, but I saw one of the old crowd in Bond Street and she told me she'd seen him with a woman, looking rather the worse for wear. He was going abroad again.'

'Was it his wife?'

'I wouldn't think so, darling. Really, Roger wasn't the marrying kind. I should have realised it, but I didn't.'

'Are you going back to London tonight?'

'No, I'm staying at Granny's. Last time I was here I was looking at her jewellery. Some of it will be for me but I wanted an emerald ring that she has which I've always admired. She wouldn't let me have it: she said it was for you.'

I stared at her incredulously.

'Oh, Stephanie, I'm sure you're wrong. Why give it to me when you're her granddaughter?'

'That's what I said, but remember that Andrew has always been her favourite. When he married you I thought she'd forget all that, but apparently she hasn't, and she's grown to like you. Of course you could always refuse to have it, tell her it should really be mine, make her see you don't need it.'

'She hasn't mentioned it to me. I'll leave Andrew to tell her that it should be yours.'

'He won't. She has other rings, most of them valuable, but I always loved that emerald the most.'

'Would you keep it, Stephanie, would you treasure it?'

'Just as long as I'm solvent, but a ring like that would be an asset, something to get me out of the doghouse when the money's gone.'

'How can you live your life like that?'

'I don't seem to have much option. It's the way I am—apparently I take after my mother, and yet I hardly remember her and I certainly don't owe her anything.'

I was glad at that moment to hear the sound of Andrew's car in front of the house, and the next minute Adrian was there and Stephanie was greeting him with a bright smile.

'What a handsome man you're going to be,' she said. 'You're like your father but I hope you'll smile more. Andrew was always so serious.'

Adrian smiled politely and then Andrew was greeting her and saying, 'I thought it must be your car, Stephanie. I don't know anybody else who drives such a rakish model.'

'I wouldn't be seen dead in your oh-so-respectable vehicle, Andrew. You're looking well. Evidently Italy agreed with you.'

So the afternoon passed pleasantly enough and Stephanie decided she would go before my mother-in-law arrived home. 'I always feel her disapproval, Andrew,' she said with a smile. 'Gosh, I wish I was going to America. Anywhere to get away from England and this gloom and doom that we're going through. We've been promised peace in our time, but don't tell me you believe it.'

He shrugged his shoulders. 'Until we hear something else we have to believe it.'

'Then why are buildings being shuttered, why bomb shelters, why gas masks and a hundred and one other things? Will it be like the last one, do you think, those rat-infested trenches, all that slaughter?'

'We will have to wait and see. Here is my mother; I don't talk about war in front of her.'

'Oh drat. I'll meet her on the drive just to say goodbye.' She kissed Adrian's cheek, saying, 'Enjoy yourself in America, darling, you two also. I'll be thinking about you and feeling green with envy.'

We watched her greeting Andrew's mother from the window, then after a brief wave of her hand she was hurrying towards her car. Andrew looked at me ruefully, and I said, 'She doesn't change, Andrew. I don't think I could ever have understood her.'

'None of us could.'

His mother joined us and she said, 'How long has Stephanie been here?'

'She came after lunch,' I replied. 'She's staying tonight with her grandmother.'

'Mmmm. I expect she's after some money. Why isn't she with her husband?'

When I didn't reply Andrew said, 'Meeting go well, Mother?'

'Very well, but there's another one tomorrow, something to do with gas masks and looking after ourselves i there is a war.'

'I wouldn't worry. We have to take precautions.'

'Well, your father's down there now. Something else i

going on; I really don't know what but he said he wasn't ready
to come home with me.'

That evening we played board games on the table in front
of the fire, we laughed and cheated and none of us could have
believed it would ever change. It was the sort of memory that
would stay with me when all we would be hearing was news
of bombs falling on British cities and how we stood alone
while the world fell to pieces around us.

Only a few days later we stood on the deck of the *Queen Mary*
looking down on a quayside where the Royal Marine band
played patriotic music and people had gathered to watch the
ship sail away. There were streamers flying, and hands
waving, and then as the great ship pulled away the strains of
'Auld Lang Syne' echoed plaintively until we could hear it
no more. I could taste the salty tears which rolled down on to
my lips, and Adrian too looked close to weeping. It wasn't
the pain of leaving that troubled him, but the emotion aroused
by the music.

Andrew stood between us, with an arm round each of our
shoulders. 'I think we should find ourselves a cup of tea,' he
suggested. 'How about crumpets, Adrian? That sounds very
civilised to me.'

Later that evening we realised that the ship was largely filled
with Americans going home and a far smaller contingent of
British passengers. The Americans hadn't liked what they had
been happening in Europe, and who could blame them for
wanting to return to a country on the other side of the Atlantic?

They felt for us, they prayed with us that next year, in twenty years, life would be the same, but there was no certainty in their entreaties, only doubt; yet it was as though the voyage had to be enjoyed at any cost. As people danced the night away there was laughter and entertainment from one end of the ship to the other. It was the enjoyment of a people determined to forget for a while any threat of disaster hanging over us.

Adrian made friends on board, and he said one morning, 'I'm going to like America, Mother. My friends have told me about the schools there and all the things they do. They don't play cricket or rugger, but they play baseball and lots of other games. I'm looking forward to it.'

When I joined Andrew in the bar that evening he was deep in conversation with another man and after introducing me he said, 'This gentleman lives in Santa Monica, Alex. Didn't we meet people who lived there on our way out to India?'

With his usual diplomacy he made no mention of Alicia by name, and the American said, 'Can you remember their name? I probably know them. Members of the golf club, perhaps?'

'Do you remember their name, Alex?' Andrew asked.

'Carsdale, I think.'

'Well, I do know a Carsdale, Jefferson Carsdale. He married an Austrian countess, beautiful woman. He shows her off very proudly.'

Adroitly Andrew changed the subject to what the Americans talked about most, the state of Europe and her dictators.

'You're sensible to get out of it,' the American said. 'I hope Europe comes to its senses and I'm glad we're far enough away from it. There's something very comforting about that Atlantic Ocean between them and us.'

Later Andrew said, 'I think we were right not to mention

your aunt's name. Remember what she said to us? "What is it about Alex that I can never be free of her?"'

'And it's true, Andrew. The family wanted to forget her, but I insisted on bringing her to life and then, as she said, she was always coming across me.'

'America's a big country; I doubt we'll meet up with them there.'

We were on deck to capture our first sight of the Statue of Liberty and the New York skyline and I felt a strange tightness in my throat remembering the picture books I had devoured as a girl depicting this very same view.

The people milling around us were looking anxiously down at the quayside as we docked, then catching sight of faces they knew their smiles were ecstatic, and that was the moment I thought about the people we had left in England and how long we must wait before we saw any of them again.

The three of us were saying our farewells to the friends we had made on board and then there was no time for anything except retrieving our luggage. We still had another journey before we arrived in Washington to begin our new life.

Adrian was weary in spite of his excitement, and we could hardly believe the pace of New York as our taxi whisked us to the hotel where we were to stay for just one night. It was throbbing tempo reflected in the traffic and the frantic hurrying populace both inside the hotel and out of it, it made me feel breathless. Not even London had prepared me for such energy, and certainly not the elegance of Vienna.

'Will Washington be like this?' Adrian asked plaintively.

'Much quieter, I think,' his father replied.

'But Washington's the capital, isn't it?'

'Yes, but this is the Big Apple, the place where everything happens. One day we'll come back and take another look at New York, but for now I can't get away from it too soon.'

We were happy in Washington and made friends apart from the English people living here. We found the American people to be warm and generous, sympathetic too when across the Atlantic war-torn Europe was disintegrating.

I can only admit to being desperately afraid as country after country fell under the might of Germany leaving England alone and defiant. The oratory of Winston Churchill inspired us and yet the news coming out of Britain was grave.

Our American friends prayed for us and wished they could do more, and Andrew was impatient, wishing we could go home, thinking he would be more use in England than in Washington. Adrian was hoping the war would go on long enough for him to be old enough to join the Royal Navy.

What strange machinations of fate changed the course of events! The treacherous bombing of Pearl Harbor brought America into the war, and then, unbelievably, instead of coming for us Hitler went for Russia, and with the help of the bitter Russian winter as well as their army Russia defeated him.

At last the tides were turning and even though there was still a long way to go hearts were lighter, hopes were braver.

Once the war was over we joined wholeheartedly in America's celebrations regardless of the fact that we were desperate to go home. Home to mist-laden mornings and church spires across the hedgerows, home to soft evening twilights and English voices; yet in some strange perverse way

I was afraid of the changes I might find there. As it turned out we had to wait several years.

Wars left a legacy of loss, of bitterness and deep-rooted resentment, and my mind went back to the aftermath of the last war. It was one evening on the boat taking us home at last that I joined Andrew where he stood looking out on a grey churning sea and I knew from his face that his thoughts were far away.

We stood in silence until he put his arm round my shoulders and said softly, 'I wonder what sort of changes we'll find, Alex. Our families will be older, my parents, your mother, and some familiar faces will have gone forever.'

'I've been thinking about that too.'

Only Adrian and I had been home to England where he was now studying at Oxford. He had been happy in America but America was not our home, and he had happily come to terms with his new life. He made no mention now of a life in the navy; instead he wrote long letters about archaeology or politics and we were unsure what to expect.

I had seen my family only briefly. Mother looked older, frailer, and so too did Andrew's parents. Andrew's grandmother had died during the war and although Stephanie had attended her funeral she had not been seen or heard of since.

We had no means of knowing where life would lead us next and as though he read my thoughts Andrew said, 'I'd like to stay in England for a few years at least, find a place somewhere that we can call home. What do you think?'

'I agree. I wanted to see the world, I've loved every moment of it but perhaps I gave it too much importance. Now I just want to find some sort of permanence.'

He smiled, and in that moment a great truth was born in

me that I loved him, not with the heady sweeping passion of a remembered youth but something deeper, stronger: the love of a mature woman who recognised the worth of all that my husband had given me, real love and stability, values that would withstand any changes we might find in the land we were returning to.

**A dramatic
saga set
against a
dazzling
background
of Edwardian
England
and colonial
India.**

When poor Lisa Foreshaw falls in love with Dominic,
the Viscount Lexican, his family are determined to
keep them apart. Unaware of Dominic's love for her,
Lisa is lured into another marriage by a family who
would rather sacrifice Lisa and Dominic's happiness
than see the family's reputation ruined. But when Lisa
discovers the truth, she vows to take revenge…

This compelling tale of wealth, privilege and love
will touch your heart.

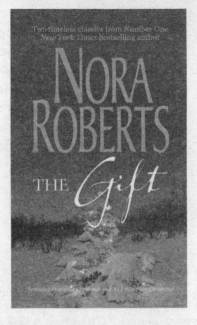
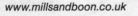